THE VICTIM

A RUFUS STONE NOVEL
PART OF THE 22RED SERIES

Graham Rabone

Grosvenor House
Publishing Limited

This book is published by
Grosvenor House Publishing Ltd
28-30 High Street, Guildford, Surrey, GU1 3EL.
www.grosvenorhousepublishing.co.uk

A CIP record for this book
is available from the British Library

ISBN 978-1-78148-721-1

ACKNOWLEDGEMENTS

When I started writing this book, I never imagined all of the essential 'backroom' work it would entail. The complexity, determination, creative thinking and support Jayne has shown is incredible. Writing some words was the easy part, refining, polishing and getting them in front of the public is the hard part. Jayne has shown such belief and has done all of that backroom work: created the web and social media pages, proof-read, bullied and cajoled me, praised and loved me throughout and I can never repay her.

It would not have been imaginable, never mind possible, without the assistance of some invaluable experts in surveillance, SAS medic training, and general military aspects, who I cannot name but they know who they are. Thank you.

Angela Clarence, who explained the difference between 'showing' and 'telling' as well as many other literary guidelines.

To Rowena and Mike Bird who offered support above and beyond that of friendship and were the first to read the completed manuscript – you make things possible.

Mandy at Grosvenor House, who edited the manuscript for me.

Whilst *The Victim* is a work of fiction, I have tried to make the book as realistic as possible, without giving away policing or military secrets or tactics. The police usually investigate once a crime has been committed and the prime objective is the prosecution of the offender. A Crime in Action is completely different because the crime is continuing and there is a life (lives) at risk. The SIO must *always* put the life of the hostage above any other consideration.

The setting in Tanzania is accurate, with its wonderfully chaotic naming of roads, its street scenes and majestic beauty all bombarding your senses. All characters are fictitious, except for Maura and Moez, who do indeed run the amazing beachside complex of Butiama on Mafia Island; they gave their permission to use their names but all other references to the story around them are indeed a work of fiction.

GLOSSARY OF TERMS

Beat the Clock	Get back safely
Booties/Bootnecks	Slang for Royal Marines
CHIS	Covert Human Intelligence Source, informant
COBRA	Cabinet Office Briefing Rooms
Counter	Counter Surveillance operative
CRB	Criminal Records Bureau
CROP	Covert Rural Observations Post
DA	Deliberate Action
DSF	Director, Special Forces
FOB	Forward Operating Base
GCHQ	Government Communications Headquarters
HCNU	Hostage and Crisis Negotiation Unit
HoS	SIS Head of Station
Humint	Human Intelligence
LUP	Lay Up Point
MI5	British Security Service
MSR	Major Supply Route
Nod/Noddy	New Royal Marines recruit (due to nodding off in lessons)
OP	Observation Post (See CROP)
RVP	Rendezvous Point
SAS	Special Air Service
SBS	Special Boat Service

SRR	Special Reconnaissance Regiment
Sigint	Signals Intelligence
SIS/Mi6	British Secret Intelligence Service
STAG	British Army term for sentry or guard
TAB	Tactical Advance to Battle
TPDF	Tanzanian Peoples' Defence Force
UKSF	United Kingdom Special Forces (SAS/SBS and SRR)
WRENS	Women's Royal Navy Service

Chapter One

Victoria Conway's cell phone rang on the table next to her. She was about to hear the voice of a man who would become her nemesis. A voice she would learn to hate more than anything in the world.

The young junior doctor looked at the display and saw that it was her mother calling from Tanzania.

"Hello Mum," she exclaimed in a bright, cheerful voice.

"This is not your mother. Listen very carefully. We have kidnapped your parents and you will not see them alive again unless you do exactly as I say."

Victoria caught her breath, removed the phone from her ear and checked the display "WHAT? Is this some kind of sick joke? Who are you? What are you doing with my mum's phone?"

"SHUT UP AND LISTEN," shouted the man, "we are holding your parents..."

"What do you mean? Holding..."

"I SAID SHUT UP AND LISTEN. We have kidnapped Deidre and Martyn Conway. You must pay $10 million for their release. You must not tell anybody. If you do, we will know. You must not go to the police. If you do, we will know. I have many brothers in the police and they will tell me. I will call you again in two hours with further instructions." The phone went dead and he was gone.

Use the contact list on the hostage's phone. Begin with the same surname. Keep calling numbers until somebody answers. The first person that does becomes the victim. Simple.

Victoria looked at her phone and checked the number. It was definitely her mum's. She sat stock still for a few seconds, screwing her face into a fierce frown, she pressed re-dial. The phone rang twice, clicked, and then all she could hear was a slight hissing, signalling a bad connection perhaps.

"Hello? Mum?" she said tentatively.

"I said I will call you back in two hours. Do not call this number again, unless I instruct you to," said the voice and cut the call.

He'd been lucky this time and got through on the first call. He hadn't even planned what he was going to say.

+++++++

She tried again, she HAD to do something – but this time the phone was switched off.

Victoria was not a young woman prone to panic, as a junior doctor she was used to dealing with emergencies, but this was completely off the radar.

She didn't know the first thing to do; she didn't know anybody who might have any idea about what you do in a kidnap. She had to think logically, but her brain felt as if it had been dipped in dry ice. She calmed herself and took some deep breaths, closed her eyes and allowed herself to think.

Hang on. Maybe there is a simple explanation. *Mum's probably left her phone somewhere and some chancer has picked it up.*

She pulled her parents' itinerary up on her iPad; checked the date: a transfer day from Zanzibar to Dar es Salaam. She found the contact number of the Serena Hotel, Dar es Salaam and called it.

"Hotel Serena, Dar es Salaam, how shall I direct your call?"

"Um, reception please?"

"Reception, thank you, connecting you now."

The phone rang for what seemed like a lifetime.

"Reception, Hotel Serena Dar es Salaam, Hyacinth speaking, how can I help you?"

"Good... is it morning or afternoon there?" said Victoria looking at her watch, 11:23 am.

"Good afternoon. How can I help you?"

"I'm trying to contact my parents, who should be booking back in today; Mr and Mrs Conway?"

Victoria could hear the tapping of the keyboard in the background and Hyacinth came back on the line.

"Hello, yes, they are due to check back in today, but they haven't arrived yet."

Shit.

"Could I leave a message please? To call their daughter, Victoria, when they arrive?"

"Yes certainly ma'am. Do they have your number?"

"Yes they do thank you. Oh. No. On second thoughts," she said, remembering they probably did not have their phone, "you'd better take it please," and dictated her phone number to the receptionist. "Could you make sure they get the message, it is rather important."

"Yes of course."

"Thank you. Thank you very much."

"It's a pleasure. Is there anything else I can help you with?"

"No, that's it thank you. Goodbye."

"Have a nice day," came the ubiquitous, unfeeling, robotic response and the line went dead.

Victoria found the website of the Hilton Double Tree Hotel in Zanzibar and called the number. After going through the same procedure, she discovered that her parents had checked out early that morning and were on their way back to Dar. Why hadn't she been more insistent that they both take their phones?

"We'll have double the roaming charges and double the hassle. Anyway we're not planning on splitting up at any point," her dad had said, "don't worry I won't let your mother get into any trouble!"

She was still inclined to think that their phone had been stolen and checked her watch again. One and a half hours to go. She kept trying to dispel dark thoughts from her mind, after all, what were the chances of her mum and dad being kidnapped? No, she was worrying over nothing. She picked up her iPad and opened the search engine, she skipped to the news absurdly thinking her parents might be mentioned, then went back to Google; she typed 'Kidnap' into the search engine, her finger hovering over the 'enter' key. *What if they know?*

She quickly deleted the search as if its mere presence on her screen might alert them. The clock watching nearly drove her insane: the hands were moving as if they were being held back by unseen gremlins inside the timepiece, tormenting her and laughing at her discomfort, each minute feeling like five – proving Einstein's theory of relativity.

She picked up the phone to call Craig, a colleague she respected and admired, and then skipped to her friend, Kerry, whose husband was in the police. *What if they have been kidnapped? What if the man could tell if I speak to somebody? Perhaps they've hacked my phone? How am I going to find $10 million? What if I pay but they aren't released? What if one of them is dead? What if both of them are dead? How do I get the money to kidnappers?*

+++++++

Hot sweet tea was what she needed. A glimmer of common sense told her she was in shock, feeling dazed, shaky and confused. She went into the kitchen, struggling to remember where her mum kept the teabags. She opened the fridge twice without taking out the milk. If she'd been in her own flat she could have slipped across the hall to talk to that unemployed fellow opposite who had worked in Africa and the Middle East on oil rigs. She froze. Was he involved? She wandered listlessly into her parents' room, looking sadly at their double bed with its Laura Ashley throw, the pretty dressing table and the silver picture frame with a montage of Victoria as a baby; on a swing; climbing Snowdon; getting her degree; outside the hospital and posing like Princess Di in front of the Taj Mahal.

God: just two years ago and look how I've aged. She looked in the mirror, squinting slightly to compare the two images. *I looked good back then with that tan. Look at me now– frown lines, bags under my eyes. And is that a fucking grey hair?* She examined herself, disappointed with what she saw.

She checked the phone signal and battery, checked the volume was up, checked she hadn't missed a call and checked it all again, feeling paranoid.

She reached for another biscuit and realised she had nearly finished the packet. As time went on past the two hours, she tried to convince herself that it was a good thing they hadn't rung: that a kidnapper would have called if he really had her parents. And in a complete volte-face, she thought perhaps they were already dead and that was why the man hadn't phoned. Or was someone watching the house waiting for her to make a move? After nearly two hours and forty-five minutes of anguish, the phone rang – her mum's number.

"Hello?" answered Victoria suspiciously.

"Miss Conway. Listen very carefully. If you do not interrupt me I will let you talk to your mother. My associates – of whom there are many – and I, have kidnapped your mother and father, Mrs Deidre Miriam Conway, born 22.12.1952, and Mr Martyn Gerald Conway born 14.8.1950, and we will hold them until you pay $10 million..."

"But..."

"DO NOT INTERRUPT..." boomed the caller. Victoria tried to picture him in her mind, listening to his sonorous voice. *Is he African? He sounds African, and a little American, and well educated.* Her imagination saw a large, well-built black man. She tried to visualise what he was doing, whether he was smiling or glowering; how old, whether he wore glasses.

"...You will pay $10 million in cash for their release. When you have the money, I will inform you how you will pay it to us."

"But..."

"Miss Conway, you are going to get one of your parents severely injured, do not interrupt, do not give me excuses. We are trained professionals and we know what we are doing. We have spies everywhere: in the police, in government, even in your British police. If you do as we say, then no harm will befall your parents. If you tell anybody, if you try and find us, your parents will die. Now just to prove we are serious, here is you mother."

Is he reading from a script? thought Victoria. Then came the unmistakable voice of her mother.

"Hello love."

Victoria almost dropped the phone; until that point she had been trying to convince herself that she had been over-reacting, worrying unnecessarily. At last she really grasped the situation and started to shake.

"Hello Mum? How are you? What's happened?" Her mother was talking but Victoria's brain could not focus on what she was saying.

Where am I going to get $10 million? How am I going to get it to the kidnappers? How am I going to cope? I can't do this on my own. I need help, who can I contact? I'm scared, scared shitless. I need to be calm for Mum. What if I can't get the money? Shit I ***can't*** *get the money. You can't just walk into a bank and ask for $10 million to pay a ransom. What am I going to tell the hospital? What am I going to do about work? Is somebody watching me? Is Mum playing a sick joke? Will I have to go to Tanzania? What do I do when I get there? How do I find them? What if they kidnap me?*

The thoughts tumbled through her head like leaves falling from a tree in autumn, fluttering and dancing uncontrollably in the wind. At last she tuned back into her mum's voice–

"... these gentlemen have kidnapped us in Dar es Salaam. Now don't you worry about us dear, just make sure you keep yourself safe."

Victoria could hear the tension and fear beneath the façade of calm. The man came back on the line.

"I will phone you tomorrow at midday with instructions. If you contact the authorities or tell anyone, we will kill your parents." And the phone went dead.

She called back again, but the phone had been switched off.

Shit shit shit. What am I going to do? What did Mum mean by 'make sure you keep yourself safe'? Does she think I am in danger? Why would they want to kidnap my mum and dad? Who are they? Was Dad alright? I hope he's alright. What if Grandma and Grandpa phone? What if the kidnappers phone them? A torrent of questions assailed her. *"Make sure you keep yourself safe." Why had she said that?*

Victoria checked every window and door making sure they were locked. She made herself another cup of tea, sat down and tried to focus, forcing herself to think calmly and logically. She went over a number of options and jotted them down in illegible spidery script:

- Go 2 police, <u>GO</u>, not phone in case bugged.
- Go 2 Kerry and Stuart 4 some advice.
- Bank – ask 4 $10 million??????.
- Foreign and Commonwealth Office.
- Craig.
- Fly to Tanzania.
- Private detective.

She crossed out a couple of the options and pondered those she had left. She looked at the damn clock on the mantelpiece again and noticed the edge of an envelope.

The letter her mum and dad had left for her 'in case of emergencies'.

She had laughed at the time, chiding them for being anal but now she retrieved the envelope with a beating, hopeful heart. Her fingers trembling, she looked at it blankly before finally drawing out the sheets of paper inside. The first one was covered in her mother's neat handwriting. A list of instructions on what to do if one or both her parents died on their trip; contact number for the funeral director; the order of service; the name of their solicitor; and a full photocopy of their travel insurance document. Victoria's brain lit up. She skimmed through the policy until she spotted the word Kidnap! She took in a great gulp of air realising she hadn't been breathing. KIDNAP Insurance! Kidnap Insurance was an automatic benefit! *'Don't tell one soul'* she heard the kidnapper say in her ear. *'Fuck you'* she whispered back stuffing the papers into her handbag,

She considered her options again and decided to visit Craig. She grabbed her coat and keys and left by the back door.

She crept slowly to the front of the house and looked up and down the avenue. She looked at the cars parked in the road and at the passers-by. Were they watching? Trembling, she got into her car and tried to put the key into the ignition, crunched the gears and stalled before she finally pulled off the driveway.

Victoria trusted Craig: they had graduated together: she remembered back-packing through India, when she had persuaded him to take part in the Rickshaw Run: a 3,500km adventure crossing the sub-continent, in a seven horsepower glorified lawnmower; he had helped her with some of the more technical computer problems she'd had; and now he was a fellow doctor from the hospital, on the same rota.

It took her just fifteen nerve-wracking minutes to reach Craig's small terraced house. She'd been checking her rear view mirror just like they did in the movies and was fairly certain she hadn't been followed. Nonetheless, she parked Colin, her battered old Renault Clio, in a side street and got out of the car. She walked around to the passenger door, opened it and reached across to lock the malfunctioning driver's door and secured the vehicle. She looked up and down the street, before taking a little path that brought her round to the back of Craig's row of houses. She vaulted over his back garden gate and walked swiftly across his lawn to the kitchen door and quietly knocked.

When she heard his footsteps coming down the hallway to answer the door she felt an overwhelming sense of relief that he was in.

"Vicky, what the hell," said Craig staring at her through the glass panel. The look on her face was enough to let him know there was a problem. He raised his bushy eyebrows in that ridiculous way, which usually made her laugh, and she managed a weak smile. God, it was a relief to see his moon-shaped, smiling face.

He opened the door and said, "You'd better come on in and tell me all about it," and led her through into his little sitting room.

When she had finished he said incredulously, "Are you absolutely sure about this?"

"I DIDN'T FUCKING WELL DREAM IT if that's what you mean," she yelled.

"Ok. Ok. apologised Craig. "But this is so off the wall. Why would anybody want to kidnap your mum and dad?"

"That's exactly what I've been asking myself. Would you please give me the benefit of the doubt and assume that I'm telling the truth for a moment. What would you do next?"

Craig shook his head and said, "I think you should contact that insurance company. I know you've been told not to tell a soul but you've already told me and I'm really glad that you did, but the insurance company will know what to do – probably. They must have had experience of this sort of thing. There's always stuff about kidnapping in the papers these days."

"Not helpful."

"Sorry."

"I don't know. I'm just not sure."

"You need professional help."

Victoria thought for a few seconds, nodded and said, "Can I use your phone then? I don't want to use my cell, in case it's bugged."

She fumbled for the insurance document and found the number, "Just tell them what you told me," said Craig. "Where's the gutsy, feisty Vicky that I see in A&E rallying the troops, giving out bollockings to time wasting patients?"

"I don't know where she is. She's disappeared. AND you didn't believe me. What if they don't believe me?"

"I'm sure they'll be able to tell whether it's a hoax or not. Have you got the policy number?"

She nodded.

"And all the details: Where they are; when they went; when they are due back."

"Yes."

"Ok. then, let's call."

The phone was answered after just one ring.

"Extension 2169 please," said Victoria.

"Abigail speaking. Do you have your policy number?

"Um, yes, yes it's P24503982," Victoria was a little taken aback by the perfunctory manner in which Abigail answered the phone.

"Thank you, and the policy holders' details?"

"Yes my mum and dad, Deidre and Martyn, with a "Y", Conway."

"And your name please?"

"I'm Victoria Conway."

"Thank you, may I call you Victoria?"

"Yes of course."

"Thank you Victoria. Sorry to be so brusque, it's just that I have to get the details before I can bring up my AIM or Automated Instruction Menu for your particular policy. Ok, can you tell me what's happened, please?"

Victoria retold her story:

"My mum and dad have been kidnapped in Tanzania."

"How do know they have been kidnapped?"

"Because the kidnapper fucking-well phoned."

"I know this is upsetting Victoria, but I have to get all the details down accurately so I need you to stay calm for me."

"I'm sorry, I'm really nervous.

"That's ok. When did the kidnapper call?"

"About eleven o'clock this morning and again err – close to two o'clock this afternoon."

"What were the exact words the kidnapper used?"

"Oh, I don't remember the exact words. I was too shocked to take it all in. He said I had to pay $10 million or my parents would be killed. That I was not to tell anybody and that he would know if I had and that he had spies in the police and the government."

"And did you get the phone number he was calling from?"

"Yes it's my mum's."

"What makes you think he is telling the truth?"

"Because he put my mum on the phone and I spoke to her and she told me that they had been kidnapped."

"When was the last time you saw your parents?"

"What? Er, about two weeks ago, just before they left for Tanzania."

"And what were they wearing?"

"What on earth has that got to do with anything?"

"I'm sorry Victoria, it's on this AIM list of questions I need to ask."

"Oh I don't know, Dad was in beige chino's, a blue shirt and a linen jacket, a sort of typical Brit in Africa, and Mum was wearing a floral dress I think."

Victoria felt as if she was being triaged with a nurse assessing the situation before deciding if and where the incident should be directed. A human filter, whose job it was to sort out the wheat from the chaff.

"Ok. Thank you for the information. I know you must be in shock and one of our consultants is going to call you very shortly. He will use the name Charles McHugh.

"Charles McHugh?" queried Victoria, writing it down.

"That's correct. What is the best number to reach you on?"

"This one, if he calls soon. I'm at a friend's house. I didn't want to call from my own phone."

"Your friend is aware of what has happened?"

"Yes, he is."

"Victoria, it is extremely important that you tell no one else. Do you understand?"

"Yes alright. I won't tell anyone else."

"Good, now I need your friend's details."

Victoria gave Craig's name and address and phone number and then the woman said goodbye.

"Well she clearly believed you," said Craig, "I think it was the right decision –, the only thing you could do."

"Oh God Craig, I don't know. I don't know what is right and what is wrong, I don't know who to trust, or who to believe. I should have just stayed at home and done exactly what they told me to do. I might have got my mum and dad killed."

"Right, let's have a cup of tea, or would you like something stronger."

"I think I'd better keep a clear head."

"I think a drop of brandy in a cup of sweet hot tea should do the trick," said Craig, "in my professional opinion!" Want something to eat? I bet you haven't eaten anything?"

They walked through into his galley kitchen, which looked out onto a long narrow garden. The sun came out from behind the clouds and illuminated a clump of peace lilies – her mother's favourite flowers. Victoria felt tears welling up as she thought of her mother being threatened with a gun.

Craig handed her a mug of tea spiked with a good dollop of brandy, "Here you are this should help a bit."

Victoria took a sip and perched herself on a stool by the window and looked at the lilies again. Her mother had sounded tense but focussed on the phone. She, Victoria, must try to stay focussed too.

"So what's the plan?" asked Craig as he turned up the gas and threw some streaky bacon into a pan. When she didn't answer he said, "Bacon and egg sarney is on the menu – just what the doctor ordered to keep you going."

"They said a man called Charles McHugh would call and I'm not to tell anyone else and I don't think they were pleased I told you."

"Well I am very pleased you told me – no way can you handle this on your own. Come here." He took the tea out of her hands and put it on the counter, pulled her off the stool and gave her a great big bear hug.

"Let it go, girl, you'll feel a whole lot better."

Victoria cried for several minutes as the bacon crisped, then charred and finally set off the smoke alarm.

"Lucky it was two-for-one at the Co-op today," said Craig tipping the bacon into the bin, wiping the pan and starting again with four new rashers.

They'd just finished their sandwiches and a second mug of tea with lots more brandy when the phone rang. Craig picked it up.

"Hello?"

"Hello, this is Charles McHugh. Is Victoria Conway there please?"

"Yes she is, hold on." Craig passed the phone over to Victoria.

"Hello, Victoria speaking."

"Hello Victoria, this is Charles McHugh. I understand you are expecting my call?"

"Yes, yes I am, thank goodness you've called me back."

"That's ok. First I need you to tell me what has happened."

"I've already told Abigail."

"Yes I know, but I'd like you to tell me please, reading it off my computer is not the same as having you tell me."

Victoria began to recount her story but McHugh kept interrupting, asking her for the minutest details, which was exasperating and she found it difficult to keep her temper.

The interrogation went on for about thirty minutes, at the end of which McHugh said, "Take down this number. Call me if you need me, but be sure to call from your friend's phone or a pay phone. Don't use your own phone. I'll bring you a new one when I come to see you tomorrow."

"Do you think my phone's bugged?"

"I doubt it very much Victoria, but it's better to be safe than sorry, isn't it? I'll come to your house tomorrow morning in plenty of time to take the call and we can take it from there. I'll be with you by about eight."

"Thank you, thank you so much," said Victoria, feeling relieved that a professional was now in charge, however obnoxious he was.

Little did she know she was about to be catapulted into a terrifying world of deceit, where she would learn to doubt everything and everybody, including herself, where she would witness events that she had only ever heard of in news bulletins or read in newspaper columns.

Chapter Two

Two weeks ago in Tanzania

It had all started so well. Deidre and Martyn were on the holiday of a lifetime and they loved it. When an insurance policy had matured, they had decided to splash out on an extravaganza of safaris, beach resorts, tropical islands and cultural improvement in Africa.

The three-week holiday in Tanzania, East Africa was booked on a whim, after seeing an advertisement. They had seen snippets about the country in newspapers and on television, but until they started looking at brochures neither had even known where Tanzania was, never mind what it had to offer: the wildlife, mountains, stunning scenery, beautiful white beaches with crystal clear water and so much more. They had awaited their holiday with excited anticipation, looking at *YouTube* video clips, exploring the websites of the lodges and reserves where they would be staying, as well as researching the abundant wildlife.

Flying out on Qatar Airways with these stunning images in their heads, they had to suffer the trauma that is Dar es Salaam before they got to the lush, tourist hot spots,. Touching down just before eight in the morning at Julius Nyerere International Airport the heat was already intense.

They followed the other passengers off the aircraft along sweltering walkways, finally struggling down a steep flight of stairs into the arrivals hall and came to an abrupt halt faced with the bun fight for Visa applications. There was no discernible system. There was a row of windowed booths in front of which stood miserable looking passengers at the mercy of even more miserable looking customs officers sitting behind plexiglass screens. Deidre, impatient to get to the bottom of the 'system', extracted herself from the crowd and approached a floorwalker, wearing a uniform.

"Excuse me," she said, "do we have to apply for a visa?"

"Yes madam, just queue up with everybody else," he said, indicating the heaving mass of people she had just left.

She re-joined Martyn on the edge of the crowd when a friendly American lady said, "I think you are in the wrong place. Have you paid your fifty dollars yet?"

"No. No we haven't," replied Deidre.

"Ah well, you have to go to those booths back there, hand over your passports, the applications we filled out on the plane and fifty dollars each to the officials. Then come back here and wait for those other officials over there to call you. It IS all very confusing. It's always the same here. It would never happen in the States," she said, shaking her head.

"Thank you, thank you very much," said Deidre and Martyn in unison before retracing their steps back to the very first set of booths they had past. They stood for several minutes trying to make eye contact with the officers. Finally, fighting off their British diffidence they approached one of the windows. A female official looked up reluctantly, put out her right hand to receive the visa application, passport and banknotes and then simply turned away leaving their papers on her desk. Nonplussed and vaguely uneasy, they re-joined the other passengers hoping desperately for the best.

The other set of bored, disinterested officials, were at last calling out the names of the lucky passengers whose Visas had been processed and granted. Deidre and Martyn waited in vain for their names to be called but, as is the Tanzanian way, the immigration officer had been calling "Mr Marteeen" and Mrs "Deidre" in a thick Tanzanian accent. Consequently, they were the very last to receive their passports duly stamped. Sticky with sweat and slightly anxious they past onto the immigration desk, only to be re-directed to another exit through to the grandiosely entitled baggage reclaim hall to find just one working carousel straining under the weight of a pile of baggage that appeared to have been abandoned.

They extricated their cases and found their way out of the terminal looking for a placard announcing their courtesy bus to take them to the hotel. They were immediately surrounded by swarm of taxi drivers offering them 'best rates' jostling and haranguing them until Martyn spotted a young, smartly dressed man holding the Serena Hotel placard on the other side of the road. He greeted them politely, checked their names off his list and asked them to follow him. They crossed several service roads into a car park, where they finally boarded their bus under the glare of all the other passengers who had been waiting in hot claustrophobic conditions for these final two stragglers.

Before they had even taken their seats, the white-knuckle drive began. It was approaching rush hour and by the time they reached the centre, the traffic was heavy and congested. The bus was hot and stuffy; horns blaring; normally sanguine people cursing each other, and cars cutting each other up for no apparent reason. The local buses, known as Dala Dala's, were driving on the footpaths or down the wrong side of the road and forcing their way into gaps that even bicycles would have struggled to get through. If traffic rules and regulations existed, nobody appeared to obey them. Chaos reigned.

They saw women with brooms sweeping the infinite supply of dust and dirt off the road, which the wind blew straight back –they later discovered this was part of a job creation scheme. Street beggars hung out at every junction – not western-style beggars who had dropped out of society, but genuine, no hope, no social safety net, no legs, no hands, no parent, beggars, imploring the passing motorists to part with a few shillings.

At the junction with Lumumba Street the bus was besieged by five street urchins with filthy faces, rags for clothes, no shoes and making the international sign for food – fingers and thumb pressed together poking at their open mouths. Deidre was filled with dismay as she watched their agonised little faces contorted with pain and hunger. She had been warned by the young man with the placard not to open the windows of the bus and give money to beggars on the streets. As an altruistic liberal, it broke her heart to ignore the children, five out of an estimated three thousand the man in the opposite seat informed her, so she forced herself to avoid eye contact, staunchly looking straight ahead.

They reached the Serena at long last and were greeted with wet face towels to clean their hands and faces; a fruit drink to wash away the dirt from their mouths; and sweets to suck on to help them forget the two hour bus journey they had just endured. When at last the bellboy opened the door to their room it was hard for them to credit the luxuriant scene that greeted them. They gazed in wonder at the perfectly manicured gardens being watered by automated sprinklers; gardeners attending to hedges and rose bushes; waiters and waitresses in starched uniforms serving guests relaxing under parasols out on the lawn; and a magnificent swimming pool glistening in the morning sunshine. Beyond the boundary of the hotel lay the Gymkhana Cricket Club to the North; the Golf Club to the South, and straight ahead forming a glorious backdrop was the Indian Ocean, fringed by swaying palm trees and a white sandy beach. Deidre felt a deep sense of shame, and despite their exhaustion, demanded that Martyn go down to the foyer, get her some shillings so that they could go back to the main road and dispense some money to the poor unfortunate people they had seen.

Martyn was no match for Deidre and meekly succumbed to her wishes. He wasn't exactly henpecked, it was just that Deidre was more forceful and determined. And Deidre was determined to make a difference; a resolve which continued throughout their holiday. No matter what Martyn said, no matter how objective and rational he was Deidre remained adamant. These people needed help and the Conways were in a position to give it.

She gave to beggars whenever possible and initiated a policy of never haggling with traders. She had fallen in love with the local arts and crafts and insisted on buying carvings, furniture and ornaments. She had bought so much they would have to have them crated and shipped. Still, their life assurance policy had matured at just over £250 000 and so she felt it immoral to haggle with people who clearly had nothing or perhaps less than nothing.

Deidre had also taken to tipping generously. They tipped the guides in Ngorogoro Crater; at the Serengeti, and at Mount Kilimanjaro; the taxi drivers; their porters; the bar staff and the waiters and waitresses. All these recipients viewed the whites, or mzungus, as they are known in Swahili, as cash cows and these two mzungus, especially the lady, like hole in the wall cash dispensers.

Her extravagance continued when they moved on to visit the island of Zanzibar on the Spice Trail. Deidre just couldn't help herself. She thought she was being kind and generous toward those she endowed and it never occurred to her that perhaps her generosity might be viewed as ostentatious or even demeaning to some.

The non-descript man who had been watching them since they had first arrived in Tanzania silently cursed everything about them – their health, their faux generosity and sympathy and he ridiculed their naivety and innocence. He was a 'spotter'. His boss, a man named Wisdom, had told him to look out for these two mzungus at the airport. The spotter was good at his job and with his practised eye, had easily recognised the Conways. He was an idealistic man whose anger fuelled his life as he pondered the politics of the world.

What would have happened if malaria had been a European or an American disease? What if it had killed over one million people in the West instead of Africa? The governments and the pharmaceutical companies would invest billions to find a cure. If they had, my mother, my first born son, my second daughter and my brother would still be alive. The mzungus would have found a cure if it had affected them and the whole world would have benefitted. And why had they only given anti HIV drugs to mzungus and not to the Africans, who needed it so badly. They had virtually eradicated HIV as a killer in the West, but not in Africa. No, in Africa, my brothers and sisters are still dying.

Watching the mzungus living in their opulent luxury, he often reflected on his childhood growing up in a mud hut and his daily two mile walk to the water hole and the backbreaking walk back carrying five gallons of filthy water, which weighed nearly fifty pounds. His long trek to school with more than three hundred children crammed into the classroom to learn English – so that they could 'get on' in life. He thought about his friends who had been taken prematurely to a 'better place' by the mzungus' Lord – at least that's what the priest said at the funerals.

He had nothing against these two mzungus personally. They were just two more tourists who could afford to give him and his people some of their vast wealth.

Why do they have to come to my country and think their paltry acts of charity would make them popular? The Europeans took everything from our country until the father of our nation sent them packing and led us in a wonderful revolution which has freed us from the yoke of the imperial colonialists. True, we have squandered much money. True, the politicians are corrupt and take for themselves the money that is meant for the people. But the mzungu governments and charities should be more careful when donating their money and should make sure it gets to the right place. Who wouldn't take a bit for themselves if they could? Exactly. We all would. So the donors should be more prescriptive with what happens to the money and then my country would be prosperous. If the mzungu multi-national corporations employed locals as senior managers instead of their own kind, then the money would be spread around the country instead of going back to America or Sweden or Australia.

From the moment he had first seen them, he was convinced they would be targeted.

Chapter Three

Deidre and Martyn had had a perfect time in the Tanzanian interior, being treated like royalty; seeing fantastic sites at beautiful locations, and moved on to their beach holiday in the North of Zanzibar from which they were returning to the mainland of Tanzania by ferry. They paid the extra $10 to travel "business class", which just meant the deck they were on was full, rather than below where the people were crammed in like sardines – in Deidre's eyes it was money well spent. Just looking in on the lower deck made her feel claustrophobic. After the two-hour ferry trip they couldn't wait to get off and feel dry land under their feet once more, but as usual there was no sign of a queue to disembark and they found themselves bumped, barged and jostled to the back of the frenzied horde of passengers struggling to squeeze down the exit ramp. Nobody quite knew why they were rushing, or where they were rushing to, because as soon as they got off, they slowed right down to the natural walking pace which was, to any westerner, bewilderingly and frustratingly slow to Western sensibilities. The Tanzanians conserved their energy in the oppressive heat and humidity by loping along at a gentle pace.

The spotter was waiting on the wall at the top of the slip road. He hadn't felt it necessary to follow the

Conways to Zanzibar, he had simply bribed the right people to discover their itinerary and had saved himself extraneous time and effort. He knew their kind. They were not like backpackers who changed their plans more often than he changed his socks. No, these two were organised and regimented and would be sticking to their itinerary, barring disaster, and a disaster was exactly what he was about to set in motion. He spoke quickly into his mobile phone in Swahili. Even if his targets had overheard him and picked up a few words like “rafiki” “mambo” “asante” and the world famous “hakuna matata”, they would have had no chance of understanding anything else he said.

He watched the couple exiting the ferry. She wore a bright local T-shirt, in the colours of Tanzania’s national flag: Green, Black, Yellow and Blue, announcing “I love Tanzania”, and shorts, and was adorned with local bracelets and necklaces. She seemed completely at ease with her surroundings and style of dress, even though it was far more relaxed than what he assumed would be her usual style. He wouldn’t have been surprised to see her with braided hair or in different circumstances, with a Masai Warrior.

He, on the other hand, seemed very ill at ease. His thin lily-white legs seemed lost in his cargo shorts. He wore a safari waistcoat over a short-sleeved shirt and had the usual mzungu accoutrements: sun hat, sun glasses on a cord and a bum bag no doubt containing sun cream, mosquito spray, phrase book, wallet, phone, tissues, and a printed hotel confirmation. He was clearly very self-conscious and uncomfortable, almost worried and scared.

As they walked, or to be more precise, shuffled and stumbled up the jetty towards Kivukoni Road, they were intent on keeping hold of their luggage as they had heard horror stories of bag snatches and pickpockets, especially around the docks.

When they reached the slip road, the scene that greeted them was beyond chaotic, beyond anarchic, it was simply pandemonium. A multitude of cars were wedged together, unable to move forward or backward with people yelling and horns blowing in complete and utter confusion. Deidre and Martyn struggled through the mayhem at the same trying to avoid the hawkers who grabbed at them selling mass produced 'genuine' local ornaments; a fish tank, complete with gallons of water in which swam a multitude of fish, balanced on a young man's head; tickets for the ferry they had just got off; not to mention the insistent taxi drivers.

The two travellers managed to cross over the slip road and onto the main road where they came across a respectable-looking taxi driver leaning against his ubiquitous white, second hand Toyota, which the Tanzanian's buy from Japan in their thousands. The man was well dressed and made no attempt to hassle them. He merely held the back door open with his right hand and welcomed them in with his left.

"Karibu," he said, which they understood as "Welcome".

After the bedlam from which they had just emerged this taxi seemed to be heaven sent. The driver took their luggage and stowed it into the boot with Martyn watching to make sure he secured it before joining Deidre on the back seat. Silence and tranquillity washed over them. They felt relieved and rather pleased with themselves. They had navigated their way through the chaos; found a decent taxi; remembered to watch the driver shut the boot and were still in possession of money, passports and phone.

"Where to sir?"

"The Serena please." replied Martyn,

"Samahani, Serena tafadhali," Deidre said correcting him.

"Ha ha, nzuri sana, very good lady," replied the driver looking in the rear view mirror and smiling at the couple as he pulled away from his parking space without even checking over his shoulder for oncoming traffic. It wasn't long before they joined the Dar es Salaam rush hour with its four lanes of traffic on a two-lane road; the locals blocking the junctions, blowing their horns, and upbraiding each other's inconsiderate driving. Their taxi driver expertly changed lanes ignoring the protestations of the other drivers whom he had cut up, and like all the other Dar drivers, drove on the pavement, drove on the wrong side of the road, took short cuts the wrong way up one-way streets, while shouting at the other drivers for being idiotic and incompetent. He got them on to Bibi Titi Muhammed Street, much faster than they anticipated and threw a left onto Uhuru Street.

"Excuse me," said Martyn. "We are at the Serena."

"Yes I know boss, there are jams down the main road so I am going the back way."

They had entered a suburb of Dar known as Kariakoo, a contemporary labyrinthine, Dickensian slum. A criss-cross of streets and alleyways lined with shops made up of two-storey pre-fab units measuring ten by forty feet, where street urchins controlled by modern day Fagins look for easy pickings, and where the filthy roads throw up great white dust clouds coating cars, people and shop-fronts alike, giving the area an almost extra-terrestrial feel. Deidre felt distinctly uneasy crawling along these alien alleyways without names, while Martyn wondered how the shops could support themselves or the three men sat outside every one, apparently doing nothing but watching the passing cars, rickshaws and the Tanzanian equivalent to a pick-up truck, the tricycle. Young boys used every fibre in their bodies to turn the pedals of these clapped out machines while transporting sofas, iron girders and even telegraph poles. They saw one skinny fellow on his tricycle with another enormous man on the back holding an outboard motor. Barrow-boys wheeled impossibly heavy loads to goodness knows where and young men walked around with huge machetes in their hands, apparently for chopping wood transported by the barrow boys.

Deidre felt thoroughly downhearted. Just minutes away lay avenues of high-rise office blocks occupied by corporations and banks with computers; air conditioning; water coolers, and banks of phones connecting them to the Western world. There were elaborate buildings housing foreign embassies and smart restaurants catering to foreign tourists. All the trappings of twenty-first century living in stark contrast to this squalid, filthy rabbit warren which she realised represented the norm for most Tanzanians.

Martyn knew that they were moving further and further away from the Serena Hotel but what he couldn't know was that their nightmare was just about to begin. Good, respectable, law-abiding people like Deidre and Martyn don't get kidnapped. They live in a modest, nicely furnished house in Bedfordshire. They drive a year-old Ford Mondeo. He mows the lawn every weekend and keeps the garden immaculate. She does voluntary work at the local hospice. And sometimes they cycle along country lanes admiring the local wildlife.

They are, in short, a typical English middle-class couple.

The attack, when it came, was deliberately dramatic. The speed and ferocity of the strike designed to subjugate and disorientate the hostages and dehumanise them in the eyes of the kidnappers. The taxi came to an abrupt halt and four armed men in masks opened the rear doors shouting and screaming. Deidre and Martyn couldn't understand a word but the meaning was abundantly clear – out of the taxi now! The men grabbed and pulled at the shell-shocked couple, putting hoods over their heads and slipping cable ties over their wrists before bundling them into an adjacent building.

Deidre was screaming and sobbing. Martyn tried to speak but his brain wouldn't function. This could not be happening! Not to him! Hands searched his pockets removing his passport, wallet, mobile phone, Swiss army penknife and then his watch. Fists punched him on the neck, shoulder, arm and finally in the stomach.

The kidnapping had begun and it could only get worse. The show of force was designed to give the kidnappers psychological superiority over their hostages and to intimidate anyone fool enough to play the hero and try to intervene. A kidnapper must maintain absolute and total authority. It's not personal, it's just business. The kidnapper needs a commodity, nothing more, nothing less. The hostage, as a mere commodity, had better hope that someone will pay the asking price, if they want to get out alive.

Chapter Four

Martyn's pulse increased to an alarming rate of 205 beats per minute; much higher than his safe limit, but his blood pressure dropped dramatically, getting weaker, causing him to faint, and he was very close to being in a life threatening decompensated shock.

This shouldn't be happening to me was all he could think.

The kidnappers shoved them into two separate rooms and locked and bolted the doors. After several minutes, or several hours – Martyn wasn't sure how much time had past– he started to focus his mind and think. He listened intently. He could hear the noise of the traffic, the high pitched engines of the bajajes; he could hear the constant background noise of people talking, haggling, greeting one another or arguing. He could hear the sound of car horns, beep-beeping continuously.

But he couldn't hear any noises within the room. He tried to 'feel' the atmosphere to sense if somebody was in there with him, giving off electricity, transmitting a human presence, he listened intently for any breathing. After several minutes he decided he was alone, he nervously raised his bound hands to his face to remove the hood, and tentatively lifted one corner trying to take in the surroundings. Even though he was sure nobody was in the room with him, he was petrified and waited for the thud on the back of his head; eventually he looked all around and established that he was alone. Taking the hood off completely he stood up to physically examine the place, that in his panic, he was convinced would be his tomb. There was a dirty urine stained mattress in the corner and that was it.

The door opened without warning and he held his breath. Two masked men came in shouting at him pulling his hood back onto his head and over this face. They frogmarched him out and shoved him into another room and cut his cable tie. This felt different, different atmospherics, silent and darker. *Why have I been moved? Where is Deidre? Is she dead?* His mind wandered to a story he had read, about a couple who had been kidnapped by Somali pirates, could these people be pirates? *Are they going to kill me? What is going to happen to me?*

+++++++

In another room the bandits were organised by their unopposed leader: Wisdom Mwakimbwla. Wisdom was Masai by birth and although he rarely dressed in traditional Masai clothes, one could see his stature and bone structure was from the ancient and noble tribe: a tall, handsome, almost elegant man. He had become educated and well-travelled, having gained a bursary to study at university in England. Unfortunately he never completed his degree in Business Studies because he was too busy enjoying himself and putting into practise what he was learning. That left very little time to actually study or complete his assignments.

He'd returned to Tanzania an idealist, convinced he could use his degree – he would never tell anybody he had dropped out – to make a success of his own safari company: *The Masai Experience*, but things hadn't gone according to plan. A few friends from uni had been enthusiastic about entering into the venture with him, promising him investment and clients, but neither had materialised. Too few visitors arrived, preferring instead to go to Kenya, where the marketing of the country was better and more aggressive.

He had ventured into kidnapping westerners by accident after a trip to Mexico, and was now making a very reasonable living out of it, with minimal risks.

He ensured his men went through all of the Conway's possessions, searching the suitcases, rifling the hand luggage. They put everything out on a table, including the possessions they had initially taken from the couple. Wisdom surveyed their haul. He would let his men have their choice of whatever they wanted, but he needed the phone and their passports.

He picked up the phone and examined it. He was quite disappointed: it was an old-fashioned Nokia 6200, a good workhorse, but surely such rich people could afford a more modern Smart phone?

He ordered one of his men to find him the charger as he interrogated the contacts list.

These two mzungus were very organised and methodical, and had recorded everybody systematically by last name, then first name, and even had an ICE entry of "Conway, Victoria" very easy to find. If necessary, they would move onto all of the 'Conways' stored, and find 'Peter & Annie', 'Norma' or 'Terry'.

Such apparently irrelevant, minor details, can define the course of our lives.

He called the mobile number stored in the phone's memory and after a few misconnections he heard the phone ringing, and unfortunately for Victoria, she answered. If she had not, he would have moved on, until another member of the family answered, it didn't matter to him which one; just somebody to pay.

Chapter Five

"Hello Babu?"

"Hello," answered Nick Cooper, Head of Station of the British Secret Intelligence Service, Dar es Salaam.

"I am looking for a new car." Code for *I need to meet you urgently at the Quality Centre, Julius Nyerere Road.*

"What is your price range," *What time?*

"I'm looking to spend 11 million shillings," *11 a.m.*

"I have a large selection in that price range and I'm sure one of our cars will suit your wallet," *Ok see you there at 11.*

Cooper sat and mused for a few minutes. It must be urgent and could be something good. Many agents, or contacts, were too eager to call urgent meetings but not this one, no, if he was asking for an urgent meeting it could only mean one of two things – he was in trouble and needed help, always a possibility in this game, or he had some very important information to impart. Cooper naturally hoped it would be the latter as he never liked losing agents. Of course when he did have to sacrifice a source to protect either the service or himself then so be it. Cooper was deeply ambitious. He had taken the Tanzania post after being assured that it was 'up and coming' and could open the door to other, better postings – if he did well.

Nick Cooper drove to the Quality Centre, a journey of about seven miles. The rush-hour traffic had eased but it was still chaotic. He pulled off the main road and parked in the rear car park of the modern shopping mall, as far away from their meeting place as he could. Cooper was an Oxford graduate, fluent in Japanese and Spanish, thirty-two years old and although fit and athletic, the air conditioning of the mall was a welcome relief. As he walked past the stores selling international brands found in just about every mall worldwide, he checked the reflections in the window displays for tails. He took the stairs to the Cineplex cinema where he pretended to look at the listings before retreating to the opposite side of the atrium for a better view of the people coming and going. When he was satisfied that he was indeed alone, he made his way to the Lemon Tree Bistro and waited for his contact. He ordered an espresso and browsed through a copy of The Citizen, one of a few English language newspapers printed in the city. A little later a man approached the table next to him.

"Excuse me. Is this table free?" *Are you alone?*

"There hasn't been anyone using it since I came in," I've *checked and I haven't been followed. You are safe to sit down with me.*

The man pulled up a chair and ordered Coke, a baguette, fries and a pastry, knowing that Cooper would pick up the tab.

The contact was code-named 'Kumi', Swahili for 'Ten' and the information Kumi supplied was always Ten out of Ten. They exchanged a few pleasantries before moving on to business. Cooper listened with growing interest to the information that a local criminal gang had kidnapped an English couple. Cooper could hardly contain his excitement as possibilities tumbled like slot machine numbers falling one by one into a perfect row of sixes.

This insignificant couple could be just the right bait to tempt Abu Faud out of the shadows. A much bigger fish than this tu'pny ha'pny gang of low level crooks.

His mentor and sponsor within the Secret Intelligence Service, otherwise known as SIS, or MI6, Sir Peregrine Dennis, loved to espouse that "One has to see the bigger picture, and there is always a bigger picture." Abu Faud, the notorious Somali clan leader controlling Al Shabaab and piratical activities, had ventured down from Somalia twice and eluded Cooper both times. If Cooper could embellish the importance of these hostages, they might prove just the right bait to draw him out again. Since George Bush had initiated the War on Terror following the September 11 attacks, it had overtaken all previous objectives, including the Cold War; the Irish Republican Threat; and even nuclear proliferation. If Cooper could be seen to be waging the War on Terror here in Dar, it might just get him out of this backwater posting.

Cooper paid and left Kumi in the café with a generous payment for his information and hurried back to the High Commission where he secreted himself in his office to make a call to another 'contact' codenamed Esther. Compartmentalising contacts was a basic principle of running agents, especially when they were working on the same operation. One could not know the existence of another and on this occasion it was absolutely essential that these two didn't have an inkling of the other's presence.

Chapter Six

Charles arrived at the Conway house at 0811:37 precisely. Victoria was clock watching again, and was annoyed that he was late. She had taken an instant dislike to him on the phone and his tardiness only confirmed her opinion. He greeted her politely in an icy sort of way and gave her the new phone with his number programmed into it, together with the charger and instruction manual.

After what felt like another interrogation from him, he proceeded to make a leisurely tour of the house as if he was looking for clues. Victoria followed him.

Why's he looking at the picture of Mum and Dad's Pearl Wedding Anniversary? And I'm sure you've seen the Hay Wain before, it's Mum's favourite. Get your hands off the sideboard as he walked past the walnut piece of furniture, stroking it. *Why are you looking at my graduation photograph so intently and put that vase down, I'm surprised you haven't turned it upside-down checking the provenance.*

Victoria snapped, *she* was the customer, *she* was employing *him*; her parents had paid his company money to do them a service.

"What are you up to?" she demanded.

"Admiring your parents' house while we wait for the phone call," he replied with a haughty arrogance.

He reminded her of one or two of the senior consultants at the hospital who had 20:20 hindsight. The 'shoulda squad', people who were great at giving advice after the event, but never seemed to be there when it mattered, or when the tough decisions had to be made.

"It is customary to ask to look around somebody's house before you start wandering about, you know."

"Actually, I do need some photographs, of you and two or three of your parents, together and separately. Have you got a photo album...or?"

"Why didn't you say so? There are a couple of albums in the book case."

Finally the man was doing something sensible.

It was difficult looking at pictures of her parents. She tried not to let the vision of them lying dead by the roadside take over. She was determined not to let the tears pricking at the back of her eyes well forward. Holding onto her emotions, they picked out some photographs which Charles McHugh slipped into an A4 envelope and put in his briefcase.

"There's one thing that might be useful. Have you taken any notes of the phone calls?"

"Yes, so as not to forget what they bloody said."

"I've got a portable scanner here and if I could just..."

"I can't believe you'll find them useful...but well, alright." Victoria opened a cardboard file in which she'd placed a sheet of notes from the two phone calls, her 'to do' list, the letter from her parents with the insurance document and a scrap of paper with Charles McHugh's name on it. She gave him the sheet with the notes.

She couldn't bear to watch him struggle with the scanner and went into the kitchen and made up a tray with coffee and a plate of chocolate digestives, her mum's favourite. She had to take several deep breaths to stop the tears, for she was doubly determined not to let this idiot see her falling apart. When she came back into the living room McHugh appeared to be checking his emails. He thanked her for the coffee and then excused himself and went into the kitchen to make some phone calls.

On his return he asked Victoria if he could record the telephone conversation with a little microphone he would attach to her phone.

"Of course," she said, relieved once again that he was showing some initiative.

"There are a few things that might be useful for you to know, Victoria," McHugh said, "my company insures over a hundred thousand people against kidnap every year and less than 0.005 per cent ever have to claim."

"Oh?" said Victoria.

"Yes and technically *you* are the victim in this, not your parents."

"What? How does that work? They are the ones that have been kidnapped. They're the ones being held hostage."

"Exactly. They are the hostages and you are the victim. I suppose it does seem a little strange doesn't it?"

"More than a little, which genius thought that up?"

"Oh, I don't know. But what else could we call you? As a generic term I mean; 'the person of whom the demand is made?' Doesn't exactly trip off the tongue, does it?"

Victoria was beginning to regret her decision to involve the insurance company. This insipid idiot with his pasty white skin, slicked back hair, and piggy eyes didn't inspire her with confidence. She decided to ask HIM some questions.

"Do you deal with many incidents like this?"

"Well I can't give you specifics Victoria, but I do deal with a large number of similar enquiries. Clearly I can't go into detail, but let's just say you're not my first."

"And what is the success rate?"

"We measure success," he said, making quotation signs with two fingers of both hands, "in different ways for different incidents."

"What will 'success'," Victoria mimicked his quotation mime, "be for my mum and dad?"

"Erm, well clearly, a successful," making the quotation signs again thinking he and Victoria were on the same wavelength, "conclusion in these circumstances would be the safe release of Deidre and Malcolm."

"Martyn."

"Pardon?"

"Mum and Dad are Deidre and Martyn, not Malcolm."

"Oh, I know. Did I say Malcolm? I know your dad is Martyn."

Fucking hell, what sort of idiot is this? What have I done? If he can't even remember Dad's name, what chance have we got of getting them back? I think I'm just going to tell him to go and take my chances. I can't do any worse than him. If I was as incompetent in A&E as he is I'd be struck off... Don't be stupid Victoria, you haven't got a clue what to do. You can't get hold of the sort of money they are asking for without this idiot's access to the insurance company's funds. He must know what he is doing to have got the job.

Just gone midday the phone rang; they could see it was Deidre's number and Victoria grabbed the phone:

"Hello?"

"Listen very carefully," said the voice on the other end, "I represent a group of professionals. We have intelligence and surveillance officers and we have built up a picture of your parents – and you. We know what we are doing."

Victoria's knuckles were white as she gripped the phone in fear, every word he said spreading more distress and anxiety through her body.

"You parents will not be harmed as long as you do exactly what we say: You must not tell anybody about the kidnapping; if you do we will know, we are very technically proficient. Do not go to the police, we have informants in the police and we will know. Do not try and locate us, we will know. We know everything about you. You will pay $10 million dollars in one week and both of your parents will be released, unharmed. There will be no negotiations. If you comply with our demands your parents will be well looked after. If you do not, then you will never see your parents again. Do you understand?"

"Um, I haven't...."

"DO YOU UNDERSTAND?"

"YES," Victoria shouted back down the phone and the call was terminated. Victoria looked at McHugh and thought he had been as much use as an ashtray on a motorbike. She'd thought he was here to help. He had done nothing.

"Right. Thank you Miss Conway," said McHugh. "I'm satisfied that this is a genuine claim on your behalf and I will be instructing a specialist to contact you..."

"A specialist? What are you then?"

"Oh, I'm the company K&E Coordinator"

"The what?"

"Kidnap and Extortion Coordinator, it's my job to assess each incident and hand-pick the specialist with the requisite skills."

"So you are not the specialist?" Victoria asked incredulously.

"Not in kidnap negotiating no. I'm the company coord..."

"Yes, company K&E Coordinator. Well I suggest you get hold of your 'specialist' and get him or her here as soon as you can, because so far I have not been very impressed with the service I have received. My mum and dad are being held hostage by some psychopath in Tanzania who is threatening to kill them if I don't come up with ten million and you are pissing about 'assessing'," and she mimicked his penchant for making the quotation signs, "the veracity of the claim instead of actually doing anything."

"We have to follow our procedures to eliminate bogus claims, which are made on a surprisingly frequent basis. Please be assured, I am taking your allegation..."

"ALLEGATION," shouted Victoria, "you heard the guy. He's going to kill them and you're talking about allegations."

"Until we examine all possibilities, we don't know what we are dealing with, that is all I mean. We are treating your alle... sorry, claim, as genuine, which is why I will be instructing a specialist to contact you."

McHugh took his leave of Victoria and as he drove away, he reviewed his morning's work. They had received the call, which he had recorded. He had had a good look around the house, which helped to gauge the character of the hostages, and had been able to assess Victoria's demeanour. He put her anger down to the terrible stress she was under; not unusual in the circumstances. He thought this was a genuine call and feeling quite pleased with himself he decided to use his in-car hands free to call in the contractor.

Charles tried to spread the work evenly among his trusted contractors. He had his favourites, the ones who weren't too greedy, picky or pushy and got on with the job without giving him too much grief. One such contractor was a small outfit called 22Red led by an ex-military man called Rufus Stone.

"I think I may have a job come in, which is right up your street," said Charles when Rufus answered the call.

"Go on," replied Rufus.

"One can never be hundred per cent certain but a couple appear to have been kidnapped in Tanzania. I've just been with the daughter while she took a call."

"Tanzania eh?"

"Yes, first one I've heard of there, it's normally a quiet country from our perspective, so, you know, they could be a pair of con artists, living it up out there hoping that the insurance policy could pay for their holiday and then some... it's happened before, but having heard the call, I don't think so."

"Mmm."

"I'm on my way back to the office and could meet up with you about four if you are interested?"

"Yeh sure, in principle. Where do you want to meet?"

"At the club?"

"Ok. Just a couple of questions Charles, so I can brief the others... when was the first call received?

"About eleven yesterday."

"How many calls in total?"

"Three."

Rufus wanted to bellow down the phone. *THREE? Three fucking calls and you have only just contacted me you incompetent cretin.* But staying in control, he said, "What's the demand?"

"$10 million dollars."

"Whoa, that's big bucks. What are you prepared to pay?"

"We can discuss that later."

"What's the victim's name?"

"Victoria Conway, a junior doctor."

Rufus noted the hesitancy in Charles' voice and asked, "Have you given her advice about friends, family and work?"

"Well, she er appeared to have all that under control," he replied hesitantly.

That's a no.

"Have you advised what to do if she receives another call?"

"Abby and I did that yesterday."

That's a no as well.

"Did you get proof of life?"

"I think Victoria did yesterday."

Another no.

"What welfare and support have you put in place for her?"

"She was holding up well and I thought if we meet up this afternoon, you would be able to take over straight away."

A whole lot of nothing then.

"See you at four at the club."

Rufus had decided there was no point asking any further questions as he was only getting vague responses for the most basic actions such as code words or phrases, reassurance, contingency plans or willingness to pay. He had learned from bitter experience that he would have to spend time and energy repairing the damage other people caused in these cases and this was a classic example.

He couldn't even phone Victoria to begin to rectify things because he hadn't been given the job yet. What annoyed him most was that he had prepared a paper notifying all the insurance companies how important it was to call in the consultants at the earliest possible moment. Rufus was even prepared to do the first consultation for free, no strings, just to ensure that things were done correctly from the off.

He phoned his partners, Orla and Don Ward, and briefed them on his call, arranging to see them just around the corner from the club at 1545.

Chapter Seven

Rufus, Don and Orla Ward, met Charles at the Special Forces Club in Knightsbridge, West London. Based in an Edwardian townhouse in a quiet street behind Harrods, it is a little oasis founded in 1945 by men and women who had served in the Special Operations Executive, or SOE, who wanted to ensure that there would always be a location in London where like minds could meet in a welcoming and discreet environment. There is no name plate and nothing to advertise what it is. The décor is understated and unlike other clubs in London it accepts men and women as well as all ranks, reflecting the spirit that exists in the Special Forces community of classlessness.

The three colleagues qualified in their own right to enter the club, Don and Rufus having retired from 22 SAS and Orla from the Special Reconnaissance Regiment or SRR: the only UKSF regiment to include women in operational roles.

They had taken very different paths into SF: Orla had started as a WREN and applied to the 14th Intelligence Company, or Det as it was colloquially known. Don had joined the Corp of Royal Signals, before opting for selection with the SAS, and Rufus had arrived at the same place via The Royal Marines.

Don and Orla had met when Don was an Electronic Warfare, IT and Communications instructor at the

Det, the forerunner of SRR, and Orla was a student on the course.

Their contact Charles McHugh did not qualify to enter. His line of work led him into contact with ex Special Forces soldiers on a frequent basis and whenever he could he chose to conduct meetings at the club. It was partly convenience, as it was close to the office, but primarily for the feeling it gave him: kudos by association. He had become such a frequent patron of the establishment that normally he was, unusually for non-members, allowed in before his guests arrived.

They met in The Prince Bernhard Room, as for some inexplicable reason this was Orla's favourite room.

"Why do you like this room so much Orla?" asked Rufus, the accepted leader of the group, as they walked in.

"I just like the photographs in here more than the other rooms. It gives it more character, more history. Something I thought you'd have understood with all the reading you do now."

"It's philosophy, neuro-linguistics and psychology – not interior decorating. A room is a room to me. Especially here."

"Barbarian," said Orla. "And what are you smirking at?" she said to her husband Don.

"Nothing my little sugar plum," said Don teasing her.

"Good to see you again Charles" said Rufus, and as they approached McHugh's table he rose from his chair to greet them.

"And you Ru. Don, Orla how are you?" rejoined Charles, "You are looking as radiant as ever." He said to Orla.

"Absolutely bloody brilliant," said Don.

"Thank you Charles," said Orla thinking he was slightly sleazy.

"Can I get you a drink?" asked Charles.

The three of them had a few little foibles and traditions, and while they were not superstitious they liked to pay their respects in their own way to their fallen comrades. One such little tradition was to have a Bloody Mary as the first drink at the club in honour of their friend and colleague Carl, a Captain in the SBS, killed in Afghanistan. It was always his drink when he came here. Sometime ago they realised that they had never asked him why, but they kept up his tradition and toasted him and the start of another job when their drinks arrived.

"Cheers," said Charles as all clinked their glasses together.

"Salute," said Rufus.

"Prost," said Don.

"Slainte," said Orla, calling on her Irish ancestry.

"To Carl," Don, Orla and Rufus said, took a drink from their glasses and sat down to business.

"I have a job in which I think you will be interested," said Charles. Rufus smiled inwardly. Charles was as rough and common as they were, he used to call himself a "rag arse builder" from when he did some labouring as a young man, but he had re-invented himself when he joined the military on a Short Service Commission and had read that "One should never end a sentence with a preposition" so he always tried to speak correctly. Since joining the insurance company he had become even more pretentious.

"What's that then Charlie?" said Don in his broadest Mancunian accent, teasing him. Don was proud of his roots, his accent and his ability and would not change for anybody or anything, not even for Orla, the undoubted love of his life.

Charles reached for his document case, bridling slightly at Don's tease, and extracted three small files which he passed to the people sat in front of him.

They sat back and read quietly, sometimes going back over a paragraph muttering to each other, sometimes shaking their heads in incredulity. They felt under no pressure to finish the document quickly, they all understood the importance of this initial briefing and they wanted to understand the facts before they started talking.

There were photographs of a very unassuming middle-aged couple, posing at what appeared to be a Christmas dinner, another of them arm in arm, apparently very comfortable in each other's company, they all looked for any tell-tale signs of friction, through body language, but none were apparent. There were individual photographs of each of them. There was a brief financial summary: a print out of their joint bank current account, with £2567; their savings account showing the recent deposit of £254 000; their mortgage was paid; and some other minor investments and savings.

There was a photograph of their daughter, Victoria, a twenty-five-year-old single woman, a recently graduated medical student from Liverpool University, now living close to her parents in Biggleswade, Bedfordshire. Her finances were very different to her parents' and she had built up a hefty student debt, which is the norm in England and did not cause them any suspicion at all.

They read from the AIM Abby had started: it was impossible to put themselves in her shoes, even though Rufus had told them that was what they had to try and do. He had been trained in Hostage negotiating in

London and in kidnap negotiating in Manchester by the British police and he was trying to give his two colleagues an insight into his specialism. Rufus knew that she would be panicking, feeling isolated and alone. It didn't matter how clever or resilient she was, in fact it was almost a natural law: 'When a person becomes a victim of a kidnap their ability to cope is inversely proportionate to their IQ', and being a doctor, she would have a high IQ. He thought that she, like the vast majority of the population, had never imagined herself in this position and her intellect would probably be playing havoc with her ability to rationalise and think cogently. Good people, nice people, don't get kidnapped.

They continued to read the document: Lunchtime today, Victoria received another call, this time in the presence of Charles, again from her mother's phone.

"Ok Charles, to save us reading this, can you brief us first hand?" asked Rufus.

"Um, yes, of course. Unfortunately I can't give you a verbatim record as my recorder failed to activate on the call. But fortunately I jotted down some notes, which you can see in your files.

In your panic you failed to record the conversation, thought Rufus.

"These are your notes?" asked Don as he looked at a photocopied sheet of A4 paper with a few instructions scribbled down and read out, "'$10million' 'No police' 'Professional' 'We will know' 'Ghost' 'Everywhere'. Can you remember anything else?"

"No, those are the salient points," retorted Charles defensively.

"Ethnicity of the kidnapper? Ambient sounds? Pace, pitch, tone of the voice? Proof of Life?" Don asked.

Rufus let his best mate have his head. He knew Don could be blunt, very blunt, and thought now was the right time for some straight talking. "What was Victoria's reaction? How was she coping? Did you try and keep the bandit on the phone to gather more intelligence? What were the threats?"

"Miss Conway didn't want any guidance she seemed to have it all under control," said a bridling McHugh.

"'Under Control'? If she has, she is Superwoman, Wonderwoman, and Lara Croft rolled into one. I've seen and heard recordings Ru has brought back and they are unbelievable. People go to pieces: she has got responsibility for the lives of her parents, and you expect us to believe she had everything 'under control'?" said Don, struggling to keep his voice down and his anger in check.

They turned the page and could see another photocopied sheet of handwritten paper containing what they assumed were Victoria's scribbled, frantic notes with "$10m to be delivered by me to DeS, or one of them dies", written clearly at the bottom of the page and underlined three times.

"Charles," started Rufus, "when this is all over we really must sit down and discuss your company's first response. If you are not comfortable with us doing the training, I'll put you in touch with some police trainers I keep in contact with who will give you some basic guidelines, but I guess now is not the time."

"But, but..." Charles was about to emit a litany of excuses, however, he could see by Rufus's face that they would not wash..." Yes ok. Ru, when this job's over, we'll get together."

Chapter Eight

"Mmmm," said Orla opening the discussions after finishing reading "this could be difficult" as the opening salvo of the forthcoming negotiations on price. She was actually thinking "Bunch of fuckin half-wit amateurs"

"I would have thought you would be quietly confident Orla," said Charles. "My clients have the couple insured for £2 million ... each."

"What's the deal then, Charles?" asked Rufus.

"£50k expenses, then 5% of whatever you save my clients."

"Five per cent of which figure we save them Charles?" asked Don.

"Of the sum insured for kidnap of course," said Charles.

"How much is the pay-out for death?" asked Rufus.

"They haven't been killed," said Charles, fully expecting this bargaining tactic.

"One of them might be in four days' time," said Orla, "and what would be the pay-out on that?"

"Ok seven point five per cent of the sum you save my clients on the kidnap figure"

"Twelve point five."

"Ten," said Charles. "That's still a tidy sum and you know it."

They knew he had acquiesced too quickly and calculated 10% of £4 million was £400, 000; they could afford to offer up a considerable sum of money and still be well in profit, even if they got paid half of that much it would still be worthwhile. They prided themselves on their ethics, honesty and integrity. They knew that a young woman was worried sick about her parents and time was of the essence. They knew Charles was well within his authorised offer, but didn't want to push him; this was a win-win as far as they were concerned. They passed unseen glances between each other.

"Ok Charles, we'll do it," said Orla, speaking for the team.

"Excellent," said McHugh, pleased that it was the more conciliatory Orla speaking, rather than her Rottweiler husband.

Don excused himself while Orla and Rufus asked Charles more questions over drinks. Most of which he was unable to answer as only Victoria would be able to answer some of the more personal details about her parents and herself.

After a few minutes they were re-joined by Don who had been checking flights and hotels on his tablet, he sat down and gave them the thumbs up.

They discussed basic plans and logistics.

"There's a Qatar flight leaving Heathrow tomorrow evening, I've booked two seats on that," Don informed them.

"Excellent Donald," said McHugh.

"Business class," said Don, staring at him pointedly "On Xs".

"Um, yes, right of course," stammered McHugh.

"I've reserved adjoining rooms in the Kilimanjaro Hotel in Dar in your alias of 'Lionel' Ru, Open ended. On Xs."

"Thanks Don," said Rufus.

"Naturally," said McHugh.

"What else have you got for us Charles?" asked Orla.

"We have phone numbers, email addresses and Victoria's Facebook address. We have the Conways' Skype names, passport details and itinerary."

"There's very little I can do with Skype. That's why we use it when the guys deploy." Don told McHugh. "Anything else you can give us?"

"Not at the moment. Our loss adjustment team are working on gathering as much information as they can, and when they get it, I'll get it to you," McHugh told them.

They concluded their meeting with handshakes all round and Charles told them he would have the contract ready for them to formally agree and sign within the hour. Essentially he just had to put the figures in the spaces left and print it off.

"One last thing please Charles," said Rufus. "Can you call Victoria now, from your phone and make the introductions? It will be a lot simpler and quicker that way."

"Oh yes, of course."

Victoria could see that it was Charles McHugh phoning, and was tempted not to pick up the call, as the idiot had not really helped her at all so far, but of course she had to.

"Hello Charles," she answered.

"Hi Victoria. I have just finished my meeting with some colleagues and have briefed them on the state of play and I'd rather like to pass you over to Rufus who will be dealing with you from now on."

Victoria could hardly bear the thought of dealing with yet another idiot, somebody else who would want to listen to the entire story, just so he could fill his forms in.

"Yes ok." she said in a distracted monotone voice.

Charles handed the phone to Rufus. Don quickly attached a small microphone to the handset as Rufus went into a corner of the room so that he could concentrate and not be distracted by anybody else and spoke to Victoria for the first time.

"Hello Victoria, my name is Rufus and together with my two colleagues I have been asked to help you."

"Right," said Victoria, *another bumbling idiot I've got to tell the whole story to.*

"I just can't begin to imagine what you must be going through. Are you alright?"

What?? Here is the first person to ask me how I am feeling rather than what has happened.

"NO I'M NOT FUCKING ALRIGHT," she screamed down the phone, venting her spleen on Rufus. "MY PARENTS HAVE BEEN KIDNAPPED, THREATENED WITH DEATH UNLESS I GET $10 MILLION, WHICH I HAVENT GOT. I'M SAT HERE FRANTIC WITH WORRY, NOBODY IS DOING ANYTHING TO HELP AND YOU ASK IF I'M ALRIGHT."

Rufus was used to this sort of reaction, and did not take it personally, emotions run very high and things are said which are often regretted afterwards.

"IT MUST BE TERRIBLE VICTORIA, I'm really sorry for you," was all he said. Initially matching

Victoria's pitch and volume, deliberately, then bringing it down, moderating his voice to control her.

Victoria's voice moderated too:

"It is terrible, I don't know what to do. I don't know what to say. I don't know who to trust, I feel so responsible and so... so impotent."

"Well we have to do one thing at a time, a little like when you are diagnosing a patient; you take a step at a time, methodically, and systematically, until you have built up a fuller picture. That's what we will do together." Rufus had deliberately used the simile to get Victoria thinking in a different way, a way she was used to and understood, rather than trying to think in alien terms. "First of all I will text you my phone number, to the phone you are using now, I will also text you details of my colleagues Orla and Don, so if for some reason you can't get hold of me, you can get them."

"Thank you," said Victoria fighting to hold back tears.

"From what I have been told, even though I don't think we will get another call this evening, I will give you some dos and don'ts should the kidnappers call you before I get there."

"Ok." sobbed Victoria.

"Because we have only just been told about you, it's going to take me some time to get home, sort my gear out and drive up to you, but I will be as quick as I can, and if it's alright with you, I will come and stay the night with you?"

"Oh yes please." The flood gates opened, *at last some support, I just hope that this guy will give me some help and guidance not like that McHugh idiot who just sat there and did nothing, just thinking about himself.*

Rufus could hear Victoria crying and started talking to give her a little time to compose herself.

When Rufus thought Victoria was mentally with him again, he gave her some simple 'holding' instructions. Although he had said do's and don'ts to her, he actually only gave her some 'do's' and no don'ts. He believed that the subconscious mind cannot process negative information, and that's what he wanted to influence: so if he told Victoria **NOT** to think of something, that's what she would focus on, it was vitally important for him to get her to concentrate on positives.

"Ok Victoria, just a few simple instructions until we get there, are you ready?"

"Yes, yes, I'm ok now."

"If they call back, then answer the call and try and record the conversation. If you forget, just make a note of the time and the salient points. Reassure them that you are going to get their money, but that $10 million is a lot for anybody to raise and will be very difficult. Ask to speak to Martyn. That's all I want you to do until I get there. Have you got all of that?"

"Yes, I've jotted it all down. Thank you," said Victoria.

"Ok. I will be with you as quickly as possible and remember, only use the phone you are using now to contact us."

"Yes I know... Rufus?"

"Yes?"

"How long will you be?"

"I'll be as fast as I can, I have to get out of town, go home, pack some things and drive to you. So it's a good few hours. I'll call you with updates as I go. One last thing Victoria: what is your favourite band?"

"Um, oh, 'The Editors' I guess. Why?"

"To avoid any confusion, and so that you know it is me, if I phone you, and when I arrive I will use the code words 'Deacon Blue', it will probably be in a sentence and you should reply that you prefer 'The Editors'. It's just a simple little technique I use so that we both know we are talking to the right people AND you are free to speak."

"Oh. Alright. Do you think it is necessary?"

"Probably not, but until we know for certain, I'd rather to be safe than sorry."

"Can't you get here any faster? It's just that everything seems to be happening so slowly. I feel so alone and so powerless," implored Victoria.

"I will be with you as fast as I possibly can Victoria, you see I plan to fly us out to Tanzania tomorrow and ..."

"What? TANZANIA? TOMORROW?"

"Yes, it's important we get out there as soon as we can to show you are serious."

"Well of course I'm serious, it just came as a bit of a shock that's all."

"Yes, I guess you are going to have to adjust from nothing seeming to happen, to bouts of frenetic activity, back to nothing happening, that's the way these things work."

There was silence on the other end of the phone.

"Victoria? Can you hear me?"

"Yes, I can hear you, I'm just a bit stunned, that's all."

"Sorry about that, where was I? Oh, yes, and there are certain arrangements we have to make and logistics to be sorted out, I've asked Don to get all of this done before we fly. I promise you we are doing everything as fast as we can. We are trying to get us on the evening flight tomorrow from Heathrow, so I have to get everything prepared before that. I promise you we are working hard. You won't always see the work we are doing, but it is important preparatory work to ensure we get Deidre and Martyn back safely."

Rufus gesticulated to Don, Orla and Charles that he was leaving without breaking the conversation with Victoria and walked out of the building towards the tube, leaving them to finalise the contract, before Don and Orla joined him.

They continued talking as he walked. Rufus asking a few questions, but mainly letting Victoria talk, a deliberate tactic on his part. Not interrupting her, or telling her about worse incidents he had dealt with. She wouldn't care about other kidnappings, *this* was the most important thing in her life at the moment and how this ranked in terms of difficulty was immaterial to her: this was *her* mum and dad.

Rufus finished the conversation with the most sensitive of subjects, and trod carefully.

He knew there was no point trying to lie to Victoria about it; she was a doctor after all.

"I would like you to collect some personal belongings of your mum and dad's: toothbrushes or combs, anything that can get us a DNA match that we can take with us."

"Why? Do you think they are dead?"

"No I don't. I wouldn't be going with you if I thought that, you would need other specialists not me. No, if we find somewhere we think they might have been kept, what we call a stronghold, we might need to take samples to double-check that they were there. It helps us build our intelligence picture," he told her the partial truth.

"Oh, ok."

"And also some comfortable clothes for them. When we get them back they might want to change into something fresh and familiar". Rufus deliberately used the word "when" a presupposition which would subliminally get Victoria to think and hopefully visualise getting her mum and dad back. Again he was being economical with the truth. Yes, of course they would want fresh clothes, but perhaps even more, they would want to get out of the orange overalls that they were probably being kept in, as quickly as possible.

Chapter Nine

Martyn felt around the pitch black room, trying to adjust his eyes to the dark, he couldn't see a thing. It was oppressively hot and airless.

His other senses kicked in and were working in overdrive. He kept imagining he heard small animals scurrying along the floor; he WAS imagining it wasn't he? Because adrenalin was surging through his veins it made his skin react and tingle as if something was crawling over him, but he didn't realise that was the cause. He felt things touching his face, arms and legs, what was it? Spiders? Mosquitoes? He felt his skin itching, feeling the tiny creatures scurrying over him, biting him, stinging him. Or was it all his imagination? As the sweat trickled down his legs and arms, it felt like bugs crawling on him. Had the little bastards bitten him? Panic swelled in his head again, what if it was a poisonous spider? He didn't want to start shouting or screaming as that would show weakness, but he needed to talk to them to explain they had got the wrong person. His dark thoughts returned, *shit was that a sting on my foot? Calm, calm, keep calm and think.* Martyn took deep breaths; he had to get control of himself, think. Think logically, objectively. Surely they would realise they had made a mistake and they would let him go soon. He wondered what had happened to

Deidre. Was she alive or dead? How could he make them realise they had made a mistake? He could say about four words in Swahili, Thank you: Asante, thank you very much: Asante sana, You're welcome: Kariboo and good: mzuri, and that was it, that was all a Mzungu tourist needed to get by, smile and say thank you. He wasn't going to get very far with that.

He felt the walls and found what he assumed was the door. He started banging on it, he had to attract their attention and explain somehow, find somebody who spoke English. They hadn't really hurt him yet, perhaps they wouldn't. His bangs got progressively louder. Nothing, no response, nothing at all – not even somebody telling him to shut the fuck up, or threaten him. He felt the panic starting again. He could hear rats or mice in the room, he was sure of it, and that smell, he'd noticed it before, as if a rat had died in the room some time previously, *Oh my God*, the thought of it, rats in the room, mice would be bad enough crawling over his sandled feet, but rats... he felt bile rising in his throat. And what if he fell asleep and the rats attacked him. He'd heard stories of rats eating people, he'd read a book about a Mafia hit man who filmed rats eating his victims. Martyn couldn't contain his fear any longer and was sick, his puke splashed all over his shins, ankles and feet; the smell of it making him gag again.

He had to get control of himself. He moved to the farthest corner of the tiny room, away from his vomit. The fetid smell was overpowering and cloying, making him feel claustrophobic in the small, hot, airless room. He stood in the corner, trying to control his breathing and his mind, the contact with his shoulders and back against the wall somehow giving him some comfort, as he knew nothing could be behind him.

Just as he was getting control over his nerves something ran over his foot, he wasn't imagining it. Something definitely ran over his foot, he rubbed it with his hand to take away the feeling of four little feet that scampered over him, and as he did so he realised he was rubbing his hand in his sticky, clammy puke. *AAAHHHGGG* his head screamed, he wanted to cry, he wanted to clean his hand, but what could he clean it on? His clothes? The wall? He didn't want to do either, but he had to clean his hand somehow. He remembered he had a pack of tissues in the right side cargo pocket of his shorts. He couldn't use his right hand to open the pocket and rummage around for the tissues, so he had to fumble with his left, to extract the tissues and eventually cleaned off most of the mess from his hand. He used the remaining tissues to clean his feet and legs as best he could.

He felt like collapsing, but the thought of the rodents creeping over him, smelling him with those long whiskery snouts, biting him, made him shudder. He'd also read that rats are doubly incontinent so they would be pissing and crapping on him at the same time. He had to get out of there, he would give them money, he would give them anything, just let him out.

He started banging on the door, again, he could hear it reverberating through the building; the place, wherever he was, sounded large and empty. He shouted Deidre's name and waited for the reply, but couldn't hear anything. Panic and dread filled his mind, where was she? Who were the kidnappers? Why had they been kidnapped?

Chapter Ten

Rufus ran his hand over his 'go-bag'; the Sand and Storm tan, cow hide leather holdall he'd bought in Nairobi on a previous job, pre-packed with the basics of what he needed for any job to which he was deployed. One of his passports, a few toiletries, minimal changes of underwear, two plain white T-shirts, power adaptors, tissues, pens, note pads, and his iPad. There are not many places in the world these days where you can't get a few essentials. While business class was liberal in its interpretation of hand luggage, his experience of yomping thirty miles across Dartmoor with a twenty-five pound Bergen and the SAS selection hike navigating forty miles across the Brecon Beacons with a sixty pound Bergen, influenced his decision to always travel light. He loved the smell and feel of the tardic portmanteau into which he could easily fit everything he needed. Don was preparing a few IT essentials but there'd still be plenty of room for those.

After his time in the military Rufus never underestimated the importance of good footwear in looking after one's feet and as he would only take one pair, they had to be good ones. It takes up to eight weeks to produce a pair of Church's shoes in Northampton, each undergoing over 250 detailed manual operations before they leave the factory. He appreciated this attention to detail, and were his favourite "work" shoes. They were comfortable, hard wearing and appeared to be indestructible. He had abused them outrageously on deployments but had only needed to have them 'refurbished' once. He couldn't believe how good they still looked.

He chose his clothes, which had to be multifunctional, carefully and deliberately. First impressions count and 'you only get one chance to make a first impression'. He selected his dark brown Ralph Lauren mole skin chinos and his favourite white cotton shirt, tailor fitted from Boss, along with his sand coloured Paul Smith linen blazer. Finishing off with an Oliver Sweeny tan colour leather belt and his regimental Breitling watch, he was good to go.

He mused to himself that if he told his parents how much this outfit cost, they would choke. It easily added up to more than their first house. Although never one to be sartorially extravagant, he kept these few key pieces in his wardrobe that would stand the rigours of travel and be comfortable enough should he find that they were the only clothes available to him over extended time periods.

Don phoned to confirm the Qatar Airways flight QR002 departing Heathrow at 2030, via Qatar, then heading on south to Dar es Salaam, two seats in business class. Since BA had stopped flying to Tanzania, it was about as direct as you can get.

He showered, dressed and examined himself in the mirror. He wondered if he should wear a tie. He held up his two favourites, a Pal Zileri and his Duchamp and decided against either, they looked too flash. Not the image he was looking for.

Rufus had only one vice and that was cars. He had a Lotus Elise, which he had bought with the profits from a previous job; a Caterham Seven 620R, which he had wanted for as long as he could remember and which he loved racing on the track; and a Jag XF automatic. He had bought one when he retired from the Regiment and as his 'company' car had upgraded several times. He'd better take the Jag, it made the right impression and he thought it made a statement about him: not too ostentatious, solid, reliable, understated and British.

He put a bottle of water and his holdall into the car and slid off the driveway, the 3 litre V6 engine effortlessly pulling the 1,770kg car away. He loved driving this car, it had all the power, comfort and room that he needed. Rufus had opted for the automatic and now couldn't understand why anybody would drive a manual; the technology was so good. If he wanted to, he could always put the car into manual, but why bother? He kept it spotless, absolutely pristine, as he had his weapon when he was in the army.

En route to Victoria, Rufus employed some anti-surveillance measures that Orla had taught him watching for any reaction from possible adversaries. Although he didn't think he would be followed, or watched as he approached Victoria's, it was important for him to stay alert, to always treat everything as if combating top-class opposition, that way he could never be taken by surprise.

He arrived at the Conways' house in Biggleswade, with the aid of his inbuilt GPS without incident. He got out of the car in the evening sunlight and walked up the short path, the gravel crunching beneath his feet, through a very pretty, quintessential English garden which spoke volumes about the sort of people they would be trying to bring back. The lawn was neat and even though they had been away for a couple of weeks, one could still see the mow lines in the grass. There were roses and clematis climbing up the wall of the house, while the lawn was bordered with hollyhocks, lavender and marigolds giving the garden a welcoming aroma and colour. A small herb garden was also trim, laid out in a geometric pattern.

Victoria opened the door just as he was about to ring the bell and burst into tears. She had been determined not to, but she couldn't help it. The stress, pressure and tension had proved too much and the arrival of Rufus sent her over the edge. She forgot about code words and security and simply buried her head in his chest as the tears cascaded down her cheeks. Rufus let her sob her heart out. He could feel her whole body shaking against his as some of the pressure transferred from her to him. After a minute or two, she began to regain control and he reached into his pocket and produced a pack of tissues. She blew her nose and dried her eyes.

He hadn't been followed so there was no need to take evasive action and simply said "Your clematis is stunning and just look at that beautiful buddleia."

This was completely out of the left field for Victoria, who looked at the flowers in the garden for the first time in two days.

She started to sob and laugh at the same time as the relief kicked in. This was the first 'normal' conversation she had had for thirty-six hours, the first time she had thought about anything except the kidnapping.

"You're right," she exclaimed, "It's such a pretty garden. Mum's got green fingers and Dad's very meticulous. It does look good doesn't it?"

She was petite with creamy skin, large green eyes that looked sunken and dark from the stress and lack of sleep with a thatch of dark hair cut in a practical bob. She wore a pair of dark green fitted jeans and a paisley country and western style shirt with mother of pearl press studs that seemed to hide rather than enhance her figure. Rufus had the impression of an honest, hardworking young woman.

"Is the herb garden patterned on the old Elizabethan shape do you know," he asked quietly. Surprised, she looked at this smart, ordinary looking man in front of her. She didn't know what she had been expecting, some sort of super hero, she guessed, someone who could wave a magic wand to make everything better. He certainly wasn't that, but everything about him exuded confidence, without arrogance, perhaps even with a touch of humility. She noted the quality of his clothes, his watch and his shiny smart shoes. He was handsome enough, clean shaven with a strong jawline and an engaging warm smile, which transmitted resolve and professionalism. But it was his eyes that really struck her, symmetrical large and filled with wisdom and warmth. Were they blue or green? Were they smiling at her?

Chapter Eleven

They moved inside. Rufus smiled to himself *she has forgotten all about the code words we've agreed.*

"I've always liked Deacon Blue," said Rufus smiling at her, forgiving her basic error of believing who he was without checking first.

Victoria looked at him with a blank expression. Rufus made his code words as simple as possible.

"Deacon Blue?" repeated Rufus "Do you like Deacon Blue?"

"Oh, Oh yes," exclaimed Victoria "Erm, I prefer The Editors."

"Yes they're good too, I particularly like *Bricks and Mortar*."

"Oh I'm sorry Rufus, you are Rufus aren't you? Oh, I feel such a fool, but I just can't think straight, thank God you are here you will get them back won't you? I just feel so helpless, they will be ok won't they? Where are the rest of you, how are you going to get them back?" was blurted out in one machine-gun breath, and Rufus let her get it all out. She had so many questions racing around her head, and until now, nobody to ask. Rufus was grateful that Charles hadn't spent too long with her, as he would have made even more mistakes than those he had already committed and that would mean even more hard work and time spent for him.

Two of Stephen Covey's "7 Habits" Rufus practises religiously are: begin with the end in mind; and put first things first. This was exactly what he needed to do now. He had become a voracious reader of self-improvement, language and psychology books and he thought Covey's philosophy transcended all three, it was his favourite aide memoire; easy to pick up at any point in the book when he had some down-time, and refresh his practises.

As well as giving Victoria the support she badly needed, he would be demonstrating his commitment, building up his kudos with her. He had allowed time for this phase of rapport building; an essential aspect to his long-term plan. He had learned time and time again, he could influence people's actions, if he had built this essential trust with them and that's what rapport building was all about, only then could he move on to eventually reach the end game.

"Take a seat Vicky," he eventually said in a calm assured manner. "I'm Rufus. Rufus Stone, I work with Orla and Don, she's the surveillance side and he's the technical side of the team and they'll be along to do some clever things to your phone if that's ok? Most people call me Ru, except my mum, who always calls me Rufus. Oh and you might hear Don or Orla call me 'Pebble' sometimes. Any of them are fine by me."

"Pebble?"

"Yeh, it started when I joined the Royal Marines and stuck, you know, the sort of thing, the training staff said I wasn't big enough to be a Stone, so called me Pebble. Some old colleagues only know me as that. Right you need to know a little bit about me I think. Why am I here? What gives me the ability or credentials to come and help you? Well, I'm a retired soldier and I've been trained by the British Police in negotiating in crises and kidnap situations; and I will make you two promises:" Rufus held his right thumb up to signify the number one. "I will be with you throughout what I can only imagine is a living hell for you;" Rufus held up his right index finger "and I will do everything in my power to get your mum and dad, Deidre and Martyn, back safely." He deliberately used their names to personalise them, to make them real people. Names are a powerful tool.

"Now, can you tell me from the beginning what happened, and if it's alright with you I will be recording what you say, so that if I need to double-check something I can. Ok?" And he put his phone on the table.

Victoria nodded her assent and said:

"I can't understand it Rufus. I'm a doctor. I see casualties in A&E every day. I make life and death decisions every day. But I've completely gone to pieces. I bet you are thinking I am a stupid, young girl who can't cope?"

"And when you are in A&E you are in control aren't you?"

"Yes, I suppose so."

"You say something and it gets done?"

"Well yes."

"You've had seven years' training in what to do?"

"Yes and it's on-going."

"And how many times have you operated on your mum and dad, wearing boxing gloves and a blindfold?"

"What?"

"That's the equivalent of what you are doing? You feel you have your parents' lives in your hands and you don't know what to do. That's why I'm here. If I'd broken my arm, I'd come to you."

"I understand. Do you think they will be ok?" asked Victoria.

"I hope so, and we must work together to ensure that they are."

"Have you done many of these things?" she asked, almost to the script that Rufus had in his head from previous jobs. Everybody wanted to know how many he'd done.

"I have lost count now Vicky, when I was still in the military I used to be invited by my friends in the police to go to some of their kidnaps as an observer, and they would let me help out as well. Since I retired from the army I've been involved in quite a few now, all over the world."

"How many?"

"It must be well over fifty all told."

"Fifty? Really? Are there that many? And do you always get them back?"

"Not all of them no," he said with a tinge of sadness in his voice, but he maintained eye contact "but the ones I failed in were because people didn't follow my advice and thought they could do a better job on their own. I'm being completely straight when I say that. Kidnap negotiations are a mixture of process and flair, and you have to know the process before you can cut corners or improvise. A bit like your job, until you are an experienced doctor, you follow the rules, your training and the process, but once you know it, you can use your experience and instinct to make faster better informed decisions."

"I see what you mean," said Victoria, pulling at the sleeve of her shirt.

"We need to work as a team, a team that is unbreakable, whose trust in each other is unwavering,

I will ask you to say things which are counter intuitive and you must trust me. Don't worry if you make a mistake. Mistakes happen and we will use them to our advantage. I'll explain all these things to you in more detail later, we will have lots of time to talk and discuss things. Now, can you tell me what happened?"

Victoria spoke for about forty minutes re-telling her story for the fourth time: this time there were no interruptions, he just let her talk, and talk, sometimes jumping from one subject to another, but telling the story the way she wanted to tell it, not to conform to a pro forma. If anything he enabled her to flow more freely and got more information. He listened to her, maintaining an interested look without staring at her; she could emphasise what she wanted to emphasise and talk about her feelings and thoughts, which to a form-filler are irrelevant, but to a negotiator, essential. She could see him nodding in agreement, or raising his eyebrows at certain parts; cocking his head to one side or another; or grimacing when she re-told a particularly painful memory; sometimes he would just "Hmm Hmm" or echo her last couple of words, showing her all of the time that he was listening to her.

He took in her body language, or para-language, as best he could. He noted that she played with her left cuff with her middle and ring finger, pulling it down towards her hand when she got anxious. She worried the right side of her bottom lip, with her canine tooth when she got upset.

Those were the only two signs of anxiety he could detect. Everything else told him she was telling the truth. She maintained eye contact, not staring at him, but was open to him. Her eyes would momentarily dart to the right, accessing her memory. She kept her hands away from her mouth, and rarely folded her arms, the only time she did was when she recounted her mum coming on the phone. Many people might have taken that as a deception signal, but Rufus was able to see the rest of her body and read it as a comforting action. Most of all he tuned in to her pace. Victoria was quite a fast talker, she had a natural rhythm which was slightly faster than his, almost certainly a sign of her intelligence and speed of thought, which he processed and analysed and knew that he would have to speed up his natural rhythm in order to build rapport more quickly. He always thought of it as the same as walking with somebody: if you wanted to you could change their pace by matching it initially before subtly slowing down or speeding up to suit your purposes and most of the time the other person would unconsciously follow suit.

He needed Victoria to know that she and her parents were the most important people to him at the moment. Rufus had often argued with people, mainly, but not exclusively, ex-military colleagues, who espoused that Active Listening Skills were a complete misnomer, and a waste of time, but he knew different: he had seen the way people react to being listened to and the power and influence it gave him. Victoria was pleasantly surprised that he let her talk the way he did. She was already feeling better, because as she spoke, he acted like a sounding board, just reflecting her words, letting her think and work things out for herself. Almost like saying a prayer. It's a one-way conversation, but somehow helps to clarify one's thoughts.

Only when Victoria had finished did Rufus start to ask questions, confirming to her that he had been listening.

Rufus's voice was calm and unflustered, which made Victoria feel her senses were being massaged; it reassured her and made her believe that he knew what he was doing and he was telling her the truth: even the unpalatable part about not always getting people back alive, somehow gave her confidence in this man who she had only just met. He could have bullshitted her easily and said "Yes", but he didn't he told her the truth. She was beginning to feel calmer already.

"I've got quite a few questions as a result of what you've told me. Are you ready?"

"Yes, go on."

"What does Martyn do for a living?"

"He's retired now, but he worked in a bank. He had several different jobs for them: at one point he was a Bank Manager, but they seemed to get rid of all of those didn't they? Then he was in charge of one of the call centres, but they closed that down and moved it abroad and they offered him voluntary redundancy, so he took it and busied himself in the garden and his ramblers group. He's on the Parish council and a member of lots of groups. He keeps himself really fit and active."

"And Deidre, what does she do?"

"Mum did admin work for various charities, and she took a lot of courses, she studied body language, now I come to think about it she's quite cerebral, loves crossword puzzles and Sudoku. They're quite conservative really, hence my name, you can't much more traditional can you? Dad the bread winner and Mum the home maker while I was growing up. She retired shortly after Dad did. Dad has decent pension off the bank, but not millions, just enough to live comfortably," she finished, indicating the living room as confirmation of what she was saying.

"But you don't know who she worked for or exactly what she did?"

"No. I don't really. When she started work I was such a swot, studying for exams, I didn't pay that much attention. And once I was at uni and living my own life...I don't believe in living in your parents' pockets." They offered to pay all of my loans off, but I've refused, it's my life my decisions, my responsibility. I don't want them to have any leverage over me. If I want to take a sabbatical and go back to India with Médecins Sans Frontières, I can and will. Why? Is it important?"

"I don't know. You never know what is important. I just like to have as much information as I can, so that nothing can surprise us. Again, in your job, if somebody is brought in, you ask lots of questions, some of which may be irrelevant, or they may not be, but you don't know until you get the answer. And even then people don't think things are important enough to tell you, or choose to withhold it."

"Oh I know exactly what you mean there. We ask people if they are on medication and they say 'No' next minute they're having a reaction because they forgot to tell us about what prescriptions they are on. I understand and I'll have a look around to see if there are any wage slips or anything like that if you want?"

"That's a good idea Victoria. It may be of no use whatsoever, but I'd like to know. Just a few more questions first though. What did the guy who phoned you sound like?"

"I was confused by his voice. He sounded African. Don't ask me to explain what I mean, but he did. He sounded quite well educated and I imagined him as a big man. He had a big voice. He used some polysyllabic words, but they didn't sound natural to him."

"Were there background noises on either call?"

"Um, it sounded quite echoey, like he was in a big room."

"What time exactly were the calls made?"

Victoria checked her phone and said:

"Ten to two for the second one ..." she went back through her history... "and eight minutes past eleven for the first one."

Rufus's phone rang and he could see it was Don calling, as there was a natural break in the conversation he took the call. All Victoria heard were some grunts and monosyllabic replies from Rufus, she was curious about who he was talking to and what was being said. *Are they talking about me? Is it bad news? Is it somebody out in Tanzania?* She tried to interpret Rufus's facial expressions, but he wasn't giving anything away.

After a few minutes the call was ended and Rufus turned to her and said, "Orla and Don will be here in a few minutes," and left it at that.

Chapter Twelve

Don had updated Rufus on the end of the meeting and other things: Charles had let a little more information out; the insurance company had been carrying out background checks with the High Commission at Dar es Salaam; they had started full financial checks on the couple and Victoria; they had initiated CRB checks; National Insurance and employment checks, in short, they had started a comprehensive intelligence and data trawl about all of the Conways to evaluate the validity of the claim. He said that he and Orla had been at the Conways' premises for the last thirty minutes, observing all movements and anything untoward around the house. After they were satisfied that they were not being watched they had placed sensors around the house and garden which would alert them if anyone approached during their stay. But Victoria didn't need to know any of this, Rufus needed her to concentrate and be focused on her role, not worry about technical details.

"I'll put the kettle on for them," said Victoria. "Do you want another cup?"

"Yes please."

She stood up and walked quickly into the kitchen and he got up and followed her, looking around, confirming the conclusion he had come to in the lounge:

a neat and tidy kitchen; standard white appliances with nothing out of the ordinary.

Rufus watched her and thought some of her self-assurance and young invincibility was returning. In the kitchen she went about her task smoothly and efficiently putting the kettle on, rinsing the tea pot, getting the tea caddy, milk, sugar, spoons and biscuits, all confirming Rufus's impression of her natural pace. They chatted in the kitchen until his phone rang, telling him that Orla and Don were at the front door. He told Victoria they were there and she opened the door to the sight of two workers dressed in delivery uniforms carrying a rather large box. She looked around at Rufus, with a look of confusion and anxiety on her face.

"It's Ok Victoria, it's Orla and Don, you can let them in."

The two "workers" carried their large box into the house and shut the door behind them, they put down the heavy looking box and extended their hands to Victoria.

"Hello Vicky, I'm Orla."

"Pleased to meet you Orla," said a bewildered Victoria.

"And I'm Don, Orla's lackey, or husband as it's more conventionally known."

They all shook hands and Victoria still looked bewildered, looking back and forth from Rufus to Don and Orla.

"Even though we are pretty sure that everything is alright here Victoria, we take a lot of precautions to be on the safe side, this is just a little ruse we sometimes use to get into places without attracting too much attention," explained Rufus.

The four of them sat in the lounge and drank the tea Victoria had made, making small talk. As he got to the bottom of the cup Rufus addressed Victoria again.

"I said I would ask you to do things that might seem a little odd, and my first request is for you to give both of your phones to Don now, as he will need to make some adaptions to them for when we are in Tanzania."

Victoria gave the phones to Don, and without any hesitation whatsoever, he went into the kitchen with his lap top and small tool kit. He shut the blinds to hide from any prying eyes, even though he was sure the kidnappers were not anywhere near them, and closing curtains and blinds would be quite natural at his time of the evening.

Rufus continued with Victoria, while Orla sat and seemingly just drank her tea, but like Rufus, she was taking everything in. Orla was even more observant that Rufus. She had been trained by the best of the best in the 14th Intelligence Company or Det, and then the SRR. She had survived because of her observational abilities, noticing when something was amiss or out of the ordinary. She had been an unusual recruit into the Det because she was an Irish Catholic: born just outside of Cork, in a small village with one school and two pubs; a grass track as a main road, where a visit to the big city was an adventure. She attended the Sproid Naomh primary school, before moving to Birmingham, England with her parents when she passed the eleven plus entrance exam to get a place at Rose Hill Road Grammar School. From there she had joined then WRENS, before applying for selection at the DET and being deployed back to Ireland.

"Who else knows about this Victoria?"

"Nobody," she said.

"What about your colleague Craig, and the insurance company, who did you tell there?"

"Oooo, I didn't think you meant that, I thought you meant other than them."

"No I need to know anybody at all, or anybody that asked any strange questions," said Rufus. The prospect of an 'inside agent' had been hammered home on the numerous training courses that he had attended, and myriad examples had been given, which had proved invaluable to Rufus and had saved him a lot of time and his life on more than one occasion. The world of kidnap had proven to be a world of smoke and mirrors in which he adopted the Police Investigators' maxim of ABC: Accept nothing. Believe nobody. Check everything. And at that very moment Don was downloading data from Victoria's personal phone to run cross checks on all of the calls and texts she had made and received. He would also load software onto both phones to allow him to monitor their usage and location nearly anywhere in the world. None of them really suspected Victoria of having anything to do with her parents' kidnapping, especially with the easy way she handed the phones over, but it was one of their standard operating procedures.

"Oh, oh Ok. Um, the first person I told was Craig, who advised me to phone the insurance company, I told the first person I spoke to there that they had been kidnapped and she put me through to Charles McHugh and I've told him everything. He told me not to mention it to anybody else."

"And you haven't?"

"No. No, I promise."

Don reappeared and gave Victoria her phones. "From the briefing we have been given, your mum and dad have only taken your mum's phone," said Don.

"Yes."

"Do you know where your dad's phone is, so I can have a look at that as well please?" he asked.

"Dad's? Why do you want Dad's?"

"Well just in case any messages have been left from the kidnappers, you never know. They might have tried your dad's phone before yours."

"Oh, ok. I'll get it for you," said Victoria rising from her seat to get the phone. "That's strange, I was sure he'd left it in the bureau." She checked her parents' bedroom and still couldn't find the phone. "I'm sorry Don, I don't know where he has left it."

"No problem Victoria, it was only on the off chance anyway."

Rufus continued to double-check the information he had until he was satisfied he had over 90% of what she knew. People would always forget something important, or withhold something which they had either overlooked or thought was irrelevant to the incident, but that would come out in time. It was almost impossible for it not to, as he and Victoria would be together for sixteen to twenty hours a day.

When he had exhausted her, she went back to her parents' bureau to look for any documentation pertaining to her mum's work.

After about another fifteen minutes she returned to Rufus and said, "That's strange. I can find all of Dad's employment paperwork and pension papers, but I can't find anything of Mum's."

By this time Don was finished and so Rufus said, "Well don't worry about it now, we'll get Don to make some National Insurance checks and see if he can find anything while we are flying. I'm sure it will all be ok."

It troubled all three of the colleagues that there seemed to be a piece of the jigsaw missing about Deidre: Why would that be? Was Victoria lying about not knowing, or not being able to find any documents? These were things that Rufus knew he would have to leave to Don.

Rufus excused himself from Victoria while he conferred with his two colleagues. Don gave him a small wash-bag which didn't contain any toiletries, he looked at the bag as Don explained:

"Well you can't take too much through customs, so I've put some things in, that I think you might need in somewhere like Tanzania," he said with a smile on his face.

Rufus examined the bag and found: sticky tape, Blu-tac, a wooden wedge, sandpaper, a safety razor, a pack of cocktail sticks, some para-cord, a coat hook, a pack of three condoms, some wire, a small mirror, some garden cable ties, a wind-up torch with USB attachments, and talcum powder Hardly hi-tech *James Bond* equipment, and looked at Don quizzically.

"They all have a potential use out there. I can't give you knives and guns because you won't get them out of the country, or yourself for that matter, and I can't give you anything that runs off a 4G platform, because it just won't work there, so this is low-tech equipment that we can adapt. I've kept it to a bare minimum because I know how precious you are about your luggage weight."

Rufus smiled at his friend and held up the coat hook. "And what the fuck's this for?"

"It's a pin hole camera you troglodyte, you stick the coat hook to the wall in an inconspicuous place and the fish eye camera will give you a pretty good image."

"And this?" holding up a comb

"To comb you hair, of course," Don started tittering to himself. He knew Rufus would ask and he just couldn't help putting an innocuous item in the bag, which could be used for the purpose it was made. I've given Orla the same equipment, even down to the jonnies, I just hope she doesn't have her luggage searched, they'll think she's on the hunt for a Masai Warrior husband."

Orla play punched Don on the shoulder, which Rufus noticed that even though it was in fun was a perfectly formed fist, straight jab.

"You'll need this as well." He handed Rufus a dummy passport. "It's for Victoria. It won't get you through an airport check, but if you need to show ID at the hotel or to the police, they'll never be able to tell the difference."

Rufus examined the document. "Jeez, Bamm. This looks really good. It would fool me. 'Rose Gardener'? Any significance in the name?"

"None whatsoever, I just thought of a name that isn't Victoria Conway and used it," said Don.

"Thanks a lot mate, that'll be really useful."

Don and Orla made a show of leaving the house together, ostensibly to go home, they said their goodbyes to Victoria and wished her well, put their delivery uniforms back on and took the now flattened box out of the house with them.

"You take right, I'll take the left," said Orla as they exited the house. Don scanned the road to right, while Orla looked up the road to their left, to see if anything had changed, but everything looked the same. She saw that one car had gone, but could not see any that had not been there before. They drove out of sight of the house and said goodbye to each other: Orla transferred to another car while Don went home to start work.

Orla stayed on plot, carrying out her anti-surveillance duties, watching their backs, making sure nobody was observing them or would follow them from the house. A little over the top, here, but again, it was their Standard Operating Procedure or SOP and had served them well in the past and until they knew exactly who they were dealing with and their opponents' capabilities they would continue to be very cautious.

From their military training they had been taught Sun Tzu's philosophy: if you know your enemies and know yourself, you will not be imperiled in a hundred battles; if you do not know your enemies but do know yourself, you will win one and lose one; if you do not know your enemies nor yourself, you will be imperiled in every single battle.

They did not know their enemy yet, or even how many enemy they would face, or where they would come from, but they were on their way to do something about that.

Chapter Thirteen

Sir Peregrine Dennis was on the secure Satellite Video conference from Vauxhall Cross, irreverently known as Legoland, the Headquarters of the British Secret Intelligence Service, to his subordinate, Nick Cooper at the British High Commission in Dar es Salaam. Both of them prided themselves on their patriotism and dedication to their country, and their ability to turn opportunities into realities.

Cooper briefed Sir Peregrine on developments in the Conway case:

"Intelligence suggests that a local criminal group have kidnapped the Conways and are holding them hostage in the Kariakoo district of Dar."

"Where?" asked Sir Peregrine in his cultured, slightly nasally voice.

"A compact commercial area, within the city centre. A rabbit warren of an area, that is near impossible to carry out any sort of surveillance activity. They are being held in separate rooms of the same building and he is in a worse state than her apparently."

"What is the provenance of this intelligence?" asked, Sir Peregrine.

"From our source, Kumi."

Sir Peregrine knew of Kumi, he did not know his true identity; he didn't need to, but knew that Kumi meant "ten" in Swahili, and understood why his handlers had given him that particular nomenclature, which had been well before Cooper's tenure at the High Commission.

"Ah, excellent" said Sir Peregrine, realising the potential value of the intelligence, "and what do you propose to do with this information?"

Sir Peregrine was already thinking three or four steps ahead; of the machinations this would afford him. He was never one to act quickly or rashly. He always considered the bigger picture and how he fit into it. *Intelligence is the life blood of any organisation, it is a valuable commodity and should be used wisely.*

"I've already started the ball rolling with Esther, Sir, as we have previously discussed for this very scenario."

"Excellent, excellent. Not too fast though Cooper, these things can't be rushed. I was always counselled 'Slowly slowly catchy monkey' and that's what we need to do here. This has too much potential to be reckless or impatient. Have you had any reaction at all?"

"Not yet Sir," said Cooper, grateful that his attempts to push things along, had, so far, failed. "But this is Africa, and things do move at a different pace to back there. And I've told Esther to be cautious and patient." He lied. "They might not take the bait at all, it all depends what is going on back in Somalia. I haven't heard back from Esther yet, but I'm sure I will as soon as possible. If the pirates make a move I will know."

"That's all good, because you see we may have an obstacle to overcome before it would be prudent to entice our friends down."

"An obstacle Sir, I'm not aware of any obstacles."

"Ah well, yes, precisely, you wouldn't be aware we may have another problem, emanating from here. I'm informed that some Kidnap Consultants have been hired by the insurance company to get the couple back, now while I can't actually shove a stick in their spokes, I can ensure they are not given any assistance from any Government agencies. Let's just hope they are not in a hurry to get them back. That would rather scupper our plans."

"There are some people here I could use to slow things down a little, just make them take their eyes off the ball, give us a better chance."

"Excellent Cooper, excellent. Not too much disruption though, very low key. We don't want to draw attention to ourselves, or put our friends off joining the party."

"Understood Sir," Said Cooper

Chapter Fourteen

Rufus and Victoria spent what was left of the evening preparing in their separate ways. Victoria emptied her trusty rucksack and suitcase onto the floor of the lounge. She was making three piles on the floor, 'definitely needed', 'possibly needed', and 'not needed'. Her pile of what she thought was essentials was much bigger than the other two piles put together.

"Whoa," said Rufus as he walked back into the room after reviewing his conversation with Victoria, jotting down a few questions. "Remember, I said 'essentials' Victoria."

"I need all of this."

"Need, or want. What did you take on that trip to India you told me about, for how many months?"

"Three."

"Three months, and you took everything in this?" he said holding up Victoria's rucksack, still showing, the evidence of her exploits, festooned with badges, and ornaments hanging off the straps and rings, with a solar panel built into the top flap for recharging small items.

"Ok Victoria, first of all ditch this rucksack, it's too vibrant, too recognisable, we need to be grey, to be able to disappear. This rucksack will be like a beacon, instantly recognisable."

"Oh, I would have thought it would fit in."

"Not from a surveillance perspective. It's an identifiable object that could be followed. Have you got a plainer one?"

Victoria disappeared to her parents' bedroom and came back with her dad's boring old-fashioned rucksack, just a khaki space to shove clothes in, without any of the modern accessories she was used to.

"Is this better?"

"Perfect. Now let's go through what you've got here. These two piles have gone. If you don't think they're necessary; they're not. Ditch them. Now, think about it as if you're going backpacking. Essentials only. I'll make us a brew while you do that, if that's ok?"

"Yes please," said Victoria looking at her pile of 'essentials'. She decided to make two piles: 'essential essentials' and 'essentials'.

As Rufus was making the tea she let out a shriek, Rufus rushed back into the lounge, expecting some kind of emergency: a news report on the TV or a text from her parents. He found Victoria frozen, in a state of horror. He couldn't see what had frightened her so much.

"What's the matter?" he said.

Victoria held up her passport, that she had put in her 'essential essentials' pile.

"I only have four months left. I'm not going to be able to go."

Rufus let out a big sigh of relief, "Oh ok. That's not a drama Victoria we'll go to the Peterborough passport office in the morning and get you a new one, we might cut things a bit tight, but if we go for the Premium Service they can give you a new passport in four hours. It's a bit more expensive, but we'll charge it to the insurance company. It just means we will have to get things sorted quickly in the morning."

"Are you sure?"

"Yes trust me. We've had to do it a few times, when our passports have got too full, or close to the expiry date. Let me have a look please."

Victoria handed him the passport.

"You're going to need a new one anyway. You need two clean pages together to get through their immigration, and... as far as I can see..." he said slowly as he examined the document, "...you haven't. It's ok. We can make some phone calls on the way. Get to Peterborough by eleven, submit the application. More phone calls. Pick up the passport at three, or I might be able to get it done a little more quickly if we talk nicely to them. Down to Heathrow, I've booked the valet parking on line, so we are only a few minutes' walk from the terminal; we are business class, so there won't be a queue."

"You make it sound so easy and effortless."

"Money does make things more effortless and if the insurance company are paying, then let's make it easy for us. Money can't buy you love or happiness, but it can help things along."

They went to separate bedrooms fairly early and Victoria tossed and turned: she had a strange man in the house, alone, she was going to leave for Tanzania tomorrow, without a passport, without any foreign currency, to hopefully rescue her parents: *oh shit I should have started taking malaria tablets; what am I going to do about work? How am I going to pay the kidnappers the money?* She had a nonsensical recurring dream throughout the night of her shooting her parents with a bow and arrow on a yacht, while being watched by the Dalai Lama. Unfortunately it wasn't one of those pleasant dreams she wanted to recapture, yet couldn't, it was a dream she just couldn't get rid of. Every time she woke from it she would hope that that was the end, but it just kept coming back, again and again.

Rufus should have been more disturbed than he was; he should have felt bad that Orla was outside, wide awake in a car; he should have felt uncomfortable in a strange bed, in a strange house; he should have felt a little apprehensive about travelling to Tanzania with the responsibility of the lives of three people, but he fell asleep as if he had taken a bottle of sleeping tablets, and although he would have woken at the slightest noise, he slept soundly through the night: the sleep of a confident, competent, courageous man, who trusted his own ability.

The next morning Orla called him in the middle of his exercises. She told him she was going off plot now that it was day light and would see him later. She would only need a couple of hours' sleep, before she was fully revitalised and able to assist Victoria and Rufus in any way they needed. Years of such discipline had acclimatised her to the rigours of surveillance. He showered and joined Victoria in the kitchen, sat at the breakfast table as Victoria prepared the food and chatted. It took Victoria's mind off her parents momentarily as she fixed him his breakfast.

"Will an omelette be ok?"

"Fantastic. Yes thanks."

"Tea?"

"Let me help you do that. I feel guilty sat here being waited on."

"It's ok."

"No, really. It will make me feel better," and stood up. He made coffee for himself and tea for Victoria.

I can't believe how comfortable I feel with this man. Perhaps it's because of the situation? Perhaps it's 'cus he clearly doesn't fancy me, no sleazy comments, no innuendos. No hidden agenda. No post coital awkwardness.

He exuded confidence and warmth that drew her to him. She had cooked breakfast for a few men over the years and this felt so different. *He didn't expect to be waited on and actually helped out. Perhaps it's the older man in him? Or perhaps it's just the way he is?*

They continued to chat over breakfast of the most fantastic three-egg omelette Rufus had ever tasted, before Victoria could ask him questions about his personal life. Rufus decided to divulge a little about himself, as a way of getting her to open up a little more.

He told her about his childhood, which sounded quite austere by modern standards, his drifting in adolescence unsure of his role in life until he found the marines.

"I tried my hand at a few things. I went to university for a year but dropped out. I got a job in the City, but that only lasted a few months, I couldn't stand it. I think I shocked everybody when I announced I was going to join the Royal Marines. The recruiting officer tried to persuade me to apply to be an officer, because of my background and qualifications, but I knew there was a lot of theory and class work, which I'd had enough of by then, so I declined the offer."

"I know what you mean with the studying. A few times as an undergrad I felt like packing it all in. I felt like all I had ever done from the age of five was study. But it's been worth it. I love my job: great people, long hours and such a rush when I do a good job on a patient."

"It must be very satisfying. As Maslow would have put it, having that respect and self-esteem in your position."

"You've studied Maslow? You weren't a normal soldier were you?"

"You'd be surprised what Special Forces get you to think about and study. We're not mindless killing machines you know. As it happens I read Maslow and Attachment Theory after my negotiating course with the police."

"WHAT? You were Special Forces? Like SAS?" said a shocked Victoria, as he was not what she imagined an SAS soldier would be like, "and now you're a negotiator? Isn't that a little weird?"

"Not at all, there's usually an SF guy on their course. Guys from the Regiment get into all sorts of things, theology, management, entrepreneurship, technology, anything and everything. It gives you a certain mind-set, an 'anything is possible' outlook. The negotiators' course just helps us in some theatres of operation."

"Which you are not going to tell me about..."

"Which I can't tell you about."

They finished breakfast and got on with their preparations, chatting as they went about their chores. Rufus loaded the dishwasher, and Victoria cleaned up, making sure the kitchen was spotless and ready for them to leave. The more she learned about him the more her respect grew.

When they had finished they sat back down and Rufus shifted to work mode.

"We've got a busy day ahead of us Victoria, lots of little things that need to be done. I suggest we make a list of everything we can think of that needs to be sorted out before we leave."

They went around the house ensuring timer lights were put on, doors and windows were locked, the boiler was turned off, the fridge was emptied of perishable food; she phoned the newsagent to cancel the paper delivery until further notice. She vacuumed, so the place was tidy when her parents returned.

It wasn't all necessary, but Rufus had an ulterior motive. He was planting the thought into Victoria's mind that her parents were coming back, giving her positivity.

They went to see her grandparents nice and early. While Rufus stayed out of sight, Victoria explained that she was going to Cornwall for a few days with friends and would be in the middle of nowhere, so she probably would not have a signal.

As Rufus was driving to Peterborough Victoria called work and explained that there was a family emergency and she had to take leave of absence. Human Resources were not very impressed and told her that she couldn't just take leave like that. She told them that it was non-negotiable and she HAD to go. The two of them discussed the advantages and disadvantages of telling a senior HR manager, but decided that they should not and when, Liz, the Director of HR called back asking for details, she was stonewalled by Victoria, with encouragement from Rufus, who was adamant he didn't want anybody else knowing what was happening.

"You CANNOT just take leave of absence without any prior notice. There are policies and procedures to follow."

"Liz, you haven't listened to me. I'm not ASKING, I'm TELLING you. Surely you know I wouldn't do this if I had a choice?"

"Well what has happened? You can at least tell me that."

"I can't explain now, and I promise I will tell you everything when I get back."

"What am I going to tell the trust?"

"Tell them what I told you. I have a family emergency. Now I've got to go, I'm driving," Victoria lied. "I'll see you when I get back."

"Victoria, you may not have a job to come back to."

But the line was dead. Victoria didn't care. What she was doing was more important, and anyway, she knew she could get another job if necessary.

Rufus listened to the conversation and mused: *What a good girl. Very different to the Victoria I first met, just* ...he looked at the clock on the dash... *twelve hours ago.*

She contacted friends by text saying she was going away for a few days, leaving it quite bland. She phoned Craig and reinforced the need for him to keep everything secret and told him of her conversation with Liz.

Chapter Fifteen

It took Rufus less than forty-five minutes to travel the forty miles to the Passport office and they were there by ten-thirty. After they paid their money and handed over the passport application, they based themselves in a coffee shop while they waited: Rufus contacted Don

"Morning Pebble. Everything sorted?"

"Hi Don, I think so yeh, a few last minute arrangements to make... like getting Victoria a fresh passport."

"Really? Which office are you going to use? Peterborough? It's got to be the closest, and they're pretty good there, better than Liverpool."

"Yeh, it's the most direct one for us as well. We've dropped the passport in, I've schmoozed the clerk and we're just waiting to get it back. I've seen the booking confirmation for Qatar and for the Kili, thanks. Any other news?"

"Not yet, no, just started on the intel again, so I should have a full briefing ready for you by the time you land."

"Ok, thanks Don, speak to you tomorrow."

"Beat the clock," concluded Don, wishing him a safe journey.

Rufus returned to Victoria, who was full of questions: about kidnap, her parents, his experience; his life.

"Do you think they are still alive?"

"I would think they are. The bandits have asked for money and Deidre and Martyn are their bargaining tools. Unless something has happened we don't know about, it is in their interest to keep them alive."

"Do you think they're hurt?"

"I don't know, I wouldn't think so. From what you've said about them, they wouldn't have put up a fight, so there would be no need."

"How long to do you think it will take?"

"Ah, now I really can't give an opinion on that one Victoria, some last a few hours, some last days, even weeks or months."

"Months?"

"Yeh, I've been involved in jobs which have lasted that long."

"Really? It must play havoc on your family life."

"I don't have to worry on that score Victoria, my ex-wife Tina divorced me some years ago. She got frustrated with being a soldier's wife and annoyed with my constant deployments abroad, especially in the Regiment. I can't say I blame her: the stress of not knowing where I was, or if I was safe; bringing up the girls on her own..."

"You've got daughters? How many? How old are they?"

"Two, Myree and Suvee, they're twins."

"They're unusual names."

"In Britain, yeh. Tina is German and she chose them. I liked the names, they were different, gave the girls' character. Anyway Tina used to try checking with the Regiment, even though she knew it was futile as they would not give any information, and even if they did, she knew they would all lie for me if necessary. So she fell out of love with me, divorced me and went back to Germany."

Victoria could see and hear he clearly loved his two girls and blamed himself and his own selfishness and dedication to the Regiment for the break-up of the marriage.

"And you, what's your story? Is there a boyfriend in tow?"

"No, it's nothing like your story, nowhere near as exciting. With the hours I do as a junior doctor the only people I see are patients and other doctors. I've dated a couple of the doctors, but it's not the best idea. Things can get a little complicated at work when you are both under pressure or on opposite shift patterns."

"What about Craig? You evidently like him."

Victoria was surprised he had remembered Craig's name as he had only been mentioned a couple of times and they had not met.

"Oh no, he's a confidante and friend and that's about it. No, I'm destined to be a spinster."

"What? Now you are being silly or fishing for compliments," he teased her, "there is no way you are going to be a spinster, unless you choose to, you're still young and very attractive, so you will meet 'Mr Right', just make sure his first name isn't 'Always'."

Victoria smiled at the old joke and thought back to some of the men she had dated, who were just that and thanked her lucky stars that she had escaped.

"Time to go," said Rufus rising.

"How do you know?"

"I gave the clerk my number and she's just text me, your passport is ready."

They collected the passport and were on their way to Terminal 4 of London's Heathrow Airport. Rufus knew his way through the terminal very well, after collecting $2000 from one of the many bureaux de change they were able to take advantage of their Business Class status by using the Fast-Track facilities and eased their way through to the Business lounge.

Victoria collapsed into one of the huge leather armchairs, after what seemed like a completely surreal experience: she had lied to her grandparents, she had lied to work, she had lied to everybody. She was jetting off with a man she had only just met to rescue her parents from kidnappers in the middle of Africa without the first idea of where to start, wondering, not for the first time, what sort of world she had fallen into. She needed a drink.

Rufus went to the free bar and ordered two glasses of champagne, he hoped that the champagne, fine wines and food would get Victoria to relax a little and let him find out some more about her. It did the trick and soon Victoria was talking non-stop. A lot of it was about her childhood and growing up under the loving care of her parents.

"I was home educated for a while. Mum thought she could teach me better than the local school. I was quite rebellious as a youngster though, and I needed other kids of my age, I felt restricted with mum teaching me."

"I know the feeling."

"So they let me go to school and I flourished. Got straight A's at A level and went to Liverpool to study medicine."

"You did well."

"Thank you. I want to be an oncologist, one of my friends died recently from bowel cancer and I'd really like to make a difference to cancer victims."

"Do you think you will be able to? I don't know how you get promoted or chosen to specialise in a hospital."

"I think so yes. I'm getting good reviews and assessments, and would like to go to The Royal Marsden, which has a really good reputation, or even the UVA."

"Where?"

"Sorry, University of Virginia, I've been offered a placement there."

She relaxed and went on to tell him how she wanted lots of children as she regretted being an only child, but her parents had not been able to have any more children; wanted to work abroad to make a difference in India or Africa; wanted to find a cure for cancer; wanted to put some ethics back into medicine as she thought too many consultants were riding a gravy train; but most of all, she wanted to get her parents back – alive.

Rufus was the consummate listener, alert and attentive, never butting in, never trying to compete with her. He was working, he was working hard, it didn't seem like he was, he looked relaxed and comfortable, but he was alert. He picked up on her body language again, noting the occasional tug of the left sleeve with her two fingers and the worrying of the bottom lip, when she spoke about her friend who had died and her parents. He had not come across any classic deception signals yet and he had not really expected to. Victoria was an open book, with nothing to hide from him, no reason to as far as he could see she just told him the truth.

He was in a good state of mind, able to listen to Victoria, who was more relaxed and assured now. He let Victoria talk away about anything and everything; he had to get a gauge of her non-verbal signals, the pace, pitch and tone of her voice so that he could assess her when she was under pressure. Unless very skilled, most people need time to see and hear slight differences when people are lying, Rufus was good, but not that good, he couldn't take one signal in isolation and draw a conclusion from it, he needed a benchmark and clusters of signals to work from.

Rufus got up and went to the bar and by the time he returned Victoria was fast asleep, stretched out in the big comfortable armchair. She had talked herself out.

Rufus took the opportunity to get on with some work, formulating ideas, ruses and getting his thoughts in order for various scenarios, only disturbed once by a text from Orla, who had been 'third eye' for them from Peterborough after a couple of hours' sleep, to say "Good luck and bon voyage, you're clean."

He woke Victoria after their flight was called for the third time. They left the lounge and walked along the never ending walkways to their gate. Rufus knew his way around, knew there was no need to rush, just to queue to get on the plane and as it was they walked straight on turned left and found their huge seats. Don had booked the two centre aisle seats, 3 E and F of the Boeing Dreamliner, so that they were side by side. More free champagne was offered prior to take off, which Victoria thought was a little excessive and they settled down for the flight to Doha, for the connection to Dar es Salaam.

Rufus was seasoned enough to know he had to make the most of the opportunity to sleep and quickly settled down on the lie flat bed provided in business class.

Victoria was drowsy through all of the alcohol, but she was amazed how Rufus was seemingly able to just turn a switch and fall asleep. They landed at Doha at 0615 and Rufus was immediately awake and alert, even though they were only transiting through the airport. They just about had enough time to get to the business lounge and have a shower to freshen up, before boarding the next flight at 0730 which would get them to Dar es Salaam at 1325. Doha airport was modern and bright and Victoria thought under different circumstances it would have been nice to shop and browse.

The connection was on time and they made good progress down to Dar es Salaam, flying over Mt Kilimanjaro in the mid-morning sunlight. Victoria gawped out of the window with lots of other passengers at the magnificent ice-capped mountain. It was amazing, it looked so close to the plane, it felt like she could reach out and touch it.

Chapter Sixteen

They landed in Dar but had a completely different experience to Deidre and Martyn: Rufus was au fait with the airport and its bureaucracy.

"Stay with me," he said as he positioned them so they were virtually at the front of the queue to get off the plane. When the doors were opened Rufus sped past the few slower passengers that were in front of them and Victoria had to virtually run to keep up with him, but there was a good reason: Rufus got to the Visa desk first, handed over the $100, and a little more as baksheesh to ensure their application was processed first, and moved to the processing desks to await being called. After less than two minutes they were called forward, their passports handed back to them, stamped and entry authorised for ninety days.

They had no baggage to collect, which could have delayed them by another hour, and Rufus led her out of the airport to the taxi desk, agreed on what he regarded was a mutually beneficial price and they were off to the Kilimanjaro Hotel, overlooking the harbour. The ride into Dar was very similar to that of Deidre and Martyn's some two weeks earlier, and Victoria's reaction to the abject poverty she could see, was very similar to her mother's. And she vowed there and then to return one day to carry out some voluntary work, using her medical skills to make a difference. She wondered, *if the commercial capital is this bad, what is the rest of the country like?*

They made their way through the chaos of the harbour to their hotel, where like her mother before her, the dichotomy of the opulent hotel and the surrounding squalor struck her even harder.

They waded through the thick red carpet, announcing their arrival at the luxurious, modern hotel. After a twenty metre walk along the sumptuous carpet, they arrived in the stark, minimalist reception; all chrome, glass and marble, and could be forgiven for forgetting they were in the middle of Dar es Salaam.

Rufus checked them in using his false passport and Victoria's dummy passport, and his covert credit card in the name of Lionel Baker to secure rooms and services for their stay and was escorted to the lift by the porter. He had asked for two key cards each so both could have access to the other's room if they wanted it, plus it was interconnecting suite, so he should always be able to get into Victoria's room if she needed him, unless she had locked the interconnecting door and the entrance door from the inside. The porter was very attentive, and Rufus noted his name tag said 'British'. Rufus deliberately called him by his name and introduced himself and Victoria as Lionel and Rose.

"How long have you worked here British?"

"Six months sir," said British, standing a little more erect as he answered.

"Do you enjoy it?"

"Vely much sir."

Victoria noted for the first time, some East African's habit of sometimes exchanging "L's" and "R's".

"I bet you see all sorts of things here don't you?" asked Rufus.

"Yes sir," said British.

Rufus saw the way British looked at the two of them and just knew he was thinking that she was his mistress, or 'little house', why else would he have a much younger, beautiful woman with him? A perfectly reasonable thought process because of the prevalence in East Africa for older men to have several younger women as 'nyumba ndogos' as they are euphemistically known.

"Do you work every day?"

"No sir, I get every second Sunday off."

"One day every two weeks?" Victoria said incredulously.

"Yes ma'am and I go and see my family in Mtwara and take them money for them to rive."

"Who's still at home?" asked Rufus.

"My mom, four sisters and two blothers. I am the oldest and the man of the house since my father died," he said, accepting his responsibility with pride.

"I'm very sorry to hear that British. Would you like to earn a little more money? Just by keeping your eyes and ears open for me. You see the lady is an English celebrity who has come here to do some charity work and some reporters from London might try and find her.

"Yes sir..."

"British, stopping calling me sir, my name is Lionel, and I've told you this is Rose, please call us by our names."

"Preased to meet you Rionel, Lose. What do you want me to rook for?" said British with a beaming grin on his face. The thought of some extra money for his family as well as helping this friendly Englishman pleased and excited him.

"That's a difficult one to answer really British as so many people visit hotels, but if you see the same faces coming in, who are not guests, who you might not have seen before then let me know. They will probably just be hanging about rather than having meetings. They could be taking more interest in guests than usual, you know they type I'm sure, they are looking around the room or the lobby all of the time."

"Yes sir, I know the sort you mean."

"And British, stop calling me sir," Rufus said with a smile.

By this time they had reached Victoria's room. Rufus passed Victoria 5000 shillings as British opened the door for her, went in and explained the facilities of the room. Rufus stayed at the threshold watching the interaction between the two of them. British was very attentive, taking pride in explaining everything to the flagging Victoria.

"Will there be anything else Lose?" asked British when he had finished explaining.

"No thank you, that's great, thanks," and she handed him the 5000 shillings in the conspiratorial fashion of the closed hand, which British deftly slipped into his pocket without checking the denomination of the note.

"Thank you, Lose," he said as he backed out of the door.

"Rufus looked over the top of his head and mouthed, "I'll be back in a few minutes."

British showed him to the room next door and went through the same procedure, Rufus slipped him 10000 shillings when he had finished; British glimpsed the flash of red of the note, recognising it immediately as he gratefully took it and slipped into the same pocket.

After unpacking his few things Rufus opened the interconnecting door to find Victoria had already unlocked her side: he saw her lying on the bed.

"You need to get some sleep, you look exhausted. I'm going to go out to reacquaint myself with the city. I won't be too long and I'll put the *Do not Disturb* sign on both doors. Stay in the room, and keep the doors locked until I get back, I don't care who it is. You've got my number haven't you?"

"Yes, we entered it into my phone if you remember."

"Are you ok with that?"

"Yes I'm whacked; just let me get a couple of hours' sleep."

He knew Dar was changing fast with foreign investment pouring in and he needed to re-acquaint himself. He had been here previously when he was in the Regiment, training Tanzanians, part of the HMG's heart and minds policy in relation to ex-colonies. He had picked up some Swahili quickly and had visited Dar es Salaam on a few occasions since then, brushing up on the pan East African language. He had kept in contact with a couple of the guys he'd trained and followed their progress with interest, keeping up on social media and e mail. He usually tried to have the odd beer with them when he was in Dar, if they could get together. This time might be different.

Issa Baramu was now a General in the TPDF, while Projest Massare was an Inspector General in the Police. They had both always invited Rufus to their promotion ceremonies and he had attended when he could, but when they reached their current ranks he'd been tied up on operations and couldn't make it. He liked both of the men, and they appear to be two of the very few senior officials in Tanzania who are honest. Intelligent, articulate men with an understanding of the difficulties their country faces, whilst remaining realists, knowing that things could not be changed overnight, and there is a lot of vested interests in keeping the status quo of the system. They even sometimes played Devil's Advocate arguing that perversely theirs was a more honest corruption than the West's corruption, which is denied and legislated against, but still exists.

Rufus kept in touch with both men because he liked them and respected them, and at the moment he was pleased he had, as he might just need a helping hand at some point, but he didn't want to let them know he was in the country yet, as they would expect to meet up, have dinner, take him to meet their families, which he loved to do in normal circumstances, but he couldn't afford the time on this trip.

Although he was sure he hadn't been followed he still took some anti-surveillance measures: in his room, he removed one of the cocktail sticks, the talcum powder and the coat hook out of Don's equipment bag: he positioned the coat hook to record anybody that might enter. He couldn't link it to his phone as Tanzania doesn't have the requisite technology, but he would be able to review it later if he needed to: he sprinkled some of the talcum powder on the floor of his room as he exited, not a lot, just enough to leave a feint impression which would let him know if he needed to review the recording. As he passed Victoria's room he broke the cocktail stick, and put the two halves in the door jam. He didn't want to take the same precautions on her side of the rooms as he thought it would alarm her, and this way he could tell if she had got up and left the room for any reason without telling him.

CHAPTER SEVENTEEN

While he was walking he ensured that nobody followed him as he carried out his recce of this small part of the vast sprawling city. He scanned the lobby as he exited, noting memorable attributes of the few people that were there. He got outside and made a show of realising he had forgotten something and re-entered the hotel. He got in the elevator and rode up and down and returned to the lobby. No one paid any attention to him.

He walked around the perimeter of the hotel first of all, surveying the egress and entry points. He noted the location of CCTV cameras and the few blind spots that were there. He observed the security on the car park, which seemed more ornamental than any real use: the walls were too low, the fences were not topped with barbed or razor wire; trees overhung the whole perimeter and there were masses of cover.

The black security staff implemented a reverse racist policy: letting the whites through virtually unchallenged, while they checked the black visitors thoroughly. Using mirrors to check under the vehicles and questioning them about their attendance.

Once he had seen enough he walked away from the hotel. He used the windscreens and shop windows as mirrors to check if anybody was behind him and crossed the road frequently, checking for a three man foot follow who would have to mirror his movement in a reverse manoeuvre. Once he was satisfied he was alone in this city of three and a half million people he walked further afield, along the harbour, noticing there were many more container ships moored up than there used to be.

He approached the ferry port, sat on a bench in a small park overlooking the harbour, taking in the sights, sounds and smells. He felt the full heat of the sun now that he was exposed in a shadeless grassed area. The sea looked beautiful in the distance, and the sky was a cloudless deep blue, but in the foreground the security fence around the harbour was falling to pieces: it was rusty and there were holes everywhere. Groups of young men sat around inside the compound, looking sullen, gutting small fish they had caught either with home-made spears or on makeshift fishing lines. The smell of rotting fish, diesel, oil, exhaust fumes and body odour penetrated his nostrils and bombarded his olfactory receptors. The toot-tooting of car horns was incessant, mixed in with the sonorous ships' horns as they moved around the harbour, *No it hasn't changed that much really*, he thought, and phoned Don.

"Hi mate," he said.

"Habari," said Don, one of the few Swahili words he knew.

"How's everything going?"

"I'm not sure Pebble," said Don, "there is some strange activity going on."

"Bravos?" asked Rufus, the phonetic "B" being shorthand for "Bandits."

"Don't think so."

"Inside agents?"

"Don't know mate," said Don. "There is something going on which I can't quite get to the bottom of. Just watch your back though eh?"

"Bamm Bamm, that's not much good to me, can you give me anything specific?" said Rufus running his right hand through his hair using the nickname Don had been given in the Regiment because the pair of them had been inseparable, and if Rufus was Pebble then Don just had to be Bamm Bamm.

"Sorry mate no, not at the moment, I hope I will be able to after your first contact. Do you still plan that for 1500 Zulu?" as they still referred to Greenwich Mean Time from their military days: with operations across the globe NATO has to work off one uniform time to avoid any confusion and GMT was the natural, logical choice.

"Yeh, I'll drop you a text just before we put the call in. I don't want to do it smack on the hour, so it will probably be a little after." said Rufus, not pushing the point that Don had brought up. He knew Don would tell him as soon as he had anything concrete to say and any conversation now would be pure speculation.

"How's Victoria holding up?" asked Don.

"She's sleeping like a baby now I imagine. The lounge did the trick, got her to relax a little. I've left her in her room, with a couple of counter measures, should we have any unexpected visitors, which I didn't think was very likely until you just said what you did. She's a good girl, very switched on, which you would hope for as a doctor. Now we're over that initial shock, feeling like she was in free fall without a parachute, she'll do well. She picks things up quickly and asks questions if she is unsure, rather than carrying on regardless."

"Good, that sounds promising."

"Ok, Bamm, I've got to go and I'll speak to you later – and Don, I don't like it when you are not sure, you make me nervous."

"Sorry Ru, I just wanted you to be aware and be extra vigilant. I know you are anyway, but you'd curse me if I didn't tell you what I was thinking."

"Yeh, thanks mate. Did you get anywhere with the checks on Deidre and Martyn?"

"That's another thing that's bothering me, I've found all of Martyn's history, but I can't find anything on Deidre, nee Dench. I've got her school, a very posh girls' school in Buckinghamshire. She went to Keeble College Oxford from there where she got a first."

"In what?"

"Philosophy and theology."

"Oh shit, well that doesn't help us much does it?"

"And then she disappears. Nada, zip, not a trace."

"What do you think that means?"

"Well, either she was a housewife for the whole of her adult life, but we know that's not the case, or she worked for the government in some covert capacity."

"Oh shit. What are you thinking, 5 or 6?"

"I guess so. Can you ask Victoria if she used any aliases ever? I don't know how you will introduce that, but I need a different starting point. I've tried her maiden name, her married name and her mother's maiden name of Robbins but I can't find her at all under any of those three."

"Ok. mate I'll ask her somehow, but there may be a simple explanation to it."

"Or we could be dealing with an ex spook. And if we are I'm surprised Vauxhall and Thames aren't all over us."

"Exactly. That's why I think there could be an innocuous explanation."

"Ever the optimist hey Ru?"

"It was drilled into me at Lympstone, Don. Cheerfulness in the face of adversity."

"Bollocks, you are always glass half full, which is why I love you."

"On that amorous note, I'm going and I'll speak to you later."

"Ok. Ru, stay safe."

+++++++

Rufus continued to reconnoitre the area. Local knowledge was invaluable to any surveillance he might have to carry out, he didn't want to follow somebody into a blind alley or worse, be followed into a blind alley. He couldn't rely on the app on his phone as it just wasn't fast enough or accurate enough in Dar: the signal was very poor in most areas and he couldn't take the chance. He walked to the ferry port and was mobbed by shipping agents trying to sell him tickets for the ferry to Zanzibar. The place hadn't changed THAT much since he was last here. They jostled for position, pushing each other out of the way, promising him the best rates and best seats, trying to direct him to their booking office, which in reality was a wooden shack. After wandering around for a short time, he headed away from the seafront and walked across Bibi Titi Mohammed Street, into Kariakoo. If he had to put money on Deidre and Martyn being anywhere it would be here. He walked slowly trying to take everything in, finding himself landmarks by which he could navigate if he had to. He watched the groups of men watching him. He meandered like a tourist, taking pictures, pretending to marvel at unusual sights. He entered a hardware store, and ordered a grappling hook he thought he might need: a bespoke piece of equipment, which he knew he couldn't get through customs and arranged to collect it in thirty minutes; an electric screwdriver, a multi tool cheap imitation; a crowbar; hammer, and a glass cutter.

He found a little a little firework shop and bought some firecrackers – not as good as the M84s or flashbangs he had used in the military, but they might serve a purpose.

He meandered his way to the open air spice and fruit market where he bought some fresh fruits to take back to the hotel. The market was a fusion of colour and aromas, spice sellers next to herb sellers, next to the green grocers, all trying to get the custom of the mzungu walking through the market. Rufus marvelled at the aroma, which was a welcome contrast to that of the docks, especially from the spices and herbs, which the country had become famous for. He knew the place was a haven for petty thieves and pickpockets, and carried his phone and wallet in the vice-like grip of his hands rather than risk them in his pocket.

Chapter Eighteen

After a couple of hours Rufus returned to the hotel, checked the cocktail stick pieces were in place as he walked past Victoria's room and quietly let himself in to his side of the rooms. The dusting of talc was undisturbed, which was good news after what Don had said and he easily brushed it into the carpet. He peeped through the interconnecting doors and saw Victoria was fast asleep. He walked quietly into her room and sat on the edge of the bed and looked at her. *God she looks young and vulnerable. The poor woman is going through hell.*

He considered letting her sleep, but knew he had to be cruel to be kind and wake her, if he didn't she wouldn't be able to sleep tonight. He put his hand gently on her shoulder and roused her. She woke slowly, making cat-like purring noises as she stirred, gently moving in the bed, the sleep that had overcome her trying to maintain its power over her brain and body, refusing to let go of its grip without a fight, dragging her mind back into the darkness of unconsciousness. If it hadn't been for Rufus fighting the sleep off for her, it would have won the battle over her will power easily and she would have slid back under the covers, promising herself "Just five more minutes", but the voice and the hand were insistent and hounded and harried the sleep out of her head, as it disappeared into the ether, soon to be forgotten, like dark giving way to the light. She looked straight at him and gave him a smile. She looked into the face of the man that she was putting all her hope and trust in, and she liked what she saw.

"For a moment I thought it was all a terrible dream and I was waking up back at home," she said.

"Unfortunately not. It's for real and we have got work to do." Rufus stood up and said, "I'll be back in thirty minutes, that'll give you time to get yourself up and showered."

He walked to the door and happened to glance in the mirror to see Victoria's gaze watching him as he walked out of the room back to his own side.

She heard him first, and wondered what on earth he was doing. She forced herself out of bed stretching her arms above her head and pushing her head back to stretch her shoulders, and walked to the interconnecting door to see Rufus transitioning from burpees to press-ups. She watched his lithe body easily pushing up his body weight. After a quick fifty, he lay on his back do some sit-ups, Pilates style, slow and controlled; it was only now as his head came back, he saw Victoria watching him.

"Come on lazy bones," he said as he was doing his stomach exercises, without a hint of strain in his voice, "shake that sleep out of your body."

"I don't know how you've got the energy, I'm shattered."

"It revitalises me, gives me more energy. It should be you telling me how important it is to exercise and keep fit. You're the doc."

"Do as I say, not as I do."

Rufus changed to a different exercise, which Victoria again assumed was Pilates, alternately stretching out his opposite arm and leg. His exercises were smooth and more rhythmical; he was making her tired just watching him and she wandered back to her own side.

After a few minutes she heard him turn on the shower, erasing the Dar es Salaam dirt and the stickiness of the long-haul flight.

She decided she should follow his example and jumped in the shower herself, and got herself ready.

Exactly thirty minutes later, Rufus tentatively tapped on Victoria's door, not wanting to catch her unaware, in a state of undress.

"Come in Ru," she shouted, "you don't have to knock."

As he entered he smelled her freshly washed hair, the clean fresh womanly smell he loved so much. She was showered, with hair dried, and minimal make-up on, and looked a different woman, all in the thirty minutes. Rufus was quietly impressed. Not many women could get ready that quick and look so good. Still, she had the benefit of age on her side.

Rufus walked into the room and took a few minutes looking around deciding on the best configuration for them to work.

"What's the matter?" asked Victoria.

"Nothing. I'm just deciding where to put the furniture." He started to rearrange the room to get ready for work. He could have been in any multi-national hotel, anywhere in the world. The same pictures, hung in the same places. The colour scheme gave a slightly 'African' feel. The writing desk and mini-bar in the same place, as

that telephone call and test different scenarios. It might seem a bit childish, but believe me it works."

"What like play acting? Like children?"

"Not like children – this is key. When you have an exam, you revise don't you? If you have a practical test, you run through the test, this is the same, we are just preparing for what might happen, if we rehearse it, it will seem more natural when you are talking. Now remember you are alone, you've come to Tanzania on your own."

"Ok."

"What if they say they saw you with a man getting off the plane?"

"I'll deny it," she said.

"No, we stick to the truth as much as we can, say something like we started talking on the plane and found out we are staying at the same hotel, so we just decided to share a taxi. Ok?"

"Ok."

"I doubt if they'll ask that, as I checked pretty thoroughly when we got here. Next. What if they ask you where you are now?"

"Ooh, I don't know."

"That's fine Victoria, that's why we are doing this. Would you really tell people who have kidnapped your parents where you are? These people are dangerous and you don't want them to know where you are. And don't worry, I've booked us in under pseudonyms, you are Rose Gardener and I am Lionel Baker, so they won't be able to phone reception asking for you."

"Are you joking? Rose Gardener? Seriously? Don't people automatically think it is a joke name?"

"Believe it or not no, and certainly not here."

"Would they do that?" Victoria looked worried.

"Do what?"

"Phone the hotel asking for me, trying to find me?"

"I have known it Victoria. Sometimes it might just be to follow you, to get more intelligence on you so that they can intimidate you. You know, just say a couple of words to let you know they know where you are staying, or what you are wearing, things like that. Or they may want to confront you to really put the frighteners on you. This is why I am here with you, to look after you and get you Deidre and Martyn back. This is what I do, what I get paid for and what I am pretty good at. Ok then, the way I expect the call to go is this..."

Rufus explained what he thought from his experience would happen, how they would try and pressurise Victoria, but he reassured her that he would be with her throughout the call, giving her signals, operating silently. He prepared for all foreseeable eventualities and majored on four: they would try and find out where she was; they would accuse her of going to the authorities; they would accuse her of not caring about her parents and they would threaten one or both of her parents to ramp up the pressure on her, they might even torture one of them and make her listen.

They role-played these four areas with Rufus playing the part of the kidnappers and to start with, Victoria was very hesitant and self-conscious, but after a short time she lost her inhibitions, forgetting about the falseness of the situation and got into the swing of things and at last she was ready.

Finally he said to Victoria, "A lot of people think communication is about talking, but there is something far more important: listening. When they want to talk we listen. No matter how good a point we think we have got to make, we listen to them, we will learn more by listening, whereas we won't learn by talking."

"But how do I tell them to do anything if I don't talk?"

"I'm saying we give them priority. When they want to talk we let them until it's our turn, then we use what they've said to influence them."

He sent a text to Don a few minutes before 6pm local time or 1500 Zulu, and after a couple of minutes received one back.

Victoria made the call. She was a bundle of nerves, and Rufus gave her a squeeze on the arm, believing that the physical contact and his close proximity would reassure her. They had a few false starts, with bad connections and the phone just ringing out, which made Victoria even more nervous, but on the fifth attempt the phone was eventually answered.

"Hello?" said a curious deep masculine voice on the other end.

"Hello. This is Victoria Conway, you called me a couple of days ago about my mum and dad, Deidre and Martyn."

"WHERE THE FUCK HAVE YOU BEEN?" the voice screamed down the line at her "WHAT THE FUCK ARE YOU PLAYING AT, DO YOU THINK WE ARE FUCKING GOING TO KEEP THEM FOR FUCKING EVER YOU STUPID BITCH!" Victoria and Rufus could hear the guy screaming down the phone, his breathing out of control. Rufus gave Victoria a reassuring thumbs up. This was good, good for Victoria, good for him. The man continued to bellow down the line, in a nonsensical tirade. Victoria looked very worried, not expecting this explosion down the line. She looked at Rufus quizzically.

He held up the prompt: *Let him vent.*

"YOU DON'T UNDERSTAND WHO YOU ARE DEALING WITH. WE KNOW YOU'VE BEEN TO THE COPS. WE HAVE MEN EVERYWHERE, IN THE COPS, IN GOVERNMENT; WE KNOW YOU'VE BEEN THAT'S HOW WE KNEW YOU WERE GOING TO CALL. WE'RE GOING TO FUCK YOUR MUM AND FILM IT WHILE WE ALL TAKE TURNS ON THE OLD COW..."

Rufus held up the prompt *Keep calm...*

"WE'RE GOING TO SLICE UP YOUR DAD, the pussy, you should hear him crying, because of you, you stupid bitch," the voice started to moderate.

Victoria took a breath as if she was about to talk, but Rufus shook his head and put his hand on her knee to steady her and raised his finger to his lips, he wanted the guy to vent, and an interruption would just fuel him and start him off again.

"You've caused this by delaying; you've made us hurt them. You've got us mad. Do you know what we've done? We've cut your mum's ear off and posted it to you. You should have heard her scream, her mzungu blood was everywhere. I had to stop my guys from fuckin her there and then, so you had better tell me what I want to hear. Where are you?"

Rufus tapped the *Too scared* prompt and showed it Victoria.

"What?" asked Victoria.

"Where the fuck are you? You stupid bitch?"

"Why do you want to know where I am?"

"I know where you are, I just want to hear whether you are going to tell the truth."

"I'm too scared to tell you that. All you need to know is that I am here, in Tanzania."

"I'll fuckin tell you what I need to know and I need to know where you are. NOW!" he bellowed down the phone.

Rufus held up the same prompt to emphasise it to Victoria, quickly followed by the *Help* prompt, but Victoria either wouldn't or couldn't use this prompt and continued on her tactic of being scared. Perhaps two prompts in one go were too much for her at this moment.

"Sorry, but please understand I'm scared and if I tell you where I am, you will hurt me."

"Have you got our money you fuckin bitch? You think you are messing with amateurs? We'll fuckin show you." Then, as if talking to somebody else, the voice turned away from the phone and said, "You. Fuckin go and get the old man and bring him here and we'll fuckin cut him up so the fuckin bitch can hear."

At this point Rufus let Victoria loose; he wanted a reaction from her now, a genuine, emotional reaction so that the kidnappers could hear her. He didn't need to tap his *emotion* prompt, she would give it anyway.

"No please," she sobbed, "please don't hurt him." She continued to cry down the phone, uncontrollably sobbing. Her eyes and nose were running and the sound of this was worth its weight in gold.

After allowing her to cry for what seemed like an eternity the voice said, "Fuckin bitch. That's right, you just be polite and we might not cut him up."

Victoria continued to sob down the phone, shaking uncontrollably. Rufus wanted this from her, it wasn't play acting or rehearsed, but he knew how effective it was. Eventually she said, "I promise I haven't been to the police, you told me not to and I haven't, I just want my mum and dad back."

"Lyin fucker."

"I'm telling you the truth. I just want them back. I'm here on my own to give you your money and get my mum and dad back safely."

The phone went dead.

Chapter Twenty

Rufus put his finger to his lips and ensured that the line was definitely disconnected, then said, "That was fantastic Victoria." He knew she would be feeling like shit, and reassuring her that she had done well was of paramount importance. He also knew he had to prepare her for the next call which he thought would be coming back into them immediately.

"I expect him to call back straight away, so when he does, he will ask about the money which you mentioned. Ok? So clearly you haven't got that much and it will take you some time to get the cash. So we lower their expectations and buy some time ok?"

The phone started ringing.

Rufus calmly started his iPhone recording again and gave Victoria the thumbs up to answer the call tapping "time" and "difficult" on his tablet.

"Where's our money bitch?" the voice was the same but a little calmer.

"I haven't got it with me, I've arranged to transfer it to a bank here so I can withdraw it, but it will take time. I couldn't get you as much as you wanted..."

"What the fuck? Do you think I am fuckin stupid? Stop playing games with me. $10 million is what it will cost you, you fuckin idiot."

"I haven't got $10 million dollars..."

"Ok so we kill one of them. Which one of them do you hate the most? Your choice. Which one will I kill?"

Rufus spelt out *neither* on his tablet, as he had not got that word pre-programmed.

Victoria burst into tears again, "Please, please, let them both live." Even in her turmoil she had remembered Rufus's coaching about trying to phrase and frame things in the positive. "I love them both so much, please..." Victoria continued to sob down the phone just managing the word "please" between sobs.

"Yeh bitch, you fuckin cry. We'll call you back tomorrow, when you had better have our fuckin money, or you decide which one dies and you can listen while we do it."

Rufus was pointing at his watch and tapped *time* on his tablet.

"What time?" Victoria sobbed down the phone.

"What?"

"What time will you call me?"

"Fuck off. So you can have Askari waiting for me."

"What? What do you mean?"

"So you can have the fuckin police waiting."

"I promise, I'm here alone, I've done what you told me, I just need to make sure I'm awake and near the phone after my long plane journey."

After a few seconds of silence, at which point Rufus put his finger to his lips again, the voice said "Be ready at two o'clock," and the phone went dead.

Rufus indicated silence, disconnected the line and call and date stamped the recording, not that he would ever be using this in any court, it was just for his own references. As soon as he finished he hugged Victoria and she burst into tears on him again. He let her cry reassuring her at the same time.

"You did brilliantly, you did everything I wanted, and it went as I predicted and rehearsed with you. That was fantastic."

"I'm going to have to decide which one they kill," Victoria sobbed, "oh my God, how can I do that? How can I play God with my parents?"

"They're not going to make you do that Vicky. I'll give you a few minutes to calm down, and clear your thoughts, while I talk to Don, then we'll go through the call together. Ok?

Rufus disappeared out the door, leaving a stunned and shaken Victoria alone with her thoughts.

"Oh my God," she said out loud, "what have I done? I've got them killed. I shouldn't have listened to him. I should have just come and paid them the fucking money. I knew it was stupid to play these silly fucking macho games. It's alright for him; it's not his parents we're dealing with. I'm going to tell him to just leave me alone, I'll tell the insurance company that he's done it all wrong and he's going to get them killed." This was quickly followed by, "They said everything he said they would say. Almost to the word. He got everything right. In our stupid fucking role-play he predicted everything." Then another complete U-turn, "Oh, does that mean he is in on the kidnap? He has told them what to say? Oh no. But I trust him, he wouldn't lie to me." Her head was spinning with conflicting thoughts and she felt she was going to go mad, not knowing, not understanding what was happening.

Meanwhile, Rufus was on the phone to Don getting an update on the kidnappers' phone, and Victoria's call had certainly prompted some activity that would keep Don busy for the next few hours and probably through the night. Rufus had given space for Victoria to make calls as well, and the two colleagues were waiting to see if she made any "unauthorised" calls and if so, to whom. After five minutes Victoria had not sent any texts, calls or been on her laptop and they were both happy with her bona fides. Not that Rufus had any doubts, but again it was one of their SOPs, to double-check their instincts with facts.

Rufus returned to the room and saw Victoria pacing up and down, looking very worried.

"How are you feeling?" he asked.

"How do you think? You've made me get one of my parents killed. They are going to fucking gang rape my mum. So how do you think I'm feeling?" She ran into the bathroom to get away from him.

Fortunately she didn't lock the door and after a couple of minutes Rufus, followed her in.

"You're right," he said, "it was a stupid question, I'm sorry. Come on." He put his arm around her shoulder. "Come back in to the room and I'll run through things with you, because believe me, that went really well, you did brilliantly. I know you don't think that at the moment, but honestly it went really well."

Victoria half cried half laughed as he led her back into the bedroom and sat her down in the same chair she had sat when she was on the phone. He moved back slightly, but he was still able to take her hands in his and he started talking:

"Hear me out before you jump to any conclusions. Ok?"

Victoria nodded her head, still very emotional.

"I told you that this was going to be a tremendously pressurised period for you and that I would be here to help you, and I'm sorry Victoria, the pressure is just going to crank up from here on in. I also told you what was going to happen when they answered the phone, and I think I got it pretty well right."

Victoria was nodding, still in an emotional state, wiping her nose and eyes with a tissue that Rufus proffered.

"I thought that went really well and I will tell you why: one," he held up his forefinger, "they threw the bit about you going to the police in, and they soon forgot about that, you convinced them straight away that you haven't and all their bullshit about having people everywhere is just that, bullshit; two: they think you are a weak feeble woman and that will make them underestimate us, that is what I want, I want them to relax and feel they are dominating you, you did that perfectly; three: you'd listened to everything I'd told you and you did it, you did it brilliantly, you looked at me for prompts and you understood them, a lot of people will shut down under such pressure, I have even seen experienced police negotiators turn away and lose themselves in their own world, not accepting help, you didn't do that, you stayed with me throughout; and four: you reacted in the right way in the right places, you cried, when it was right to cry, and next time I might want you to get angry with them to perhaps even threaten them. As I told you, I will be asking you to do things which are counter-intuitive. Ok?"

"Ok," she said through the laugh-sobs, her eyes wet with tears, but smiling at the same time.

"We must play the conversation back, so we can pick out the important bits. He will have made verbal errors, slip ups which will tell us things and that is why I record them, so we can analyse it and be objective. Was that the guy you spoke to back in England?"

"No, I've never heard his voice before."

"Ok, so we know there are at least two of them." Rufus made some notes in his book. When he finished he looked up at Victoria. "First of all, do you want anything to eat or drink, because you have had a hard day, I've thrown a lot at you and it's been an emotional rollercoaster?"

"Yes, I've just realised how thirsty and hungry I am."

Rufus didn't expect any calls back from the bandits, but again he wasn't going to take any chances. He got Victoria to give him the phone, double-checked it was locked and put it in his pocket. He had a system by which he always kept his personal phone in his right pocket and any other phones in his left pocket. They went down to the Sushi restaurant on the mezzanine floor and ordered food. Rufus didn't drink when he was working, but he knew that Victoria would want a good stiff one to settle, her down. He didn't mind, as he was quite sure they would not get another call, and if they did, he had enough reuses up his sleeve to explain virtually anything away.

They settled at their table and Victoria was curious.

"So Rufus Stone, you know lots about me, my parents, what I do for a living; tell me a little bit about yourself."

"What do you want to know?"

"Anything. Everything."

"There's not much to tell really Victoria, I got a bit lost as a teenager and joined the military."

"Why did you choose The Royal Marines?"

"When I went into the booties' recruiting office, they just made more of a fuss, made me feel like they wanted me."

"Booties?"

"Yeh, the Booties, that's what the other arms call them, or the Royals or Muscles Are Required Intelligence Not Essential."

"Ha ha. You're not like that though, you're quite cerebral?"

"No, I never got into the macho thing. We all had to carry heavy weights over extreme distances. The final test for the Commando course is a thirty mile yomp, with twenty-five pounds of kit, plus weapon and water. SAS selection is even tougher: forty miles with a sixty pound Bergen, weapon and water over the Brecon Beacons in under twenty-four hours."

"That's inhuman."

"It's a grueller, so I always think: why carry any more than you have to? Either kit or body mass. I always pack the bare minimum."

"Girlfriend?"

"Not really. After Tina left I was wrapped up with the Regiment. Never in one place for long enough to hold down a relationship." Rufus was not going to explain Rachel, an FBI Special Agent working out of Quantico, to Victoria, it was just too complicated.

They'd met at Hendon on the police negotiators' course and hit it off immediately: she helped him a lot in the first few days, explaining theories and methods which are common to both the Americans and the British and other SOPs which were completely different, because of the different societies. He was able to see the rationale from both sides because of his military background and familiarity with weapons, he understood the American caution at a siege and because of his Britishness he understood the need to sometimes go face to face; a complete anathema to the Americans.

A Chicagoan, with a broad accent, tall, virtually as tall as Rufus, and to Rufus was stunningly pretty, but she tried to hide it; Rufus wasn't a psychologist, but he thought the conservative way she dressed and appeared was because she was in the macho world of Hostage Rescue and she was competing with men, and wanted to be seen as an equal and the way to do that was to be as masculine as them.

The chemistry had been strong from the first public introductions and they'd sought each other out at every opportunity and a romantic relationship had developed.

They'd met again a few months later when they engineered attending the same kidnap course.

They kept in touch, both accepting their long-distance relationship. Their brief spells together being frenetic and charged with passion and energy.

"Hobbies?"

"I love my cars. As well as the Jag I've got a Lotus and a Caterham. I like track days and sometimes go hill climbing with a mate in his car a Radical Clubsport 1400 ZX14. It's just a bit of fun really. I do the odd triathlon, a bit of parachuting, mountaineering, and caving."

"Oh my God no, I can't bear the thought of pot-holing, crawling around in the wet, cold and pitch black. I get the other stuff, but pot-holing?"

"It's not everybody's cup of tea is it?"

+++++++

Sir Peregrine had been busy liaising with the American cousins. He had not got them too excited at the moment: the Brits were dealing with a low-level gang who had kidnapped a British couple, in an ex colony – as far as they were concerned it was a British problem.

He got back to Nick Cooper in Dar:

"How are things developing over there Cooper?" he enquired.

"Coming along nicely at the moment; Cheltenham has been able to give us some pretty good help," referring to their sister intelligence service of the Government Communications Headquarters, or GCHQ. "We know the Conways' daughter is here, with a contractor hired by the insurance company and we know they have been in contact with the group holding the couple. Our man is keeping me updated and I've set things in motion to lure the quarry into our trap.

"Excellent," said Sir Peregrine, more to himself than to Cooper. "What do we know about the contractor?"

"Um," said Cooper checking his files, "his name is Rufus Stone, ex Regiment, partner in a small crisis management company called 22Red. A well-respected, handy bloke."

"Well, we can't let sentiment get in our way Cooper, he might be well respected but there is a bigger picture here, as you are well aware, and he is expendable, if he starts interfering with the strategy we will have to consider a different course of action. This is potentially far more important than one, two or even three lives."

"Yes I understand that sir. It's just that you asked me what I knew about him... he's been involved in quite a few jobs around the world. The company is only three people strong: Stone; and another couple, Don and Orla Ward, both ex SF."

"Right," said Sir Peregrine in a distracted tone, as he moved from his rosewood desk and looked out of the window across the Thames. He was Rhodesian by birth, of Welsh extraction. At best a panjandrum, at worst a deceitful, egocentric psychopath, in the way he dominated his staff and never felt any remorse for his actions, not matter how unjustified they were. His parents had returned to Britain with him when he was a boy, attended Monmouth Boys' School on a scholarship prior to gaining a place at Cambridge to read The Classics and joined the Royal Welsh Fusiliers on a Short Service Commission, before joining SIS: a man of considerable intellect, ability and power.

In the time it took to get up and walk to the window he had imagined a whole host of scenarios, most of them involving the removal of Rufus Stone.

"All I am saying Cooper, is that we have to do whatever is necessary to protect our freedoms and way of life. Do you understand?"

"Perfectly sir."

"I want twice daily briefings on this. Don't let me down now, will you old boy. I'll speak to you later," and abruptly terminated the call.

He had one hour to prepare for the first 'COBRA' meeting of the kidnap and he had to control proceedings. This was potentially too important to divulge what he knew and what he was planning. He would have to control Braddock from GCHQ, who would know too much. SF would be there and they may have a backdoor into the op, as no doubt these do-gooders would have let their old colleagues know what they were up to.

Sir Peregrine looked on Special Forces with disdain, with their classlessness and what he perceived as damned incivility, the way the ranks spoke to their officers. The police would be there, trying to get in on the act, but he didn't have to worry about them, they knew nothing at the moment, and he would keep it that way. The politicians would just do as they were advised, and it would be him giving the advice. He just had to ensure Braddock was kept in his place and keep a weather eye on SF, they could always be loose cannons, with no respect for how things should be done. He returned to his desk and planned his tactics for the meeting. The meeting in the Cabinet Office Briefing Rooms from which COBRA gets its name: the subterranean, secure, soundproofed suite of rooms, was attended by senior politicians: Dame Alexandra Cunningham-Black, Foreign Office Minister of State with responsibility for the Commonwealth, and Joanne Harper, the Under Secretary of State for Counter-terrorism; civil servants, Sir Peregrine represented MI6; Fiona Wade, MI5; Robert Braddock GCHQ, and the Head of Station (HoS) Cooper, was on the Secure Satellite link from Dar es Salaam. The military, newly appointed Government Liaison Officer or GLO, Major "Mad Frankie" Fraser of 22 SAS, members of the Metropolitan Police Service's Counterterrorism Command (SO15), Detective Superintendent Richards and his batman Detective Inspector Willday, and head of the Hostage and Crisis Negotiation Unit (HCNU), Detective Superintendent "Stringbag" Stringer. All of the participants had been vetted to at least Developed Vetting (DV) level, some a lot higher, with "strapping" and to levels that are never published or known about.

Even in such secure company everybody had been searched, had all forms of mobile communications and photographic equipment removed before they were allowed into the subterranean modern day Faraday Cage, securing all communications within the room. All those present was very guarded about putting their head above the parapet to disclose how much they knew, because that might reveal the extent of their networks, or in some cases, lack of them.

There are inter-departmental rivalries, and budgets, reputations and standings to consider in the nepotistic, savage world of counterterrorism. The real work was carried out away from the formal meeting room, with alliances forged or broken on the unyielding anvil of power and influence.

Sir Peregrine looked upon them all with disdain: when he had started in the service, none of this irrelevant trivia would have taken place. But all of this openness and accountability that afflicted them led to this bureaucratic nonsense. Good God, even SIS had a website. In the old days, SIS would have directed GCHQ what to do, nobody would have known anything about it until SIS had accomplished the safe release of the hostages, or got them killed. The point was that he and his colleagues knew what they were doing, had the contacts and know-how to accomplish things that are best left to the experts, without all of the meddling by politicians, military and police.

The meeting was amiable enough, and to the uninitiated it would appear a lot of intelligence and information was shared. To the practised observer though, it was clear that nobody actually contributed to the cumulative knowledge at all. They all confirmed what was already known: the time date and place of the kidnapping; the antecedents of the hostages; the belief that they were being held in the Kariakoo district of Dar es Salaam and the fact that an ex-Special Forces soldier was in Dar es Salaam with the daughter of the hostages attempting to affect their safe release.

"Colleagues," said the minister, "is there anything HMG could or should be doing to help these private individuals in their endeavours to secure the release of, um," she quickly looked at her briefing papers, "of, um Mr and Mrs Conway within the parameters of the British Government's continued stance on not negotiating and of no substantial concessions to terrorism?"

No one wanted to give their opponents any reason for accusing them of being soft on terrorism, or to give the government's critics, foreign or domestic, any ammunition in being able to link the government to the negotiations. The silence was deafening.

The minister decided to continue. "I think it would be prudent to maintain the stance that HMG is monitoring the situation and is aware of communications between interested parties. However, we should reiterate our long standing policy of not negotiating with terrorists, even though we have no intelligence to suggest that the kidnappers are terrorists."

Sir Peregrine kept his council, knowing that the kidnappers were indeed mere criminals.

"Interms of practical assistance," she continued, "I have asked the High Commissioner in Dar and Ms Harper to lobby local contacts and officials to put pressure on the kidnappers. I understand she had met with the president and expressed our concerns regarding the incident. We have been promised full co-operation by the Tanzanian authorities who will allow our teams into the country should we gain accurate enough intelligence to mount an intervention."

The HoS in Dar, Nick Cooper, started to talk via the satellite link but Sir Peregrine cut across him.

"Yes ma'am, I have an update from Dar and I can also confirm the Tanzanians are assisting. They are aware that an SIS surveillance team is providing low level protection on a CHIS." Sir Peregrine never explained acronyms or abbreviations to anybody, "they also assured me that should we deem DA necessary they will provide all and any assistance possible."

Of course Cooper hadn't told the Tanzanians the details or his plans, but he had to play the game and make them aware of the British interest.

Major Fraser, the Special Force liaison officer said:

"We have a team "on exercise" at a holding point on the Chagos Archipelago in the British Indian Ocean Territory. We are two hours from Dar es Salaam, where we have a F.O.B organised, through a contact in the TPDF should you wish us to move forward."

"Very good Major," said the minister. "I am becoming quite accustomed to forward military planning, and I guess the prospect of a few days in the Indian Ocean helped push things along a little?"

"Well, I don't suppose it hindered the plans at all ma'am," he said, imagining his colleagues sail boarding, scuba diving and fishing in the blue waters of the Indian Ocean.

The other attendees looked jealously at the major, knowing the minister, like some of her predecessors, rated Special Forces highly and trusted their input and judgement more highly than any others.

"Do you need any assistance from any of our other colleagues and stakeholders?" The minister looked around the room at the other departmental and agency representatives, knowing that they were either withholding information or didn't want to reveal the paucity of their intelligence.

"I understand that Sigint could be very interesting," said Major Fraser, having been told through the Special Forces old boy network of Don's concerns. "So I need to be briefed up on any BJ's provided by JTSL to the Firm," the major lapsed into jargon, meaning he needed to have sight of any Blue Jackets, an antiquated term dating back to when the Firm, or MI6 were briefed by GCHQ's predecessors and the files were denoted by the use of a blue cardboard folder, or jacket. JTLS, or the Joint Technical Language Service of GCHQ would provide the intelligence on any communications traffic that had been monitored.

"Mr Braddock?" said the minister, looking straight at the man from GCHQ.

"I'd anticipated the request Minister, and prepared a BJ for the major with the relevant intelligence," as he leaned forward and handed over the file. He was put out that Sir Peregrine had not been in contact to either confirm receipt of the intel, or to share any intel he might have to further GCHQ's understanding of the situation. He regarded Sir Peregrine, a descriptive name if there was one: as the bird of the same name is large and powerful, swift and agile – it famously swoops down, from a great height to come in for the kill. He'd always been like that; everybody knew it and he always got away with it. Others regarded Sir Peregrine as an anachronism, a dinosaur. Braddock reminded himself that dinosaurs roamed the Earth for millions of years and in terms of longevity, were far more successful than humankind.

"Ma'am," interjected Sir Peregrine, glaring at Braddock, trying to block the passing over of the intelligence, "I have not had sight of the BJ yet and protocol dictates that it should come through our offices, prior to further dissemination."

"Thank you Sir Peregrine," replied Dame Cunningham-Black. "But in these circumstances in which time may be of the essence, I think it is safe for our military colleagues to start their planning."

"These are the exact circumstances that the current protocols are designed to protect ma'am. There has to be coordination of the intelligence and action, which is the role of my offices, to ensure there is no unilateral action, or even worse no blue-on-blue," objected Sir Peregrine.

"Ma'am," interjected Major Fraser, the epitome of everything Sir Peregrine hated about Special Forces. A working class oik, who had risen through the ranks to gain the Queen's Commission, and be given the rank of Major. "There is no question of unilateral action, however, it is imperative that as the operational unit which will be tasked with any intervention, we are fully up-to-speed on ANY intelligence." Fraser stared at Sir Peregrine. "And that doesn't just mean Sigint from Cheltenham. We need to know who the opposition are; their capabilities; their intentions; whether we have any sources within the group who we might need to protect. This is precisely the forum for this intelligence to be shared to ensure we all on the same page and can contribute to the collective knowledge."

"The BJ was forwarded to Vauxhall this morning ma'am. I don't know whether Sir Peregrine has had sight of the document yet though as I have not received a reply to the communication."

Damn that Braddock, thought Sir Peregrine:

"Not as yet ma'am, it has to be assessed by the analysts and the Tanzania desk before I read it." He told a half truth, to explain his dereliction of duty. "I would suggest that my staff be given the opportunity to thoroughly research the intelligence prior to it being disseminated."

The other attendees' expressions did not change one iota, all keeping their professional masks in place, but began searching for something to occupy their hands and eyes while this power struggle ensued. Most agreed with the major, but SF liaison officers came and went, the minister's tenure was in the lap of the gods, but Sir Peregrine was a permanent fixture. He seemed to have been involved forever and had a great deal of influence. Not a man who you wanted to get on the wrong side of.

"Thank you Major, Robert, Sir Peregrine," said the minister – Sir Peregrine noting he was the last to be addressed. "I agree, with the major this is precisely one of the reasons COBRA was initiated, to share information and to act as a Tasking and Coordination Group. I suggest that you manage your staff in order prioritise their work in accordance with governmental policy."

There was a slight hiatus in the meeting as everybody searched for something useful to add to the discussion and diffuse the tension. Most of the attendees were seasoned enough to understand what was going on and decided to keep out of it – it wasn't their fight– the internecine warfare raging in front of them was fun to watch, but dangerous to get involved. There was one exception.

"Of course, former Squadron Sgt Major Stone has been through our courses," said Detective Superintendent Stringer of the HCNU. "I would therefore expect his strategy to be that of obtaining proof of life, delay, intelligence building, lowering of expectations and the identification of a third party intermediary. Based on that supposition I would expect this to be a long drawn-out process, with no prospect of a negotiated release or possibility of an intervention in the immediate future."

Nobody came to his rescue as the minister looked at him quizzically, wondering what point he was trying to make.

"Excellent, um, thank you Detective Superintendent," she said eventually.

Sir Peregrine had to get back some control of the meeting and decided to divulge a small amount of information:

"Our intelligence suggests that al-Shabaab are linked to the kidnapping." He chose his words carefully, "and while I have the deepest sympathy for the Conways, this unfortunate event could provide us with a longer term strategic advantage."

"What is that supposed to mean?" asked the minister.

"It means that the national interest, and that of our partners, may well be better served in the long run if we maintain the status quo and leave this, um, this Stone fellow to his own devices. That we offer no support, tacit or explicit, to him and his team and maintain the government's stance, while we monitor the situation from afar and gather intelligence. Our cousins at the Company have a dearth of intelligence here, and this could give us some leverage with them, as well as assist the tasking of our boys out there."

The minister looked around the room.

"Are you suggesting that we sacrifice the lives of two British citizens?"

"Not sacrifice ma'am, no. But their short term predicament may well lead to a longer term benefit."

"But you just said 'offer no support, tacit or explicit', which appears to me that you are suggesting that even if we identify where the Conways are, we do nothing."

That was exactly what he was suggesting

"No ma'am, obviously I do not mean that. I mean that we do not provide Stone with any support which we may be in a position to offer at the moment. That we monitor events and time any action we choose to adopt to maximise its effect. That way we will entice the kidnappers out into the open."

"Ah, right," said the minister.

"And at that moment we would share all of the intelligence, when it has been analysed and assessed, after all ma'am erroneous intelligence is worse than no intelligence at all and can lead to misjudgements and miscalculations. No, it is better to wait to ensure the facts are given to our friends in the military who, as we all know, do such a fantastic job on our behalf and I wouldn't want to endanger them."

Major Fraser saw straight through Sir Peregrine's rhetoric, it might be his first COBRA but he had been warned about how manipulative Dennis was and marked his cards for the next meeting.

Braddock knew and thought Sir Peregrine Dennis knew that with a little more effort they could identify fairly accurately where the stronghold was, and with a little more Humint, which he suspected The Firm had, they could probably pinpoint the target precisely, Dar es Salaam is a labyrinth, but not that bad, and he was reasonably certain that at the moment al-Shabaab were not holding the Conways and that an intervention using Special Forces would be relatively simple against a gang of criminals, instead of trained and motivated terrorists.

Clearly the politicians needed to know this, but he had already crossed Dennis once during the meeting and was not prepared to do it again, not without more clear support from the minister or the other attendees. The only one with the bollocks to stand up to Dennis was Mad Frankie, but he hadn't got the guile or connections that Dennis had got and anyway his orbit around government was on a completely different trajectory to his own and Dennis's, which were inextricably linked. No, he would have to bide his time and gauge when it was appropriate to divulge this to the politicians.

Sir Peregrine was withholding information from the politicians for different reasons to that of his colleague: he regarded politicians as a little too emotional, unreliable and loose-lipped for intelligence work, and of course too short-term, always looking at the next election. This operation was part of a much greater strategic plan and was best left to the professionals, who have the skill, knowledge and experience to handle this kind of situation, as well as having the long term national interest at heart.

Dame Cunningham-Black was persuaded by Sir Peregrine's eloquent argument and concluded that now was not the time to share the raw intelligence with the military. She drew the meeting to a close and summarised the conclusions, thanked everybody for their attendance and set the date of the next meeting for two days' time.

The participants left the meeting collecting their phones and laptops from security on their way out, splitting off into their natural alliances, discussing the meeting in guarded voices.

The police contingent all walked back to New Scotland Yard together, but Detective Superintendent Stringer, was in his own little world of reverie, he thought he had done rather well on his first COBRA meeting. He had emphasised the importance of his unit by telling the minister that they had trained Stone. He'd explained the negotiating strategy and put forward a cogent argument for a long process, giving him even more exposure to the minister who seemed quite impressed with his performance. A good day's work, he thought to himself as he strolled back with the others across Horse Guards Road, through St James' Park, across Birdcage Walk, along Queen Anne's Gate to The Broadway and New Scotland Yard. He didn't hear a word the Counter Terrorist chaps were saying. Yes, he concluded to himself, things were looking up for him.

'Mad Frankie' Fraser and Robert Braddock walked a short way together, both very unhappy at the way the meeting had ended. They concluded that they should set up an unofficial back channel to each other in order to share their information, which would be a 'one-way' street for the time being, but Braddock loathed Dennis and saw the major as a kindred spirit and thought it was worth the risk of going behind the back of the devious curmudgeonly old spy.

The politicians left the basement offices together to walk up the stairs. They all knew that the minister had been out manoeuvred by the old spy, but none of them wanted to broach the subject with her, they knew her well enough to realise that she was aware and would make amends when the time was right.

The only one to leave on his own was Sir Peregrine Dennis, he neither invited or sought company from any of his 'colleagues' as the very politically correct minister insisted on calling them. As far as he was concerned none of them were his colleagues, certainly not his friends, peers or confidantes. He knew that Major Fraser would not be out-smarted so easily next time, it was after all, his first COBRA, but he would be ready for him in two days' time.

Chapter Twenty-One

Victoria and Rufus got to the Sushi bar and Rufus nonchalantly chose a table that was side on to the entrance so that he could use his peripheral vision to check anybody coming in. They ordered food and chatted away, discussing the phone call and their own hypotheses about the kidnappers all in hushed conspiratorial voices.

"Forget the phone call for a few minutes, because neither of us will remember it exactly, we'll go back to the room and play it back when we've had something to eat." Rufus said eventually.

"Ok, I'll try, but his threats about cutting Mum's ear off and raping her keep playing in my head."

"I guess they are, but let's listen to the recording and we'll dissect everything as we go through it. Have you ever been through the island personality test?" Rufus asked in an attempt to stop Victoria replaying the conversation in her head.

"I don't think so."

Over the course of dinner Rufus led Victoria through a series of hypothetical scenarios after being stranded on an island. It was not scientific in anyway, but it had the desired effect and distracted Victoria.

When they finished he caught the waiter's attention and paid the bill on his room account, because he didn't want to spend too long in the public areas of the hotel. He noted that although the waiter was dealing with him, he was actually watching Victoria. From everything he had seen of Victoria, his assessment of her was that she did not realise how beautiful she was, and the effect she had on most men.

They caught the elevator to their floor and for some reason of morality and ethics they walked in their separate doors, just to see each other on the other side as they entered their rooms.

Rufus went through to Victoria's side.

"We need to review today's call if you are up to it?"

"Please, I think I need to get it all straight in my head."

"Good. From my point of view it went according to plan. How do you think it went?"

"Oh Ru I don't know. My head is spinning with possibilities. All sorts of irrational thoughts: Are you a good guy or a bad guy? Are my parents still alive? Are they ok? Do I need you, playing your stupid mind games or should I just go ahead and deal with these bastards myself. How did you know what they were going to say? It was uncanny, like you had written the script for them, a little bit too convenient. I don't know what to think, who to trust or what to do."

Rufus was used to this inner turmoil and didn't take any of it personally; he knew he had to give Victoria a reality check.

"I can understand everything you say, honestly, and the reason I can understand it, is because it has happened to me before. Let's look at the facts Victoria, I don't want to sound big headed, but we're good, we're very good at this and that's why the insurance company come to us. They trust Don, Orla and me because they know us and they know we get the right results for them and their clients. I've told you that we have worked on kidnap cases before, lots of them, and I've told you that the only ones that have gone wrong are when people took unilateral action, when people in your position lost faith in us. But the vast majority have believed in us and their faith has been justified."

Rufus was using a technique called "social proofing". "Yes I predicted what they said yesterday, and let's face it, if I couldn't do that, I wouldn't be much use to you would I? I will make another prediction, if you choose to go it alone, not only will *you* be taken hostage, your mum and dad will not be released and the three of you will be held for a long time for a lot more money than they are currently asking for. I will always have your parents' safety and best interest as my primary goal, except in one circumstance – and that is if it puts you in danger. It's not about machismo, or scoring points off them or playing games. Everything we do, we do for a reason that I can explain, and has been thought through."

"On Rufus, I'm sorry, I'm sorry I doubted you, it's just that I feel such an enormous pressure, the fate of my parents is in my hands."

"Our hands, Victoria. We are a team remember, I've told you that right at the start."

Victoria nodded in agreement and smiled at him.

Rufus could see Victoria was getting stronger, only yesterday she would have started crying at the thought of the responsibility she had for her parents' lives, but now she was ready for it. They prepared themselves to review the day's conversation together.

"I'm sorry," she said again.

"You don't need to apologise Victoria."

As they listened, Rufus referred to his notes forewarning Victoria of important points arising. They nick-named the bandit 'Samuel', after Samuel L Jackson, as Rufus always liked to give people names by which they could refer to them when discussing the calls. They listened to him rant, and claim that he knew lots of facts. Rufus stopped the play-back and said, "That's all lies isn't it? Think about it logically: one, you haven't been to the police; two; no-one knows you are here, you've seen how chaotic and disorganised the airport is; three; he wasn't expecting your call as he claims – you caught him off-guard. It was all bullshit and one of the reasons he ranted so much was because he was unprepared. Inner and outer emotion. Are you familiar with that?"

"Mm," said Victoria trying to assimilate everything Rufus had said.

They played more of the recording until Rufus stopped it again.

"See, he can't have posted you your mum's ear, he doesn't know where you are. He hasn't done that. It's all just bluster to get you on the back-foot, and that's exactly where we are going to let him think you are."

They listened to the kidnapper calm down and show signs that he accepted what Victoria said.

"You happier now?" asked Rufus after they had finished, do you understand why I thought the call went well?

"Yes, yes I can now you've explained it all to me."

Rufus suggested that they shut, but not lock the interconnecting doors, so that Victoria could have privacy, but if the phone went in the night he could still rush through and assist her without any delay. The other thoughts he had were so that he could protect her more easily if their whereabouts were discovered, and he would hear if she tried to make any phone calls. He had experienced his victims trying all sorts of things: leaving the room to go to a prearranged meeting; sending texts; making phone calls; phone sex; asking for advice from friends; phoning the press and publishers to try and get a deal; swapping SIM cards in the phone to make untraceable calls – it never ceased to amaze him. But Victoria readily agreed with Rufus, not suspecting that he was thinking any of this at all.

Chapter Twenty-Two

Victoria was woken at 7a.m. by Rufus knocking the door and calling her name.

"Come in Ru," she called.

His face appeared around the door first, smiling and vibrant. When he could see she was ready he strode into the room and she could see he was showered, dressed and ready to go.

"You make me sick," she said. "I bet you've done your exercises as well?"

"Of course I have. It sets me up for the day and gets me ready for breakfast. I've woken you up so that you can get over the jet lag a bit more easily, if I let you lie in you will feel worse."

Victoria sat up in bed, pulling the bed sheets up to her neck as she did so.

"How did you know I didn't want to come to the gym with you?"

"First of all, I haven't been to the gym, I've worked out in my room, so that I could be close to you if you needed me. Second, I think the right amount of sleep is marginally more important for you than exercise at the moment."

"What?" exclaimed Victoria. "The great Rufus Stone extolling the virtues of sleep over exercise. Hold the front page."

"Touché," said Rufus smiling, "Now get yourself ready, I've ordered room service for breakfast and then we need to rehearse."

"Yes SIR," said Victoria teasing him, giving her best salute to Rufus, making sure the bed clothes were still firmly in place with her other hand.

Rufus smiled a broad grin at her and disappeared to his own side. He thought of phoning Don, but a quick calculation told him it was only 4a.m. in the UK.

After thirty minutes Victoria knocked the interconnecting door and walked into his room. He was sat with headphones on and his notebook out listening to the previous calls, again making notes, preparing.

God, thought Victoria. *he never stops, he's inhuman, I've never seen him sleep, if he does he falls asleep after me and wakes before me, he never relaxes, switches off or gets caught unawares.*

Rufus looked up at her and mouthed "two minutes" as he continued to listen to the recording, jotting down notes. As Rufus finished there was a knock at Victoria's door. He checked the spyhole and could see it was a waiter with their breakfast and let him in.

They prepared for their next call, over breakfast. Rufus explained that he thought the bad guys would concentrate on the money. He explained to Victoria the actual logistics of arranging such a large amount of cash:

"You can't just walk into a bank and withdraw that amount of money, even if you have it in your account. The banks don't carry that sort of cash and it would be impossible to walk out with it, so their focus on the cash would actually be good for us because we can lower their expectations again and offer $1million, or nearly two billion Tanzanian shillings. This is still a considerable sum of money to anybody."

"Do you think they will go for that?"

"It's my job to make sure they do. One million is not to be sniffed at Victoria." And while he had no intention of actually paying any money, he had to make things realistic.

Victoria listened intently, trying to get to grips with his plans. He spoke so authoritatively, as if he absolutely knew what would happen. *How can he be so sure?*

He predicted that negotiations would be taken over by a calmer more objective bandit, and that wasn't so good, so Victoria would have to be careful. She would have to be more alert, more thoughtful and they would have to rehearse more. Rufus usually found that the calmer the voice the more dangerous and sinister any threats made seemed to the victim. It was easier to fall into their traps and they didn't give you as much thinking time as an angry person.

Rufus explained his and Don's theory, that they were dealing with criminals or bandits rather than a group like Harakat al-Shabaab al-Mujahideen, more commonly referred to simply as al-Shabaab, or 'The boys': a supposed religious terrorist group, an oxymoron if ever there was one. What both he and Don were worried about, but he wasn't going to tell Victoria this, was that the bandits were in contact with al-Shabaab, trying to negotiate a better deal with them, so pitching the right amount and offering it up relatively quickly was of paramount importance. Fortunately thanks to Don's technical expertise, they had the inside track on this, but there was still something worrying Don, which Rufus couldn't put his finger on.

Dealing with criminals was a lot more straightforward than dealing with terrorists; criminals wanted two things: the money and their freedom. Sometimes they would even settle for one, the money, reasoning that they could do the time and come out of prison to the cash. Happy Days...

Terrorists are a different breed entirely, and their demands can be varied and extreme, from publicity, to freeing of comrades, to money, to intelligence gathering. And they could be a lot more brutal, especially to the infidel. The infidels' lives were worth nothing to a Muslim extremist. He definitely did not want Deidre and Martyn to be given to al-Shabaab or any other al Qaida affiliate. He knew, though, that once they showed their hand as to what they wanted he would be able to manage it. If it was still money they were after, then that was the easiest, and he could deal with them the same way he would deal with criminals. It came back to Sun Tzu, knowing what motivates your enemy. But if they wanted glory and were prepared to die in their jihad, then Rufus's task would become virtually impossible. His only hope would be to buy time and gather intelligence to mount an intervention.

He wanted Victoria to get "proof of life" he didn't use those words to her, but emphasised how important it was for her to speak to her parents and they discussed ways she could persuade the kidnappers to give her the proof they needed. Rufus set the room up again and asked Victoria if she was happy with the way they worked yesterday.

"Definitely, I felt more reassured that you were there, but at the same time, you weren't there. It felt good to me."

They rehearsed the second call, this time Rufus kept his voice even and business like, making evil threats to Victoria that made her take a sharp intake of breath, but she was a fast learner and started to think for herself, playing her part superbly.

Rufus made some last minute preparations, checked with Don that everything was ok and they were ready for the call.

Chapter Twenty-Three

Victoria answered it on the second ring, after Rufus gave her the thumbs up.

"Miss Conway?" said the sonorous voice on the other end; a well-spoken man with an African accent, to whom Rufus immediately gave the nomenclature of 'James' after James Earl Jones.

"Yes," said Victoria.

"You spoke to my associate yesterday and I understand that protracted negotiations were initiated, for and on behalf of my organisation, and that during said negotiations, my colleague unfortunately made numerous unseemly comments, which were unnecessary and in the larger scheme of our said negotiations were, not to put too fine a point on it, unhelpful."

Victoria stared at Rufus, although he had told her about jobs where the bandits put airs and graces on to try and give the impression of professionalism and education, it still took her by surprise, and if the situation had not been so serious, she would have burst out laughing.

Rufus winked at her and gave her the thumbs up again.

"Yes I did speak to somebody yesterday," she replied.

"I apologise unreservedly in absentia for my colleague's boorish and frankly unhelpful conduct and

I hope that we can resume negotiations on a more even footing."

It sounded to Victoria like he had swallowed a thesaurus, and it was just like Rufus had told her. But she had to stay in role, the role of the solitary, vulnerable naive child who wanted her mummy and daddy back.

"He was horrible to my mum and dad, I'm so pleased that you are talking to me now and I'm sure we will be able to arrange to get you your money, but I can't get anywhere near the $10million you asked for."

"What can you get?"

"I can get you $1million I think, that's nearly two billion shillings."

"You have the temerity to offer a paltry $1million for the lives of your parents, I would..."

"That's correct."

"Please do not interrupt me while I am talking, I find it most offensive. You must understand that my organisation is extremely numerous in number and we have many mouths to feed, police officers and officials to look after who provide us with protection and information on your whereabouts. We are like the Minotaur of Greek mythology, with many heads and you will not be able to destroy us. If you remove one of us, more will take their place."

Victoria had to suppress her giggles again at this mistake. It sounded to Victoria and Rufus that he was actually reading from a script; in fact Rufus was certain of it. Victoria would have been paranoid that she was being surveilled, if it wasn't for Rufus, reassuring her that they would claim this sort of complex structure and omniscience.

"I don't want to destroy you, I've seen the poverty in your country and I sympathise with you, that's why I want to get your money to you."

"DO. NOT.IN.TERR.UPT.ME," the voice said, he didn't shout but he said each word carefully, each syllable separately.

Rufus was holding up the prompt *Let him Speak*, but Victoria tried to engage him

"I'm sorry, I thought you had finished, I didn't mean..."

"Miss Conway, do not mistake my civility, upbringing and manners for weakness, if you interrupt me again your parents will suffer severely."

Victoria drew a breath as if to speak, but Rufus knew he was testing her, and shook his head, holding his finger to her lips for emphasis.

"If I return with your offer to our executive meeting they will find it most insulting. I'm sure that I will not be able to control many of my colleagues who already think we should adopt a harsher regime against your parents, but for the moment, my reasonable stance has prevailed."

Rufus still had his finger on her lips, and when he was certain the voice had finished, he took it away and nodded to her and tapped *thank you* on his tablet.

"Thank you," she said, giving her own thumbs up acknowledging Rufus's indication towards the prompt on the screen "Thank you so much Mr ?..."

"My name is of no importance Miss Conway, just think carefully before you make your next offer."

Rufus was holding up two fingers.

"I can try and get you two million, but you must..."

"Hahahaha."

Rufus's finger was on her lips again.

"NO, Miss Conway, YOU must understand, that you are not in any position to tell me what we must do. I will tell YOU what YOU MUST do, you do not tell me. I am in control here. I am the one with all of the aces, not you."

Rufus's finger was on his lips again, negotiating was about listening, not talking; and when he was certain the voice had finished he pointed to the *Sorry* prompt, quickly followed by the *Emotion* screen.

"I'm sorry, I didn't mean to tell you you must do anything, I was trying to explain that I just can't get the sort of money you are asking for. If I raise money against my parents' house and get money from friends and family I still might not even get to $2 million, but that is what I will try and get for you. But you must... sorry, sorry, that's just an expression, I really need to know that Mum and Dad are ok before I can do anything, people won't lend me the money if they are..." Victoria started to weep and Rufus smiled inwardly, he thought the emotion sounded genuine, and it was perfect, "... sorry, um, you know, that um, that they are ok."

Rufus was giving her thumbs up, rolling hand over hand and nodding, indicating that she should continue and then brought up the prompt *Talk to them please.*

"Can I talk to them please?"

Rufus often thought he was like a conductor of an orchestra, not actually playing the instruments, but responsible for when to bring in each new element: the timing, the synchronisation, the intensity and the subtleties using his hands in a similar way. He thought it was a good analogy, as the conductor and the orchestra have a symbiotic relationship, just like the victim and the negotiator.

"That will be very difficult to arrange," said the voice.

Rufus tapped the *PLEASE* prompt and then *Emotion.*

"PLEASE," said Victoria with emphasis. "I need to know they are ok, I am worried sick and I can't think straight not knowing if they are still alive. I can't sleep and I keep bursting into tears thinking that I might never see them again. If I know they are ok, I can concentrate on getting your money," Acknowledging the *Money* prompt that Rufus had shown her.

The pair of them were now working like a well-oiled machine, Rufus silently conducting Victoria's responses and Victoria providing the realism and emotion necessary.

"I will call you the same time tomorrow, I am warning you Miss Conway, no police, no paramilitary, and when you have heard their voices I will demand our money and you had better have it ready for their sakes."

Rufus showed the *More Time* prompt for Victoria, but the line went dead. He went through his routine of double-checking the line was cut off before he time stamped the call.

"Well done," he said. "I thought you did brilliantly again. Just think what he said towards the end, "I'm the one with all of the aces, not you." That is just perfect for us. You have played your part fantastically. Right, if he calls back, and I don't think he will, I want you to emphasise the amount of time that getting that amount of money will take, also, if you can, ask him to release one of your parents. Ok?"

Victoria was much more controlled now. She looked at Rufus and felt a real sense of trust and a bond with him. When he had been pointing at the prompt screen or putting his fingers on her lips, she trusted him implicitly, and wished that she had met him in different circumstances, but she hadn't and she had to concentrate for her Mum and Dad. But she had to remind herself that this was not normal, this was an extraordinary circumstance in which she found herself and she needed him.

"I feel much better after that one Ru, but what was all the crap he was coming out with at the start? I nearly burst out laughing."

"I know you did. I didn't dare catch your eye for a few seconds, or I think we would have both gone. And didn't he sound like a supercilious James Earl Jones?"

"Oh yes, yes, that's it, I was trying to think what you would call him. It was just like James Earl Jones. But he couldn't pronounce his words properly; they are clearly not part of his usual vocabulary."

"Well done Victoria, you're starting to think, instead of react. I'll be able to put my feet up soon and just let you get on with it."

"Oh no you don't Mr, I need you; you give me confidence and keep me focused."

"You're doing great Victoria, believe me, I'm really pleased with the way things are going. Now I need to phone Don again and see if he has anything for us."

Chapter Twenty-Four

Rufus went to his own room and made the call. He didn't really understand how Don did what he did, but he did it bloody well.

"Hello mate. What have you got?"

"That was really good Ru. Got it all recorded and I'm just tracking this phone now, I've got quite a strong fix on this one."

"We're calling him James," said Rufus.

"Well James is just leaving a gaff off Chole Road, Masaki, if you know it? I've got a surprisingly strong signal from him and he seems to be heading into the city according to mapping. I don't understand how it's so strong when you keep dropping in and out."

"Ok, I need the exact details of the place and I'll go and recce it tonight. I know that part of town pretty well, and fortunately it's on the peninsular where all the ex-pats live, so I won't stick out like a bulldog's bollocks. I also need the address of where he is heading now and I'll make an assessment on that one. Did he call anybody before he left?"

"Yes one call, it lasted about ten seconds, as if he was checking somebody was in and he'd be on his way over. My guess is he is going to check on his prize $2 million Christmas parcels," said Don.

"And mine, and that's why I need that address."

"Ok mate I'm working on that, and you be careful hey? There is something going on, which I can't quite fathom out; a lot of activity on Deidre's phone. I haven't seen activity like this before, so I'm still trying to understand what it is. She doesn't seem to be changing SIMs, but she might well be playing for both sides."

"So that's what's been worrying you. Why didn't you just say?"

"Because I'm not sure, that's why. I don't want to set hares running for no reason."

"Ok, so what's the motivation for her? I'm just testing your hypothesis here."

"The two main ones are money, or shagging of course. There's the insurance money pay-out and she could have set him up to go halves with the Bravos."

"Risky business Don. What would stop them taking the money and cutting her out?"

"Yeh I know, but I've got no data to tell you if she was in touch with anybody beforehand. So shagging then? See if Victoria can tell you anything."

"Oh right. Brilliant idea", said Rufus jokingly. "I'll just go in and ask Victoria if her old lady puts it about. Speaking of Victoria, I don't know if you listened in, but she did really well, a very fast learner."

"Yes I was listening. I thought James was a bit of a Barclays Banker though. What was all that bullshit he was coming out with at the start?"

"Well if you'd done the course with me like I told you to, you'd understand wouldn't you, I can't give you all my expertise. You stick to your technology and I'll deal in the real world."

"Ooooh", said Don. "On a serious note, I want to send Orla out to you. I think it's better to be safe than sorry and she will give you that bit of flexibility, and me a bit of security that I'm going to get a payday."

"I was thinking along the same lines myself. I took a walk yesterday and this city is growing fast, and although I recognised most places, I don't want to get caught out."

"I knew you'd agree with me, so I've already booked the flight for her this afternoon. I've booked her into *New Africa* which is only around the corner from you," said Don.

"Mmm. I know it. I'd rather her be in here with us though. If things happen quickly I'd like her watching my back straight away."

"Ok. What rooms are you, and I'll make sure she's on the next floor up."

"I'm 515 and Victoria is next door in 517," said Rufus.

"Right I'll get her onto the sixth floor then. Is there anything else you need?"

"Not really thanks mate, everything seems to be going pretty much according to the script. As soon as James stops moving let me know will you and the exact address of where he was when he made the call."

"You'll be the first to know."

+++++++

Nick Cooper was having a very similar conversation to that of Rufus and Don. Cheltenham had been able to get a fix on the phone call and listened in on the conversation. He was phoned and given a brief resume of the call, with a promise of a full transcript within two hours.

Cooper terminated the call and contacted his boss and mentor, Sir Peregrine, back in London.

"Thank you, Cooper. Let me be very clear about this: our strategy depends upon you taking robust action forthwith otherwise this Stone character might just negotiate the release of these people. This is a golden opportunity and we can't let it slip through our fingers. We are relying on you to make this happen. This is strictly a black op. We cannot be seen to be endangering the lives of a few British citizens, even if it is to save the lives of thousands of our compatriots."

"Yes sir. As soon as I've finished with you I'll make the arrangements."

"Well don't let me keep you." And the line went abruptly dead.

Cooper was used to his boss's lack of interpersonal skills but still looked at the phone in amazement and said to himself:

"'Thank you very much Nick, you're doing a great job and if this comes off, I see bigger and better things for you. Speak soon'. You're fucking welcome sir."

Cooper picked up another telephone and called Kumi. After establishing that he was free to speak, Cooper arranged to meet him at the pseudo British pub, The George and Dragon in Masaki, to give him his instructions. He picked up a third phone and made another phone call, making a promise to send Rufus Stone's service photograph as soon as he terminated the call.

Rufus went back to Victoria, who was jotting down some notes, trying to remember what had been said and what it meant. She would have some valid theories and Rufus would include her in all discussions; decision making, theory building, and planning. She was a clever woman and Rufus would listen to her over lunch. The basic human need of belonging would also be fulfilled by making sure she knew she was a critical part of the team. To feel ostracised leads to resentment and potentially a lot worse.

After discussing the call and preparing for another one, they went to the bar. Rufus took all his usual precautions in the rooms, ensuring he would know if anybody had entered them.

Originally, he had been taught to sit in the corner of the bar, or restaurant or any public room, so that he couldn't get taken by surprise and he could survey the scene. Orla had given him a different theory though and now he always avoided the corner. Any adversary would immediately look into the corners of the rooms and ping you straight away, so any advantage was minimised. Yes you could see them, but they could also see you. Orla taught Rufus to be inconspicuous; he would use mirrors or changes in sound, ambience and atmosphere to know when somebody entered the room, which he preferred. Victoria was his best radar today, as she was still on super alert and looked up at everybody entering the bar, whoever they were. He chose a table in the centre of the room, mixed among all of the other guests and one that afforded him an unobstructed view of the picture window which acted as a perfect mirror.

Many people entered the bar over the next hour and Rufus assessed them all. Most people fitted in to one of two categories: they walked in and looked for friends or colleagues, or they walked straight to the bar. Few people walk in and deliberately survey their surroundings. Yet one guy did just that, taking particular notice of the corners, so Rufus paid attention to him. He might just be very cautious and like to know where emergency exits are situated, should there be a need, but Rufus doubted it. He looked ordinary enough, but he would wouldn't he? Surveillance operatives try to look ordinary. The guy tried to look inconspicuous, but wasn't succeeding. He was looking around a bit too much, trying to be nonchalant.

Rufus had the advantage of using Victoria as camouflage, he leant forward so that his mouth was next to Victoria's ear his face in her thick hair, and said in a low voice.

"Don't take this the wrong way, I'm really not some pervy old man, I just need to talk quietly to you, so that nobody can hear what I am saying," he lied, as he didn't want to alarm her unnecessarily.

Victoria felt a shiver go down her spine as Rufus leaned in closer to her. He cupped his right hand against Victoria's left cheek and ran through the day's events, while watching the guy. He was convinced it wasn't James, certain that James was a local guy, but it didn't make Rufus any less concerned about this ordinary man. He was white, like most of the rest of the patrons in the bar, average height, average build, nondescript clothing, nothing with brands, labels or memorable images to grab the attention. No glasses, no cigarette, not chewing gum or carrying anything untoward. Rufus looked for a feature he could remember without staring at the guy and noticed a slight deformity of the ear lobe, that lobe stuck out more than most people's: a sort of right angled kink at the bottom of the ear making it look like an aerofoil. Rufus got a look at his shoes: a pair of blue deck shoes.

He was on his phone, not looking at Rufus and Victoria at all, and to all intents and purposes behaving quite naturally, as if he was waiting for a date or a friend, but Rufus didn't like it. The sixth sense, his sub-conscious, had kept him alive all this time and it was telling him something was not right.

He sat back and texted Don.

Anything for me?

Got the addresses, replied Don.

Nothing else? texted Rufus.

No.

Thanks, speak later.

Rufus and Victoria went through to the sushi restaurant, again. He chose the same table. After a few minutes the guy appeared, who Rufus had christened 'Loafers' because of his footwear, talked to the Maître de and left. Rufus didn't believe in coincidences, excused himself, claiming he needed to go to the restroom and walked out of the restaurant, down the stairs into the lobby, where he watched Loafers disappear out through the main doors. He took the opportunity to phone Don and get both addresses, and then told him what had just happened.

"I've got none of our targets showing anywhere near you mate. I can't help, sorry."

Rufus had to make a decision: follow Loafers, let Loafers follow him, which he would if his gut instinct was correct, or wait for Orla to turn up. He decided he couldn't afford to leave Victoria alone, even if he put her in her room, this could be a decoy and anybody could get into a hotel room in ten seconds flat. No, he would do it properly, if he was being overcautious, tomorrow would tell him.

He went back into Victoria and acted as if there was nothing wrong at all. They had a light lunch together swapping theories, testing each other's hypotheses. Victoria drawing on her medical training, Rufus using his extensive life experience. Victoria wanted to pigeonhole both of the bandits she had spoken to, but Rufus explained that they were acting their parts, just like she was acting hers. They both agreed that James was not well educated by Western standards and was trying to exaggerate his eloquence. Clearly he was trying to give the impression of an intelligent businessman, heading a corporation. Rufus reassured Victoria that he was no such thing.

"It's like they are just playing 'good cop, bad cop' isn't it?"

"Exactly that," said Rufus, "they've probably watched a few Hollywood films and they'll just swap the calls between them to keep you guessing and on edge."

Victoria knew everything Rufus was saying was right. But even though she knew he was right, she still had that little nagging voice in the back of her mind; the 'what if' voice.

Chapter Twenty-Five

They went to their rooms and Rufus checked that both bedrooms were exactly as he had left them, taking a little more care now. He contacted Don again by Skype, believing that even the NSA and GCHQ hadn't quite cracked how to intercept the calls, plus it was always reassuring to see Don's face, even if it was slightly distorted.

The two colleagues briefed each other on what they knew and what they thought they knew. Rufus brought Don up-to-speed on Loafers, but knew there was nothing Don could do about that and Rufus would have to wait until tomorrow morning for Orla's help.

They finished their call and Rufus returned to Victoria, who was lying on the bed, her eyes looking really heavy. He knew she was physically and mentally tired but didn't want her going to sleep yet as he believed that she would not sleep well during the night and he needed her fresh for the morning. It was difficult for him to explain the ebbs and flows of a kidnap, in which long periods of inactivity are interspersed with brief moments of high tension and drama.

"Where were we on the island?" he asked referring to the personality test they started yesterday.

"Um, I'd just described the inside of my log cabin. Can I change what I could see inside? The luxury I've described would be impossible on the island I'm imagining."

"No you can't. That's not the point of it, it's not meant to be realistic; it's your imagination at the time, your spontaneous sub-conscious reaction."

They spent the next half an hour finishing off the profile and Rufus explained what each of the answers theoretically meant. Some Victoria thought were spot on, but she rationalised it was like a horoscope and one could make the answers fit if you wanted to.

This was a part of a job that Rufus found the most difficult: it was the calm before the storm; he couldn't keep rehearsing the next call, or reviewing the last, he had to occupy Victoria so that she didn't start mithering over what was, or perhaps more accurately was not, happening, but the time had to be filled. He didn't want to go out into the public area of the hotel too much, because of Loafers.

Eventually the evening arrived and they went for dinner, after the now obligatory precautions on the rooms, to The Palm restaurant, overlooking the hotel's gardens.

Victoria was trying to stay awake asking him questions about Tina and his daughters. He didn't often talk about them to his clients, but he was quite happy to tell Victoria all about them and how much he loved and missed them.

When they finished their meals Rufus finally relented and said it was time for bed. He could see Victoria was really flagging and he guessed that by going to bed now, she would probably sleep all night.

They got back to their rooms, and he suggested to Victoria that they followed the same procedure as the night before. Even if she had any different thoughts, she was too tired to bother expressing them and agreed. As soon as Rufus closed the doors she collapsed on her bed, fully clothed, exhausted, leaving the lights on.

After a short time, Rufus quietly looked in on her. He decided to take her shoes off, put her into bed and turn the lights off. He considered taking her trousers and top off to let her sleep better, but imagined the scene if she woke just as he was removing her trousers. She could cry rape, it would ruin their relationship, the job, everything. No, shoes and only shoes was a much more sensible decision. He went back to his own room, did some more work, spoke to Don, then got into bed and was out like a light.

After a few hours Victoria woke. She had everything whirring around in her head. Was Rufus right? She had heard about state sponsored criminality in Africa, how did he know that these guys hadn't got all of the facilities the state could offer them? How did he know there wasn't any army of intelligence officers, surveillance officers and technical geeks who were tracking their every move? Why couldn't she just get the money the insurance company had assured her was available and pay the bastards that had her mum and dad?

She undressed and got back into bed fighting to get back to sleep, dreading the fatigue she was going to feel in the morning and the more she tried the worse it got, eventually dropping back off to sleep at about 3a.m.

Rufus was up at 0600 as usual and silently peeped through Victoria's door to check she was asleep. He exercised in his room again: stretches and core exercises, followed by 1000 sit ups in reps of 200; 300 press ups in reps of 60, ten minutes of burpees to get his heart going through the roof, and was ready well before he had a text from Orla. He texted her his room number and she was with him in a couple of minutes.

He gave her a succinct briefing and they discussed a plan of action: they both agreed that they had somehow been compromised but neither could understand how or why. He had taken all his usual precautions and was sure that nobody had followed them. They were booked in under false names, which nobody knew, other than the four of them. The four of them... Victoria knew where they were and what names they had used. Could she really be the inside agent? Rufus doubted it, but he couldn't be certain. They decided to flush out the opposition by allowing them to surveil Victoria and him. They worked on the details and Orla left silently at 0755.

Rufus opened the door and checked the corridor before letting Orla out and saw British, the Bell Boy stood at the door with a big grin on his face, Rufus quickly invited him in to talk to the pair of them. He told them of some mzungus who had been hanging around the hotel and asking questions.

After a brief conversation Rufus thanked and paid British handsomely, telling him any further information would be equally well rewarded. After British left, Orla and Rufus discussed the information that he had imparted. It confirmed their fears. Orla silently disappeared, leaving Rufus to go and wake Victoria.

+++++++

Nick Cooper read the overnight briefing from the contractors, Surveillance And Security Ltd and from GCHQ, with interest. The S&S contractors had, with the help of information supplied by GCHQ via Cooper, traced the subjects to the Kilimanjaro Hotel, although it had taken several bribes staff at the hotel to actually identify their targets. He now knew their pseudonyms, room numbers, and had images from the hotel CCTV of both of them.

Naturally he knew Victoria's cell number as GCHQ had reverse traced the call from Deidre, but he still did not have Rufus's, although he was confident that would come easily now all of the pieces of the jigsaw were falling into place.

Next he read his text from Kumi. He could, if he wanted, conclude the kidnapping now as a result of what Kumi told him. He had all of the information required; he had the necessary personnel and he would be able to get the agreement of the Tanzanian authorities without too much hassle, but he was waiting for contact from Esther to update him on any reaction from al-Shabab.

He phoned Kumi giving him precise instructions, terminated the call, checked his clock and saw that it was still only 0600 in London and Sir Peregrine would not start work for another hour, so he sent a secure report to him, which would be on his desk when he arrived.

When Victoria was awoken by Rufus at 8.15 she was completely unaware of Orla's presence in Dar es Salaam, or that British had seem them. She got up, showered and breakfasted in the room with Rufus. Rufus had a voracious appetite and helped himself to the fruit platter, made up his own enormous cereal bowl with fresh fruit; rolled oats, nuts raisins, berries and seeds with about a gallon of natural yogurt. She was going to say something about the quantity he ate, but one look at his lean frame told her that he knew his own body and knew how much fuel to take on board. She was just amazed where he put it all.

He lifted the serving tray and checked the sausages and bacon, but never touched them, he just put them on one side; perhaps he WAS getting full. Over breakfast Rufus suggested they go to one of the local shopping malls, after the call, as long as everything went according to plan, just to get out of the hotel, the air conditioning and the stifling atmosphere to clear their heads. They decided to go to Mlimani Mall as it would be relatively easy to get to.

Rufus tidied up all of the crockery and cutlery and put them outside the door, placing the *Do not Disturb* sign on the handle, locking it and jamming it. He put the sausages and bacon he had ordered in a doggy bag, and put them aside in his room.

Victoria looked at him quizzically.

"Just in case I feel peckish later," he said sheepishly.

They worked quickly and rehearsed well, all of Victoria's self-consciousness now disappeared, and they were soon ready for the call. Rufus hoped he had predicted the content of the call correctly as it would help him assess Victoria better. They didn't have to wait long, until the phone rang.

"Good morning Miss Conway. I trust you slept well?"

"As well as can be expected."

Rufus was showing *ask him.*

"And you?"

"We were busy with our preparations and planning Miss Conway. We will accept five million US dollars. Do you have a pen and paper?"

"I've explained, I CANNOT get $5 million, it's impossible. The most I might be able to get is two, I can guarantee you one, and might be able to get close to $2 million, but I'm not sure."

"Wait."

They could hear murmuring and muttering in the background and eventually James came back on the line.

"We will accept $5 million, but not a penny less. Now, do you have a pen and paper ready?"

"Um, hold on," she said looking at Rufus, who was signalling ok to her, while getting her a pen and paper as he really wanted her to make a note of the instructions as well as him. "Yes, I've got them."

"The money is to be used US dollar bills, printed no earlier than 2006. The denominations must be a mixture of $20 and $50 bills, nothing lower or higher. You will put the bills in three black Nike bags which can be bought from the Sport Store at either the Quality Centre or Mlimani City. You will deliver the money to us, alone, at a time and place of our choosing. Should there be any deviation from these instructions we will kill one of your parents. Do you understand?"

At Rufus's insistence Victoria had remained quiet throughout the instructions and now he prompted her to repeat what James had said.

"Excellent," said James when she had finished, "I can tell we are going to work well together. I will call later."

"When?" asked Victoria, at the same time Rufus was mouthing the word to her, but the call had been cut.

"I can never raise $5 million Ru, what are you doing?"

"I know you can't, but it won't come to that, trust me."

"I hope you know what you are doing, this is my parents' lives we're dealing with."

"I know it is Vicky, they are on my mind every moment of every minute."

"And that's spooky that we are going to Mlimani isn't it?" said Victoria, her suspicions and curiosity heightened again.

"Not really Vic. There are only two shopping malls catering for the westerners and he mentioned both of them. I think it actually falls into place really well and we can go to the Sport Store and buy the bags ready. It will give us a whole new topic of conversation when he calls back: how we were lucky getting the last three, how big they are, how cheap or expensive they are, what good or bad quality they are and most importantly how $5 million will never, ever fit into three bags."

Victoria found herself between a rock and hard place again. She trusted Rufus, but things kept happening, which just seemed too coincidental, too convenient. She hated herself for doubting him.

Chapter Twenty-Six

They ordered a cab from the concierge for ten minutes time and after a few minutes to freshen up, they made their way to the lobby, tipped the concierge a couple of dollars and were off.

Rufus had already told Orla where they would be going, as he was pretty confident he would be able to persuade Victoria where to go, especially as she didn't know the city at all.

Orla got herself a bajaj, a three-wheeler menace of a vehicle, common in Asia and Africa, and positioned herself away from the hotel, on the Bagamoyo Road: a natural pinch point en route to the mall; ideal for her in her role as counter surveillance, or just 'counter' in her language.

After they passed her she told the young driver to wait while she noted the next ten vehicles that came along. Because the traffic was so heavy, she noted the last three figures of the license plates on each of them and then instructed the young driver to take her to Mlimani.

"Don't go too fast, I don't want to be weaving in and out of all the traffic and I want to keep well back from that taxi I showed you."

"Yes ma'am," said the sullen looking driver, who didn't want to waste time driving slowly.

"I will pay you double," said Orla, seeing the look on his face.

"Asante sana," said the boy, beaming.

They stayed well back, as the traffic only moved slowly, she could afford to allow more distance than usual and allowing ten to twelve cars in-between her and Rufus's vehicle at any time. Slowly but surely, some of the vehicles she'd noted, turned off, stopped or overtook Rufus's taxi, leaving her with four cars and a motorbike still behind them. She pinged two cars and the motor bike that raised her suspicions: the motorbike, a Kawasaki Ninja 300, could have overtaken easily, but held station. The two cars had two male occupants each and the three vehicles would alternate position, with one of them always two cars behind Rufus at any time, while the other would drop back for a few minutes, then make their way forward again.

They clearly hadn't been able to put any sort of tracker on the taxi, as they hadn't known which vehicle Rufus would be using beforehand and so they had to keep an eyeball on the taxi at all times, which had made it easier for Orla to spot them.

"You definitely have company Ru. One bike and two cars," she shouted into her phone above the din of the bajaj.

"Thanks," was all she got back, Rufus still not wanting Victoria to know that Orla was with them.

Rufus and Victoria arrived at the shopping mall, followed by the three tailing vehicles, then Orla. Rufus and Victoria were dropped off by the taxi driver and walked into the mall, without looking round or appearing to be aware of anything untoward at all.

Orla observed the three surveillance vehicles, follow the taxi into the car park: the two cars disgorged their passengers and immediately drove back out of the car park to plot up on the road, as a safety net on the 'straight on' line and in the 'reverse' so they had both directions covered.

Standard surveillance technique, thought Orla.

The passengers followed Rufus and Victoria into the mall.

The biker gave himself a discreet visual of both foot entrances into the mall, using distance as cover and providing him the necessary arc of vision.

Orla phoned Rufus and updated him, while she held station outside in the car park, the bajaj disappearing into the camouflage of the dozens of similar vehicles waiting to be hired.

Rufus and Victoria continued shopping. In order to give Orla more of a chance to find out who they were, Rufus had to let the watchers believe that he was unaware of their presence. They window shopped their way through the mall, Rufus used the window panes as mirrors; his apparent confused disorientation to turn around and walk in the opposite direction and conversation with Victoria, all to assist his observations.

He spotted both men after a few minutes. They were alternating their wide and narrow lines: the wide line giving the surveillant a good arc of vision, while the narrow line was much trickier. They went to the Sport Store and bought the three black bags as instructed.

They whiled away a good hour wandering in and out the shops in the mall. Rufus, silently bemoaning the fact the out of town shopping mall was being cloned all over the world, creating homogenous cities everywhere, he would not have known whether he was in Dar es Salaam, Dallas, Detroit or Durban, they all looked the same to him.

While having a coffee and pastry Rufus observed the two watchers follow them into the café, positioning themselves at separate tables so they could monitor things anonymously, or so they thought. They could arc the room, covering each other and their targets.

If there was any doubt whatsoever in Rufus's mind that it was these guys that were following them, this clinched it for him - he was able to get a good look at them: again non-descript men, one black one white, they were clones of Loafers from last night. He got a good look at their shoes; they might be able to change shirts, jackets, hats and glasses, but almost certainly wouldn't change their shoes. From what Orla had told him, he knew that there were at least five guys involved in the surveillance, and he didn't know if the five included Loafers as he hadn't looked around at all. He closed his eyes and tried to memorise the faces and give them names. He named the black guy 'Brogues' and the white guy 'Converse'. He texted Orla the names he had given them.

K was the only reply required from Orla.

Victoria was oblivious to all of this, she just enjoyed getting out of the hotel, seeing a little of Dar es Salaam and having a relaxing coffee with Rufus. She even let her mind wander from the predicament that her mum and dad were in for a few seconds of reverie, imagining what it would be like to be here under different circumstances.

Rufus was assessing all the scenarios and hypotheses. He was sure Victoria was not involved; she was too naïve, too trusting of him; so who were these guys?

Why were they following them? What was their objective? Where were they from? He was pleased that they had taken the decision for Orla to join him: not only did it give him a third eye, and therefore some protection, she gave him greater flexibility and potential. Two are way better as twice as good as one.

They returned to the car park and caught a taxi back to the Kilimanjaro. Orla observed Brogues and Converse exit shortly afterwards and make their way to the waiting cars, the biker pick Rufus and Victoria up as they exited the car park, to be joined by the cars as they made their way back to the Bagomoyo Road.

She told her bajaj driver to follow them again, and they slipped in at the back of the virtual convoy. Orla had photographed all five members of the surveillance team, photographed the cars, the license plates and the motor bike with her Canon EOS 500. She tried to send the pictures directly to Rufus but the signal wasn't good enough to take the data.

Everything else seemed to be going smoothly, until the bajaj came to a stuttering stop.

"Two minutes lady, Asheida Matata, no worries," the driver said as he hopped out, without a care in the world, and got his petrol can out of the little compartment at the back and calmly and unhurriedly began to top up his petrol tank. Orla was trying to hurry him up, but urgency is not a national characteristic and the young man, well more of a boy really, sedately continued with his routine.

Orla was furious, she was letting Rufus down. She considered leaving this driver and getting another one, but the policeman's law was in play and she couldn't find one now she wanted one. Even though the traffic was moving slowly it had progressed too far for her to regain her position she could only watch in frustration as the line of traffic continued south back into the city centre.

She phoned Rufus, and told him what had happened over the din of the traffic and blaring horns. "Don't worry, it's not your fault, so don't blame yourself. It's one of those things. Speak later."

He was actually quite confident that he would recognise Loafers, from last night as well as Brogues and Converse from today; he'd been able to get a good look at all three.

Victoria looked at him quizzically.

"Orla," Rufus explained. "She was going into London to do me a favour and has broken down," he lied easily, using his own maxim of sticking closely to the truth.

"Is she alright?"

"Yes, she's fine thanks," he said, deliberately not expanding.

Chapter Twenty-Seven

They arrived back at the Kilimanjaro and went to the elevator. Rufus knew they were still being followed. This time the two guys who had been driving carried out the foot follow, not wanting to expose any members of the team too often. They entered the elevator and Rufus deliberately pushed the wrong button, taking them up to the seventh floor. He stood with his back towards the display so that Victoria couldn't see he had made a mistake and correct it.

"Oh shit," said Rufus as they sailed past their floor, spinning around to look at the display, "I must have pressed the wrong button. Sorry Victoria, but we can walk back down the stairs to our floor, is that ok?" said Rufus, not realising his little charade had been a complete waste of time. Victoria nodded her head, oblivious to this sub plot going on around her.

They got to their rooms and Rufus checked his countermeasures: all still in place. He needed to talk to Orla and Don to get updates on the day's activity and called Don first as he knew Orla would be struggling back through the traffic. He went to his own side of the adjoining suite and called Don.

"Who are these fuckers on our pitch then Don?"

"Mate, I wish I could tell you. There's lots of traffic. In fact, there was so much traffic and data I've brought Ed to chart it all for us."

Rufus knew Ed as they had used him in the past. He was an ex-police analyst, and really good.

"Ed and I have been working our bollocks off trying to sort this mess out, but it's going to take us a bit longer to sus out who the fuck they are. But I don't like it. I don't like it one bit."

Don continued to update him, telling him what he already knew, that the bandits had been using Deidre's phone to make the calls to Victoria, and then told him what he didn't know: the same phone was being used to contact and receive calls within Dar, including one UK registered number, and also was being used to contact and receive calls from Somalia. The Dar group was growing exponentially, emanating from a phone which was pretty well constant, while the Somalia grouping was still quite small. The intelligence chart was growing by the hour and those three distinct groupings were the ones Don and Ed were concentrating on, but it was difficult to prioritise without more specific intelligence. The Dar grouping appearing to be the fulcrum, in communication with the other two, but these other two groups not communicating with each other. All communications seemed to be going through the bandits and predominantly Deidre's phone.

Their analysis showed calls being made to this phone, usually from the Dar group, and immediately afterwards a call would be made from the same phone to the Somalia group. Occasionally it would be the same in reverse.

Don could see connections spreading from the epicentre of Deidre's phone, like a spider's web. The question he couldn't answer was: who was the spider? Rufus knew that Don thought it was Deidre, and it was beginning to look that way, but from everything Victoria had said, he couldn't bring himself to believe it. *Still stranger things have happened. Like a bride being killed on her honeymoon in South Africa by a contract killer and the husband being suspected of setting it up. People do strange things, for myriad reasons.*

"Do me a favour, please Don. Do some research around the Brit phone that Deidre is in contact with? If you're right it could be her bit of fluff, if you're wrong it could be the spider you are talking about."

"Ok. mate. It might take us a bit of time though."

Next he asked Don for the address off Chole Road, where James had called from yesterday, but due to the confusing way property is addressed in Dar es Salaam, Don couldn't give him specifics, but told him it was showing close to Lukas Bar and it was just off the main drag.

Rufus smiled to himself hearing Don describe the Chole Road as a "main drag", thinking that Don would never depict the Chole Road in that way if he ever saw it. It was a minor road at best by Western standards, narrow and pot-holed. "I'll send you an animated map to your phone, showing the route to the premises. You'll be able to follow it exactly then."

"Thanks Bamm."

"The place in Kariakoo is a nightmare though. There are no road names or addresses, just a maze of alleys, markets and bazaars which I can never guide you through without being pinged by somebody straightaway. Orla might have a chance, though, she could wear a burka, which she's done loads of times before, and pass for a local."

"That could work. There's a large Muslim population in Dar and she would be able to blend in nicely."

Rufus thanked Don for the update and they arranged to talk later, he phoned Orla who had just got back. They still thought it was better for Victoria not to know of her presence and that Rufus would recce the Chole address tonight and she would do Kariakoo in the morning.

Rufus decided he would move the pinhole camera into Victoria's side, strategically placed in the room when he left, to enable Orla to watch Victoria from her own room. Although he was quite confident that Victoria was playing it straight, he wanted to be absolutely sure. With Orla babysitting Victoria he would feel comfortable leaving her.

While he was talking to Orla, about his plans Victoria's phone began ringing unexpectedly. He cut the call to Orla and hurried through to Victoria seeing the display of *Mum* on the screen.

He gave Victoria the phone, turned his own phone on to record and gave her the go ahead.

"Hello."

"Hello Miss Conway," said James. "How are you enjoying the Kilimanjaro?"

Rufus had got all sorts of prompts prepared, but he deliberately hadn't prepared this one to see Victoria's reaction.

Victoria looked at him like a rabbit caught in the headlights, frozen, her mouth open trying to formulate words but nothing came out.

Rufus calmly leaned forward and turned the phone off. That was the reaction he was hoping for: further evidence of Victoria's innocence in all of this. He didn't think she was that good an actress that she could have faked that reaction. *But if not Victoria, then who?*

Was Don right? How did these guys know we're at the Kilimanjaro in the first place? He thought, *I was really careful, I'm sure we weren't followed.*

Were the men following them really part of the kidnap team? Did they really have surveillance teams and informants everywhere? They were potentially fighting a battle on two fronts, so he had to gather information to assess the risks and dangers to Deidre and Martyn, as well as his team.

This thought process took a millisecond and as he looked up Victoria looked even more startled and horrified at this apparently reckless action.

"Say you dropped the phone in shock, say you WERE in the Kilimanjaro but you've moved as you thought you were being followed, be really frightened, ok? I want a lot of emotion from you."

"Fucking hell Ru, he'll never..."

The phone rang and Rufus gesticulated she should answer and mouthed "trust me".

"Hello, Um, I'm really sorry about that, I dropped the phone."

"Eh?"

"I dropped the phone, I thought I was going to shit myself, how did you know I'd stayed at the Kilimanjaro?"

"I told you Miss Conway, our organisation is vast and well connected."

"Well I've moved from here," she made the verbal slip and wondered whether James had picked it up. She was looking at Rufus who had, but it was gone and there was nothing he could do about it, so Akuna Matata. She spoke and used the lines he had prepared for her.

"Anyway, where I am is not important, what *is* important is my mum and dad and your money, and if you are going to frighten me like that it will take me longer to get your money as I will be too scared to go out."

"I am merely demonstrating the futility of you trying to resist our collective power."

"I'm trying to help you, not resist you. I want to give you your money, I want my mum and dad back, and I want to go home with them, safely."

"Where you are is of no consequence..."

Rufus was furiously typing out prompts to explain his presence should James ask who he was and decided a fellow junior doctor whom she had known from university was the best option; a relative could be challenged; a representative of the insurance company would alert the bandits to large sums available, so a mature friend would be close enough to Victoria and distant enough from Deidre and Martyn to hold up to any questioning. But the question never came. He couldn't understand it, surely if the surveillance team was in touch with James they would have said Victoria was escorted by a man. He kept the prompts ready and concentrated on Victoria again.

"I will phone you again in two days, as I have some other important business to tend to, so you had better have some good news for me to deliver to my colleagues, or you just might find yourself dealing with my associate who you spoke to first. I am sure you will concur, it was not a pleasant experience."

"I will do my best, but I can only do it if I feel safe to get out and arrange money transfers and deposits, and I am not worrying about my parents."

"Ah, speaking of whom, I have somebody you might want to talk to," a hand was put over the phone and a few muffled instructions were given, a few seconds later Victoria burst into tears as she heard the strained tones of her mother.

"Victoria? Victoria love? Are you there?"

Victoria could hardly talk through the tears of joy and worry.

"Hello Mum," she said. "Are you alright?"

"Yes we are ok darling. They are treating us ok, but please hurry up and get them their money so we can come home."

Rufus was pointing at *Dad?* on his screen, but before Victoria could ask about her dad James came back on the phone:

"Are you happy you are dealing with the right people now? You have two days Miss Conway."

"Yes, yes and can I speak to my dad, I can't give you your money until I know both Mum *and* Dad are alive and well."

Chapter Twenty-Eight

The phone line went dead and Rufus went through his usual post call routine.

"Well done Victoria," said Rufus. "You recovered from the shock really well. I thought you did superbly again. So we know they've got mum and we need to make sure dad is alright."

"Oh my fucking God, Ru. They know where I am, they DO have people everywhere. What am I going to do?"

"It's critical for us to remain calm and focused. The worst things you can do in a crisis are freeze or panic so let's think about things. The two most important aspects of that conversation are: we've found out your mum is alive. Closely followed by them knowing where you are. I don't know how. I know how they didn't do it: they didn't follow us in the UK. They didn't follow us from the airport; they didn't phone around the hotels and get your name from reception, which means, either we have a leak, or somebody with access to some pretty good technology has told them.

I've got a couple of plans to find out how. I'm going to phone an old friend who has a beach resort called Butiama on Mafia Island, just off the mainland. It has a small airstrip and you can only get there by prior arrangement, because they have to come and collect you from the airport. I'm going to send you out there for a day or two."

"Oh no Ru, I'm not leaving you, and I don't want to go to some island with small landing strips and jets, I want to get my parents back. I'm not here on a fucking holiday." At which she stood up and marched into the bathroom.

Rufus took the opportunity to place the coat hook camera in line with the rest of the hooks and texted Orla to check the picture.

Victoria came back into the bedroom with a defiant look on her face.

"First of all Victoria, we have got two days in which I can act without worrying about you. I promise you, you will be safe there with Maura and Moez, the owners of the resort. They're great people. Secondly, when I say a small landing strip, I mean just a gravel runway, with bumps and dust and, who mentioned jets? It just means you'll be safe and secluded, while I can build our intelligence picture."

"I'm not going."

"Maura and Moez will know in advance of any arrivals as they have to collect them from the strip to take them to the beach lodge. They've done a fantastic job there, and what's more I trust both of them implicitly; you'll be safe, and I need to get on without worrying about you."

"Rufus, I'm not going."

"The place is in the middle of paradise, you can't find it on mapping, you can't drive there, you'll be safe. And you are not going on holiday. I will need you fresh and focused when we bring you back, because things are going to get pretty hairy."

"I want to stay here with you, I feel safe and useful like I am really part of this team you keep talking about."

Victoria sat there, internalising her emotions. As much as the thought of just getting away for a couple of days was appealing, she had the contrary feeling on needing to be in Dar, needing to be on the phone and needing to be doing something proactive to get her parents back and being with Rufus. She wouldn't feel right going off enjoying herself in paradise in the Indian Ocean.

Rufus looked at her and assessed his options: he could carry on trying to convince her now; or he could let her think about what he'd said and return to it later, by which time she would probably have virtually convinced herself that it was the right thing to do.

He had to maximise the opportunity of the next forty-eight hours; fortunately Orla was here and they could share the workload. Between them they could work virtually non-stop if they had to, and get some control of the situation, because at the moment, if Don was right, they hadn't really got a handle on what was happening. Rufus's ace up his sleeve was Orla; as far as he knew, nobody knew she was there and she was acting as his eyes, ears and back up.

He excused himself from Victoria, claiming he had to go to the lobby and left the room. He went up to Orla and they checked the camera which was working fine. Orla showed Rufus her laptop with the photographs she had taken of the surveillance team. He studied the images to commit the faces to memory, but he already had one of the faces locked in his head: Loafers, he was driving one of the cars.

She labelled Loafers, Brogues and Converse and looked at the other two men in the team.

"Nike by the look of them," said Orla.

"I'll give you that one. Nike it is then. And the last guy? "

As Orla renamed Nike's photograph she said, "What's he got on his feet? Are they Cowboy boots? What sort of surveillance operative wear Cowboy boots?"

"What's it to be then? Cowboy or boots?"

"It's got to be 'Cowboy'. Right: Loafers, Cowboy, Brogues, Converse and Nike. That's five we know of, I wonder how many more there are and who they are working for?" said Orla.

"I've asked Don to do some digging on that for us. If, and it's a big if, they are working for the bandits, we are in trouble, and more to the point Deidre and Martyn are in the crapper."

They had an informal mini briefing, something they found essential in all aspects of their work, so that they were both singing off the same page. They discussed where they were up to, what they had learned, their thoughts, strategy and tactics for the next two days and came up with a plan of action. They both knew that the best strategy rarely survived first contact with the enemy, but it is good to have a plan that could be adapted to the changing circumstances.

Next they detailed what they didn't know; a list that was getting longer by the day, instead of shorter.

Rufus returned to Victoria and told her that he had to go out; she should order room service for dinner and not leave the room. He asked her for her phone, telling her that he didn't want her worrying if it went off.

"Where are you going?" she asked, slightly hurt that he was leaving her.

"I've arranged to meet an old friend at The Coliseum Hotel. He's a senior officer in the police here and may be useful to us," he lied easily to her.

"Why can't I come?" she asked. "It would look more natural if we were together, we would look like a married couple."

Rufus looked incredulously at her. "First, we would not look like a married couple, we would look like a pervy old bloke and his mistress. Second, I want to be incognito, you turn heads wherever you go and draw attention to us, all of the men stare at you..."

"That's not tr–"

"Third, the guy I'm meeting is very private and if I am asking him to do us some favours, it must be on a one to one basis, without anybody else there."

"Mmmm, but I don't want to stay here on my own, I want to come with you," she said almost pouting at him. "I feel safe when I'm with you. I can just sit in a corner and you won't even know I'm there. I promise."

Orla was watching the unfolding scene in the room below, giggling to herself. She could tell Victoria was pleading with Rufus, and liked him a lot, but he was such a klutz he was oblivious to the effect he had on women, he just thought they either liked him as a friend, or respected him for the job he did for them. It was an endearing quality. For one so worldly wise, so experienced in every other way, he was unsure of how to handle women. *Perhaps it's just as well. He'd be off shagging everything if only he knew.*

"I can't take you Vicky. He's specifically asked me to go alone. He trusts me, and I respect him and we may well need his influence. I don't want to diminish my friendship with him by going against his wishes."

"Ok, but I still think I could have sat in the corner. You could take me if you wanted to."

"I really don't think it would be a good idea. Have you thought any more about going to Butiama?" Rufus asked. "I've spoken to Moez and they would be more than happy to have you as a guest for a couple of days."

"Um, I guess you are right about that too, it's just that I feel my place is here with you on the phone negotiating their release."

"And you will be Victoria. James said he would call back in two days. That means you will be sitting around with nothing constructive to do and at the moment we don't know enough about the opposition and I have got to change that. I can't do the things I need to do while you are locked up in here, it's not fair on you and I don't want to take unnecessary risks."

"Ok, I guess you know best. But be careful, I don't want to have to negotiate for you as well," she said smiling at him.

"Good decision," he said placing a reassuring hand on her shoulder.

Rufus returned to his room and prepared for his journey to Chole Road. After putting a couple of items Don had given him and some he had bought in Kariakoo in a small backpack, he ran back upstairs to Orla, gave her the phone to baby sit and told her how to book the flight online with Coastal Airlines, from Dar to Mafia.

Orla considered the pros and cons of telling Rufus how much Victoria thought of him and decided against saying anything, it would only complicate things if he started modifying his behaviour around her.

He put the counter-measures on his room and caught a taxi to the Hilton Double-Tree, on the Peninsular. To ensure he wasn't being followed they took a circuitous route to travel the four miles, eventually getting to the hotel after a thirty-minute drive. He paid the fare and walked into the sports bar just off the lobby, ordered a soft drink and sat down, pretending to watch the football on one of the massive screens in the bar, waiting to see if anybody came in after him.

He was just about to get up when Converse and Cowboy walked in. They surveyed the room and settled on two bar stools.

Rufus texted Orla *Picked up a tail.* As he wondered how they had found him, *I'm sure I haven't been followed from the Kilimanjaro, so how have they found me? The only two people who knew where I was going were Don and Orla and it's not them. I know I haven't been followed, I'm absolutely certain.. They could have set up the taxi so that they knew which one I was using, or they could be better surveillance operatives than I thought.*

He had to make a decision: let them know he knew they were following him, or lose them without them knowing. He chose the latter.

He walked into the rear garden overlooking the bay, which was full of holiday makers and business meetings. Children were splashing and playing in the swimming pool, screaming and shouting, the way only children can, without any inhibitions and cares.

He walked to the hotel's private pier and once he was behind a hedge and out of sight he vaulted the balustrade landing on the beach about ten feet below. He jogged under the pier along the shoreline and walked up the jetty to the Slipway next door to the hotel. He guessed that would buy him some time, but would it be enough? And who were they?

The Slipway is a colourful, vibrant local attraction catering for the ex-pats and locals alike, offering some "authentic" local artefacts, a supermarket, and restaurants where he could disappear in the crowd. Set on the north westerly edge of the peninsular it is a favourite for sundowners as it catches the setting sun across the bay beautifully, allowing diners to sit by the water's edge while sipping their favourite cocktail or ice cold beer.

He phoned Orla to check everything was ok as he sat at the Waterfront Restaurant and watched the sun go down with the rest of the customers and tourists who were furiously snapping the setting sun as it set the bay alight with reds and amber hues making the still waters glow as if there was a huge cauldron on the sea bed. You could virtually set your clock by the sun rise and sun set in Tanzania, and in fact the Tanzanians do, and treat 6am as the start of the day and 7am as one o'clock, which can be confusing when they call a meeting at 3am- really meaning 9am.

Chapter Twenty-Nine

As the sun disappeared, a total darkness fell on the city, from bright daylight to darkness in the matter of a few minutes. Rufus left and walked back towards Chole Road and phoned Don. He put his earpiece in so he could hear Don, who was following him, and James, electronically and monitored his progress towards the target premises. Unfortunately, the signal was poor and Don kept losing his signal and his location and more importantly the same went for James' signal in the city centre, just not quite as flaky.

Don was very uneasy about the situation. He couldn't give his friend the support he wanted to give him; he felt isolated and powerless and wished he was there with Rufus. He falteringly guided him left onto Chole Road, passed the Treasures of Africa antique shop, and as he passed Lukas Bar and Restaurant, Don told him to slow down so that the signal could catch up. He reassured him that as far as he could tell James' phone was still in the city centre and he was good to go.

It had only taken him ten minutes to walk, but it was already pitch black. He used the cover of the darkness to check he wasn't being followed. Don lost his GPS fix completely and could only talk him through from where his last fix was; directed him next right, which on Don's screen was shown as Transit Supermarket Road;

in different circumstances they might have given the road names some thought, but neither had the time or inclination to think about where the Tanzanians got them from. Rufus assured Don there was no road name, and in fact no road, just a dirt track. They had to go with their gut instinct as Don was now blind and could only go off mapping, not knowing exactly where Rufus was in relation to the map. He instructed him to walk along the track for approximately 150 yards. Don could see a U.N. building marked on his screen and told Rufus that if he reached that point he had gone too far.

Rufus knew he took 120 paces to 100 yards, something that was vitally important in Special Forces and counted 180 steps up the track. He could see a large walled compound on his left. There was electric fencing topping the wall, but Rufus noted the ivy and vegetation growing on the wires and the trees' branches brushing against it as he walked past.

Through the gate he could see the elderly guard, dressed in dirty, unkempt uniform, reclined in his chair, feet up on a stool inside his small guard shelter, lit by a make-shift tubular light resting in the branches of a small tree. Rufus guessed he was a live-in guard, who was retained more for his honesty and loyalty, rather than his expertise and skills. He didn't want to feel too optimistic but he felt this would be a relatively easy.

He was pretty sure the electric fence didn't work and he was equally as sure the guard would be asleep in the next hour. *Who can blame him?*, thought Rufus *he's probably worked sixteen hours already and only earned a couple of dollars.*

Rufus disappeared like a phantom into the shadows cast by the trees in the moonlight. *Thank fuck there are no street lights around here.* He picked his observation post with practised expertise from his CROP training. The greatest compliment for a CROP operative is to have a dog piss on you, but Rufus wasn't hoping for that tonight, he wanted to be in and out quickly as he had to take care of other business.

He took up his cover and waited. He watched for the guard's routine and waited to see if Converse and Cowboy appeared. He used the time to enhance his night vision. His training told him it would take between five to ten minutes to attain primary night vision as the rhodopsin in the rods of his eyes changed shape and had full effect after thirty minutes. Rufus was practised at enhancing his night vision. He avoided looking at car headlights and other light sources, used his peripheral vision, which employed the rod cells in the eyes, as they have better lowlight detection, enabling him to see better in the dark; just enough to give him an advantage. To not look where you are going seems crazy, but with the amount of practise Rufus had he was able to utilise this medical fact to his benefit.

By eight o'clock he could hear the guard snoring and there was still no sign of his two tails. The guard wasn't the type of enemy the British Army had spent thousands of pounds training him to fight, but he didn't choose his enemies and for tonight, this guard was the enemy, not that he intended him any harm.

He walked silently along the side wall to the second tree and pulled himself effortlessly up onto the first branch. While he conducted a quick visual examination of the house he tossed a few scraps out of the doggy bag from this morning onto the lawn and waited a few minutes. When he was satisfied there were no dogs about, he tested the electric fence with his electric screwdriver he had bought in Kariakoo: not a flicker. He knew the tester worked as he had tested it at the hotel, so he put his hand on the fencing quite confidently.

The guard was asleep now and he didn't want to wake him so that he could alert either the police or James. Rufus wasn't concerned about the police, but he was worried about James becoming suspicious. He checked the lane again for any signs of Converse and Cowboy and dropped down silently over the wall. He'd already seen that all of the windows were shut and the ground floor doors all had grills on.

He took out the small grappling hook, and glided to the rear of the house where he found what he was looking for in a small balcony overlooking the rear lawn. He tossed up the hook, attached to para cord and it caught first time. He climbed the wall easily. As he climbed he heard Don tell him that he had completely lost James's signal and that he should be ready to move with short notice. The security on the door was pretty good: it would have taken him about thirty seconds to get through that, but what was the point when the window to the side was slightly open, just protected by the mosquito screen. Rufus removed the screen and opened the window; he memorised the order in which the few ornaments on the window sill were arranged, and moved them to the side. He was through the window and inside in no time, the snores of the guard only drowned out by the bullfrogs' deafening croaks.

As he made his way carefully through the house, Don updated him that he had a signal again and James was on the move, but still some way away.

He moved silently and quickly, thinking to himself that he would have made a good burglar given different circumstances. He could hear Don talking to him, but the signal was too weak and he couldn't understand what was being said.

Once in the lounge he looked for the best place to position a bug, knowing that although time was now a crucial factor he had to find a place which would give a good signal and remain undiscovered for as long as he needed it.

He found some letters lying on a desk and photographed the address to do some research later and continued his work silently.

Don came back in his ear, clear this time telling him that James was getting closer. "Mate I can't give you up-to-the-minute updates as the signal is too flaky, there could be a ten-minute time lag. Just be careful eh."

Rufus's mind churned through various options: Had Converse and Cowboy phoned James to tell him that Rufus was prowling around, were they working for him? Had he blown everything? Would he leave to find a reception committee waiting for him? Where were Converse and Cowboy now?

Rufus didn't want James to discover him; he wanted him on the loose so that he could lead him to the stronghold. He couldn't take the risk that the bandits had an alert system in place and would kill Deidre and Martyn if they discovered he was looking for them. This was his first rule: the primacy of the hostages' lives and not to put their lives in danger unnecessarily. Not until he was sure of where they were and he had a good chance of effecting their release or rescue.

The obvious place for the bug would have been the telephone, but like the rest of the world, Tanzanians very rarely use the landline, and prefer to work off their cell phones, ignoring the virtually obsolete phone on the coffee table. He placed on bug in a table lamp and gave Don a sound check.

"Strength R 4," Don told him, "and he's getting pretty close mate, you need to hurry."

"Roger that," said Rufus, calmly looking for the next place to hide a bug.

"He's just turning onto Haile Selassie Road, I think you've got less than three minutes, if my signal is accurate." Don imparted the information in a calm manner. Rufus knew what he was doing, and Don didn't want to fluster him.

"Roger."

Rufus went to what was obviously the master bedroom. He found the perfect place for the second bug, and saw the headlights pull up to the gate.

"Chole Road," said Don.

"Roger that, but he is back already," as he calmly placed the audio bug and concealed it.

"Passing Slipway Rd," Don clearly hadn't heard Rufus's response as the signal was dipping in and out and making their conversation next to useless.

"Roger thanks, I'm done; just a quick signal strength test."

"R zero," said Don, hearing Rufus on the phone, but not through the bug.

Rufus didn't need to question whether Don was sure, just as Don didn't question Rufus had activated the bug.

"Transit Supermarket Road," said Don, the flaky comms playing havoc with their conversation as Don monitored three different systems: the GPS signal, the bug transmission and the telephone conversations. Rufus saw the angle of the headlights change as the car pulled into the driveway.

"Roger," said Rufus as he removed the bug and replaced it with another. He heard the car door slam shut.

"Signal strength test."

"R5, and he's on top of you, you need to get out of there," said Don.

"Roger. I'm done and fox-trotting."

Rufus heard the door open and footsteps in the hall. He climbed out of the window as he heard footsteps coming up the stairs. He looked back into the room to double-check he had remembered everything and saw the failed bug which he had tried first on the coffee table.

The footsteps were continuing up the stairs as Rufus boosted himself back through the window.

The voice of the man on the stairs called back down to the guard in Swahili, telling him that he expected guests in a few minutes, it sounded so close that he could have been in the room.

Rufus scooped up the tiny device and sped back to the window, climbed though it in one easy movement as the door to the bedroom opened. James went straight to the en suite bathroom and urgently relieved himself.

That assuaged Rufus's mind a little, if James had come back as a result of a call from Converse and Cowboy he would have come in looking for Rufus, not telling the guard he was expecting guests and going for a piss.

Rufus took the opportunity of the cascade of liquid hitting the porcelain to lean back in to the bedroom to rearrange the ornaments on the window sill, gently close the window and replace mosquito screen as he saw lights coming on in the bedroom, flooding light through the windows into the void.

Rufus stayed in the shadows, knowing that James would not be able to see out from the light into the dark and he was confident that the guard would not be making a patrol yet, not with guests expected in a few minutes. He would wait at the gate house to let them in as soon as they arrived.

He pressed his back against the wall of the house to make his profile smaller and waited for any reaction and for his breathing to normalise.

He removed his grappling hook, hung off the balcony and dropped down onto the lawn below and stealthily made his way around the side of the house.

He couldn't afford to move any further as the guard was now awake, having been disturbed from his slumber to open the gates. He could see car headlights coming up Transit Supermarket Road, bouncing all over the trees as the driver negotiated his way up the pot-holed dirt track. A small beep of the horn and the guard was up and opening the gate.

The headlights of the arriving cars illuminated the opposite side of the garden and Rufus used the distraction to move through the darkness and slip out of the gates, disappearing without a trace, as the guard was showing the visitors where to park and his night vision would be useless.

"Hi mate," he said down the still open line to Don.

"Hi Ru. I've got nothing on you, but strength R4 in the house. They are talking in Swahili though, which isn't one of my strong points. I'll have to create a WAV file and send it down to you to review when you get back to the hotel."

"Ok. Thanks. That was a bit closer than I would have liked, plus I've got Converse and Cowboy following me."

"What? How? Where are they? How do you know?" the questions tumbled out.

Chapter Thirty

"Two of the team followed me to the Double Tree, where I think I lost them. How? I don't know. It's really bugging me. And how do I know, they walked into the Double Tree a few minutes after I got there and I don't believe in coincidences," Rufus said.

"They might be staying there, or meeting someone there."

"Yeh they might be, and I might be the president of the USA, but I ain't."

"I'm just saying never assume, as you keep telling me," Don concluded.

Rufus got back to the hotel and checked on Orla and Victoria. He could see on the monitor that Victoria was fast asleep and he had no intention of disturbing her. So he and Orla briefed each other.

"Nothing at all," said Orla. "She has done nothing to arouse any suspicions. She's showered and pampered herself a little; it's a good job you weren't here to watch that."

"What do you mean?"

"She's a very pretty young woman and while she was grooming herself, I was able to turn off, and not watch, but I don't think you would have been able to. That's all. It would be quite natural for a bloke. You bunch of lecherous old pervs. Anyway, she laid on the bed and watched the TV until she dropped off. No phone calls, no visitors, nothing."

Rufus rolled his eyes choosing not to give Orla the satisfaction of protesting.

"Good. I was sure she's been straight with us and I think you've just confirmed it."

"I think so. And what's your update?" asked Orla.

Rufus filled her in on the evening,

"Ok," said Orla. "There are a few possibilities here. We can rule Victoria out as I said. They could have a spotter in the foyer, waiting for you to leave, somebody we haven't clocked yet; they could have bribed a member of staff; they could have got a patch into the hotel CCTV. I'm pretty sure it's internet based, so they could do that from their phones or laptops. They could have planted that taxi, so you had to use it, although that would be difficult with all of the comings and goings. Did you call the taxi or did the concierge?"

"The concierge."

"Oh, well, that's quite simple then, they could have paid the concierge, he just waits, then orders the right taxi. It wouldn't cost much to pay for the taxi for the night and bribe the concierge; they might be a bloody good surveillance team and followed you without you clocking them. Although from what I saw, they aren't that good. However they did it, we need to change hotels."

"Roger that," said Rufus, "but I'm going to the bar to see if I can flush any of these bastards out, I want to know who they are working for. It isn't, um... he pulled the camera out of his cargo pocket, "Wisdom

Mwakimbwla aka James, that's for sure. So if it isn't him, who the fuck is it?"

"Ok. be careful."

+++++++

"They lost him?" asked a frustrated Nick Cooper talking on his mobile from his home.

"Yeh, they picked him up leaving the hotel, after one of the receptionists we are paying gave them the heads up. The GPS on his phone is just so unstable, they kept losing him. Eventually they got a fix at the Double Tree, by Slipway," explained the team leader from S&S contractors.

"I know where the Double Tree is."

"Anyway, they picked him up again there and lost him again. His signal just kept coming and going."

"Do they think he clocked them and lost them deliberately?"

"They said not. They are convinced he hasn't pinged them at all."

"I want a full briefing on my desk by 0800." He was pacing the floor, considering his next move. He had banked on the team's surveillance expertise to keep tabs on Stone and Conway, what was he paying them for if they couldn't even do that? He would have to speak to Sir Peregrine about a change of tactics.

+++++++

Rufus walked into the bar on the eighth floor that had a beautiful view of the harbour, and there, sat in the corner was Nike.

So at least three of them working then, he thought to himself as he ordered a beer, with no intention of drinking it. He wanted to give the impression he was continuing to drink as he took a handful of cashew nuts off the bar and clumsily dropped most of them trying to shovel them into his mouth. He sat as far away from Nike as he could, who he could see was using his cell phone. Rufus assumed he was giving somebody a sit rep and/or asking for back up. Sure enough Brogues walked into the bar a few minutes later.

At least four. He surveyed the bar to see if he could make anybody else. Brogues looked towards Rufus, also pretending to have a casual look around the bar, but his eyes rested on Rufus a fraction of a second too long. *They're not THAT good then. Orla would have forty fits if she saw such amateurish surveillance. Just the two of them in here, let's see what happens.*

He got up and swayed slightly, and made his way to the restrooms. He got out of sight and quickly got into the gents', found an empty cubicle and sat on the toilet lid. A few seconds later he heard the washroom door open and heard a set of footsteps enter. He could hear the familiar sound of a man relieving himself at the urinal, and the footsteps come back towards the cubicles, and the doors being gently pushed open. The footsteps stopped and Rufus knew the guy was looking beneath the door to see his feet. After a few more seconds he stood, and readied himself.

He slid the bolt back noiselessly and jerked the door open, giving him a split second advantage over Brogues who was stood in front of the door, baton in his right hand, waiting to strike.

He threw his arm back to get maximum impact. Rufus lunged in to the space provided by the amateurish move. The baton came down. Rufus blocked with his left forearm. Simultaneously head butting Brogues on the bridge of his nose. The forward momentum and the power in his neck delivered a crushing blow to the fragile nasal bone. Head butting was far more preferable to punching, a skull is much more robust than the twenty-seven bones in a hand, and Rufus had given up punching people in the face a long time ago. Anyway, Brogues wasn't playing by the rules either, his baton would have caused Rufus some serious injuries. Brogues let out a scream of pain. He belatedly brought his hands to protect his shattered nose. Rufus, stepped back slightly and kicked through and down on his right knee. They both heard the sickening sound of the joint breaking.

Brogues emitted an even louder shriek of pain as he collapsed on the floor.

Rufus felt arms wrap around his body and trap his upper arms in a bear hug. Another stupid mistake: his sub-conscious took over, he didn't need to think; thinking could be fatal.

He threw his hips to the left, flicked his right hand backwards in one fluid movement, caught the attacker in the balls, making his head come forward in a reflex motion. A perfect target for Rufus's head moving backward providing a combined energy impact as he back head butted his attacker on the nose and knocked him out.

Rufus looked down at Brogues and Nike on the floor of the washroom. The whole thing was over in seconds, just the way he liked it. He moved to the entrance door and put out the *Cleaning in Progress* sign, which would deter most people for a few minutes at least, he returned to the two immobile bodies on the floor and searched

Nike: he found cash and a phone, nothing to identify him at all. He took the phone and slipped it into his left trouser pocket.

He grabbed Brogues by the scruff of the neck and shook him back to consciousness.

"Who are you fucking wankers?" Rufus asked.

"Fuck off Stone," said Brogues. "If I were you, I'd get out of this country and leave the Conways behind. You don't know what you are getting yourself into."

Rufus detected a Geordie accent.

"I said who..."

Rufus was interrupted by a knock on the washroom door, and shouted, "Closed for cleaning sir."

He stood on Brogues's broken patella causing him to scream in agony.

"Who are you?"

"What's going on in there? I really need the rest room," shouted the voice from the other side.

Rufus heard the door open and the man looked in, gasped at the scene in front of him and closed the door quickly. Rufus, expertly frisked Brogues, removed his phone and stamped on it, calmly got up and walked out of the washroom, careful not to attract any more attention.

He could see the guy who had looked in the restroom, in animated conversation with the bar staff. He turned away from the bar to the elevators and phoned Orla.

Chapter Thirty-One

"The shit's hit the fan, we're bugging out. Meet us in the lobby asap, overt."

Orla didn't need any explanations, she guessed what had happened, but that was immaterial, she would get the "why" later.

He returned to his own room and woke Victoria telling her to get herself ready as they were leaving straight away.

"Why are we leaving at this…"

"I'll explain everything later; just get your shit together as quickly as possible."

Rufus's tone left no room for discussion. He went into his adjoining room and was ready in seconds. It took Victoria a few more minutes to get her clothes and toiletries together, but he was still impressed with the speed she was ready to leave and they made their way to reception.

Orla was already there, had asked the concierge for a taxi and was keeping watch discreetly for anything suspicious. She saw an ambulance come to the front door and the crew quickly walk in and get the lift. She kept watch as Rufus settled the bill in cash, and the three of them left to get in the waiting taxi.

As Orla joined them Victoria gave a double take.

"What? How long have you been here? Why didn't you tell me?"

"I'll explain everything as soon as we get ourselves out of here," said Rufus. He guessed they would be too identifiable in all of the usual mzungu hotels: the Hilton, the Holiday Inn, The Serena, probably even New Africa, so he decided to get out of the city.

"The Kigamboni Ferry, please," said Rufus to the driver.

As they travelled, Orla sat in the back with Victoria and kept watch out of the rear window, looking for a tail. Rufus turned in the front seat and spoke to Victoria.

"Orla only arrived this morning. I didn't tell you, because I didn't want you worrying more than you already are. We have thought that somebody has been watching us for a couple of days now, but I needed – and still need – you to concentrate on your job, which is on the phone, and leave the other stuff to us."

"Watching us? Who? Is that how James knew I was in the Kilimanjaro? Why didn't you tell me?"

"There are lots of questions we've all got Victoria. Let's get settled at another place and we'll explain everything we think we know."

It was only a short ride to the Kigamboni Ferry, which took them to the other side of the harbour to the south side of Dar and the district of Kigamboni. It was relatively quiet with only a few dozen foot passengers, instead of the thousands during the day. After a couple of minutes, they headed along the coast road a little way to the South Beach Hotel.

Rufus paid the taxi driver and waited for him to leave. They got into another taxi and drove a few minutes farther south to the Kijiji beach resort. He asked the driver to wait, while he checked availability and entered the thatch covered lobby.

"Good evening Aziz," said Rufus, noting the man's name tag.

"Good evening sir," said the tired looking night receptionist.

"Do you have three rooms, just for tonight please?"

Aziz checked the computer.

"I only have one double sir. An executive double."

"We'll take it. I'll just go and get my friends, and pay the taxi."

He returned to the taxi, paid the driver and the three of them entered the rustic hotel. He handed over his passport and credit card. "I know this isn't ideal but we've got to share the room. You two can share the bed, if that's ok, and I'll take the floor," he said, turning to the two women.

The two ladies shrugged their shoulders accepting the situation and handed over their passports to the receptionist.

Aziz showed them to their rooms and Rufus tipped him handsomely.

"Are you on duty all night Aziz?" he asked.

"Yes sir."

"I wonder if you can do me a favour?" Rufus handed the porter another ten thousand shillings. "These ladies' husbands might come looking for us, if you understand me?"

"Yes sir, I understand," said Aziz with a knowing look.

"If any men come looking around asking about us can you wake me? It doesn't matter what time, just phone the room and I'll wake up."

"Yes sir." Aziz made his way back to the reception while the three of them sorted themselves out in their room.

"I think I'm owed an explanation," said Victoria, looking at her two roomates.

Rufus explained what had happened during the day and evening, being very economical with the truth, leaving out his evening excursion, as Victoria didn't need to know that, or about his little fracas back at the hotel; just the five-man surveillance team following them. Orla took everything in, the soldier in her appreciating the Accuracy, Brevity and Clarity of Rufus's resume. Victoria sat agog and scared. Scared for herself, and scared for her parents.

"Who are these people?" she eventually asked.

"I'm not sure Victoria. Orla and I have a few theories. But what we are both fairly sure of is that they are not directly linked to the kidnappers. From what Don has told us, there may be a connection, but not a direct connection. I can't be any more specific than that. What we have got to prepare for, is if they tell the bandits what has happened, and that precipitates a call.

"How can you be sure? How do you know you haven't just got my parents killed?"

"I can't be a hundred per cent certain Victoria, but from everything we've pieced together we are pretty sure that these guys are not directly connected to the kidnappers."

"Well who are they then? Who else would want to follow us and find out where we are except the kidnappers?"

"There could be a few reasons Victoria. It might be another gang, who have heard about the kidnapping and they are trying to find the stronghold as well; it could be Tanzanian law enforcement, military or spies, trying to investigate; it could be something to do with our own government."

"Or it could be the kidnappers," said Victoria, unconvinced with his argument.

"Well we will know if it is the kidnappers soon enough, because they will be on the phone, trying to find out who I am. If they do, this is what I suggest..."

They agreed in rough terms what Victoria would say: they would stick with the story that Rufus was a university friend and was on the uni karate team. When the two goons attacked him, he defended himself and they fled. They role-played the scene until Victoria was comfortable. They waited another hour, but the expected call never materialised.

Victoria started to doze off again, so Orla and Rufus decided to turn in for the night, taking it in turns to take stag, just in case. Rufus opted to take the first stag and took the opportunity to examine the phone he had taken. He tried to unlock it but couldn't. He tried *1234*, *0000* and *password* but after that he was pretty much stuck. He saw no point in keeping it any longer so he removed the battery and SIM then threw the handset out of the window, more in frustration than anything else, annoyed that he couldn't get past a simple 4-digit security code.

Victoria's phone rang at 0236. Rufus was still on stag so was awake anyway. He could see it was Deidre's phone calling, and walked to Victoria's side of the bed, to rouse her, but the call was disconnected before she could answer.

"Don't worry, he'll call back," said Rufus taking his own phone out of his right pocket, preparing to record.

"How can you be so..." started Victoria.

Both the women looked at him as the phone started to ring again. Rufus pressed record on his phone, and said, "Deep breath", to Victoria and pressed answer, then loud speaker on her phone.

"WHAT THE FUCK IS GOING ON?" screamed the voice down the phone.

Rufus immediately recognised the change of voice, back to Samuel. He knew Victoria was going to have to ride this tirade out.

"What do y...?" started Victoria, thinking she had been asked a question. Rufus put his finger to his lips again, and Victoria nodded her assent and understanding.

"DON'T FUCKING INTERUPT ME YOU FUCKING LYING BITCH WHORE. WHAT ARE YOU DOING?"

Rufus waited for a couple of seconds to make sure Samuel had finished, but he knew as soon as Victoria opened her mouth, he would rage again, but then if she didn't say anything he would also rage, so he tapped *What do you mean?*.

"What do you mean?" said Victoria.

"WHAT DO I FUCKING MEAN? YOU LEAVE THE COUNTRY AND ASK WHAT I MEAN?" he screamed.

They all looked at each, bewildered, Rufus's brain trying to assimilate the information. A number of scenarios raced through his head: one: they are testing Victoria; two: a corrupt customs official has given them the wrong information, a "false positive" in effect, or three: the surveillance team had given them incorrect information, for whatever reason.

"I don't know what you mean," Victoria said acknowledging Rufus's prompt.

"ARE YOU FUCKING STUPID? YOU FUCKING STUPID MZUNGU. I'M GOING TO GO AND FUCKING DO THEM. DO YOU UNDERSTAND ME? WHICH ONE SHALL I DO FIRST?"

Rufus was speedily preparing prompts for Victoria, and she acknowledged each one.

"Please, please," implored Victoria "I can't understand you when you shout so loud, and I don't know what you are talking about. Please don't hurt them, I am still in Tanzania, I promise you. Why would I leave when I want my mum and dad back? It doesn't make any sense."

"Where are you then?" said Samuel, a little calmer. In Rufus's experience most people could not keep a full blown rant up for too long, as long as you didn't fuel it.

"I'm still in Tanzania," she said.

"Where exactly?"

Get angry was the prompt.

"We've been through this already; I am NOT going to tell you where I am. And because I know you are looking for me, I am moving around anyway, with friends and contacts that I know who are here, which is just delaying everything. ALL I WANT TO DO IS GIVE YOU YOUR MONEY AND GET MY MUM AND DAD BACK AND GET OUT OF THIS DAMN COUNTRY." Victoria replied, getting louder and more forceful. "HOW DARE YOU ACCUSE ME OF ABANDONING MY PARENTS."

"Ha, ha, ha, Miss Conway," said James, taking over from Samuel. "Please forgive my colleague's unseemly behaviour. I understand your frustration and of course we know you are still in the country, I think he was trying to test you. I myself see no justifiable objective reason to test you and please accept my apologies for my colleague's false accusations."

By the tone of his voice Rufus imagined James giving Samuel daggers on the other end of the phone because he had revealed a hole in their intelligence.

"Well I just don't need all of that," Victoria said in a raised voice.

"Calm down Miss Conway."

"CALM DOWN?" screamed Victoria, "FUCKING CALM DOWN? YOU ACCUSE ME OF ABANDONING MY PARENTS AND LEAVING THE COUNTRY, THREATEN TO 'DO' THEM AND YOU ARE TELLING ME TO CALM DOWN?"

Rufus had given Victoria her head again, letting her full range of emotions loose on James, getting him on the back foot for a few moments.

"Please Miss Conway," said James.

Rufus smiled as he knew Victoria had got the upper hand for a moment and so he decided to press home their advantage and tapped out a prompt.

"Now listen to me," said Victoria. "I want to hear my Dad. I want to know he is ok and I want to hear him at 5pm tomorrow. By that time I will have your money arranged and IF I know that both my mum and dad are alive, I will give you your money. Do you understand?"

"Miss ..."

"DO YOU UNDERSTAND?" Victoria balled.

"Yes. 5pm tomorrow."

Rufus cut the phone off and after double-checking it said, "Well done Victoria. That was superb. You got them exactly where we want them and that's on the back foot. I would think they are having a right bust up now after that, they've lost all the initiative. We can control things now, as long as we are subtle about it. I guess when they call back they are going to want to put you under pressure. So we could well hear threats to Mum or Dad.

"What? Why?"

"Because they have to try and re-gain control over you and that is their most potent weapon. They made a mistake. They revealed a chink in their intelligence to you, which has let you off the hook psychologically. Before they could say they knew where you were or what you were doing, and now they can't. So they will play tricks with your mind over the phone. You can't see what they are doing and they use that to torment you. But we have the same advantage; they can't see what we are doing either. We have a little over thirty-six hours to prepare. We've got lots to do in between now and then, so you try and get some sleep and we'll wake you in good time."

Chapter Thirty-Two

They woke Victoria just gone six and after a light breakfast took two taxis to the old Dar es Salaam airport, a quaint throwback to colonial times, which caters for domestic flights only. They all thought that two taxis were probably overcautious, but Rufus and Orla decided to take no chances; it allowed Orla to be third eye again, running counter for them and remain unobserved herself. Her invisibility was a great asset at the moment.

Victoria and Rufus were in the first taxi, followed by Orla. They decided to avoid the ferry as it was effectively rush hour and they could queue for two hours to get on the small ferry delivering the labour force from the suburbs to the city; thousands of foot passengers and hundreds of cars, all funnelled into a hopelessly overcrowded service road and ferry. Rufus had used it a few times in the past and was amazed there had never, to his knowledge, been a major disaster.

They drove the long way along the B2, or Kilwa Road through suburbs of Kipara and Mtoni. Through the small shanty villages, until they reached the sprawling conurbation of Dar, when the houses and shops became more compacted, the roads, slightly better maintained and wider.

The journey was uneventful and Orla called Rufus to tell him that they were definitely not being followed, they chatted about Maura and Moez and how it would have been good to go and see them, but both knew it was completely impractical on this trip. On the outskirts of Dar es Salaam, at the junction of Kilwa Road and Nelson Mandela Road, Orla saw a Toyota Land Cruiser, with three occupants accelerate across the junction and "T Bone" Rufus's taxi. She saw Cowboy in the front passenger seat pointing at Rufus's car and urging the driver to go faster. Rufus had seen it coming too:

"GO, GO, GO!," he shouted to the driver while he pulled Victoria away from the offside over towards him on the nearside. Unfortunately the driver had not seen the Toyota at all and wasn't trained in the same way the two former soldiers were: he didn't react to Rufus's command in the way Rufus hoped, instead he hesitated, not sure what was happening, then braked...HARD, wondering what was happening in the back of his car, and why this mad mzungu was shouting what he thought was: "No no no" at him. He didn't know anything about the Toyota until it impacted on his door, crushing him and trapping him in his seat. There were no air bags in his twenty-year-old Toyota import and he was either knocked unconscious or killed immediately, Rufus didn't know which. Their car careered to the left, barrel rolling once, throwing Rufus and Victoria around the inside of the vehicle, disorienting them. They came to an abrupt stop as they collided with the massive, immovable Baobab tree. The car's front passenger door impacted against the tree, warping and twisting the old vehicle.

Rufus regained focus and his bearings first. He couldn't see the two passengers jump out of the Land Cruiser and walk towards them, but Orla did. She recognised them as Loafers and Cowboy, armed with Heckler and Koch MP5s; the guns levelled at Rufus's taxi. This was evidently pay-back for last night and the damage Rufus had caused with his bare hands to their colleagues.

Rufus didn't need to see them to know he had to get Victoria and himself out of the vehicle as quickly as possible. He tried the door, but it was jammed tight in the twisted wreck of a vehicle. He leaned back and kicked the window through spraying glass all over the ground and climbed out in one easy movement.

He looked above the top of the car just as they opened fire on the taxi. Rufus dropped back down and pulled Victoria out of the window and took cover behind the tree, probably the safest place anybody could be when being shot at.

The two shooters continued to fire, out of anger and frustration more than with any expectation of hitting their target, intending to keep then penned down while they moved in for the kill.

Rufus assessed his limited options, knowing he was powerless to do anything against two men armed with MP5s, if they attacked him with purpose and determination. He looked around for any type of weapon to use against them. There were a few branches he could use to either throw or use as an old-fashioned staff, but realistically his odds were poor. Cowboy and Loafers were a little wary of approaching the vehicle as they had seen the damage he could cause and didn't know whether he was armed or not. They did not want to end up like Brogues and Converse.

Orla watched the events unfold in front of her. She had travelled in the front passenger seat for just such an eventuality; she had made her driver stop and wait, there was no point rushing in blindly to end up in the same predicament as Rufus; she had been trained by the SRR how to use a vehicle properly in all types of scenarios including how to use it as a weapon.

She acted quickly and her right elbow caught the driver sweetly and unexpectedly on the temple knocking him out; she had no time to get out of the car, run round to the driver's door, open it, take off the seat belt, drag him out, get in the driver's seat, take control, and she knew that it was impossible to push him out of the car, with his seat belt on and the door shut. She made all of these calculations in a millisecond. She put the car in drive, stretched her leg across the central divide and stamped on the accelerator. The front wheels spun as they desperately sought traction on the dusty road and she sped forward towards the two attackers.

Fortunately the noise of the car accelerating was masked by the cacophony of sound all around them, people were shouting and screaming, drivers were sounding their horns in annoyance and frustration as Orla hurtled towards Cowboy and Loafers. They were concentrating on Rufus's position; the red mist was down and had lost their edge, because they were so intent on getting even with him, while at the same time being wary of him. They stood no chance as they did not see Orla until the last second when they turned to look at the taxi which was speeding towards them. It was too late: Cowboy was able to level his weapon at the car, and get a couple of rounds off but fortunately for Orla, aimed at the driver's position.

Orla was still in the passenger seat lying back to reach the accelerator which gave her a modicum of protection, the car impacted with Loafers milliseconds before it struck Cowboy and sent them both flying like rag dolls, slow motion into the air.

She went speeding past them, braking as hard as she could to avoid other vehicles and pedestrians and make her closing distance on Cowboy and Loafers less. She was out of her vehicle as Rufus appeared from the tree and they both ran towards their would-be assailants.

She was shouting to Rufus.

"You take Cowboy and I'll take Loafers," pointing as she said it.

The local population were all transfixed watching the scene unfold in front of them. People were screaming and running for cover. Rufus had blood running down the left side of his face, two men lay motionless in the mud and another two were slumped at the wheels of the vehicles. Victoria was still cowering behind the tree and saw nothing of the attack, not understanding what was happening or why. A few days ago she was enjoying a normal life in a normal village in England. Now, she felt like she was in the middle of a war zone with Rambo and G.I. Jane.

When Orla and Rufus reached their attackers they were lying dead or unconscious in the mud, neither of them checked to find out which – that was not their primary concern they had to prioritise and eliminate the immediate danger. They both looked at the Land Cruiser, the driver of which was flustered and trying to get the vehicle into drive, to finish off the attack. They heard the engine revs increase as the driver eventually fumbled the automatic shift into drive and accelerate towards them.

Orla had freed the MP5 from Loafers slightly before Rufus untangled Cowboy from his weapon. She took aim and got off a one second burst through the windscreen, at 800 rounds per minute, killing the driver instantly. The vehicle continued towards them and they both leapt out of the way just in time as the Toyota ran over both prostrate attackers, making sure that if they weren't already dead, they were now. It continued on its path until it crashed into the wall of the Amin Linen and Fabric Store, air bags inflating, hazard lights initiating and the horn blaring, the rear end bounced into the air and came to a dead stop as the vehicle stalled.

Rufus pointed to the two dead men and shouted, "Ammo. I'll get the driver."

He ran to the Land Cruiser and opened the driver's door and checked the attacker was dead. He could see a GPS handset in the foot well, where it had been thrown off the seat, he reached in, grabbed it and realised that these guys had been tracking them somehow.

Orla understood and emptied the two men's safari jacket pockets finding another four magazines. She quickly and efficiently searched the rest of their bodies and found a Glock 17 on each of them. She took the pistols for good measure, looked up to see Rufus running back to the Baobab tree to get Victoria.

She stood and surveyed the scene, looking to identify the next source of danger. None was apparent; these guys had been in one vehicle and had no back-up. Sloppy. The locals were keeping their distance, either hiding in shops or standing a good way off. The cops were nowhere to be seen.

Rufus got to Victoria who was sobbing where he had left her and checked she was ok. She was crying and scared out of her wits but otherwise she was ok. He reached into the upturned vehicle and grabbed their bags. He put them down next to her and went and checked on the driver. He could feel a pulse in the carotid artery and punched in 911 for an ambulance as he walked back to Victoria and lifted her easily off the ground. He carried her away from the wreckage, still with the phone to his ear.

He saw Orla had run to her taxi and dragged the still unconscious driver out of the car. She too checked for a pulse and injuries before doing anything else.

She gave him the thumbs up, indicating the driver was still alive she put him in the recovery position and inspected the vehicle. There were two huge dents in the bonnet/hood but the engine was still running. She got in the driver's seat and put it in reverse testing the mechanics. It wasn't great, but it was running.

When the phone was eventually answered, he requested several ambulances to the scene. Rufus had carried Victoria to the taxi and placed her across the back seat, while Orla was clearing what was left of the shattered windscreen away. They both jumped in the front seat, Rufus took a deep breath and calmly said, "Ok" to Orla.

Every natural instinct of Orla's told her to floor the pedal and get out of there as quickly as possible her pulse was racing her blood pressure up and adrenalin coursing through her veins; while every training session and instructor's voice told her to remain very controlled, to drive calmly and sedately away from the scene of the carnage so as not to draw any more attention to themselves than they had already had. Rufus's calm demeanour helped her and so the training won and she drove them away, slowly and carefully. She looked in the mirror and could see people coming out from behind buildings and from out of shops to see what had happened.

"Give me your phone Orla," Rufus said.

She reached into her pocket as she was driving and after a bit of wriggling gave him the phone. He got his out of his pocket and asked Orla to pull over. He gave their fully functioning useable Smart phones to two young men stood at the side of the road who immediately ran off with their haul.

"That should keep whoever it is busy for a few hours at least," he said.

He took Victoria's phone out of his left pocket and removed the battery, putting the phone back in his pocket and the battery in his back pocket.

"What are you doing?" both Orla and Victoria asked.

"They've been tracking us. I can't believe we didn't realise before. How else would they have found us in the hotel? We'd used false names? How did they follow me last night?"

"They followed you last night?" said Victoria.

"Yes they did, but I lost them for a short time until they showed up at the hotel again. And how did they know EXACTLY where we were today? It can't be the cars, we keep getting different taxis. I've checked my clothes and shoes so it must be through the phones. I'm not sure if it possible to track without the battery in, I can't see how, but remind me to ask Don."

"Who are these people?" Victoria asked for the second time in under twelve hours.

"I honestly don't know Victoria, but they are pretty well informed and equipped. They were tracking us with a GPS in the Toyota, the guy last night knew my name, and they have these babies," he said, patting the Heckler and Koch MP5s. This was an unexpected bonus, as he and Orla were very familiar with the best-selling MP5, or Maschinenpistole, version 5.

"We need to find out who they are, which side they are on, where they are getting their information and why they are trying to fuck us up. It could be any one of a number of people, but if we concentrate on who they are, the rest of the answers will fall into place."

Orla continued to drive calmly back towards Dar es Salaam, as ambulances, police cars and fire trucks sped the other way to the scene of the carnage they had left behind.

CHAPTER THIRTY-THREE

"Did you kill those men?" asked Victoria.

"You mean those men who tried to kill us?" asked Rufus. "Very probably... yes. It was them or us Victoria, and I'm sure you think we chose the right option?"

"It's just that we don't know who they are, or whether they could have led us to my parents. And you should have let me check them and tend to them until the emergency services arrived."

"I doubt that very much Victoria," said Orla, joining in the conversation. "From what we have discovered and Don has told us, we don't think they were directly connected to the kidnappers."

"And you were in no fit state to look after yourself fifteen minutes ago, let alone anybody else," said Rufus.

"That's not the point," said Victoria. "I'm a doctor and people were injured or dying, some of them are innocent and I could and should have done something about it. People should not be dying to save another two lives, even if they are my parents."

"We checked the taxi drivers who were both still alive and mine certainly had a strong pulse."

"So did mine," chipped in Orla. "Just a flesh wound I think."

"And the other guys damn well tried to kill us and nearly succeeded. If they had impacted a few feet further back they would have got you, not the driver, which seems to be where they were aiming, if he hadn't braked they would have struck a few feet further back and we might not be having this conversation. Whoever they are, whoever they are working for, whatever they are trying to do, they are the bad guys, not us. We just defended ourselves and you. If you remember I said the only time our priorities would change would be if you were in danger. Well you were, and we had to do something about it. If Orla hadn't been here we would both be dead."

They drove on in an uneasy silence, Victoria consumed with guilt, Rufus concentrating on the route to the airport, occasionally giving Orla directions. He couldn't let her follow the signs as he could have in most other cities, as there are none - the metal having been stolen to sell on or utilise in the making of something more important to the local population.

As they approached the Julius Nyerere Road, Rufus had to make a decision which way they would go: left to the airport or right towards the city.

"I still think we should stick to our plan and you should go to Butiama, Victoria. There is no way they will know you have gone there, whoever they are."

"You said they wouldn't know where we were before Ru, but they did."

"I know, I'm sorry, but now we have got rid of our phones and disconnected yours they won't be able to track us. Orla and I will get some throw phones and I'll contact Moez. He's a good guy; I'd trust him with my life. There is only one way to get there: by plane to the airstrip, where they or one of their staff will pick you up. We can vet everybody before they arrive and it will only be for a day, then we'll fly back for you. It's just that Orla and I have some work to do which will need both of us and I can't leave you alone, I won't risk it. Not anymore."

"What if they phone?" asked Victoria.

"We don't answer. They set the deadline and we will stick to it, there are enough excuses here for us not to answer the phone: lack of signal; lack of power as you had the power cable nicked; lack of power because of power cuts; turning it off to get some sleep, turning it off while you were in the bank negotiating the money – that's just off the top of my head without giving it any thought. Don't worry about that."

"Ok. I'll go. But I want to come back tomorrow and get Mum and Dad back. No more fighting, no more heroics, I just want them back safe and sound."

"Good, it's the right decision," he said. "Right here, Orla," he interrupted himself and continued to Victoria, "We will be back to pick you up tomorrow."

They drove out of town along the chaotic main road, past the main International Terminal round to the old airport car park, and locked the car. There was no security on the car park, no barriers, no guards and most importantly, no CCTV.

The domestic terminal was a very relaxed place, a throwback to colonial times; small, under-equipped old-fashioned, and had an air of nostalgia, almost like a family run business, with security and procedures taking a back seat to friendliness and informality.

They put Victoria's baggage through what was meant to be a scanner, while Rufus and Orla blagged their way through the security check, claiming they were all on the flight. They looked at the scanner and could see that although there was a monitor, it wasn't working, and nobody viewed it anyway. They chatted to the friendly guard who was impressed with Rufus's Swahili and Orla's breasts while they waited for the small bag to appear. After a few seconds the guard reached into the scanner and pulled Victoria's bag out with a big smile and gave it to her.

"I think you pulled again there mate," Rufus said to Orla.

"You are all the same aren't you? The world over, a small flash of cleavage or leg and you can't take your eyes off it."

"If you've got it, flaunt it, I think that's what you used to say wasn't it?"

"Absolutely," she replied, laughing and grabbed Rufus's arm, putting hers through his.

Victoria walked with them quietly. She felt quite morose; she was still shocked by the attack on them and the carnage they had caused; she was worried about not being able to answer the phone; she was frightened about leaving Rufus going into the unknown and if she was honest with herself, she was jealous of Orla's relationship with Rufus.

They walked to the check-in counter and gave Victoria's false name of Rose Gardener. Orla looked over the A4 sheet held on a clipboard by the check-in clerk as he ticked Rose's name, and chose two more names at random from the list, which had not got ticks by them. Orla memorised the names in case they needed to give them to get into the departures lounge, but she needn't have worried.

They walked, unopposed, into the small bare room, which functioned as the departure lounge.

"I've seen bigger doctors' waiting rooms than this, and certainly more comfortable," said Orla, as she sat on the wooden bench seat, trying to get some relief from the ineffectual fan.

They waited a few minutes until a member of staff shouted out the flight. Together with a handful of other passengers they strolled out airside onto the tarmac, in the relaxed informal boarding process with no passport checks or tickets, no more x-ray machines, no Advanced Passenger Information required, just a quaint roll call of passengers. They mingled with the others, and although they would have been discovered had they tried to get on the plane, no-one paid any attention to them.

They walked a little way with the other passengers, peeling off to their right back to the arrivals door, stopping for a few minutes to ensure Victoria got on the small twelve-seater plane.

Once she was aboard they walked to the arrivals door, where there was no security, and simply walked back to the car. It was more like a train station than an airport in terms of security which suited them perfectly. They retrieved their bags and guns from the taxi, put the keys on the visor, leaving it unlocked, and hopped in to another one. They didn't have to worry about CCTV coverage as there was none at the airport and the Tanzanians didn't have their fingerprints, and as long as they were calm and didn't draw attention to themselves they would be ok, even when the car was eventually discovered.

The stunning views of the Tanzanian coastline from seven thousand feet were wasted on Victoria; she was in her own little world, considering everything that had gone on. The last three days had been a whirlwind for her and she was trying to make sense of it all. They flew south-east away from the sprawling city centre of Dar es Salaam, stretching much farther than she had realised, across verdant green countryside and over beautiful white sandy beaches, across the turquoise Indian Ocean towards Mafia. Twenty-five minutes later she could see the tiny airstrip directly in front of them, made of orange sand and gravel. She could hardly believe it, it was like something out of a film or documentary; she never really believed that such places still existed. A few seconds later they touched down on a bumpy, short, airstrip serviced by a small building serving as the terminal, security, gift shop and customs rolled into one, with the word MAFIA hand painted on the tiled roof.

Victoria thought Rufus had been exaggerating, but he hadn't; it was so picturesque and quaint. She got off the plane and walked towards a small gaggle of people standing by the very rustic airport arrivals and departures building. Her own house was bigger, it was brilliant. A man with a broad welcoming smile, wearing shorts and a diving T-shirt, walked towards her. Victoria took an immediate liking to him.

"Hello Victoria, I'm Moez. Welcome to Mafia Island and to Butiama. Rufus has told me all about what happened, so don't worry. Are you alright?"

"Hello Moez, I really don't know. I feel like I am in the middle of a dream and I will wake up soon. And I feel terrible because I am thinking about me, when I'm imposing upon you and Maura, and my parents are being held hostage and what must they be going through."

"Well, I suggest you listen to Ru, he knows what he is doing and I am sure he has sent you over here for the good of your parents and not just for a bit of fun. And far from imposing upon us, we're pleased to have you here; it's always good to see a friend of Ru's."

That got Victoria thinking again *What does he mean? A friend of Ru's? Has he brought other people over here? How many times has he done this? Why would he need to send people here?*

He took her small bag off her and walked to an old Land Rover to drive her to the resort. It was fantastic, and if it wasn't for the circumstances, she would have been overwhelmed by the whole experience. The windscreen was cracked, the wipers could only be operated manually. It was a crash gearbox, so he had to double de-clutch and match the revs to get it into gear as he pulled away. It was noisy and battered, with seats well-worn from the thousands of bottoms squashing them over the years, spewing the innards out of the cracked fabric.

Chapter Thirty-Four

"FUCKING HELL. What the fuck has happened?" Nick Cooper screamed into his phone, as he watched the grainy scene on television. He didn't give the person at the other end chance to answer.

"You were told to surveil them and report back to me on their movements and whereabouts, not start a fucking war. I told you he was ex Special Forces, what did you think he would do? Just roll over and let you give it him up the arse? He really was SAS not just a muppet company using the initials." He ran his fingers through his hair in anger, frustration and concern. He had to think: *I could inform the authorities that Stone had killed three men, but then I would have to account for starting the attack; explain what they were doing and that could get messy – who was the woman that intervened? why didn't I know about her? Unless the surviving member of his team had got all confused and mistook Victoria for someone else and she had run them over and shot the driver?* No, *that was not feasible was it? Stone must have arranged back up, that I don't know about. Shit. I've got to tell the boss as well. Shit. But, the main strategy remains the same and I can still deliver him that can't I? It's just that this could get a bit embarrassing if it gets out.*

"Tell your man to keep his mouth shut, and to say that he was attacked without provocation and just got caught up in some sort of battle between two groups. That he knows nothing about either group, or what it was about, and we will look after him."

Cooper put the phone down to the Operations Manager of Surveillance and Security Ltd and called his source 'Esther'.

After speaking to Esther he was in a better mood and prepared himself to contact Sir Peregrine, concentrating on Esther's news rather than the debacle that was still being shown on the morning news bulletin.

+++++++

Martyn was in a far worse state than Victoria. He had been treated worse than a dog: he was literally and metaphorically in the dark. He still didn't know where he was, where Deidre was, or even if she was alive; why they had been captured; who had captured them; if anybody knew they were missing. Would Victoria have missed them by now? He doubted it, as they had already said there might be days in between telephone calls, as they did not realise the cell network was pretty extensive in Tanzania. He was trying to keep track of the time, but couldn't as he had no reference at all.

All he got was the local staple of ugali: goo, made from corn flour and water, twice a day, brought by a guard who didn't speak to him, didn't even acknowledge him. He couldn't sleep because of the rats in the room. He had one pot in the corner to relieve himself in. No toilet paper, which left him feeling sore and dirty. He could smell foul obnoxious odours coming off him and he day dreamed about having a long, luxurious bath to clean and freshen himself up. He tried to recite passages and verses from poems, songs and books, but the solitary confinement was taking its toll already. He was hallucinating, and he was becoming feverish. His mouth felt stale and rancid and was so dry he couldn't produce any saliva. He had banged on walls, doors and pipes to try and get some sort of response, any response, just to know that another human being was around.

The door opened without any warning, and unfortunately he got what he wished for: two men entered and grabbed him; he was too weak both in mind and body to resist them. The light blinded him and made him squeeze his eyes tight shut as they dragged him out. They man-handled him a little way and shoved him down into a chair. He sat there cowering, waiting for the attack, anticipating the strike on his body. He opened his eyes slowly, because he was scared what he might see and his eyes were just not used to any light.

As he opened his eyes he saw Deidre sitting beside him, she was looking straight at him.

"Dweedy," he mumbled, meaning "Deidre" because he couldn't make his tongue and lips work. She looked at him, seemingly without any emotion whatsoever, he couldn't understand it.

"They want us to make an audio recording telling Victoria we're ok," Deidre said in a monotone, emotionless voice.

Martyn was dumbfounded. He couldn't understand why Deidre was being so callous and emotionless.

"They want us to talk together and read this out," she held up a piece of A4 paper with words typed on it.

"Wawer," said Martyn making a drinking motion with his hand, which one of the guards took to mean water, and provided him with a grimy, dirty cup of brackish water. Martyn didn't care: what little reasoning he had left concluded that he had probably been drinking worse than that and took a mouthful and swilled it around his parched, swollen mouth.

"Deidre. What's happening? Why are you being like this?" he mumbled, bewildered.

Deidre stared back at him, giving him no sign of emotion at all.

What's happening? thought Martyn. *Why is she being like this?* He looked at her and she appeared to be completely devoid of any emotion towards him. *What's wrong with her? Is she in shock? Has she been drugged?* His brain just couldn't process the information his senses were providing.

"We need to read this out together so that they can play the recording to Victoria when they next talk to her," said Deidre.

"They've been talking to Victoria? Oh my God, no. How is she? What..." his croaky voice nearly cracking with emotion.

"Of course they are talking to Victoria; they are negotiating a payment for our release with her."

"What? How? When did all this take place?" said Martyn, confused as to what was happening.

"Over the last few days of course," said Deidre, "and Victoria has said she wants proof that they are holding us and that we are ok, so we have to read this out."

"I have to read this first bit," said Deidre. "Down to here, and you have to read the rest."

Martyn looked at the paper and could see about five lines of text for each of them. He scanned the sheet of paper and read his lines.

"Hello Victoria, this is your dad, Martyn Conway. We are being treated well and with dignity. The people who are treating us as their guests have a legitimate cause and are good and honourable people. I urge you and the people of the United Kingdom to support their just cause in the name of Allah. I watched the football game between the Seahawks and the Broncos on Saturday which ended up forty-three, eight to the Seahawks."

"I'm not saying that," said Martyn indignantly. "It's all lies,"

"MARTYN." shouted Deidre, "just fucking-well do it."

In thirty-one years of marriage Martyn had never heard Deidre swear. He stopped and checked to make sure it was actually Deidre saying it, and he hadn't imagined it. She was staring down at him with a steely glint in her eye. He hadn't got the will to resist her glare and succumbed easily. Deidre had always said she loved his avuncular nature, but now she seemed to hate him, hate his weakness. She was glowering at him with despise. What was happening?

Chapter Thirty-Five

After making a quick stop to buy four mobile phones from one of the dozens of small shops, Orla and Rufus decided on the Chichi Hotel in Biafra just off the Kinondoni Road. The hotel was cheap, but most importantly it was not frequented by tourists and was not well known. If their attackers tried to track them down by visiting or phoning hotels, it would be some time before they thought about this one. It had one more benefit in that it was close to both Kariakoo, their next port of call, and to Masaki.

On entering the lobby they quickly surveyed it, it was perfect for them: quiet, very little security, no CCTV, no flat-screen television on the wall with twenty-four hour news, and the thoroughfare was slightly obscured from the desk by a supporting column.

They checked in using yet another alias to the Lionel Blair name he had used at Kilimanjaro: they booked one double room under the name of Mr and Mrs Bobby and Tracy Moore, American nationals, with expertly forged American passports, which would certainly stand the cursory inspection the clerk gave them. Orla had suggested being a married couple as she thought it would appear normal, and sleeping in the same bed just came naturally to them, they had done it so often.

After being shown to their room Rufus went through his standard operating procedure of endearing himself to the porter, who gave his name as General, tipping well and alluded to the fact that they were actually having an affair and the real husband might come looking for them, so if he saw anything untoward he should alert them.

General went away happy with his generous tip from the wealthy American, while they inspected the room: they were pleasantly surprised by the standard of the hotel in general and the room in particular. It was on the first floor and the windows were sealed, which suited them at the moment. It was clean and tidy and more spacious than they expected, giving them the luxury of being able to spread out a bit.

They sorted themselves out, showering quickly and preparing their kit, sharing the ammunition and weapons. Orla put on her bespoke webbing which would be hidden by her burka, while Rufus was double-checking the weapons. He reduced the stock on Orla's weapon to machine pistol size so that she could secret it more easily– not ideal he thought, but better than nothing – and changed magazines, ensuring she had a full one of thirty-two rounds.

They programmed their phones with Don's, and each other's numbers and when they were fully prepared, they Skyped Don.

"Hi Don," said Orla.

"Jesus you have had me worried. Are you ok? Is Ru with you?"

"I'm here mate," said Rufus, moving slightly to let the in-built camera pick him up.

"What's going on?" asked Don. "I've been trying both of your phones, but some locals kept answering."

"Rufus gave them away." Orla went on to tell Don what had happened over the previous six hours, including their theory that their phones had either been hacked, or tracked, or both.

"Ah, that makes sense now then," said Don. "That accounts for the strange activity I was seeing. But it seemed to be "official" to me. I assumed it was our friends in Cheltenham, doing some work for COBRA."

"Well it might well be the official reason Don, but for some reason, if you are right, these guys were being fed the product. Why would the spooks try and do our legs? 'Cus it must be the spooks that have been briefing them. What's in it for them? We were damn well doing their work for them and if they'd asked us to keep them in the loop, we would have done."

"There must be another angle we haven't thought of." said Orla.

"The only one I can think of is their loss of power and influence over the last twenty years, and this is just another erosion of their empire. A few years ago they would have been the lead on a British national kidnapped abroad. Perhaps they are trying to fuck us up, sorry love." he apologised to Orla for swearing. "so that they can show we are a bunch of amateurs and they are the experts."

"So trying to claw back a bit of kudos? Is there anybody at Cheltenham you can talk to on the QT?" asked Orla.

"I think so. I did a couple of courses at Shrivenham with them, some seriously clever people with brains the size of small planets. I think I probably owe them more than they owe me, but I'll try and convince them they owe me a favour."

"If you can please Don, I'd like to know exactly what Orla and I are facing down here. And if asking them doesn't work, threaten 'em with a good regimental kicking."

"Ok. mate, I'll get straight on it."

They gave Don their phone numbers so that he could be fully back in the loop. Orla continued to brief Don, while Rufus got back to work in a quietly efficient manner. He looked up the number for "Butiama" on the internet as he could not remember it, and programmed his and Orla's phone with that and other numbers. He brought up mapping ready for a briefing by Don, frustrated with the speed of the internet. Don dropped out a few times, and kept having to reconnect to Orla. He got out the glass cutter he had bought on his first trip to Kariakoo and gave it to Orla.

He looked at some of the other equipment he had bought. He gave her an earpiece and got his own ready. He got the firecrackers that he had bought and split them into three piles: the biggest one he put in reserve, and gave Orla one of the smaller piles, he kept the third. They weren't as good as the flash bangs they were used to, but they were better than nothing and could buy a split second of reaction time.

Don briefed them on what he knew: Deidre's phone had moved from the stronghold about an hour ago he believed; the Transit Supermarket Road address had been quiet. He hadn't tracked any of the target phones there and the two bugs that Rufus had planted had been silent. He had pinged both, and he was sure they were working, but nobody was there; there had been more activity from Deidre's phone to several other numbers and Ed, the analyst was busy plotting associations. They all agreed that a recce of the stronghold was worthwhile and might give them immediate benefits. Deidre's phone was off at the moment, so he couldn't even give them a rough idea where she was.

Don took over their tablet remotely and guided them through Kariakoo to where he believed the stronghold to be. They couldn't get the clarity that they were used to in Europe, as mapping wouldn't zoom down to the same magnification, they kept losing connection, plus with the rabbit warren of houses and stores, it was difficult to tell if it was a one- or two-storey building.

There was no street view available, so they had to go with what they had, which was good enough to give them a very good idea of the target, but not the detailed briefing they would have liked. They all agreed that this was just a reconnaissance mission and that if Orla ID'd it as the stronghold, she would withdraw, they would re-group and plan their assault. If she was compromised, they agreed on a RVP. If she was captured, they agreed on an emergency action plan.

They tried to plan for every eventuality as they all knew the risk Orla was taking, because in order for Rufus not to attract too much attention he had to remain a few minutes away "browsing" at the market, with his kit in his holdall. They both memorised their way to the stronghold from their respective positions. Rufus had to be doubly sure that he knew the way, even if he was running at top speed. If Orla shouted for help, he knew that she would need it – and quick. Fortunately he could still remember some of the landmarks that he had noted and was confident he could get there quickly.

Ideally they would have liked to wait until dusk, but they didn't have the time for ideals so it was agreed that the recce would take place immediately.

After they cut the call to Don, they got themselves ready and "buddied up" to check each other over. Rufus insisted that Orla put some make up on the backs of her hands to give them some colour, but other than that she was perfect. They decided on separate taxis. Orla could speak enough Swahili and a little Arabic, a necessity of some of the missions she had been on previously, to get by so she would have no problem telling the driver where to go if he didn't speak English.

Orla walked anonymously out in her burkha, and got into one of the taxis waiting at the gates of the hotel. She attracted no attention whatsoever from anybody in the hotel, and the taxi driver accepted her as a devout Muslim without any question.

Rufus waited a minute, grabbed his kit bag and left, getting another waiting taxi and giving the driver instructions to take him to Kariakoo.

Orla was there before him, paid the taxi driver and waited at the side of the road for his call to let her know he was on the plot. She took in her surroundings and atmosphere. Unlike Rufus, she had never been to Kariakoo before and needed a couple of seconds to acclimatise to the atmosphere of the place: the smells, colours and dust, the constant noise. She had to understand what 'normal' was so she knew when something abnormal was happening.

They kept their phone call open so they were in permanent contact. She walked the short distance to the target and let him know she was there and that all was quiet, using their own form of words that they both understood, rather than talk in clear, or plain language, just in case anybody had found their new numbers and was listening. It was a tried and tested system for them; an amalgamation of different techniques they knew.

"The bank *stronghold* is like a library *very quiet.*"

"Roger that," said Rufus.

"White 1: 1 Bobby; central, 2 Microsoft 1 green, 1 red." *Front ground floor has one door positioned centrally and two windows: one on the left one on the right.*

"Roger."

"White 2: 2 boarded Microsoft green and red."

"Roger."

"Red aspect: external apples, no Microsoft" *right side has stairs running up the side no window.*

"Roger."

"Green aspect: Green 1: 1 Bobby, Green 2 Zero."

"Roger."

Rufus was inspecting some under-developed fruit at one of the fruit sellers' stalls, presumably provided by one of the millions of small scale, under-funded farmers growing sub-standard produce intended for the home market. The microphone from Orla's headset, covered by her burkha amplified all the noise and he could hear her breathing and quiet footsteps as she made her way to the black (back).

Orla was trying to look inconspicuous and at the same time be cautious; she didn't want to stumble into any surprises. She wasn't too concerned about herself she was bothered about Deidre and Martyn. If she showed out and alerted the kidnappers they could kill

Deidre and Martyn as the only witnesses to their crime. The best way to achieve that was to look natural, hidden in full view.

She quietly and effortlessly moved around the back, checking for anybody that might be watching her, listening for any movement or voices, her senses hyper-sensitive to any noises, movement, smells or change in ambience.

"Black aspect: Black 1: 1 Bobby and 2 Microsoft all boarded."

"Roger."

"Black 2: 2 Microsoft, boarded."

"Roger."

"I'm going to take a look up the red apples, the place is pudding (deserted)."

"Wait one, Orla I'm coming towards you, so I am closer."

"Roger," said Orla.

"Ok. Orla, go," said Rufus after he had positioned himself closer.

"Roger."

Orla walked to the top of the fire escape stairs, ready to bluff her way out of any confrontation by claiming she was looking for her Auntie Jazlyn, thinking that she lived there. She tapped lightly on the door, and listened. She waited about ten seconds and tapped a bit louder calling out "Auntie Jazlyn". Still nothing.

"I'm going to perform surgery," she said, and took the glass cutter from her webbing and put it against the glass of the door.

"Roger."

She silently removed a small circle of glass, reached inside and undid the lock and latch, and entered. She could feel Rufus running up the metal steps behind her, rather than hear him. He joined her inside shutting the door silently behind him.

They both readied their weapons and began a systematic search of the premises, their years of drills taking over to perform the task quickly.

They cleared the building and re-grouped. It was clear that this had been the stronghold. There were three rooms that had either been used as "cells" or the general washroom, with a bucket in the corner of each, full to overflowing with excrement. In the large communal area, it was obvious several meals had been taken around an untidy table: crumbs and grease, empty packets, and plates all over it. Five blankets were laid out on the floor where people had slept. Cigarette butts were strewn around the floor, together with bottles of water. The place stunk of stale sweat, fetid excrement, urine and cigarettes.

No attempt had been made to forensically sanitise the building, which led them both to conclude that they had left in a hurry, and/or were amateurs.

The two colleagues scoured the building for any documentation, clothing or personal effects. They found a pile of clothes screwed up and thrown into the corner. Rufus knelt down and examined the clothes, it was a mixture of men's and women's clothing, he presumed, they belonged to Deidre and Martyn and had been discarded by the bandits. He scooped them up and shoved them in his rucksack to show Victoria and evidentially secure them if needed.

Not wanting want to spend too long inside they left as quietly and unobtrusively as they had arrived. The only evidence of their visit was the hole in the glass. Rufus looked at it and decided it was too neat, too perfect and would alert anybody returning to the building. He smashed some of the glass from the outside showering shards over the floor, ran down the stairs, grabbed a rock, returned and placed the offending boulder inside the building.

Chapter Thirty-Six

They made their way back to the hotel separately, Rufus entered first and Orla walked in, still in her burka, slightly afterwards.

Back in their room they Skyped Don. Rufus gave him a quick sit-rep, while Orla got out of outer clothing and webbing and took the make-up off her hands.

"Hi mate, we got in and the birds have flown the nest."

"Shit. But I guessed that was the case and at least we know they were there, and tracking Deidre's phone worked."

"Yeh, I guess, but how did they know we were coming? From what you've said this has been a base for a few days."

"Transit Supermarket Road had come online and I've overheard the conversation there, some in Swahili and some in English. They seem to have moved them this morning. They appear to know that you were back in town. James thinks there are at least four teams here looking for them, from what he said. I don't know where they have taken them though. Deidre's phone is now offline and James didn't mention a location."

"So how did they know we are back in town? How did they know we were coming? There have been too many coincidences since I got here, I don't like it. Can you get hold of that fuckwit McHugh and see if he's spoken to anybody about hiring us? If he has I'm going to rip his head off and shit down the hole."

"Roger that."

Orla joined them in her knickers and bra and looked over Rufus's shoulder at the screen.

"Hi love. How's the other intel coming on," she asked.

"Good and bad," he said. "We now have a network of phones based in Dar, although most of them are throw phones, but the bad news is we have another network based up in Somalia, and the Somali traffic is becoming heavier. I'll send you a document with the networks on. Don't worry, we've made it as Janet and John as we can so you two trogs can understand it."

"Thanks for your confidence in us," she replied smiling. "And be sure to tell us if they start making their way down here, won't you," she added.

"That's my next point. I think two of them are already there."

"Oh shit," said Orla and Rufus simultaneously.

"I think we have got three teams working here against us," said Rufus. "One, the original bandits; two: the Somalis, I expect have come down to relieve the bandits of their packages either voluntarily or by force; and three: this unknown group of westerners – I can't see them working for the bandits, that's a non-starter, but from what you've said and we've seen there is some form of relationship there. I know we've discussed this before but do either of you have any ideas?"

"They could be contractors hired by Deidre," said Don.

"Mmmm," said Orla, "that scenario is looking more and more likely. They seem pretty well funded with weapons, coms and a good intel feed. Some of that could be coming from Deidre."

"And I have coms between Deidre and this group." said Don.

"Between Deidre's phone and them," corrected Rufus.

"Well what other explanation have we got? Deidre gets the pair of them insured for... what was it?"

"Two million quid a piece," said Orla.

"She hears and reads about kidnappings going on all the time down in East Africa, reads about that guy that topped his wife down in South Africa, and starts to think how easy it would be. She doesn't realise that we are going to be hired to come and get them back. People don't know the likes of us even exist. So she plans it all with her young boyfriend."

"What young boyfriend?" asked Rufus.

"Bear with me mate, it's a hypothesis as you would say... She plans it with her toyboy, who is also seeing a big payday. He's well connected and puts a team together to come down here and watch her back, and make sure that Martyn is topped and the money is collected. When they get back to England he can do what he likes on £2 million as he has her by the short and curlies, she can't go to the old bill, she's fucked."

"There are a few holes there Don."

"Such as?"

"They know my name," said Rufus.

"I've thought about that and there are two ways I can think of: either Victoria told her somehow, or lover-boy works at Charles' insurance company and found out we'd been contracted. Personally I think the latter holds up to scrutiny better as he would have more access to information, and other than the calls we have authorised Vicky seems to be playing a pretty straight bat. Then, the final nails in the coffin for me are that only Deidre's phone is being used AND Victoria has only spoken to Deidre and not Martyn. My guess is he's already dead and they are playing it out a bit to make it look authentic, or waiting to for an opportunity to dump the body."

"They were tracking us. That's pretty sophisticated."

"Get real Ru, we have teenagers hacking into NASA and MI6 and all sorts of shit, anybody with half a brain can do this now," said Don.

"What about the Somalis? What are they doing here then?" asked Orla.

"I've given that some thought, and they could have heard about the kidnapping on the grapevine, not knowing it's a set-up and they've come down to take care of things. You know the way the booties are patrolling the Somali waters now. It's safer and easier for them to do it this way. They've been forced in-land. Look what's been happening in Kenya. It all fits. It fits with the traffic that Ed and I are looking at, it has motive, and opportunity, it fits with the facts as we know them."

"It's a working hypothesis, I'll give you that," said Rufus, "but I have to keep an open mind."

"You've been mixing with the plod for too long," said Don.

"You might be right there, mate. My suggestion is we continue to play this as if it is a hundred per cent genuine on the negotiating front, it's the only way, and when we get Victoria back we go for proof of life with Martyn. In the meantime, Orla and I had better get busy again, seeing if we can help prove your theory. I think another visit to Transit Supermarket Road is called for," said Rufus, looking towards Orla and back to the tablet at Don.

Rufus and Orla put all the kit into Rufus's holdall this time as there was no reason for Orla to dress up in the burkha.'

They left the hotel like regular guests this time, not bothering whether they were seen or spoken to by the staff. They walked into the car park and caught a taxi the short distance to Chole Road, in the fading light.

They planned to approach the compound on foot, but as they were pulling up by Lukas Bar and before they could get out of the car, Don telephoned Orla.

"James is on the move. I've got a weak signal from him and the damn thing keeps dropping out, but he's definitely moving."

"Wait here please," Orla instructed the driver of the taxi and a couple of seconds later they were rewarded when a Land Rover Discovery emerged from Transit Supermarket Road.

They waited for it to pass and asked their driver to follow it as discreetly as he could. They only got a glimpse of the face, they assumed to be James, the first time either of them had seen the man they were negotiating with, who was threatening the lives of Deidre and Martyn, but Orla had the face memorised immediately.

The Discovery is not a common vehicle in Dar and was relatively easy to follow: they surveilled it onto Bagamoyo Road and headed out of town, passed the Millennium Towers a little way and threw a left pulling up outside a local haunt called The Hongera Bar.

They pulled up on the opposite side of the road and watched James walk into the bar area. As is usual in

Tanzania, the bar was open on two sides, and covered with a thatched roof of makumi, or palm leaves. There was seating outside of the thatch and more tables inside, with even more tables and chairs stacked up in the corner. Rufus offered the driver $10 and asked him to wait for them a little way up the road, which he was happy to do: $10 for doing nothing, of course he was happy to wait; he even said they could pay him later.

Orla looked at Rufus.

"We've got honest faces," said Rufus.

Because the bar was lighter than the now dark street, it was easier to see in than to see out and they felt quite comfortable to cross the road and navigate their way through the plethora of tables and chairs strewn around the place, and sit at a plastic table with dirty plastic chairs just outside the roof covering, in relative darkness.

when the opportunity arose. They observed the frien but serious games, yet another contradictory behavio they had noted in their time in the country. There was no discernible order in which the players took turns, but they usually knew who the next challenger was, and any disagreements were ended in a noisy but friendly way, which appeared to the two British observers as if it would end in a fight, but never did.

Their food arrived next which was 'mixed' to say the least. The intestine soup was delicious, but the chips miai was far too greasy for them, but they still ate it, under the principle of not knowing when they would eat again.

James left after about thirty minutes of what appeared to be deep conversation. They watched him return to his Disco and drive off, wondering whether they had made the right decision. But now they put their rudimentary plan into operation.

Orla had slowly but surely loosened her blouse to show more cleavage than usual and they moved forward, positioning themselves by the pool table. Rufus indicated that they wanted to play and they continued to watch the game and the target, who had returned to the table.

Orla was getting lots of stares from the Tanzanian men, who are not very discreet with their stares at the best of times, and when the game ended, she stood up to play. Strictly speaking it wasn't her turn, but after some very loud, animated gesticulating the men decided it would be fun to see the mzungu lady bending over the able and laugh at her losing.

Orla guessed what was being said about her, and it vas actually what she and Rufus had hoped for.

Chapter Thirty-Seven

Orla deliberately chose a table that had a thick bush at the rear of it, so they did not give off a silhouette to anybody looking from the inside. Rufus caught the eye of the young waitress who approached them and curtsied, which slightly embarrassed them, Orla more so than Rufus as she had never had anyone curtsy to her before and was uncomfortable with the experience.

"Kilimanjaro mbili baridi sana tafadhali," said Rufus, giving the waitress a Tsh 10000 bill. She took the money, curtsied again and went off to the bar.

They looked around the establishment and not only were they the only two mzungus in the bar; Orla was the only female customer. They took in as much information as they possible could in their sweep of the bar.

There was no security of any description in the public area, although the bar was protected by security grills. The décor was a dirty yellow colour, ingrained with years of dust and grime, there was an open drain running through the seated area; there were vending stalls around the one open corner of the bar selling shoes, perfume, books, children's toys and CDs. DJ Kulwa, as he announced himself, was playing a mixture of local and hip hop songs far too loud for the capability of the sound system, causing it to distort the sound.

Next to DJ Kulwa, an ancient analogue television, mounted high up on the wall was showing a football match, and even though a group of locals were avidly and excitedly watching the screen, Rufus couldn't make anything out: the only visible picture had reduced to the very centre of the screen, while the outer screen was a distorted, fuzzy, purple colour. However, it didn't seem to make any difference to the spectators who were enthusiastically supporting one of the teams.

Yellow plastic chairs were strewn across the seating area, where people had stood up and just let the chair fall over. A central stand extolled the virtues of Cola drinks and behind that were the toilets, which Rufus and Orla zeroed in on: set in the far corner of the bar, easily accessible and ideal to slip out to the open air, unobserved and out to the road. It was the one private area of the entire place where they could act unobserved, if the opportunity arose.

The waitress returned with their two cold Kilimanjaro beers and curtsied again. She opened the bottles in front of them, a prerequisite of all mzungus and most locals, ensuring she did not touch the neck with her hands. Rufus told her to keep the change and in Swahili increased their order to two orange juices, two bottles of water, two chips miai, and two bowls of intestine soup, giving the waitress another Tsh 20 000.

"What have you ordered?" asked Orla.

"Juice, water, a sort of omelette with chips and a local delicacy, which if it is cooked properly is delicious."

"What is it?"

"Ox gut, the whole intestinal system."

"Mmmm, sounds lovely," she said sarcastically.

Rufus reasoned that they might as well get some sustenance and fluid while they could as they didn't know how long they would be there and didn't know when their next opportunity for food would be.

They watched James talk to a man who had bee playing pool at one of the two tables in the bar. The moved away from the tables, set on the very edge of th covered area, back further into the covered area. Ruf and Orla couldn't hear what they were saying or ma out anything that was being said from lip-reading body language; it was too dark and too noisy. Wh they watched they discussed their plans and decid that with the bugs in his house James was more valua on the loose, therefore, they would concentrate on other guy.

Their drinks arrived with more curtsies, and lot smiles. Rufus told the waitress to keep the change a and she walked away, staring at Rufus as she left.

"What is it with you and young women?"

"What do you mean?"

"The way she's looking at you. Do you flirt them deliberately?"

"Who? What are you talking about?"

"The waitress."

"I haven't flirted with her, I've ordered our And given her a decent tip."

"You haven't got a Scooby have you?"

"Seeing as I don't know what you are talking the obvious answer is no," he stood up and went gents. When he returned he nodded to Orla ar "About as good as it gets."

He sat back down and they watched the playing pool and decided on a tactic of dist

As the challenger it was her responsibility to break off. She leaned over the table and wiggled her bottom, more than was necessary as she positioned her legs to take the shot and rested her boobs on the cushion of the table to accentuate them. The men were transfixed.

They were even more transfixed when she cleared the table without giving her opponent a single shot: she had a lucky break, potting one of each of the stripes and solids. The laughs and cat calling at the unfortunate man rang around the bar, who tried to argue that it hadn't been fair, to the derision of his friends.

Orla won four games on the trot, and was attracting quite an audience and would-be challengers. The noise level was increasing exponentially as people argued their case for being the next challenger; all convinced that they would be the one to beat the woman.

Rufus concentrated on their target and his opportunity arose when he left his seat to go to the toilet. Rufus had kept an eye on the gents and knew there was one man in there. He stood up, ensuring Orla had seen him and followed the target into the covered area of the bar. As he approached the washroom the smell of ammonia caused by the urine attacked his nostrils again, but he was in luck, the other guy was just leaving the washroom as Rufus walked in.

The target was standing at the urinal right in front of a Britmax fan that looked like it was made from girders used to build the Empire State building. Rufus didn't waste any time smashing the guy's head into the fan and wondered when the last time the fan had actually worked.

The guy was knocked clean out and would have collapsed on the floor if Rufus hadn't caught him. He carried him into what would usually be called a cubicle; an area with a lockable door and a "long drop" for a toilet. Rufus shoved him against a wall and supported him with one arm as he phoned Orla.

"Ready to go?" she could just about hear above the din of men laughing at their compatriot losing to the woman.

"I'll create a diversion. You'll know when."

After a few more seconds he heard the commotion and knew this was what he wanted. Orla had slapped a man around the face accusing him of pinching her bottom. The other voyeurs had jumped to Orla's aid and started attacking the man. The owner of the bar rushed over, together with his staff, to intervene. There was mayhem, with people shouting, accusing, pushing and shoving. Orla picked up their kit bag and walked away unobserved by the melee and joined Rufus as he walked out into the darkness on the far side of the bar and out into the night with the dead weight over his shoulder.

As they got close to the taxi they lowered the guy and held an arm around each shoulder and 'walked' their victim back to the taxi, pretending he was drunk and that they had rescued him.

The taxi driver looked quizzically at them, not believing a word they said. He started to drive and made a telephone call, assuming that like most other mzungus, these two would not understand Swahili. Unfortunately for him, Rufus understood every word.

"Hello, hello," said the driver, "I have two white people in the taxi who are kidnapping a man from the bar. What should I do?"

Of course Rufus couldn't hear the reply, but he had heard enough. Orla could see him reaching into the bag and silently withdrawing his Glock, she could also see that the safety was on and that he had no intention of hurting the taxi driver. Rufus tapped the driver on the shoulder and indicated he should pull over. As they came to a stop Rufus showed the driver the MP5 and said, “Kupata nje ya gari,” in fluent Swahili. The driver looked simultaneously aghast and petrified and immediately obliged by getting out of the car.

Rufus also got out of the car and took the driver’s cell phone off him. He searched him and found another phone and took that too. Rufus gave him $20 for the fare, and as Orla jumped in the driver’s seat he got back in the rear of the taxi and they sped away, leaving the well-intentioned driver at the side of the road.

Chapter Thirty-Eight

Rufus directed Orla to a headland just north of Coco Beach, while he put a cable tie around the passenger's wrists, just in case he tried anything daft and caused them to crash. He knew the headland would be deserted at this time of night and directed Orla up the bumpy driveway off Toure Drive, until they were through the trees, to the edge of the cliff overlooking the city of Dar es Salaam, across the bay.

They got out of the car and pulled the groggy passenger out with them. They surveyed the area, it was dark and they could not see clearly across the headland. The noise of the Indian Ocean surf masked all other sounds as it crashed into the small coves, covering them in a fine mist of salty water.

Satisfied that they were alone, and would not be disturbed, they lay their captive on the rocky ground and tapped his face to wake him up. It took several taps to bring him round and as he regained consciousness he looked terrified. His head was throbbing and he could feel blood had trickled down his face to one side of his nose and had dried there.

He hadn't got a clue who these two mzungus were and had never seen them before, but the man was standing over him with what he could clearly see was a gun.

Rufus spoke in Swahili to him. "I don't want to hurt you, but I am quite prepared and capable of subjecting you to the most excruciating pain if you do not answer my questions. Do you understand me?"

"Yes. Yes," said the petrified man.

"What is your name?"

"Sendoro Mashashi."

"What is the name of the man you met at the bar?"

"What man?"

Rufus rolled Sendoro over and snapped his little finger, causing him to scream in pain. He rolled him back and asked the question again.

"Wisdom Mwakimbwla," came the instant reply through sobs of agony.

"What did you talk about?"

Sendoro hesitated for a fraction of a second, but his will had disappeared: if this lunatic was prepared to break his finger for asking a question, what else would he do?

"He told me that he is going to his yacht in the bay this evening and that I must be ready to go to him at any time he phones me. He said he didn't know how long he would be because he has to go to an important meeting on the yacht where the mzungus can't listen to what they have to say. He said I should be there ten minutes after his phone call to drive somebody away from the meeting."

"Which bay?"

"Masaki bay."

"What is the name of the yacht?"

"I think it is called 'Lazy Days'"

"What type of boat is it?"

"I don't know what you call it. It is like two boats in one."

"You mean it is as big as two boats or has two hulls, two parts that go in the water and are joined in the middle?"

"Yes that's it."

"What is the man's name?"

"He didn't say," said Sendoro, looking up with fear in his eyes. "Honestly, he didn't say who it was, just that it is somebody important."

"Where have you got to go?"

"I don't know, I think it is somewhere a long way away because Mr Wisdom said to be prepared to be away from home for a few days and to ensure the car was full of fuel."

"He spoke to you for long time, what else did he say?"

"He just told me to clean my car up and be sure that I was polite and drive well as my passenger would be a very important one, who could make Mr Wisdom a lot of money."

"Where is the man from?"

"I don't know, I didn't ask and he didn't tell me."

"Is the man a mzungu?"

"He didn't say, I don't know. You don't ask questions of men like Mr Wisdom."

"What else did you talk about?"

"Nothing, honestly. We spoke about Man U and Arsenal, I support Arsenal and he supports Man U."

"How much is he paying you?"

"$20."

"Here's $50, to replace your phone and because you are not going to get there."

"But Mr Wisdom will kill me if I don't get there," implored Sendoro.

Rufus shoved the $50 bill into Sendoro's pocket, picked him up onto his shoulder for the second time in an hour and walked towards the taxi. Orla opened the boot and Rufus gently placed Sendoro in the small space available.

"We won't leave you here long," said Rufus as he shut to boot lid.

They didn't want to risk driving the stolen taxi any longer, so they walked back down the short driveway to the road and hailed the first bajaj that came along after just a couple of minutes. They rushed back to the Chichi hotel, telling the driver to wait for them, grabbed a few things they thought they would need and went back to their ride.

The bajaj driver got them to the Slipway complex overlooking Masaki Bay, they paid him and went down the steps towards the ocean. They walked through the shops, cafes and restaurants and along the man-made jetty. Orla pointed towards a yacht, which was anchored about two hundred yards away, lights illuminating its deck. It was the only yacht in the bay with its lights on and Orla trained her camera, a Nikon D3 DSLR with an 80-400 VR lens on the yacht. She checked her settings for the darkness: choosing an ISO of 6400 to allow the maximum amount of light.

"It's a catamaran," she said. "Its bow is facing us, so I can't see the name. But it must be Lazy Days." She continued to watch, as Rufus prepared his equipment.

Orla took her small tri-pod from her back pack, placed the camera on it, attached her cable release and secured it for steadiness, focused on the boat and started photographing the scene, just trying to get the name.

Eventually the boat came around to the stern under the influence of the gentle current and light breeze and she could see Lazy Days inscribed across the width of the stern.

"That's our boat," said Orla. She continued to keep observations on the yacht and take photographs as Rufus hopped over the wall reappearing a few minutes dressed in a camouflaged lightweight full body-swimming suit. He didn't need it for the temperature, just to break up his shape in the water. The makers claim that it makes the diver invisible, even from a few feet away.

He took the kit that Orla had put into waterproof zip-lock bags, and silently entered the still warm water. He swam effortlessly and invisibly towards the catamaran, trying to disturb the water as little as possible as he approached. He could hear the voices carrying across the water, and the unmistakable sound of people drinking.

Orla checked she was alone and tried to call Don, but the signal had gone. She took the opportunity to take more photographs of the yacht and the people on board.

Rufus could see lookouts on the boat, and used the shadows of the other moored boats as cover as he inched his way towards the boat, like a crocodile stalking a wildebeest at a watering hole.

It took him over thirty minutes to cover the two hundred metres, which he could swim in three minutes under normal circumstances. He reached the stern and he slid imperceptibly into the relative safety between the twin hulls, out of sight of any prying eyes.

He scanned the hulls, and the underside of the deck, checking for any glint of a lens that might be spying on him. He stayed there silent and invisible for the next ten minutes, knowing that if they did have a camera, or had seen him approaching, they would show their hand pretty quickly.

He started to relax slightly as everything appeared to be normal up on deck; no raised voices, no unusual activity. He concluded he must be safe for the moment.

He swum to the inspection hatch built into the deck of the catamaran: a clear Perspex base, topped by a honeycomb plastic insert, fitting snugly into the deck. Rufus trod water as he got out a multi tool that Orla had given him. He fitted the screwdriver into the slots of the retaining arms keeping the latches in place and gently turned them to release the Perspex base. He was able to grab both edges of the hanging Perspex and pull himself high enough out of the water to listen to the voices.

He could hear them talking, seemingly at the other end of the deck. He kept his grip and used his head to push the honeycomb insert gently upwards; just enough to give him a view. He changed his grip, as he was now able to hold onto the sides of the hatch. Nobody was looking his way. The guards were looking outwards, away from the boat for any approaching danger, and five men were having an animated discussion. He recognised one of them as James, or as he now knew him Wisdom Mwakimbwla. They were speaking incredibly quickly even for Rufus and he struggled to fully understand the conversation, but he picked up snippets about $1 and $2 million, about hostages, and al-Shabab. He guessed they were haggling about payment terms.

What he didn't know was that one of the other men was Sheikh Moktar Ali Hashi Farah known as Abu Faud, one of the leaders of al-Shabaab. Abu Faud was a particularly ruthless man from the Hawiye Clan. Abu Faud was intent on becoming the Amir of the whole al-Shabaab network. He was a very well-educated man, fluent in Arabic, Swahili, English and French, held a medical doctorate from Cairo University, which led to him becoming a surgeon, and had joined the Red Crescent to help in war zones.

He was determined to become an ally of the reported leader of al-Qaida: Mahfouz Kamel Wasfi, who believed that a vanguard of true Muslims modeling itself after the original Companions of the Prophet had to be developed. That this precursor would crystalise and mobilise all true Muslims in their right and just war against the west. Abu Faud wanted to be a part of that glorious group, earning himself a place in Islamic folklore and legend as well as a fortune along the way.

Chapter Thirty-Nine

Rufus changed his grip back to the Perspex and let the honeycomb settle back into place, steadied himself with one hand and took a bug out of his zip-lock bag, fixed it on the inside of one of the honeycomb sections. He couldn't do a signal test with Don, and just had to hope for the best on this one.

As he was finishing off attaching the bug, one of the guards looked towards his position.

Has he seen me?

Rufus remained completely still, holding his body weight almost out of the water with one hand. Fortunately the water was warm and calm which made it slightly easier.

The guard came slowly down the deck, looking about him, listening.

Rufus was sure he hadn't made a sound. There was no way the guard could have heard him. The slight movement of the honeycomb might have caught his eye, but he wasn't looking at the inspection cover. *So what's brought you down here?*

His grip was beginning to ease. He could see the guard standing right above him. If he looked down he would have to be blind not to see him, and if he didn't notice him, he might spot the small irregularity in the honeycomb that would be glaringly obvious until he replaced the Perspex.

Rufus eyed the guard's weapon: the ubiquitous AK47, capable of emptying its thirty rounds from the iconic curved magazine in three seconds. At this distance they would scythe him in half – if the guard looked down.

His curiosity about the guard's motives was answered as Rufus saw him surreptitiously look back to the stern where the conversations were taking place and put something in his pocket. Rufus couldn't see what it was and wasn't too bothered either, he just wanted the guard to go, but he continued to stand directly above him.

He had to make a decision: stay where he was and hope his motionless position would make him less visible, or risk the slight movement.

Rufus let go of the Perspex cover and slid silently back into the water, edging back towards the stern and the darkness. He hadn't had time to re-secure the Perspex to protect the honeycomb, which meant the bug would be exposed to the water and spray. The bug was in a place where he doubted it would capture much dialogue anyway, but it could act as a locator for Don, so he had to make sure his efforts weren't totally wasted.

He stayed in the darkness, waiting for any reaction from the guards. There was none. He waited until he saw the shadow of the guard disappear and slowly moved back to the hatch and very slowly closed it, securing the retaining clips in place. When he had finished, he could see the full moon was rising, giving the water a silver sheen, illuminating it so well that if he swum directly back to Orla he would be a big target in the water. Even though the makers made their claim of invisibility, he didn't want to test it with his life. He decided to head off at a tangent so the reflection from the moon didn't expose him, he swum slowly and carefully, making as few ripples and as little noise as possible.

He got back to Orla and dried and dressed himself in seconds, while giving her a resume of what had happened.

"I was able to get quite a few shots, pretty good quality too," she said with a certain amount of professional pride.

She phoned Don again, getting through on the seventh attempt.

"At last. This bloody phone system here is totally u.s. Hello love. How are you?"

"Yeh great darling', but I have to agree with you about the phone system there. What's the update?"

"There's been a change of plan and Rufus has placed the device on a boat, where we have just seen a meeting taking place. We were told they met on the boat so they couldn't be overheard or bugged."

"Ok. I'll do a signal strength test as soon as we get off the phone, but don't hold your breath, it's just so erratic."

"Ok. It's a fluid situation here, so we'll have to remain quite flexible with our planning and tactics."

"No change there then."

"Guess not, but we normally have pretty good comms to keep you updated, it just took me seven tries to get through to you. Bit like being in the same room with you really."

"HA! I'll have to go on one of Pebble's 'listening' courses then won't I?"

"Seriously, we'll try and keep you in the loop, but it might be difficult."

"Ok. I understand and I'll get back to you in a few minutes with an update on the device."

Rufus and Orla quickly discussed tactics: whether to follow the Somalis, they ruled this one out, as Sendoro had told them he was going on a long journey and as good as Orla is, she couldn't follow a car on her own, on empty roads for hundreds of miles; should they follow Wisdom, as they now knew him? Or should they follow one of the others coming off the boat? Rufus hadn't seen any mzungus on the boat, and the surveillance team was mainly white, and if his hunch was right, British. This would just be pot luck. They decided to tail Wisdom and see if he took them to a new stronghold. They settled down for the wait.

They saw the small dingy leave the catamaran with Abu Faud and the other Somalis on board. If they had known how important Abu Faud was there would have been little hesitation, as his presence was ominous, but they didn't know and they couldn't have guessed. They stayed in the shadows while Orla snapped away getting some more good photographs.

The Somalis walked out of sight, clearly expecting their ride to be waiting for them. They returned to the shorline a few minutes later, on the phone, presumably asking Wisdom where their promised ride was. Orla and Rufus decided to walk down the jetty, arm in arm, giving the appearance of having had an amorous evening on the end of the jetty.

As they approached the two men Rufus could hear the man who was clearly the leader of the group, speaking in Swahili on the phone.

"It had better be here in ten minutes – you assured me that one of your men would be waiting."

About fifteen minutes later, Abu Faud and his entourage walked through the courtyard area of Slipway, up the steps and disappeared. Orla and Rufus could still see Lazy Days from where they were but they were left ruing their decision when they saw the yacht weigh anchor and sail off into the night.

It was just after 11pm and Rufus felt like something to eat again. They couldn't do anything else now so he suggested they go to QBar, a local bordello, where some beautiful local girls ply their trade, catering almost exclusively for the mzungu clientele and Rufus knew they served surprisingly good food until the early hours.

"I'm not going to a brothel," said Orla.

"Trust me," said Rufus, "you'll love it, and I promise the food is really good."

"I'm going to kill you for this Stone. I've never been in a brothel in my life."

"I shouldn't think you have, but put it on your bucket list, it's something everybody should do at least once in their lives."

They caught a bajaj from Slipway and were at QBar in a few minutes. Orla walked in to the pub/club, which was surprisingly similar to the Hongera Bar, partly covered and partly open air.

A DJ was in the corner playing music; several TVs were on the walls some showing English Premier League Football, South African Rugby on others; a game of pool was being played at a table adjacent to the dance floor which was occupied by what she thought were drop-dead gorgeous girls trying to make eye contact with the men.

"It's just like a sports bar back home," she shouted down Rufus's ear.

The front half of the establishment was open air, with stairs on the side leading up to a balcony and hourly rate rooms upstairs, which was what provided a roof for the rear of the premises.

She watched the steady traffic of girls and punters travel up and down the stairs, unashamedly using the facilities.

They got themselves a table undercover and ordered some soft drinks and pasta dishes. While they were waiting Orla got up and danced. At first she was worried what the reaction of the working girls would be, but they were friendly enough, they were used to mzungu women coming in and they realised they weren't trying to steal their trade, or come on to them, so they were no problem. A couple of the girls even danced with Orla, admiring her moves to the oldies that were being played.

"This is a great place," she said, sitting down when she saw the waiter bring the food. "Mmmmmm this is REALLY good, I'm amazed," she said through a mouthful of food, and then nearly choked as she looked up towards the entrance.

Converse walked into the club along with another guy they had not seen before. Rufus had his back to them and relied on Orla giving a commentary. They went to the bar and appeared to be very relaxed ordering their drinks and looking lasciviously at the hookers.

The girls recognised the "look" straightaway; their radar set to pick up the tell-tale signals of a genuinely interested man, and were round the two men like bees around honey. At this late hour the girls were often tempted to do a two for one offer and the guys were too busy assessing which one, or two, each of them should have, to look in the direction of Orla and Rufus, but she still kept a very discreet watch even so.

She christened this other guy Turkish, as he looked like the Jason Statham character of the same name and kept Rufus updated, leaning into him across the table.

Rufus had switched back on after he allowed himself to relax for a few minutes and was surveying the rest of the room for any colleagues of the two guys that he might have missed; he was relieved to see that he had not missed anybody. As he had told Victoria at the very start, he would not endanger her mum and dad's lives, so he always had to play with one hand behind his back. In other circumstances it would have been easy to interrupt one of them while they were otherwise engaged with the girls and get the information out of them, but he still didn't know what the connection was between this group and the kidnap group.

He kept his back to them and continued to eat, while Orla kept them under observation. Fortunately, it appeared that both men agreed a price for two girls each and walked up the open stairs to the "guest bedrooms". Orla was a little taken aback at the brazenness of the whole thing, walking up the stairs in full view of everybody, never imagining that it was that easy.

"Have you ever been with a prostitute Ru?" she asked as she watched their legs disappear out of sight.

Rufus was half ready for the question, and despite all the years of military service and all the places he had been, he looked Orla in the eye and answered honestly,

"No."

"I think I'd kill Don if I found out he'd been with one," she said.

"Why? If he had, and I'm not saying he has, before he met you, it's not a crime, the girls get paid and the guy gets his rocks off." Rufus said, playing devil's advocate.

"So why have you never used one?"

"I've never felt the need to, but I don't denigrate the girls or anybody that wants to use them, they perform a public service somewhere like here, in my opinion."

"It's wrong selling your body for sex, they can't get any pleasure out of it."

"I don't claim that they do, just like many people don't get any pleasure out of their work, because that's what it is, work – a way to make a living and they are using their natural attributes to their best effect."

"I'd still kill him," she said ending the conversation.

They took the opportunity to pay their bill and leave for the Chichi Hotel.

"I'm really surprised,." said Orla when they were in the taxi.

"What about?"

"Well two things really. How good the place was, I expected it to be a seedy joint with creepy men and half naked ugly women with porn showing everywhere, and it was nothing like that, but also how brazen men are – there just doesn't seem to be any shame at all, no embarrassment, they just pick a girl or two and go and shag 'em."

"They don't always shag them. Sometimes they will just want the girls to put on a bit of girl-on-girl show for them."

"And the girls will do that?"

"Yeh, why not if the punter is paying them good money. It means nothing to the girls, just like shagging a punter – in fact, it might be preferable for some of them," he said smiling,

"You're dead right there Ru," she agreed, thinking about some of the sizes and shapes of men she'd seen.

They reached the hotel and entered their room, checking their counter measures were still in place. Orla stripped down to her underwear and got into bed. Rufus washed his jockey shorts in the bath with soap and water, put his other pair on and got into bed with her.

"I'll take the first couple of hours if you like? I'll bet you are shattered aren't you?" he said as he climbed in next to her.

"I am a bit, think I'm still a little jet lagged." she kissed her finger tips, put them to his cheek, rolled over and fell asleep.

They took turns in "stagging" through the rest of night, just in case it was no coincidence that Converse and Turkish had appeared. But the night past uneventfully and they managed a reasonable night's sleep.

Chapter Forty

Victoria was not having such a good night's sleep at Butiama. She had been met at the air-strip, just like Rufus had told her, and Moez had immediately phoned him to let him know that she was safe. Moez handed the phone to Victoria and they had chatted for a few minutes and she was surprised that Rufus sounded genuinely pleased to hear her voice.

She would usually have loved the drive through traditional villages to the lodge, consisting of small one roomed huts, with thatched roofs. Small corrals, made from branches of trees, interlaced to create a fence for the livestock, children playing in the gardens and road who ran to their Land Rover waving at her. Their smiling and joyous faces brightened her spirits temporarily. Fruit and vegetables built up into little pyramids in the traditional style, for sale, displayed at the front of the houses. Women in traditional dress, balancing loads on their heads and their babies strapped on their backs, other women and children down at the river bank either collecting water or washing the clothes.

This was how she imagined Africa, not the sprawling conurbation of Dar. She was frustrated that she could not enjoy the scenery and views because she was preoccupied with thoughts of her parents.

"Has Ru sent many friends over here?" she eventually asked as casually as she could.

"Some yes, they were mainly buddies from the regiment who needed to get away from it all. I never asked why, it was none of my business."

"Anybody like me?"

"Like you? No not that I can think of... he has recommended us to a few friends and alike, but nobody like you. Tanzania is a peaceful, safe place and this is the first time he has asked me to help like this."

Victoria wanted to ask him directly "Has he brought any women over?" but she didn't know how to, and anyway they were just arriving at Butiama.

She was taken aback by the beautiful resort. It was as if she went through some sort of force field when they drove through the gates, which slowed time down and made everything more tranquil and peaceful.

Maura came out of the small, informal reception to greet Victoria; she couldn't imagine what the poor young woman was going through and gave her a genuinely warm hug. They walked her down the sand covered passageways, where bare feet were certainly de rigour, to a circular thatched bar. Moez ordered her a fruit juice from the barman, while Victoria looked out the across the private beach to the ocean. It really was paradise, just like Rufus had said. No noise, no traffic, white beaches and palm trees, she lost herself for a few seconds wondering what it would be like to spend a few days here.

Maura and Moez seemed to have thought of everything to make their guests' stay a relaxing, enjoyable one, with the emphasis being on relaxation.

Maura disturbed Victoria's reverie when she approached and showed her to her banda, which was beautiful: Victoria approached the thatched cottage along more white sandy paths. At the steps to the patio there was a foot bath to remove the sand, leading to wooden decking with a hammock, and wicker chairs and tables. The double doors opened to a simple, but tastefully decorated room, which Victoria just knew was the work of Maura.

"Oh Maura, it's beautiful. You are so kind, letting me come to stay."

"It's our pleasure. Any friend of Ru's is a friend of ours." After Maura explained the facilities of the room, she could see Victoria was tired and took her leave. "I'll leave you to sort yourself out. See you a little later."

Victoria was asleep on the bed before Maura was back at the reception. She woke a little while later, picked up the complimentary beach bag and towel and walked the short distance to the beach.

It was straight out of a holiday magazine: white sandy beach, flanked by palm trees on one side and a clear ocean on the other; small fishing vessels were moored just off shore and men in dug-out canoes, using home-made masks and spears were paddling out to the ocean to catch dinner for their family, or if they were really lucky, to sell.

She put her possessions down, perfectly happy that they would be safe on the beach and walked into the sea. It was unbelievable; so clear and warm. She could see shoals of fish within grabbing distance, and crabs, which she gave a wide birth, foraging on the bottom.

She decided to take a leaf out of Rufus's book and swim hard for thirty minutes, feeling her muscles begin to ache, her breathing hard, as she changed from five strokes per breath to three, alternating her breathing the way she had been taught. The exercise felt good: she felt like she had blown some cobwebs out of her system and while she swum, she thought.

Maura joined her for dinner while Moez performed the duties with the other guests, ensuring their stay was as pleasurable as possible.

They ate a delicious dinner of fresh red snapper, caught by one of the fishermen Victoria had seen paddling out to sea a few hours earlier, and expertly cooked by the chefs. Victoria looked around the beautiful restaurant, with a sandy floor and thatched roof exposed to the open air and connected to the bar by a covered walkway massaged by a gentle breeze coming off the water.

She felt guilty that she was such poor company at dinner, despite Maura's best efforts, and went to bed early, feeling helpless and hopeless. She was reliving all the things that had gone on over the past few days and trying to make sense of it all, and erase some of it from her mind at the same time. The more she tried to forget it, the more it came back to the forefront of her mind.

The flight over had been lovely and had distracted her slightly, as she travelled across the azure sea to Mafia, but it couldn't dispel the feeling of doubt that had taken hold of her.

Why was Ru so insistent that I came out here to get out of the way? What is he doing? What has he got to hide? Why did he hide Orla's presence? Why did they have to kill those men who attacked us? What if they were trying to rescue me from Ru and they weren't attacking at all but rescuing me? Stop it, you're being silly, Ru and Orla are here to help you. Those guys were shooting at us. You saw them ram you off the road and shoot at you. They tried to kill us. They nearly succeeded, but why? What is going on?

She tossed and turned and tried to get back to sleep, but the warmth and the sound of waves rolling in, instead of soothing her, annoyed her so much she eventually got up, slipped on some shorts and a T-shirt and walked outside.

The night sky was spectacular. She had travelled quite a lot in her short life: most recently to India. She looked up and saw a celestial display like she had never seen before. Stars so clear; the moon so bright it cast clear, defined shadows on the white sand. She lay back and took in the enormity of the sky, imagining she was a Greek or Egyptian astronomer, trying to dispel all of her troublesome thoughts about her parents and Rufus.

As her eyes adjusted themselves she could see a figure in the shadows of the palm trees.

She was sure there was somebody there. The shadows moved in the gentle breeze, camouflaging her assailant's shadow. The rustling of the leaves and the waves gently lapping the shore masked any sounds he was making.

The temperature suddenly dropped a couple of degrees and she shivered for the first time.

The shadow was still and silent and appeared to be looking her way. She froze, rueing her decision to lie on the bright white sand as it emphasised her presence. The figure started coming towards her out of the shadows. She froze and held her breath, contemplating her best course of action. *Ru told me I was safe here. What to do: fight or flight?*

They had guns. *No point fighting.*

She would never outrun a man, especially on this sand, and where would she run? Her heart was beating so loud she could hear and feel it, through her chest.

Despite shivering, she started to sweat, panic rising in her.

To get to Moez and Maura's house she would have to run past him. Impossible.

Run into the sea? Where would she swim?

She lay there, motionless, hoping he hadn't seen her; that by some pure fluke the assassin was making his way to her banda to kill her in her sleep.

She watched, trying to quieten her deafening heartbeat and rasping breathing, but surely he could hear her.

The figure drew closer, staying in the shadows of the swaying palms. The wind gently blew the few wisps of clouds across the moon. As the silent attacker came out of the shadows onto the white sand, the moon light cast his shadow clearly, alerting the crabs, making them scurry back to their holes as he approached her. There was no mistake he was definitely coming towards her.

"Can't you sleep?" he asked as he got closer.

Victoria let out a big sigh of relief as she realised it was Moez, watching out for her, looking after her, the way Rufus had said he would.

"Oh Moez, thank God it's you."

"Who did you think it was?" asked Moez.

"Oh I don't know. I am seeing conspiracies and danger in everything now. I can't help it. I don't know who I can trust, who to believe. What to do. When I listen to Rufus he makes sense to me and I believe in him, but when I start thinking I just get confused. Why doesn't he just get the money and pay them to get my mum and dad back? Why do we have to go through all of these games? And why didn't he tell me about Orla? And why has he sent me up here out of the way?"

"Have you spoken to Ru about all this?"

"Yes, well no, no I haven't because I feel bad about doubting him, about questioning his judgment. I'd feel embarrassed."

"Don't feel embarrassed. Ru is used to brutal honesty. We were taught and still believe that the only way to continually improve is for complete honesty. If something is not good enough, he has to be told. If he hasn't done his job properly, if you don't believe in him unconditionally, then he needs to know and he needs to know why and how he can improve. He would be more upset that you haven't told him."

"I know, I know. I understand everything you've told me, that's what Ru has said as well, but it is still embarrassing to tell somebody that you don't trust them, or you don't think they have done their job properly."

"So how is he supposed to know then? Osmosis? Unless you tell him he won't know, he will think you are happy with the way things are going."

"You're right, I know you are, and I will talk to him later today when I get back to Dar, I promise. And I DO trust him; everything he has done and said has been spot on. He saved my life earlier today when we were attacked. It's just that, well I don't know, everything is so confusing."

"And you think he wouldn't understand that?"

"I know he does, I know he and Orla are doing a fantastic job, and they are brilliant and superb and brave and clever and everything I would want them to be, but I'm scared."

"You have every right to be scared Victoria. Rufus is one of the bravest and best men I have ever met, he has experienced more trauma and drama than any man has a right to. He is honest and ethical and he will be doing his very best to get your mum and dad back. It is more a matter of honour for him, he has promised to help you and he will, or he will die trying. I don't know Orla, but if Ru and Don trust her, then I do, without reservation, absolutely and unconditionally. Believe them, trust them and do exactly what they say."

Victoria buried her head into Moez's shoulder, to thank him for his words. For confirming what deep down she knew. She just had to trust her instincts. Another man was saying exactly what she thought about Rufus, and yet she still didn't understand what was going on. That was the problem: the confusion, everything seemed to be masked by something else, nothing was what it seemed.

She sat upright and pulled away from Moez slightly.

"Oh Moez I'm sorry, I'm sorry to be a nuisance to you and Maura. I'm sorry I said that about Rufus, who you clearly hold in the highest esteem. I will speak to both of them tomorrow and explain my feelings and doubts and anxieties. Thank you."

"Well done. They will thank you for it and they WILL understand. Now let's turn in."

Moez gave Victoria a hand, pulled her to her feet and walked her back to her banda.

"If I'm right, you are going to have a busy day ahead of you. So in the morning I've arranged a special treat for you. If it doesn't take your mind off what's happening, then nothing will."

"Oh Moez, I really don't know if I feel like doing anything, I just want to get my mum and dad back."

"Trust me Victoria, this is special. Now you get some sleep and I promise I'll stay awake for you and keep an eye on your banda."

She went to bed and this time the metronomic rolling of the waves gently rocked her to sleep, for a blissful few hours.

Moez stood guard over her all night, staying awake and alert. He knew she was safe, no one could get to the island without him knowing, they were in the middle of the ocean but he did as he promised and remained vigilant and alert throughout the rest of the uneventful night.

Chapter Forty-One

The next morning heralded a fresh start for Victoria. The sun was shining, the ocean was sparkling and shimmering; the changes in hues showing the reefs and alterations in depth in the waters. Victoria walked from her banda and straight into the ocean, amazed by how warm it was so early in the morning. As she swum in the beautiful waters she could see Moez sat in the open air bar and she wondered what favour or service Rufus had done for Moez or Maura to engender such loyalty to him. As she swum she thought about everything that had happened and realised that Moez, Rufus, Don and Orla were of the same mould: determined, honest, resourceful and she realised that she could trust Rufus with her and her parents' lives. As the ocean washed over her, it seemed to wash away her doubts and she resolved to tell Rufus about all her anxieties and concerns.

She walked out of the ocean, straight into the bar.

"Did you enjoy that?" asked Moez.

"It's amazing, so warm and still and clear."

"Breakfast, Victoria," called Maura a little way up the sandy path to the restaurant.

"You'd better have something Victoria, I'm taking you swimming with Whale Sharks and it's better to have something in your stomach."

"Whale Sharks? Are you kidding me? I'm not getting in the water with sharks, are you mad?"

"Trust me Victoria, it is perfectly safe, they are plankton eaters. You will love it."

"Good morning Victoria," said Maura as they reached her. She gave Victoria a kiss on the cheek. "Did you get back to sleep?"

"Yes thanks to Moez. This is such a beautiful place you have here."

"Thank you, we enjoy it. Now, help yourself to the buffet and Jason will be over in a minute to take your order."

Victoria and Maura made small talk while she ate, and Moez sorted out the boat to take them to sea.

Thirty minutes later, she was skimming across the water on her own privately guided excursion.

"The main school arrives in November, but for some reason we have this small one come through at this time of year. They always come to this spot, rather than the main channel between us and the mainland, where they feed. We don't advertise this because we think they might be mating and don't want to disturb them. In November there are boat loads of tourists jumping in the water with them," explained Moez.

After a few minutes, Victoria saw an enormous fin break the water, followed by another, and another. "Oh my God, they are everywhere."

"Yeh, the trick is to predict where they are going to get in front of them." He spoke in Swahili to the young man manning the boat and directed him to point where he thought the Sharks would be heading, the crew-hand opened the throttle and skirted around the sharks to intercept their path.

Moez stopped the engine and rolled backwards into the water. He surfaced. "Come on Victoria, if you come in this side, you'll have a great view," came the nasally instruction, caused by the mask blocking his nose as he trod water.

She entered the water and was immediately rewarded by a four-metre long shark gliding towards her, its enormous mouth wide open filtering the plankton. For some reason, it didn't look threatening, she thought she would be anxious, but something about the giant animal made her realise it meant her no harm. As more of the majestic animals appeared, she squealed with delight, dived down after them and actually touched one of them. It was unbelievable.

She wondered if Moez had done this on purpose, to make her think of Rufus as a Whale Shark: capable, if he wanted, of doing her tremendous harm, but no intention of doing so; somebody with whom she was safe and should have no worries.

After an exhilarating hour, in which they had the ocean to themselves they returned to Butiama and Victoria prepared to leave.

She hugged Maura as she waited to get in the Land Rover and promised she would be back, sometime, somehow, under different circumstances.

She got in the Land Rover with Moez and completed the return journey to the airstrip. She couldn't thank Moez enough and started to cry with emotion. She couldn't believe how many times she had cried in the last few days, but this time it was with happiness and resolve: a determination that she was going to get the bastards that were holding her parents.

"Your parents will be ok Victoria. Ru will do everything in his power to get them back safely for you. He is a very resourceful, extraordinary man and I would rather have him with me, than ten ordinary men, any day."

"Thank you Moez. Thank you for the comforting words, and thank you for looking after me so well. I told Maura I will be back, and I will." She hugged Moez and walked into the small building for her flight back to Dar.

+++++++

Martyn was not having such a good time as his daughter. He was not reacting well at all to solitary confinement. He had read out the preprepared script into the camera and tried to make it as monotone as possible, to give the message that he wasn't being well treated, or with any dignity and didn't mean what he said. His captors had made him do it again and again, beating him about the body. When they held a gun to his head, his feeble resistance had faded away and he gave it his best shot. He just hoped that Victoria and all his friends and family would know he was lying and being forced to say these things. He had been bundled back into his cell immediately afterwards, even though he had begged them to let him spend some time with Deidre. He was crying, pleading to let him stay in the light with some human contact, but they threw him back in his cell without saying a word.

A short time later, he could hear a commotion outside his room, with lots of shouting and rushing around. He didn't know what was happening, but it didn't sound good. His door was flung open and he was ordered out at gunpoint. He could see a crate by the door and it was indicated that he should get in. As soon as he curled himself up into the box, the lid was hammered down and he felt himself unceremoniously lifted up and put down again. It wasn't until he heard the engine start up and felt the vibrations of the motor he realised he had been placed on some sort of vehicle. The movement confirmed what he thought and he tried to imagine the route they were taking.

He had seen films where the hostage hears distinctive noises and works out where they are, but he couldn't do anything like that. He didn't know where he was in the first place, to even begin to know where he was being taken.

After what seemed to be a short trip he felt his crate being lifted and moved again. When he heard the nails being prised off the top of it he decided to spring up and attack his captors, reasoning that he would have the element of surprise, and what was the worst that could happen? They could shoot him, and at the moment that didn't seem like a bad option.

As they began to lift the lid he launched himself upwards, but his old muscles were withered and weak. His joints were stiff and he sprung with all the power of the little old man that he was fast becoming.

The guards didn't even raise their guns, but took him by the arms and shoved him into his new cell. Not that he could tell it was a new cell. It was pitch-black and seemed identical to the last one. He slumped to the floor, crying, feeling pathetic and sorry for himself. He thought of Victoria and she gave him some strength. He must be strong for her. She was still their baby and she would be going through hell when she saw the video.

He got himself up and decided he had to be physically and mentally strong for her and began to plan a strategy to keep his body and mind active. He remembered some exercises from his yoga classes and planned an exercise regime. He tried to think of the positives of the video that he had been forced to make and decided that the good things were that people would know they were alive and HMG would be doing their best to get them back.

He didn't know much about what the government did, but he was sure they would be doing something. When other British nationals had been kidnapped he had taken a mild interest in the news reports of the governmental stance and something called COBRA. He had no idea what COBRA was, or what it did, but he was aware they did something.

He had visions of teams of Special Forces assaulting the building, just like he had seen on the Iranian Embassy siege, and rescuing him and Deidre. The next moment he would lapse into depression thinking of the hostages in Beirut, such as Terry Waite, John McCarthy and Brian Keenan. He couldn't remember how long they had been held but he knew it was years. He now understood a little of what they had meant when they said they craved human contact, anything at all, even abuse was better than being isolated. His mind raced about what was happening. He still couldn't understand why Deidre had behaved the way she had. Where was she now? Where was he? Had she been moved with him, or had they been split up? He assumed they had been moved because their captors were worried they would be found. Did people know where they were?

He could hear the muffled noises of city life going on outside, but he had no idea of where he was, what time of day it was, or in fact what day it was. He tried to occupy his mind by reciting poetry and lyrics to songs.

He tried mental arithmetic and finding the highest prime number in his head. He got up to 1013 quite quickly, but he was getting frustrated that he couldn't concentrate. It seemed to take him days to get to 1481 and then quickly worked out that 1483, 1487 and 1489 were all prime numbers. He used the trial division method, but for some reason the darkness and solitude affected his ability to concentrate. First he would work out the square root in his head, so he calculated the square root of 1489 to be about 38. He then tried to divide every number from 38 down to 2 into 1489. When he found that none of these numbers would divide exactly, he moved on to 1491. He drew shapes in the air with his hands representing a long division symbol and slowly and laboriously went through every odd number not containing a 5 down from 37 until he got to 21. *Damn*, he thought, and moved on to 1493. Maths was the only brain activity he could do which would give him positive answers. If he tried to remember capital cities, he got frustrated because if he didn't know it, or had forgotten it, he couldn't work it out. He practised memory games, creating memory palaces, mnemonics, and acronyms. Every time a guard passed him food, he asked for a light and a book, but he was completely ignored. He tried to grab them, but was easily brushed aside. He was completely and utterly alone and hopeless.

Chapter Forty-Two

The same group met in the same underground, secure room as at the first COBRA meeting. They all had a briefing paper in front of them with basic details of the kidnapping to date; their own separate departmental briefing papers, including Sir Peregrine who had a comprehensive up-date from Nick Cooper.

Sir Peregrine had had the morning to consider his options: three dead, two of their contracted staff injured, plus two civilians injured, the stronghold spooked and moved, the cell siting of the phones was lost.

He had decided that the old adage of attack being the best form of defence was relevant to his circumstances and arranged a pre-meeting meeting with the minister.

"Frankly Minister, we can blame all of this... this morass, on Stone's gung-ho, maverick approach. It's a typical military reaction to a perceived threat: shoot first and ask questions later. He is responsible for all the deaths and the, not to put too fine a point on it, the almost certain murder of the kidnapped couple."

"Why would he cause this mess and draw attention to himself? Surely it is in his best interests to remain incognito?"

"One would have thought so ma'am, but my information is that he is a bit of loose cannon. To that end, I authorised Cooper to hire a local company purely to look after Miss Conway's best interests; to make sure she is safe and doesn't stumble into any unsavoury parts of Dar and to keep the F&CO and thereby HMG abreast of all the developments."

"So these dead men are part of this company working for us?" she asked.

"Yes ma'am. I can only speculate on the reasons that have driven Stone to attack the contractors in the way he has and I will ensure that the Tanzanian authorities are made aware of the full facts after Mr and Mrs Conway are either killed or recovered."

"Thank you Sir Peregrine, thank you very much. Do you think it would be more prudent for me to speak to my Tanzanian counterpart and inform him of our intelligence?"

The ever helpful Sir Peregrine had other ideas:

"I think Ma'am, given all the circumstances that it is probably better dealt with more informally, through my unofficial channels. After all, HMG doesn't want to be associated with such a mess, does it?"

"Mmmm."

"And we both know what our great British press would make of it. By the time they had finished it would look like an agent of the state is out there officially."

Unfortunately the minister believed her trusted advisor, although she didn't like him, she had never warmed to him, he always seemed to know what he was talking about, all the facts seemed to fit the circumstances as she knew them. She couldn't allow a British national to maraud around another country causing deaths and carnage without alerting the appropriate authorities.

The only two people he would have to worry about now would be Braddock from GCHQ and that up-start, Fraser.

The rest of the participants, were naturally unaware of the meeting, they didn't need to know, so they read the briefing paper to bring themselves up-to-date immediately before the start of the meeting.

Some of the other people around the table knew of the mayhem that was occurring in Dar es Salaam. All had slightly different views on the cause of the violence and deaths, but none of them, except Major Fraser, knew the details.They didn't have eyes and ears on the ground to give them a full account, but while none of them, except the politicians, civil servants and Stringer believed what they read, they hadn't got any details to challenge the account.

Mad Frankie Fraser, had received information from Don via DSF, and didn't believe a single word of the document, but had not had enough warning to carry out any research of his own. The old spy had deliberately withheld the information until the last minute, claiming it was a 'dynamic situation'.

He had been told by his SF channels, that Rufus, supported by Orla, in country, and Don in the UK had made contact with the kidnappers and were agreeing a much reduced fee.

He knew that they had encountered some local difficulties and he also knew, without a shadow of doubt, that they would not go on the rampage the way it was being reported. They would not want to draw attention to themselves; it was against all their training and procedures. He knew all three of them, knew their professionalism and capabilities, he had even put work their way.

He made a mental note to contact Don directly at the end of the meeting to get a full account from the horse's mouth, rather than through official channels, when things get misrepresented, or sanitised. But for the moment, he could not argue without any degree of knowledge that the 'facts' being presented to them were wrong.

Dame Cunningham-Black opened the meeting, with the customary formalities and asked Sir Peregrine to update the meeting verbally, which he reluctantly did in his droll manner, as if he was talking to a class of eleven year olds.

He finished without inviting questions.

"I don't believe it ma'am," said Major Fraser. "I know these guys and that is completely out of character."

"Major," Sir Peregrine said sneeringly through gritted teeth, "we all know the pressures our Special Forces are under and the magnificent job you do," Mad Frankie knew that there was a 'but' coming to negate what he had just said, "but even our Special Forces are human and fallible. There have been numerous reported cases, and some not so well reported, when ex regimental troopers have lost control of their faculties. Now far be it from me to suggest that this is the case in this instance, but the facts do seem to suggest that Stone has lost sight of his primary objective. Res ipsa loquiter."

"No the facts don't speak for themselves – the Sigint doesn't support your supposition. There is a lot..."

"I know what the Sigint is saying," Dennis said cutting across Robert Braddock, "and it is misleading, it doesn't support the Humint I am receiving from my staff on the ground. Now that may be to do with the vagaries of the Tanzanian network, or it might be to do with the red herrings being drawn across your path by the terrorists and Stone with his team. Am I right in understanding that you have now lost the intercept on Stone's and Miss Conway's phones?

"Well yes, but..."

"And am I right in understanding that you had identified the stronghold to a block of three buildings?"

"Yes and we..."

"And am I right in understanding that due to Stone's precipitative actions the stronghold has been relocated to an as yet unknown location?"

"Yes, it has moved but we don't..."

"So, far from discrediting our observations and intelligence gathering on the ground, you are actually supporting our postulation."

Most of the police detectives in the meeting knew Dennis was making the facts fit the hypothesis, not the other way round as they were trained to, but didn't know the reason. They all decided that it was none of their business, a little internal spat, in which they could only see one winner, and so kept quiet.

Major Fraser knew he had to gather hard intelligence before he spoke again and had to rule out gut feelings and knowing how Orla and Rufus operated. If the truth be known, he hadn't worked with them for at least eighteen months and he could not justify what he was saying. It didn't change his view though, but he concluded that he would rather lose this battle in order to win the war, which he knew he was going to have with Sir Peregrine Fucking Dennis.

The only person in the room unaware of the Machiavellian machinations taking place was Detective Superintendent Stringbag Stringer. His radar was not attuned to the politics of Whitehall and the internecine warfare that was taking place in front of him.

"Ma'am as you are aware, I have an international cadre of police negotiators who I could deploy to Tanzania to take over the negotiations from Stone. They have been selected for..."

"Thank you Detective Superintendent," said the minister, "however, this is not a matter for Her Majesty's Government. It is, as far as I am aware, a criminal and not a political kidnapping, and therefore not part of the Joint Protocol covering kidnap. Until Miss Conway decided to report the matter to UK law enforcement, it will officially remain a private matter. A team of Scotland Yard detectives arriving in Tanzania, would put it very much in the public domain and very difficult for HMG to plausibly deny any involvement." She turned away from Stringer and addressed Mad Frankie. "Major Fraser, don't worry, this doesn't affect your preparations and things should continue as planned."

"Thank you ma'am," replied Mad Frankie, who felt madder than ever at the moment, but was keeping his infamous temper under control. Just.

"In view of the events in Tanzania, we will reconvene at the same time the day after tomorrow," said Dame Cunningham-Black.

Chapter Forty-Three

Orla and Rufus made the most of their chance to have a lie-in and catch up on some sleep. They had still stagged each other all night, effectively halving the sleep they appeared to have, but it was still twice as much as they were used to. They lay in the same bed again, with no thought of one of them taking the chair to sleep on, and no thought of each other sexually. The night past uneventfully letting them relax a little.

When they eventually got up, they carried out their individual training regimes, to keep up their fitness, core strength and suppleness.

They breakfasted and reviewed everything with Don. They had taken a few steps forward and a couple of steps backwards, but they found reviewing their actions and intelligence was both beneficial to their understanding of what was happening, and ensured they were all singing from the same sheet.

They arranged a hire car through Dolores on reception at the Chichi, which Rufus paid for by cash, showing his American alias to book the car, choosing something standard, that wouldn't stand out: a white Toyota Corolla, which suited their purposes perfectly.

They left the Chichi a little later allowing for the Dar traffic to get to the bank to pick up the prearranged cash that Don had organised through the insurance company. It was a lot of money to withdraw in one transaction and the bank had needed two days' notice to arrange it. Rufus was asked for several forms of identification in order for the bank to release $50 000, and at one point he thought they were going to refuse to give him the money. He had to see three different managers until it was eventually sorted out. None of the managers wanted to make the decision one way or the other, preferring the senior manager there to make the final call. After what seemed like an eternity they were on their way to pick Victoria up from the airport.

They pulled into the car park, unopposed and noticed that the taxi they had 'borrowed' the previous day had gone, and they hoped the owner had got it back.

They walked into the arrivals hall, carrying the loot in a holdall, not trusting the car's security to look after that amount of money. Orla had kept a constant vigil on the rear view mirrors and was confident they hadn't been followed, but they still didn't want to leave the cash unattended. They were constantly pestered by taxi drivers offering them good rates, who wouldn't take no for an answer, and waited in the sunshine for a few minutes until they saw Victoria's plane arrive, and quickly taxi to its holding point.

The few passengers alighted from the plane and Victoria ran to meet them. She launched herself at Rufus and hugged him, and then she hugged Orla.

Orla looked over Victoria's shoulder at Rufus quizzically, and he simply shrugged his shoulders, perplexed at this show of public emotion from Victoria.

"Oh my god, I've missed you both so much," she said, machine-gun style when she finally released Orla from her grip. "I've been doing lots of thinking, and I've had some ideas, and when this is all over I want to take us all to Butiama for a holiday, it's beautiful."

Victoria's face, posture and whole demeanour changed, she'd 'switched on' as she said.

"We've been busy Victoria," said Orla. "We identified a place where we think your mum and dad WERE being held."

"WERE?"

"Yes, we got there too late. But there is more good news. We've identified one of the kidnappers, and probably the leader of the gang. We persuaded a taxi driver to tell us a bit about him. We were able to follow him to a meeting, but he left by boat, and of course we couldn't follow him. But we know who we are dealing with, sort of, and we are on the right lines."

"Damn, if only I'd gone to Mafia earlier, you might have found them."

"Not necessarily, and you know by now we don't deal in 'ifs' and 'mights'," said Rufus.

"No I know, I'm beginning to understand you. And I understand why you are doing what you are doing now. We need to get back and get rehearsing for the next call. I want to be ready for when they phone."

Rufus smiled inwardly, knowing Victoria had gone to Butiama with doubts and frustrations and guessed his old mate Moez had worked his magic – that, plus time to reflect and think about what had happened had revitalised and reinvigorated Victoria. It justified his decision even more to send her away for the day which had enabled them to get things done. He phoned Moez to thank him and let him know that Victoria was with them and got a brief update from him.

After a few minutes the porter arrived with all the baggage on a small trolley. Rufus grabbed Victoria's backpack and the three of them walked back to the car, Victoria holding on to Rufus's arm, but in a more serious business-like way. She was no longer the little girl lost. They were harangued again by the taxi drivers offering them the best rates to a destination of their choice.

They got to the sanctuary of their own vehicle and set off for their hotel, making small talk on the drive back. They checked Victoria into her own room next to them and arranged for her to come to their room as soon as she was ready.

Within a couple of minutes Victoria knocked at the door and sat down ready to be fully updated by Rufus.

Victoria looked around the room and could see both Orla's and Rufus's gear in the room and a double bed. She didn't want to think about Rufus sleeping with Orla, images and thoughts flashed through her head.

"Are you sharing this room?" she asked.

"Yeh, we thought it would look more natural as our passports show us as a married couple," replied Rufus, not picking up on Victoria's sub-text.

"Perhaps we should revert to Victoria and I sharing the room, now she's back with us?" interjected Orla, immediately understanding where Victoria was coming from. *Poor Rufus; he might be a brilliant negotiator, but he doesn't understand women at all,* she thought. "You could sleep in a bed tonight then Ru, instead of the chair," she said glaring at him.

Rufus caught up with the conversation, assuming that he was saving Orla's embarrassment of sharing the bed with him.

"Yeh, that would be good. If that's alright with you two?"

"Fine by me," said Orla.

"That seems better all round to me, I'll go and get my bag," Victoria said, disappearing from the room. She was back in seconds and placed her bag on the bed, staking her claim, so that there could be no mistake.

Rufus, briefed by Moez, set about reassuring Victoria, even though he was certain she had settled any doubts in her own mind he wanted to be absolutely sure.

"Are you ok?"

"Yeh I'm ok, thanks," Victoria replied.

"Are you sure? Is there anything you want to ask, anything you want to clear up?" asked Rufus.

"Oh Rufus, I'm sorry, but I'm sure you both understand the turmoil I've gone through over the past few days. I was blissfully ignorant of any of this prior to meeting you, and now my world has been turned upside-down and I am just reorienting myself."

"I – we – I'm sure I can speak for Orla here, understand all of that, and I'll tell you what, you have coped a lot better than some people we have dealt with."

"Really? I can't imagine anybody being as pathetic as I was."

"Believe me, you are coping really well."

"I'm so sorry Rufus."

"What's happened?"

"Nothing has happened; I'm just sorry that I doubted you."

"Is that it? I thought it was something serious. I don't blame you at all. You are in an incredibly high pressure situation. Your mind will be racing, working overtime, as well as your imagination. You will feel responsible for the lives of your parents. You have witnessed some horrific events that most people thankfully never have to go through and I have still expected you to function normally. You will probably think I am delaying things unnecessarily, and that is my fault that I haven't explained our tactics and reasoning to you. And I guess, that you even think I might be involved sometimes? Is all that about right?"

"Yes, absolutely. And I'm a doctor you would expect me to understand all of this about shock wouldn't you?"

"Not at all. You are at the centre of a maelstrom. If you could behave rationally and not be effected by it all I would think you were either heartless, or involved or both."

"Mmmm, I see what you mean."

"And the reasons we take our time are threefold: I've said to you before, what is to stop them taking you hostage if you just turn up with the money? What's to stop them taking the money and not releasing Mum and Dad and asking for more? What's to stop them taking the money and killing you and or your parents? These are desperate, dangerous people we are dealing with. They want the money, and it is our only bargaining tool. We have to ensure that when we give them the money you and your parents are as safe as we can possibly make it for you. We can only do that by doing as much background work as we can before we give them the money."

"Uh uh."

"I promise we will do everything physically possible to keep your mum and dad safe. To the criminals, they are just a means to earning some cash, a commodity to be traded, so they have a vested interest in looking after them, but purely as a bargaining tool. To me they are real people, your parents; innocent victims of other peoples' greed and malevolence. It would appear your parents have never broken a law in their lives and from what you have said are lovely, thoughtful, and caring, and I will do my utmost to get them back safely. Now you can ask me anything you like about what has been going on, or what has happened, anything you are not sure of."

"Why didn't we just give them the $10 million like they asked for?"

"A very reasonable question, especially from the daughter of the hostages and there are at least three reasons here Victoria on top of the ones I've just given you:

"One," holding up his thumb, "if we had agreed immediately they would have thought there was more available and reneged on the agreement; two," holding up his forefinger, "we would be endangering other peoples' lives by agreeing to such an extortionate sum, as it would encourage them to kidnap more westerners; and three," holding up his middle finger, "as I explained earlier, Harakat al-Shabaab al-Mujahideen have informants and agents all over east Africa and there is a very real risk that they are paying an interest in your mum and dad.

"If they thought they could get their hands on $10 million they would have taken your mum and dad off the criminals who have them and we would be dealing with them now. Now to tell you the blunt reality, there is still a risk that that could happen. $5 million is still a lot of money and that is why we are trying to get the agreement made and the cash delivered as quickly as possible, before Harakat al-Shabaab al-Mujahideen have time to organise themselves, because if they do, it changes the dynamics completely.

"I think we would have got your mum and dad back by now if there hadn't been some outside interference. Now, we don't know for sure what is happening, but to lay all our cards on the table, we believe that the bandits here are in touch with Harakat al-Shabaab al-Mujahideen, trying to do a deal. We also think they are in touch with the British Secret Intelligence Service, or MI6 as you know them, and we think it was SIS that attacked us yesterday."

Chapter Forty-Four

"What? That's impossible."

"It's not impossible Victoria, we don't understand why, although we have a few theories, but we are pretty sure it was either SIS or arranged by SIS." Rufus didn't expand on their theories as he thought he had probably given Victoria enough to think about for the time being.

Victoria was shocked, literally in shock, she thought she had got everything straight in her own mind, knew what they were doing and what they were trying to achieve, but to be told by Rufus that the men who rammed their car and shot at them were actually British spies, who were supposed to be on their side. It didn't make sense to her.

He made them all a drink, using the in-room facilities, letting Victoria think about what he had told her. For anybody not involved in his world he knew it was a vista too abhorrent to contemplate.

"Why would MI6 attack us? I don't understand," she asked while the kettle was boiling.

"We don't fully understand ourselves Victoria. We know they have been tracking us for some time. They found us in the Kilimanjaro, they followed us to the shopping centre – they even tried to attack me at the hotel."

"WHAT? What happened?" asked Victoria, learning of this for the first time.

"Two of their guys followed me into the gents' intending to assault me at the very least."

"How do you know they were going to attack you?"

"One of the guys stood outside my cubicle with a baton in his hand. Now where I'm from that is not an invitation to dinner, so I dealt with him and..."

"What do you mean you 'dealt with him'? He's got a baton and as far as I know you were unarmed, what did you do?" slightly alarmed, and at the same time proud of 'her team' as she thought of him.

"Um, I head-butted him."

"RU. That's dangerous."

"Only for the other guy," quipped Orla.

"Then what happened?"

Rufus decided to skip over the detail of smashing Brogues's kneecap to smithereens "His partner got me in a bear hug."

"What did you do?"

"I back-head-butted him," Rufus said matter-of-factly.

"You don't want to know the details Victoria," interjected Orla again, knowing the tactic well, "it's a man thing."

"When I asked them a few questions, they knew my name and told me to leave the country and leave you and your mum and dad behind. They said I didn't know what I was getting myself into. I left them in the washroom and that's when we left the Kilimanjaro."

"And you are sure they are British?"

"Absolutely. From what we've found out and Don has told us, we have no doubt. We just don't know why."

"And it's not like we can rock-up at the British High Commission and demand to know why," added Orla.

"So we are negotiating with crooks, in a fight against time with Harakat al-Shabaab al-Mujahideen, while being attacked, hampered and harried by SIS."

"OH MY GOD," said Victoria, the enormity of the situation striking her. It was bad enough when she thought she was dealing with the kidnappers, to learn that al-Shabaab, who she was hearing more and more of in the news, and MI6 were involved and also against them, was shattering.

"We can still do this Vicky. We have shaken off our tails from SIS and we were able to do a couple of things last night, which gives us an advantage, we think."

"What else happened last night?"

"There's good news and bad news," said Rufus, deciding Victoria needed to know more than Orla had told her and more than he was used to divulging.

"It was Don who identified the stronghold; he's been doing some work back in the UK. You see, the four of us have to work as a team. Although Don isn't here, he is an integral part of the operation. The only problem is when we got there they had gone."

"What? You've skipped a few steps there Ru, what happened?"

"We think SIS alerted them that we were coming because Don identified the building where he thought your mum and dad were. Orla went and took a look first and we both went in. We found these," he held up the few items of clothing they had recovered, "which we assume..."

Victoria's face told him they had assumed correctly.

"That's Mum's blouse," she said, "and Dad's shorts, and his socks... oh and that's Mum's favourite jacket. Oh, oh my God, fucking hell, they're dead aren't they? Why else would you have their clothes?"

"We think they are ok. Victoria. We think that SIS alerted them that we were coming and they moved your mum and dad, which is quite common. One of the reasons we think that happened is because of what I heard last night. We were able to follow James in the evening." He decided against using Wisdom's real name in case Victoria let it out under pressure. "I was able to listen to a little conversation on a boat."

"Ru, stop, you have left too much detail out. How did you follow him? What boat? Where? How did you get on board to listen?"

Rufus recounted the story, judiciously omitting the pain he had caused Sendoro and explained how he had swum out to the Lazy Days and was able to listen to a few snippets, and plant a bug on the boat.

This would have all been very exciting for Victoria, if she wasn't personally involved, as it was she had to internalise everything. Think about what she was being told calmly and objectively.

Rufus and Orla decided to let Victoria think about what they had told her and busied themselves, giving Victoria time to digest everything she had just been told; a roller coaster of good and bad news, subterfuge, action, deception and bravery. Her head was awash with images and thoughts that she couldn't control. She trusted the two of them implicitly, knew everything they said made sense and yet there was always a little voice in her ear with the 'what ifs' and 'whys'?'

She studied the two of them, sorting out their equipment, envying and admiring their assuredness and competence in equal measure.

Eventually she spoke to Rufus. "Had we better do some role-play Ru?"

Rufus and Orla slipped into their individual tasks: Rufus started role-playing with Victoria; Orla Skyped Don.

Rufus and Victoria sat in their now familiar, comfortable positions, she was amazed how reassuring it was to have him in such close proximity, the feel of his leg against hers giving her succour, the touch of his hand on her giving her strength.

"Now before we achieve what I want to achieve, you are going to take a serious amount of shit over the phone. They are going to come at you big style, and we have to let them. They have to believe that they have got control over you again. I expect threats to your parents, to you personally, abuse accusations, and I think they will throw the lot at you. We might be able to mitigate it by getting in an early apology, taking the wind out of their sails a little. Now what would you say was the reason for you shouting at them yesterday?"

Rufus was preparing Victoria from his lexicon of alibis and reasons that he used to justify unexpected events to the bandits. They were simple enough tactics that had been refined during numerous operations. He found that the simplest ideas were usually the best ones and he liked the victim to either come up with the ideas, or believe that they had come up with the ideas.

"I was mad. I was really mad, that they would think I had deserted my mum and dad."

"So that's what we say. Remember these guys are not thinking the same way as you. It's our job to see things from their perspective, to walk in their shoes, as the jargon goes, because they won't try and see things from your perspective. So now, what would you add to being mad?"

"Um, Um."

"Right, we've already agreed we are going to get an apology in quickly?"

"Yeh."

"And you are going to explain that you were angry and upset?"

"Yeh."

"And then you can promise them that you are getting..."

"Getting their money," Victoria interrupted, "and that they will not have to look after Mum and Dad for much longer."

"Exactly."

"And that it is important we trust each other, they want their money and I want my parents. I will not do anything to damage the trust they have in me," said Victoria.

"The only thing I would try and change there is: instead of looking after Mum and Dad in the negative, frame it in the positive, so something like "you will be able to...."

"Got it, you will be able to let Mum and Dad go very soon."

"Exactly, so in their minds they are envisaging letting your parents go, instead of keeping them captive. They're all only nuances, but even so they are really important in influencing the sub-conscious. I have a friend who coaches sportsmen and women. He is absolutely certain that when he is talking to football strikers, for instance, instead of concentrating on the consequences of missing a penalty, he concentrates on the feelings of seeing the ball go in the back of the net. So the striker sees the ball going in. Hears the crowd cheering. Sees his coach smiling and applauding. He uses as many senses to fire their imagination as he can. Do you see what I mean?"

"Yes, yes I do. I'd never thought about it before. I'm thinking how I can use this when everything goes back to normal and I am treating patients. Thanks Ru." She leaned forward and gave him a kiss on the cheek.

Rufus smiled inwardly again, because Victoria's language showed she was already thinking about the future, that this catastrophic event was only temporary and she could see herself on the other side of it. This was really important to him; he knew she would be strong for him, just because of her language.

He got down to some role-play.

Chapter Forty-Five

Orla could hear Rufus's voice rising while she spoke to Don; accusing Victoria of lying, then praising her for her response.

"Hello treacle," Don said in a mock cockney accent.

"Hi darling," said Orla. "How are you?"

"Everything is fine here. How's it going your end?"

"Quite eventful, but I think we have everything under control."

"Yes I think you do from what I can tell."

"Right, brief me," said Orla.

"We are identifying more and more phones and players. Deidre is still at the epicentre of all this and..."

"Sorry to be pedantic here Don, but as Rufus would say..."

"Ok, ok, Deidre's phone is at the epicentre of all the activity. We are getting the feed from the Lazy Days R4 but it's all in Swahili which isn't much use to us. I'm trying to find a reliable Swahili speaker to translate it for us, but all of the good ones are being used by the boffins."

"That's no good is it? I would say to send it to Ru, but I don't think he has got time to transcribe it, which is what he would need to do. See what you can do please Babe, it might be important for us."

"I know, we are working hard on that one," said Don. "We have got the Firm, GCHQ, the Company and the NSA all over this. They all seem to be taking a very keen interest. I don't know exactly what their interest is, but I have seen activity from what I am pretty sure are their assets. but they are deploying a lot of assets, both technical and human by the look of it. The trouble is, without a direct line of communication to them I am in the dark. And anyway, I am sure that if we could ask them what their interest is, our boys would only say the welfare of British citizens. And the yanks would say they are assisting their staunchest ally."

"Can't you speak to anybody there to find out? Can't you go to the DSF and explain that we are trying to get two British citizens back and that any assistance from government would be advantageous?"

"That's just it. I've been through our normal channels and drawn a blank. I've even asked McHugh if he can use his company's contacts in Whitehall, but again, nothing. It's like we don't exist."

"Even the Regiment?"

"Exactly. They are not telling them anything. Frankie has got the blokes on the Chagos Islands in the Indian Ocean. But other than keeping fit, they are not really doing anything. No intel feed. No planning, nothing. They're a token, that's all. Frankie got the lines from JTSL, but they've told him less than I can. Everybody is holding back. There are no assets being thrown at this one at all, all of which backs up my theory that Deidre is in on this. They've intercepted some comms between her and the villains and it's all a set-up, that's why nobody is bothered. They don't tell us, so we can go blundering on. HMG looks sweet and innocent, and we're the fall guys who ballsed it all up if it goes wrong," said Don.

"What do you mean if it all goes wrong?"

"If we don't get them both back. HMG can sidestep any accusations and blame us, whereas if – and this is a big if because I think Martyn is already dead – we get them both back alive, they can get the glory by association. Deidre is pulling all the strings, she set it all up. The spooks all know it. The politicians know it, I know it – it's just you and Ru who can't see it. C'mon, everything fits doesn't it?"

"Ok, let's think this through. Everything you say makes sense but what's the worst that can happen? If we just get Deidre back alive, and Martyn is dead as you say, how does that affect us? We get paid half the amount by the insurance company, until we, or they, prove Deidre did it. Then we get paid the other half when they don't have to pay out on Martyn because she, the beneficiary, had him killed. If they are both dead, well we've taken a bit of a hit, but we should still come out fairly even on the advance. I haven't done the accounts yet, but we haven't gone mad with the cash," said Orla.

"Well I'm going to go through the small print that nobody ever bothers to read. See what it says about foregoing payment," said Don.

"Ok, meanwhile we stick to our SOP. We treat every job a hundred per cent kosher. It's the only way."

"I know. I just don't want us to be stood there with our trousers round our ankles being told to bend over at the end of this."

"Ok Babe, I've got to go as it's nearly time for the call-in. Get back in touch with Frankie if you can, I'm sure between the pair of you, you can get to the bottom of what is going on. Speak to you later. Mmmwwwah," she kissed the screen to say goodbye, she checked her shoulder and could see Rufus and Victoria were engrossed in their preparations, she quickly lifted her top and gave Don a quick flash of her boobs, just to keep him going while she was away, and heard Don groaning as she turned the connection off and wandered back over to Rufus and Victoria.

"Ah, good timing Orla, we're just prepping the equipment and you can double-check everything for me so we are good to go when they call. Everything alright with Don? Any update?"

"The only update is no update from his point of view."

Orla double- checked everything for Rufus as he ran through a few last minute reminders for Orla. They tweaked some of the prompts he had ready.

"They won't phone exactly at five. They have to show they are in control, so they may make us wait, a classic, if somewhat infantile game in my opinion. Anybody need anything, water, food? Victoria, I suggest you have water. Keep yourself hydrated, it's really imp.... oh I forgot you're a doctor you know all this shit don't you?"

"I am and I do, but it's still good that you are thinking about me. So yes, I will please."

"Orla?"

"Yeh, some water please, Ru. How do you say cold again?"

"Baridi. Or Baridi sana."

"Well baridi sana it is then."

Rufus phoned room service and ordered the water. Even though it wasn't a big hotel, he didn't want to leave Victoria while they were waiting for the call.

The water arrived and Rufus gave the waitress a tip of 1000 shillings, put the *Do not Disturb* sign on the handle, shoved a door wedge under the door to ensure they would not be interrupted unexpectedly by enthusiastic maids.

At 1745 the phone had still not rung; Rufus turned to Victoria and said, "Right we have two choices here. You can either be really angry that they didn't phone at five like you agreed, or really anxious."

"I think anxious, because that's what I am," said Victoria.

"I agree," said Rufus, "which will help, because one of the first things they will do is punish you for yesterday. I don't know exactly what it will be, but they have three weapons: they can threaten you, they can threaten your parents or they can inflict pain on your parents."

"Oh no," whispered Victoria.

"Well, there is a sort of fourth, which is the one I think they will use, but we won't know until we get your parents back, and that is they pretend to harm your parents. Either way if you start off being really anxious, it will help mitigate things."

"What? So me screaming down the phone at them will get my parents harmed?"

"We were always going to reach this point Victoria. It's almost inevitable. You shouting down the phone brought us valuable time. Harming or threatening to harm your parents has nothing to do with you shouting. It's psychological intimidation. So you have to be ready to offer up the interim payment, unless they ask for it first. Ok?" said Rufus.

"Yes ok."

"Ok. Now remember all the stuff we talked about, fear and trust. So don't agree to anywhere, buy a bit of time with those things we spoke about so that Orla can recce them for us to decide whether you want to go there."

"What? You want me to go and take money to these guys?"

"No, that's exactly what we are going to avoid by doing what I've told you."

"Oh right," said Victoria.

They all settled back to wait for the phone to ring. The time dragged and Victoria had to restrain herself from checking her watch every few minutes. Rufus and Orla, well-used to long periods of inactivity, rested their minds and bodies, almost in a trance.

The phone rang at 1815. Victoria nearly jumped out of her skin. Rufus and Orla were fully alert, from nought to sixty in a nanosecond. Rufus checked the number, gave them both a nod, started recording, said, "Deep breath," and answered the phone all in one movement.

Chapter Forty-Six

"Hello. Hello?" said Victoria in a nervous voice.

Perfect thought Rufus.

"You want to hear your father do you?" said the man they knew as Wisdom.

"Yes please," said Victoria, thinking *this is good news.*

"You want to hear him screaming like a baby, because you disrespected me, do you?" Wisdom's voice took on a steely edge. "You want to listen to him having a finger chopped off and then fed to him? I will educate you in the ways of my country, Miss Conway. I have several associates in my presence who would dearly love to inflict pain on him and hear him scream and squeal like a pig. Do you understand what I mean?"

Rufus understood exactly what he meant as *Duelling Banjos* started playing in his head from the film *Deliverance*.

"Please don't hurt him. I didn't mean to be disrespectful. I'm tired and exhausted and scared and when your... your friend accused me of deserting my parents I was upset."

"For your insolence your father is going to pay."

"I'm sorry, I'm really sorry. Please don't hurt him, he's my dad and I love him," Victoria sobbed.

"You must learn the lesson of respect and manners. Something you mzungus say we Africans lack, and the way you will learn is through punishment." Wisdom kept his voice low and calm and even, sending a chill through Victoria.

"I'm sorry," she cried down the phone.

Throughout the call Rufus had been encouraging her to weep and sob.

"It's too late to be sorry, Miss Conway. You should have thought about that when you were demanding things of me. Now do you want to hear your father screaming?"

Victoria nodded as Rufus as he held a prompt up and said, "No I just want him safely home to me with Mum."

"So you don't want to hear your father?"

"Um yes, yes I do, I want to hear he is safe and being well looked after." That got an approving nod from Rufus.

"In future Miss, I suggest you choose your words very carefully when dealing with me. I studied at your Oxford University and am very experienced in rhetorical debates. You are not dealing with some street urchin. You are dealing with professionals, artisans. This is what we do. I don't like to resort to violence to establish the rules, nevertheless, if I have to I will. Do I make myself clear?"

Rufus was holding his finger to his lips, but Victoria spoke anyway. Rufus knew she was damned if she did and damned if she didn't speak.

"Yes, I'm..."

"Do not interrupt me. I had decided to be benevolent and not harm your father, but if you interrupt me,

I shall be forced to reconsider my munificence. Now I have established the rules we can continue with the business at hand."

Rufus was holding his finger up, in the 'shhhhh' signal again.

"Miss Conway?"

Rufus nodded.

"Yes?"

"Do you understand the rules?"

"Yes I do. I was waiting for you to finish, because I didn't want to be rude and offend you."

"Ah. Good, good. Now, what are you going to give me, to convince me that you should be allowed to speak to your father?"

"I don't. I don't know," Victoria acted dumb at Rufus's insistence.

"Have you got my money?"

"I have some of it."

Wisdom took the bait immediately.

"How much?" he said a little too eagerly.

"I've been able to withdraw $50 000 as a first instalment."

"$50 000? Is that all? What am I supposed to do with that?" Wisdom raged. "I have mouths to feed, organisations to run, officials to keep sweet. Many, many people rely on me. How am I supposed to look after all these people on $50 000?"

Rufus imagined the glint in Wisdom's eye as he was saying it, as the greed that infects all kidnappers kicked in. $50k for a few days' "work" wasn't bad going, but he also knew he would want more. They always do.

"Surely it is enough to let me speak to Martyn, my dad"

"When you have given me my money I will let you speak to him."

Rufus and Victoria had role-played this very point. Victoria had to be insistent and polite that she would only deliver the money IF she knew her father was ok.

"How do I know he is alright, how do I know you even have him if I can't talk to him. If you put yourself in my shoes, surely you can see that I need to know."

"I thought as much. I will let you listen to him, wait there."

Victoria, Rufus and Orla looked at each other quizzically. Rufus was the first to realise what Wisdom meant, and tapped out *Pre-recorded* on his tablet. They could hear some muffled sounds, which they couldn't make out and then they heard Martyn's wooden voice come over the phone, clearly reading a script:

"Hello Victoria, this is your dad, Martyn Conway. We are being treated well and with dignity. The people who are treating us as their guests have a legitimate cause and are good and honourable people. I urge you and the people of the United Kingdom to support their just cause in the name of Allah. I watched the football game between the Seahawks and the Broncos, on Saturday, which ended up forty-three, eight to the Seahawks."

"Dad? Dad?" said Victoria not wanting to acknowledge that the voice was pre-recorded.

"Your father recorded that for us on Sunday. Now do you accept that he is alive and that he is with us?"

Rufus was preparing prompts for Victoria as she spoke.

"Thank you," she said. "Thank you for letting me know he is safe and thank you for treating him well," even though she didn't believe that they were.

"Now, about my money... You will bring it to the car park of the Quality Centre on the Pugu Road at 10pm this evening. You must come alone with the money. I have men there and if they see any suspicious behaviour, they will inform me and I will kill your father. Do you understand?"

"That could be difficult for me," she said. "I can't just walk around with $50 000, that's eighty million shillings." They had decided to get the figure into Tanzanian shillings as it sounded a much more impressive amount. It would make Wisdom less objective and greedy. "What if something happens to me, what if the police stop me and find the money, and I can't just hand over the money to any Tom, Dick or Harry."

"Who?"

"Sorry it's an expression, it means anybody that you don't know. Let's think about this. Why don't you bring my mum or dad and we can exchange the money for one of them. You will still have one of them won't you?"

"Please don't be stupid, Miss Conway. I am not going to give you either of your parents for a mere $50 000, they are worth far more than that to me."

"I'm pleased it is a 'mere $50 000' to you, because it is a lot of money to me, and I don't want to give it away without some assurances."

"What do you suggest?"

"I want to give it to you personally."

"What, so you can go to the authorities and testify against me?"

"No, so I know it is you I am dealing with."

"Don't take me for a fool, Miss Conway. I will send my trusty lieutenant. We can agree a code word, which I will give to him so you know he is my representative."

Rufus held up the *Yes* prompt.

"Ok, but if I see anything suspicious I won't stop. You are not going to kidnap me as well."

"I have no intention of kidnapping you," said Wisdom. "Come alone. Come in a taxi, send the taxi away and wait in the car park at the front of the Quality Centre for one of my men to come to you. He will use the code word "Julius Nyerere" after the beloved father of our nation. He will have his phone on and I will be listening, if he says anything untoward or says that he can see anything suspicious, then I WILL kill one of them. Do you understand?

Victoria was looking at Rufus who nodded to her.

"Yes, that is all very clear."

"I will call you when my man gets back to let you know it all went well."

Rufus wanted to leave room for manoeuvre and so encouraged Victoria to end the call.

"I understand," said Victoria and cut the call off.

"You don't really expect me to go up there on my own do you?" she said.

"Not at all, I expect Orla to go," said Rufus.

"What do you mean? What if they have a picture of me from Mum and Dad?"

"They won't see Orla, but she will be there."

"I don't understand," said Victoria.

"You will, I'll explain everything when we've got it organised. Orla and I need to make some arrangements. First though you did really well again, brilliantly. We know your dad was at least alive until Sunday. You kept him safe and calmed James down, everything went really well. In case they phone back they might ask questions about which cab you will be in, or where you are coming from. Clearly you wouldn't tell them that even if you knew. They might make some changes, because we agreed too easily. If they do try that, we stick to our agreement; it's perfect for what I have in mind. Ok?"

"Ok."

Rufus and Orla swung into their post-call routine. Rufus went over the call with Victoria, listening for any clues or mistakes, while Orla Skyped Don.

They were both very busy making arrangements; double-checking details and making calls. The meeting might be scheduled for ten, but they wanted to be on plot a long time before that and so had to make sure their plans were in place.

They left the hotel at 1930. The traffic was still heavy heading in the opposite direction out of town, but they had a trouble free journey to the Quality Centre getting there by 2000, well before the 2200 schedule. Night had already fallen so when Rufus and Victoria dropped Orla off, she disappeared within seconds. They continued a little way up the road and parked up in the darkness of the unlit service road.

Chapter Forty-Seven

Rufus made another telephone call, talking in what appeared to be fluent Swahili, then settled back to observe, his senses fully alert to any potential surprises. In his time in the SAS he had carried out numerous ambushes, where patience was essential. He'd never imagined when he was a 'nod' in the Marines that he would progress to Special Forces, planning and conducting ambushes. He used all his and Orla's experience to ensure this one went according to plan.

At 2145 Orla texted him.

"1 B on P", meaning one Bandit had turned up on the Plot.

To which Rufus simply replied, "R," for Roger.

He then sent another text.

"Right, Victoria. In a few minutes I want you to get on the phone and ask what the hell is going on?"

"What? What do you mean?"

"The army and police are on their way here, and you want to know why?"

A few minutes later, Victoria could hear sirens. They were getting louder and she could see the blue and red flashing lights on vehicles heading up Pugu Road towards them.

Victoria timed the call perfectly. She rang her mum's phone which was answered just as the cavalcade went past. She had to shout into the phone to make herself heard.

"What the fuck is going on?" she screamed.

"What? What is happening?"

"That's what I want to know," she shouted.

"Hold on," the line went dead.

The police/army convoy continued past Rufus and Victoria; sirens blaring, lights flashing, towards the airport. Victoria's phone rang again.

"I told you no tricks," said Wisdom.

"What? What do you mean? I phoned you to ask what the hell was going on."

"My guy phoned to say that the police were all over him."

"The police were here, of course they were, you could hear them over the phone, but they weren't coming for us, they've driven on."

"What? My guy has driven off, he said they were coming for him."

"And I thought they were coming for me, you told me you have police officers working for you, I thought it was them." She looked over at Rufus who was giving her encouragement signals. "Where is he now?"

"He's on his way back here I think."

"What? Well I'm not waiting around here any longer with eighty million on me. I'll call you when I get back so I can get your money to you and we can get things moving."

At that point Orla texted Rufus telling him the plot was now clean and they returned to pick her up. Orla jumped in the back of the car and Rufus phoned his old mate, General Issa Barumu.

"Asante sana Rafiki," *Thank you very much my friend,* he said. "I will call you to let you know how things have gone."

As soon as he finished the call Orla briefed them on what had happened: "One bandit fifteen minutes prior to the meeting. No back up. He just stood around in the open, waiting; very unprofessional. And when the military approached, he took off like a startled rabbit. He ran back to his car and was off. Car parked approximately twenty yards away, like he didn't want to work too hard. If we go for a real drop, then I don't think we will have any problems, very surveillance unaware. If we had a full team, it would be a piece of cake, even around here."

"Yeh, well we haven't. Do you think you can do it?"

"You know I'd back myself against these jokers, yeh."

"Excuse me, but what was all that about? Why were the police and army coming up the road? How did you know they would be coming?"

"I told you, I have a couple of very important friends in the police and army here and they were doing me a favour. We were getting to know our enemy. We were enabling Orla to make plans about how she intends to approach the next phase."

"What next phase?"

"To surveil them and identify where your mum and dad are."

"You really think you can do that, Orla?"

"Absolutely right I do, from what I saw he wouldn't know if I was in the car with him."

"Ok. Right Victoria, when we get back I want us to put a call in to arrange another money drop. They will accuse us of trying to get them arrested. We can point to the facts that you called him to question what was happening first. The army or police or whoever they were just drove straight past, but his "trusty lieutenant" wouldn't know that because he drove off as quickly as he could, and you don't want any army or police involvement any more than they do. You can even throw in that the army would take the eighty million for themselves, if they were involved. And sometimes things just happen that we have no control over."

"How did you arrange for a convoy to be passing at just the right time?" asked Victoria.

"It's who you know, not what you know in this life," he said winking at her.

They returned to the hotel and after a few minutes' role-play they put the call in; Rufus as usual, controlling the phone and recording.

"Hello," said Wisdom. "That was a very unfortunate occurrence wasn't it, Miss Conway?"

"I thought you'd set me up at first. I thought you'd arranged for the police to come and take my money and then you could deny ever having received anything."

"And I thought you'd set me up. However, it appears that we have misjudged each other. Listen carefully though. I am a naturally suspicious man and do not believe in coincidences. I must warn you Miss Conway that any other unexpected events will have dire consequences for your parents. I have told you before not to misinterpret my civility as weakness. You will deliver my money within the next hour or I will hurt your parents."

"But I've only got the eighty million, I can't get any more at this time of night."

"That is exactly what I am referring to," said Wisdom.

Victoria acknowledged Rufus's prompt and asked, "Where and when do you suggest? Only I don't like travelling around Dar at this time of night in taxis."

"Then tell me where you are and I will come and get my money."

"You know I am not going to tell you where I am. Will you tell me where you are and I will bring the money to you?"

"Ha ha. Let us make the same arrangement as before, only a different location."

Orla and Rufus were both nodding enthusiastically. They were prepared to invest $50k for the opportunity of getting Proof of Life and potentially finding where the stronghold had been moved to. They had tested the capability of the opposition and so far found them wanting.

"We will meet you at the entrance to the Mzizima Fish Market, Ocean Road, in one hour. As I said Miss Conway, I am a suspicious man, and should anything go wrong. If my man sees any police or any suspicious activity he will alert me immediately. His phone will be open to me like before."

A clear lie, all three of them thought.

"And I will know immediately if there are any problems, one of your parents will be severely hurt if I hear anything suspicious like sirens, you do not want that on your conscience do you, Miss Conway? Your parents are old and frail, and they are getting weaker by the day."

Rufus was hurriedly preparing prompts for Victoria.

"Please, you know this city better than me and there are always sirens going off. There is always some VIP with a motorcade being escorted somewhere. You can't blame me for that. Please be reasonable. You can't hurt my parents if that happens."

"Do not tell me what I can or can't do. I repeat, if I hear any sirens or anything suspicious, one of your parents WILL be hurt. Now get my fucking money to me." The phone went dead.

Rufus double-checked the phone was off. "Great stuff, he has left us enough room for manoeuvre if we need it, but I don't think we will. Ok, no time to lose." He didn't have to tell Orla what was needed so he concentrated on Victoria, instructing her to prepare herself, while getting his work things ready.

With practised efficiency, Orla and Rufus were ready in a few minutes, and turned their attention to helping Victoria. They walked out of the hotel less than ten minutes after putting the phone down.

The roads were deserted at that time of night, which could lead to its own problems as people, who are pretty relaxed about the road traffic laws at the best of times, completely ignored them when the roads were quiet. Traffic lights and signals were invisible, one way streets become two-way streets and people liked to put their foot down in a town where the average speed was less that 10MPH.

They got to the Fish Market in double-quick time; giving them a good forty minutes before the agreed time, they were sure they were there before the opposition. After a quick recce, Rufus and Victoria got out of the car and climbed the wall of the market. Rufus boosted Victoria up onto the wall and was easily up and over in one movement to help her down the other side.

The place was eerily deserted: it stunk of rotting fish, which attracted rats and mice, cats and dogs to scavenge what they could. Victoria could hear the scampering of tiny feet across the cobbled ground and the high pitched squeaking of the rats. Dogs snarled and fought for scraps of food. The few moonlit clouds in the sky raced in off the sea casting shadows and darkness in unpredictable fashions.

Victoria held Rufus's arm with one hand and her nose with the other. She thought she was going to retch, the smell was unbelievable. She had been in morgues and been present in some gruesome autopsies, when the smell had been overpowering, but this was in a different league.

It was the years and years of rotting fish, work surfaces that had never properly been cleaned, fish blood in every nook and cranny of pavement or road. Rotting guts and heads strewn around overflowing bins which all added to the pungent odour.

They found a position that Rufus was happy with and settled down to wait.

Orla drove a little way off towards the Kigamboni Ferry, knowing that the bandits had put themselves into a small one-way system, where it would be difficult and impractical to turn the car around, she was banking on them coming past her.

They waited, stationary and silent, aware from their military days that the human eye will pick up movement more readily than a stationary object.

Rufus had his MP5 ready, but he didn't want to use it unless Victoria's life was in danger, that was not the objective of tonight.

At 0015 Rufus saw the car drive slowly from Magogoni Street onto Ocean Road, and immediately texted Orla previously prepared text:

Bandit on Plot.

Chapter Forty-Eight

The car, with one lone male occupant looking around nervously, continued down towards the ferry, and out of Rufus's sight.

Same B on P as b4, came the text from Orla.

Victoria's phone went and Rufus gave her the ok to answer it.

"Hello," she said.

"Where are you Miss Conway?" said Wisdom.

"I'm at the Fish Market. Your man has just driven past me."

"He can't see you. Where are you exactly?"

"Well I'm hardly going to stand out in the middle of the road, with your $50 000 making myself a target for anybody coming past. Tell him to come to the gates and I will let him see me when I know everything is ok."

"Remember. No tricks, Miss Conway. If I hear anything untoward your father gets hurt." Victoria could hear a strange noise and then her dad's voice, "Please Victoria, be careful love, do as he says but be careful."

"Dad?"

"Victoria, just be careful."

"I will Dad, don't worry."

"Good girl, please just do as he says, he has a gun and it is pointing straight at me."

"Don't worry Dad, I've got his money, I'll get you home soon," she said through tears of laughter, hearing her dad's voice properly for the first time in days.

Wisdom took back over. "If you want to see him alive, you had better do as he says." The line went dead.

Victoria kept herself together, knowing she had to concentrate and be careful. She saw the car coming back round from Magogoni Street. It stopped and the driver got out, pulling his hood down lower over his face to put it in shadows. He approached the Fish Market gate, clearly very nervous. He was looking around, completely disoriented, definitely not a trained observer.

His actions were jumpy and disorganised, those of a nervous man, not the professional team his boss purported to lead. Rufus knew he could take him out any time he wanted. Still he didn't relax – although the guy was clearly an amateur and nervous – that could make him jumpy and unpredictable and therefore dangerous. Rufus kept the MP5 trained on him from his vantage point in the shadows.

"Have you got the money?"

"Aren't you supposed to say something to me first?" said Victoria, agreeing with Orla and Rufus's assessment of him.

"What? Oh yeh, Julius Nyerere."

"Here it is," said Victoria handing over the holdall full of dollar bills. They had thought of giving the money in shillings, but as the largest denomination is 10000, it would have needed 80000 notes and been far more cumbersome, taken more bags and made the courier take at least two trips back and forth to the car to carry it all. It might have given them some advantages, in that it would slow the courier down as he carried the weight in the holdalls that they would have had to put it in, but in the end they decided against it. It was not worth their extra effort to gain that very small advantage: Orla had plenty of time to prepare herself anyway and they went with US dollars.

"Wait there," ordered the man and he returned to his car. Victoria and Rufus could see him put his phone to his ear and clearly have a conversation. After a couple of minutes he stood up at the driver's door and shouted to Victoria. "The boss says it had better all be there and he will call you at 10a.m.," got back in the car and drove off.

Rufus knew he didn't have to let Orla know that the target vehicle was leaving as he boosted Victoria on to the top of the wall and repeated the procedure they had used to get in. They walked the short distance up the hill to the Kilimanjaro Hotel where Rufus knew he could hire a taxi back to their hotel.

They were back in no time and let themselves into the double room.

Rufus suggested that Victoria get some sleep, and he would wait in the room for her and let her know when there was any news from Orla. She was adamant that she would not go to sleep while Orla was out risking her life for her and her parents, so the two of them sat in the room waiting. They made small talk about the hygiene of the fish market, the inadequacies of the courier and the feeling of impotence they were both experiencing, waiting for Orla, who was out there on her own, doing what she did best.

Orla watched the bandit as he drove off with the money. He actually stopped a few feet from her position and re-examined the money, making sure there was no funny money stuffed in-between the genuine notes. He made another phone call, and she could hear his excited voice through the windows.

He pulled away from the port and drove off up the hill. Usually she wouldn't have contemplated following a target solo at this time of night; she would show out too quickly. But she decided that the bandit was not surveillance conscious and if she was careful, she would be ok, especially if he remained in the city as there would be a few other vehicles around.

She followed from a safe distance out to the north on the Old Bagamoyo Road, she was lucky that she was able to keep at least one car between her and the courier, and even luckier that no one stopped at the red lights, so if he got through on green, it didn't look suspicious for her to go through if it changed to red.

They turned right at a roundabout onto the Jangwani Beach Road, which was going to be more problematic, as they were the only two cars on this road. Just as she was reconsidering her options the courier pulled off the road straight into a walled compound.

Orla drove straight passed and pulled over a short way down the road. She grabbed her kit and doubled back towards the house. She ran effortlessly and covered the ground quickly, even though she was carrying her weapon and other kit. She recced the compound and made her way round to the rear of the premises, where she found what she wanted: a tree that over-hung the compound wall. She swung herself up onto the branch and hand-over-handed along it until she could swing her legs down and drop to the ground. She got herself in position and watched and waited.

The house was large, probably 400 to 500m2. There were a few outbuildings and an archway which seemed to lead back to the driveway. The veranda covered doors and windows were grilled and well protected with large padlocks. On the first floor the windows were similarly protected. She was assessing the potential for an intervention and needed to note every strength and weakness for Rufus and her to plan the assault.

When she had examined as much of the building and its environs as she could, she climbed back out of the compound to call Rufus. He answered before it had even rung her end and she updated him, talking in a low voice.

All Victoria could hear was Rufus's responses to Orla's update, but it was clear he was quite upbeat about what she was saying:

"Mm mm, Yeh,? Great. Have you recced the whole place? ...uh uh. Ok, I'll brief up Don and Victoria and we'll put the call in asap. Do you need any more kit? ....yeh, ok."

Rufus turned to Victoria.

"Orla followed our guy back to what she believes is the stronghold. She has been able to recce the whole site. She saw James at one of the windows talking to the courier, so we know he's there. We just need to prove he has your mum and dad with him. We are pretty sure your dad is there aren't we, because you spoke to him earlier, but we don't know about mum, so I want you to put a call in to James and ask to speak to them, try for both, but if we can only speak to one, go for Mum."

Rufus continued to brief Victoria on how he wanted her to play the call. He phoned Orla to tell her they were just about to make the call and pressed the green button.

"Hello Miss Conway. I said I would phone you at 10a.m."

"I know you did I'm sorry, but I wanted to make sure you had got your money after the last time went wrong. I am very nervous because of the threats you made and I just need to know that everything is alright."

"Yes I have my money. It is fortunate for your parents that everything went smoothly."

"I know. I was very nervous about it. I was more nervous for them than I was for myself. Thank you for letting me speak to Dad and now I have shown I am serious and I will get you your money can I speak to Mum?"

"She is sleeping, and I do not want to disturb her."

"I'm sure they wouldn't mind being disturbed to talk to me, to know I am doing everything you ask and that I will soon have them home. I need to speak to them to know they are ok."

There was silence on the other end of the phone.

"Please. You know I am serious now, I have just given you eighty million in cash, I need to know I am dealing with the right person and that you are serious," said Victoria.

They could almost hear the cogs turning in Wisdom's brain, weighing up the benefits opposed to the disadvantages.

"Ok," he said. "I will allow you this concession."

They could hear muffled noises over the phone and after a few minutes Deidre's voice could be heard.

"Victoria, Victoria? Is that you love?"

"Yes it's me Mum. Are you ok?"

Rufus's phone vibrated silently in his pocket, Orla had texted *Lights on* to him. He was concentrating on the conversation as well as reading his text and selecting prompts for Victoria.

"Yes we are fine love. We'll be better when we get out of here, but we are fine."

"I just wanted to hear your voice Mum." Victoria's voice started to shake with emotion.

"Don't cry love. We're ok. Just look after yourself. Be careful won't you?"

Rufus was holding up the word *Dad?*.

"Yes Mum I will, don't worry about me. Is Dad with you?"

"He's ok, yes."

Rufus needed to know that he was there with them, but didn't want to push it too far, so he just put the word *Talk* on the screen.

"Can I talk to him?"

"Um, I don't ...."

"No you cannot," cut across Wisdom. "Do not abuse my hospitality and generosity. You have spoken to your father once tonight. You know he is in good health."

Rufus needed to know that both Deidre and Martyn were at the premises before he could mount an intervention with any confidence. If Wisdom had separated them for some reason and Martyn was missing when they went in, they would be sentencing him to death. The safety of the hostages: the first golden rule of a Crime in Action.

Rufus's decision was made for him though. At the same time as he could hear a commotion start to build over the phone, he had a text from Orla saying, *Poss Bs on P*.

Rufus and Victoria could hear shouting and a gunshot.

Chapter Forty-Nine

This time Orla ignored their SOP and telephoned Rufus, she knew his phone would be on vibrate anyway and knew he wouldn't answer if it wasn't safe.

"Gun fire," she said when he answered.

"Yeh I've just heard over the phone. Sitrep please Orla."

"Four pick-ups full of suspected terrorists arrived on Plot, approximately two minutes ago. They have forced entry, one gun shot heard. Approximately eight sus terrorists in the stronghold; two left with the cars. Small arms only."

"Stay in cover Orla, there's no point showing out with ten opposition, you've got no chance of getting Deidre and Martyn back. Just observe and get us any intelligence that you can. I'll be with you as soon as I can get there, don't do anything until I get there."

"Roger."

Rufus ended the call and spoke to Victoria.

"Vicky I have to go. You must stay here. There has been an attack at the stronghold, Orla has heard one gunshot, but we have no reason to believe that your parents have been injured. I need to go and back Orla up as soon as possible though."

"I'll come with you"

"No Victoria. That is too dangerous. We will need to switch on and back each other up. You must stay here."

"But I want to see Mum and Dad."

"Victoria. This is non-negotiable. It is too dangerous."

Rufus finished his preparations and picked his bag up. "I mean it Victoria, stay here until I get back. As soon as I have any news I will call you."

As Rufus was walking out the door his phone went and he answered Orla. At the same time, Victoria's phone rang.

Rufus had to make a quick decision: whether to get the update from Orla or to let Victoria take the call. He decided on both.

He put his earpiece in and spoke quickly and quietly to Orla. "Call coming in, I'll leave the line open."

He heard "Roger" through his earpiece as turned to Victoria, said "Deep breath," and turned her phone on.

They both heard a completely different voice on the line.

"This is the spokesman for Harakat al-Shabaab al-Mujahideen. We have taken possession of your parents and from now on you will be dealing with us and only us. You will deliver $10 million to us by Friday this week or we will kill one of your parents. This is non-negotiable and if you delay, or try and subvert our demand in any way we WILL kill one of them."

At the same time Rufus could also hear Orla giving a sitrep, "Tangos still in stronghold."

He was holding up his tablet with the prompt *Difficult*. He had to buy time. He had to get back control of the situation, which was slipping away fast. If he allowed the kidnappers to dictate the speed, then he had no chance.

"It's impossible for me to get you $10 million by Friday. ......Rufus was holding up *Banking rules* and *International Money Transfer Laws*...Victoria continued, "first of all I haven't got that sort of money, and second you just can't do it"

"Then you had better get your government to arrange for you to be able to transfer the money. Your capitalist corporations and Governments are always moving large amounts of cash around the world. Don't give me excuses. Just do it."

Rufus was holding up *Alone* and *Mistaken identity*. Victoria gave him the thumbs up, and Rufus prepared the next prompt. He had to time each prompt accurately so that he didn't bombard Victoria, but soon enough to give her brain time to process the information and formulate her own argument.

"But I am working on my own. I have come to Tanzania on my own. We are just a normal family"... Rufus was holding up *Doctor*..."If you think I work for a large corporation or the government..." *Retired* ... "then you have got the wrong people. I am a newly qualified doctor training to save people's lives and Mum and Dad are retired..." *Time*... "I will need time to raise money... *Lower Expectations*... "And there is no way I can get $10 million, I told the other people that. Please, you must believe me."

"You did not listen to what I said mzungu. $10 million by Friday, or we will kill one of them..."

Bargaining position...

"This is not negotiable."

Victoria was looking at Rufus quizzically...

"We do not make idle threats and you are dealing with professionals here..."

Two lives worth more than one... Victoria gave Rufus a nod...

"And we know what we are doing."

"AND I am trying my hardest to get you your money," said Victoria, "and surely you realise that two lives are worth more than one to me. If you kill one of them just because I cannot change banking laws, there is nothing I can do about that..." *Reality check...* "But I will not be prepared to pay as much for one of my parents as I am for both of them and I have to be honest with you, I CANNOT raise that sort of money. I am doing everything I can to raise money against my mum and dad's house, borrow from friends, arrange loans..." Rufus was giving encouragement and rolling his hands around each other, in the 'keep going' motion..."But I know I will not be able to get anywhere near $10 million. It's impossible for me. As I said to you a few seconds ago, if you think we are worth that sort of money you have made a mistake."

"How much are you parents worth to you?"

Rufus punched the *Priceless* prompt.

"They are irreplaceable, I cannot put a price on their lives..." *Reality...* "But if I physically haven't got the money, I can't do anything about it. Why aren't you asking me for $1 billion? I'll tell you why, because you know I can't raise that sort of money. Well face reality and understand I cannot raise $10 million." *British Government...* "It is impossible. And you know my government's stance on this sort of thing; they will not help me if they think I am going to pay you money. They have made it quite clear that I am on my own.... Rufus put his finger to his lips to stop Victoria. He wanted to give the new bandits time to let what she had said sink in.

There was an agonising few seconds of silence, which Victoria wanted to fill, but Rufus wanted to use the silence to their advantage. Silence could be a great tool in the armoury if it was used effectively, but it had to be judged just right. The tension filled the room as Victoria wondered whether they had accepted her perfectly true reasoning.

She looked Rufus in the eyes, gazing at his calm determined face, pleased that she had put her trust in him. She held the phone in her hand between her and Rufus, willing it to burst back into life, as she looked at Rufus's steady, deep breathing while she knew her own heart was racing, probably too quickly, pumping adrenalin into her blood, when she should be calm like him.

Eventually a voice came out of the phone breaking the silence, "How much can..." *$2 million maximum...* "you get for your parents' lives?"

Time was the next prompt that Rufus brought up.

"I don't know, I told the other people I might be able to get $2 million, but that will take time for me to arrange." Victoria was looking straight at Rufus, who was nodding gently at her and again held his finger to his lips.

"You do not have the luxury of time, when can you get it?" *As fast as I can* was the prompt that Rufus was holding up.

"I don't know. I will need some time to arrange everything. I am in the process of arranging the money and I am doing it as fast as I can."

Rufus put his finger to his lips again.

Again there were a few seconds silence on the other end.

"Phone me on this number tomorrow morning at ten and let me know when you can get us our money. The phone will be off until then," and the line went dead. Rufus went through his usual procedure to ensure the call had been ended and looked at Victoria, who was slumped in her chair. She had been so hopeful that Orla and Rufus were on the verge of getting her parents back, just to have the hope dashed on the rocks of Islamic Terrorism at the last minute.

She didn't know if her parents were still alive and if they were ok. And she had had to work hard during that phone call, having to concentrate on the kidnapper's voice and Rufus, while making sure she said the right things. She had been petrified about saying the wrong thing and getting her parents shot or beaten.

"Are you still with me Orla?" Rufus said into his hands free.

"Orla? Orla?" he looked at the screen of his phone and he was disconnected. He wasn't too worried, Orla could look after herself well enough, and she would be able to give them a full update as soon as she got back, he had to deal with Victoria, who looked like she had been five rounds in the ring.

"Well done Vicky. You did brilliantly. From them saying it was 'non-negotiable' you moved them to accepting our time frame and a lot less money. You did really well."

"Rufus. What is happening?" she said shaking with fear.

"We've had a minor temporary setback Vicky," he said stretching the truth as much as he dare with her. "We'll get straight back on to them first thing in the morning and take the initiative. We'll offer up an interim payment and see where that takes us. Hopefully they will take the bait and we will have only been put back a few hours. We'll have a few hurdles to overcome, but you have done so well up to now I am sure we can get things back on track."

"I wish I shared your optimism. My parents are being held by people you tell me are fucking al-fucking-Qaeda affiliated, terrorists, who don't give a flying fuck about their own lives, never mind anybody else's, and you are saying it is a minor set-back. What do you and fucking Action Woman plan to do next, eh? Abseil through the windows with knives between your teeth? Or parachute down on top of them and kill them all with your bare hands? For God's sake Rufus, we are talking about my parents' lives here, and you seem to think it is some sort of personal adventure. A battle of wills between you and the kidnappers. Just fucking give them the money, that's all they want, you've said that yourself." Victoria screamed at him.

Rufus surprisingly matched her tone, but not her emotion "I UNDERSTAND YOU ARE UPSET" quickly bringing his voice back to its usual level, "and I will explain why I am 'playing games'. You asked if I had ever failed, and I told you I had, with a person who didn't trust me, didn't 'follow the rules'. She thought the same as you and took it upon herself to take the money to the bandits herself, believing in the generosity of human nature and the innate kindness of the human spirit.

I found her body five days later. She had been brutally raped, multiple times vaginally and anally. She had one breast sliced off and various burn marks over her face and torso. She had teeth missing and contusions all over her body. We never did find her husband who had been kidnapped originally.

These people are devious, lying, manipulative bastards who have no regard for human life and do not think twice about breaking an agreement. They will swear on their mothers' lives, their children's eyes and they will still lie and cheat. Now I am determined to keep your mum and dad and you safe and this is the best way I know of doing it. It might seem counter-intuitive to you, and probably to most people, but it works."

Victoria, not for the first time on this roller coaster, was in turmoil. She felt the weight of the world on her shoulders. She knew Rufus was doing his best, but sometimes it felt like she was in the centre of a maelstrom, unable to understand or influence the events swirling around her.

Rufus put his arms around her and not for the first time she put her head on his chest. She knew he was right, she knew she needed him. She wouldn't last five minutes on the streets of Dar es Salaam without him. It was so hard to see where this was going and how he planned to get her parents back; the kidnappers seemed to hold all the aces; they had her parents; they knew the area; they could dictate times and places; they could just walk away and disappear if they wanted, killing her parents and disposing of the bodies in the jungle or the ocean, leaving the beasts or fish to destroy any evidence, anytime they wanted.

"Victoria. We WILL get your parents back."

"How can you promise that?"

"I can't promise THAT, but I do promise that we will do everything in our power to ensure we get them back safely. I don't want to sound conceited, but I know what

I am doing. This was always a possibility, and if you remember I told you, that's why I was pushing to get your mum and dad back so quickly, before these guys got hold of them."

"Yes I remember."

"But by the sound of it they are basically the same, they are avaricious, motivated by the money, there was nothing in their opening demands to you other than money. No political pronouncements, no demands to free prisoners, or the west to leave their country. Sometimes, some of them wrap it up claiming it is to wage a holy Jihad, others are more honest and just want the money. Money is the root of all evil and that is what this boils down to, and I will use that greed to hoist them by their own petard. It works Victoria and that is why I can objectively say it is a minor setback."

Victoria looked at him silently, sullenly, digesting what he had said. *Yeh I probably am too emotionally involved. But who wouldn't be if their parents had been kidnapped?* She felt herself shiver. *Was that an omen?* Or was it just her body closing down and her core temperature dropping? The scientist in her knew it was the latter as it was approaching 2a.m. and she had been busy and had shock after shock. The daughter in her feared it was a portent of evil things to come.

Chapter Fifty

Rufus suggested to Victoria that she get to bed, as she had had a long day. This time she knew she was shattered, and her will was weaker, she went into the bathroom to get ready. She looked at herself in the mirror and thought she looked like she had aged twenty years. She had dark rims around, and big bags under her eyes, she felt dirty and smelly and utterly, utterly exhausted. She washed her face and cleaned her teeth, stripped down to her underwear and returned to the bedroom. She slid into bed, feeling dithery and freezing cold.

Rufus had turned his attention to Orla and was trying to call her back. The phone kept going straight to answerphone. He looked up as he heard Victoria get into bed and could hear her teeth chattering.

"Are you ok?" he asked.

"I don't know. I hope it's a mixture of exhaustion and the time of night. The sooner I get warm in bed, the better."

Without thinking about the signal he would be giving her, he quickly assessed his own knowledge and knew that warmth of another human body would bring her temperature back to normal more quickly than any other method he had access to. He stripped down to his jockey shorts and got into bed next to her.

"Cuddle up to me Victoria, put your cold..." he jumped as she did exactly what he was telling her to, "feet on me. Jesus you are cold aren't you?"

She snuggled up to him, extracting the warmth from his near naked body. She wanted to stroke his abdomen and chest, and feel his shoulders, but he was completely focused on what he was doing.

A split-second of doubt about his sexuality flashed through her mind. *He does dress very well, and keeps himself really toned, well groomed and manicured. He seems oblivious to me, even now when I am semi-naked wrapped around him. Or perhaps he just didn't find me attractive? But he seems oblivious to Orla as well, and she is undeniably beautiful. That would explain a lot if he's gay.*

He kept trying Orla, but he wasn't too concerned that she wasn't answering; if she was driving she could well be in one of the many black spots in Dar. If that were the case she would be back shortly and would update him anyway.

Rufus felt Victoria's body start to relax as she drifted off to sleep. He decided to stay where he was to give her some comfort and he could carry on trying to contact Orla anyway.

He texted Orla, asking her to contact him as soon as she got a signal.

He lay in bed wide awake, reflecting on the day's events. *Shit, we were close to getting them back twice in just over twenty-four hours. It's back to square one now though, or perhaps even worse.* He thought about the tactics he would employ when dealing with Harakat al-Shabaab al-Mujahideen as he always insisted on calling them. The guy who he had spoken to sounded like Eddie Murphy when he was playing the part of an African, and that's what he would call him 'Eddie'. *We'll be able to say that we've already given them $50 000 as there is no way they will have left the money with Wisdom's gang, so we can play on that for a while. We can explain how difficult it was to just get $50 000. To get forty times that amount will take a long, long time, lots of organisation and will have the yanks and the Brits crawling all over us, making it really difficult.*

He continued to think about tomorrow's tactics as he kept phoning Orla, still without any response.

He got out of bed, confident that Victoria was fast asleep and opened a bottle of the complimentary water in the room. He guzzled the water down in one go, realising how thirsty he was. He set about preparing all the kit for the day, double-checking everything and cleaning his weapon, busying himself, trying to take his mind off Orla. After another thirty minutes, he was starting to get concerned.

He phoned her again, still nothing, and resent his text. He knew that some texts just disappeared into the ether in Tanzania, never to reach their intended recipient, while others found their way to the phone days later. There was still no reply from Orla though.

He skyped Don not wanting to alarm him, but needing to share his concerns and hopefully get some assistance in locating Orla. He woke Don who had only just gone to bed after a busy night of intercepting, plotting and charting. His wife and best mate were certainly keeping him busy.

"Hi mate."

"Good morning Ru. You've been busy haven't you?"

"Yeh we have, have you been keeping up?"

"Yeh, no problem mate, although I lost Orla this evening."

"That's what I'm phoning about. She was at the stronghold when the Harakat al-Shabaab al-Mujahideen bandits turned up, but I haven't heard from her since and I'm beginning to get a bit concerned." A bit concerned in their language was absolutely bloody frantic in anybody else's.

"She'll be ok," said Don. "She knows what she is doing."

"I know she does Don, but she has been a long time, she should have been back by now, and if not she should have called in with a sitrep."

"Mmmm, I see what you mean, and I can't locate her phone at all." There was a break in the conversation and Rufus could hear Don tapping away at keys and then he said, "Deidre is on the move, but the signal is so poor I can't give you an exact fix, but she was heading north past Bagamoyo. Do you know it?"

"Yeh I know Bagamoyo, about forty clicks north of here. It is very sparsely populated there. It's good for them, in that it will be difficult to find them, but also good for us if I have to take Deliberate Action."

"Mmm trouble is, the signal is so poor I can't give you a GPS fix, just a beacon fix, so it could take you sometime to locate them."

Don had tried to explain tracking to Rufus in the past, and although most of it went over his head, he did remember that the GPS fix was accurate in good conditions down to the square metre, but the beacon, or cell fix could just put the phone in a general arc from the mast, and could be very unreliable in certain conditions.

Various scenarios played through their minds, in which Orla had been killed or captured, her phone smashed or stolen from her. Don knew that Harakat al-Shabaab al-Mujahideen was no supporter of women's rights and dreaded to think of her potential fate if they had discovered her.

They both forced themselves to deal with what they knew and the 'now', rather than the 'what ifs'.

"Ok, mate in order of priority I need comms with Orla, then a fix on Deidre. I'll keep trying Orla, if you can see if there is anything you can do?"

"Will do," said Don, both of them now 'a bit concerned' and ended the call.

+++++++

Orla had crawled to the vehicles in which the bandits had arrived, under cover of the commotion going on inside the house, planning to disable at least one of them, to buy time, however, with the two guards left with the vehicles, that was going to be tough. They weren't that alert, but even they would have seen or heard her disabling the engines.

Very slowly and quietly, Orla unhooked the tarpaulin on one of the Toyota Hilux pick-ups and hoisted herself into the back, hoping that there was nothing under the cover that could either harm her or startle her and slid under the tarpaulin covering, pulling it back over the body work once she was inside.

It was a calculated risk and she hoped she was right: four vehicles with cabs could take sixteen people comfortably; there were ten bandits, two hostages and she didn't know how many captured bandits – she hoped no more than four. That would make sixteen, and no reason for anybody to have to jump in the back of any of the pick-ups.

She peeped out of a crack between the bodywork and the tarpaulin, watching for activity, and reached for her phone to text Rufus, but at the last second she realised that the light from the phone would light up the tarpaulin like a Christmas tree. She turned the phone off and lay motionless on the still warm metal of the floor of the flat bed. The commotion continued in the building-the speed which they spoke and the number of syllables in each sentence made it sound like they were always having a heated argument.

But Orla was convinced that on this occasion they were actually arguing, but she didn't know what about. She hoped it was whether they should take or leave Wisdom and his cronies, rather than doing anybody in. They all started to leave the house and walk towards the vehicles. She forced her body to relax as she lay in the back of the truck, the voices were all around her and she felt like they could see through the tarpaulin and knew she was there. They must be able to hear her breathing. A deaf man in a dumper truck could hear her heart pounding. Slowly doors started to slam shut, she counted them and felt three of the four doors on her vehicle shut. Fourteen... fifteen doors, there was only one door to go and it was the one on the nearside doors on her truck. Why hadn't he got in? What was he waiting for? Was he waiting for her to show out? Did he know she was there? Had one of the drivers spotted her as she got into the back? She didn't dare take a look; she had to supress her natural instincts and rely on her training, stay still and well hidden.

She heard footsteps moving towards the back of the vehicle, and unusually no talking. She imagined the bandit holding his finger to his lips, pointing at the rear of the truck as he crept towards the tailgate. She moved the weapon slightly up her body and slid off the safety. She decided that if he pulled the tarpaulin back, or peeked through a gap she would spring into action, shoot first and ask questions later. She made herself relax, so that she would react more effectively when he pulled the tarpaulin back, so that the training and the drills would take over.

The quietness outside her dark, confined world under the tarp was deafening. Her imagination could see him creeping around the back, weapon in one hand the other hand free to pull the tarpaulin back. She was in an awkward position to react and fight properly, and if she did shoot him, how could she possibly take on the rest of the gang? She steeled herself, ready for the sound and shock of gunfire.

Chapter Fifty-One

She lay waiting, nervous tension racking her body until she heard the unmistakable sound of a man urinating up the back of the truck, the gentle groan of relief as he emptied his bladder. She heard him pull up his zip and the engines start up, the last door shut and they were off.

Rufus was getting more than a little concerned now. He couldn't sleep. He was trying Orla's mobile constantly. Different scenarios played through his head, from her lying dead somewhere having been captured, to having had enough, throwing the phone and going to the airport. He knew the last proposition was a non-starter, but it still flashed through his mind.

Not for the first time he forced himself to deal with what he knew. Speculation, uninformed speculation was pointless; he had to deal with the facts.

After a couple of hours he could see the dawn starting to break and he heard his Skype ring tone sound off. He leaped up and answered Don.

"Just got a ping," said Don.

"Who from?"

"Both Deidre and Orla."

"Where?"

"It's not a good fix, but it's out west towards Morogoro."

"Morogoro?"

"Yeh about two to three hours' drive from you."

"Yeh, mate I know it. What're they doing there?"

"I don't know, 'cus I'd lost everything for a while. It appears they are together, so I can only think of four realistic scenarios. Orla has surveilled them there; she's been kidnapped and taken there with them; she's dropped her phone and they've picked it up; or they've killed her and taken the phone. I discount the first one, because she would have got in touch if she was tailing them, I discount the third one, because she would have made it back to you by now, so she's either dead or captured."

"What is the distance between the phones?"

"None that I can make out, but it is impossible to be precise, the signal is so poor."

"Ok. That changes things quite dramatically and I think I've got to go proactive. Concentrate on the location of those phones I'm going to have to call another favour in."

"Issa?"

"Yep, he still owes big time anyway, from the time I saved his ass when we helped them target poachers down south by Mtwara."

"Ok. anything I can do for you?"

"No mate, just keep monitoring those phones for me and update me will you. I'm going to get a power nap, before Victoria wakes up."

"Ok. I'll leave you thirty minutes and get on with it."

"Thanks Don. Oh and Don, if she is alive I will do my best to get her back."

"I know you will. There's no need to say it mate."

"Perhaps not, perhaps I'm just willing her to be alive as I feel responsible. And mate... if she's dead I'll exact retribution for you. I'll make them wish they were dead, they'll suffer for her."

"I know that too."

+++++++

Orla was suffering badly. She was being bounced up and down in the back of the truck on the flat bed. She had no padding or cushioning to ease the jarring effect of her body on the metal. It was a bone shaking journey. She tried to get some sort of purchase wedging between the wheel arches to prevent the worst of the impacts on her body, but it was so incessant that she had to keep changing position to stop any particular part of her body suffering too much.

She shoved the bit of hessian sacking that had been left in the back under her backside to try and give herself a little bit of cushioning; at first the relief was immense, but after just a few minutes the jarring was just as bad as ever. Some of the pot-holes they went down were particularly painful, it was almost as if they knew she was in the back and they were having a laugh at her expense, finding the deepest pot-holes to cause the most pain. There was nothing she could do: she couldn't get out, or stand up, she couldn't get a cushion; she just had to suffer the agony she was going through. She knew she would be black and blue all over and for once in her life wished she was carrying some extra padding to soften some of the impacts on her bones.

She could see the sun had risen and took the calculated risk of turning her phone on: with travelling at the speed they were and the daylight now washing over them she reasoned that it was nearly impossible for the light of the phone to be seen.

It took her several attempts to prepare the text to send to Rufus because of all the bumping around, causing her to misspell and mistype the text. Eventually she was ready and pressed 'send' only to see the phone had no service. She cursed silently and watched the phone's screen, waiting for a bar of signal to appear to give her the window of opportunity to send the text.

Rufus was awoken by a text alert on his phone buzzing. He looked down and saw it was from Orla.

"Infil'd B's truk. D&M alive. Gt D 2 gt a fx."

Rufus was pretty sure that was from Orla, but he couldn't be certain. He didn't know if the bandits had got hold of the phone, or made Orla send the text. He couldn't risk ringing to speak to her, as he might give her away if she was safe, but he couldn't reply in the open as he didn't know who had control of the phone. Fortunately they had agreed code words which appeared innocuous to a third party.

"Hi Orla. Thanks. Have you heard the news today?"

Rufus thought about the pros and cons of sending the text. He knew Orla would have the phone on vibrate if she was still at liberty and so felt fairly confident that he could send it. If she was being held, they could either force her to send the correct response, but that would take some time to get her to do that. But if they held the phone they would know that she was working with somebody. But there again, the text was harmless and she would be able to explain it away easily. He pressed send and waited, hoping he had made the right decision.

He waited for what seemed like an eternity, willing the phone to burst into life.

After a few minutes his phone buzzed.

"Yes I was shocked by the announcement."

"Are you ok?" This was still part of their prearranged code.

"No, I've got stomach cramps."

Rufus knew that Orla was ok and free to communicate. He fired up Skype and got hold of Don.

"I've got Orla texting me, she's ok, she says she's infiltrated the bandits' truck and that Deidre and Martyn are alive," said Rufus.

"Thank fuck for that," said Don. "I thought we were going to have to find a new surveillance operative." Employing their black humour to hide their true feelings, "I wonder how the crazy woman has done that?"

"I don't know, but at one point I thought I was going to have to carry her luggage back for you."

"Nah, you could have given it to charity. It wouldn't fit me. Although I suppose I could have given it to the next Mrs Ward. Waste not want not I always say."

"You old romantic."

"I suppose I'd better get working, find a location for you?"

"Yes please mate and I'll text her, see if she knows where she is, anything that can give us a clue."

They left Skype open while they worked. Unfortunately Orla could not give Rufus any clue as to where she was, she hadn't seen any signs, despite looking out the back of the truck.

Don had slightly better luck and was able to get a better fix on both the phones and located them in the Mikumi National Park area, just to the west of Morogoro.

"I know it roughly," said Rufus, "completely uninhabited out there. It's an area about twice the size of London, so I'll need a better fix than that mate. Co-ordinates would be useful."

"I know. Calm down scrum-half, I'll get 'em to you as soon as I can give you a better result."

"Sorry, mate, it's just that I feel responsible for her."

"Well don't. She's a professional, she knows what she is doing and she knows the risks, I don't hold you responsible at all."

"Thanks mate, but you know it doesn't change anything don't you?"

"Yeh, I know... and thanks," concluded Don.

Rufus had hardly slept for twenty-four hours, except for his power nap, and he knew he wasn't going to get a chance today. He had to make plans: he had to get to Mikumi and he had to make sure Victoria was safe and secure.

He made a couple of phone calls and went to wake Victoria. He let himself into her room and sat on the edge of her bed. She was dead-beat, not yet adapted to the life of a junior doctor, surviving on minimal sleep and making life and death decisions in a state of permanent exhaustion. Her hair fell over her face, as she slept soundly. The bed sheet hardly had a wrinkle in it as she had slept so peacefully and motionless. Rufus put his hand on her shoulder and rocked her gently. He heard her murmur and groan at first as she came out of her deep sleep. He could see consciousness returning to her face, washing over her body and her senses returning from their hibernation. He waited for her eyes to open and focus on him. She smiled at him, a genuine full faced smile, with her lips and eyes, and he knew she had forgiven him and was back "on-side" at least until he told her about Orla.

In reality Victoria had 'forgiven' him immediately and was thinking about how she had snuggled up to him and the warmth and feel of his body last night. It sent a tingle through her body. Then she remembered her 'gay' theory.

"Good morning Victoria," he said.

"Morning Ru. How did you sleep?"

"I haven't really Victoria. I've had about twenty minutes I think."

Victoria sat up in bed, letting the sheets fall down around her abdomen, revealing her bra. "Twenty minutes. Is that all? Is Orla back?"

"No she's not, she's followed your mum and dad to a place called Mikumi," replied Rufus, as if it was the most natural thing in the world to be sitting on the edge of a semi-naked young lady's bed telling her his colleague was following her parents who had been kidnapped by terrorists.

"Where's that?"

"It's out to the west of here, by Morogoro."

"Yeh, I'm still none the wiser. Are they ok?"

"Yes they are ok I think, but it's very difficult to communicate with Orla at the moment. The signal isn't brilliant and she has to be very circumspect when she uses the phone."...*And she won't be able to charge it,* thought Rufus.

"What are we going to do then?" asked Victoria.

"I'm glad you asked that. First of all, we have to prepare for the call at ten o'clock, so we have an hour to prepare for that. I need you up and ready in fifteen minutes. I've ordered some food for the room and we'll rehearse while we are eating. I'll be back in fifteen minutes."

"You don't have to leave I can get dressed in the bathroom, while you carry on working out here." She got out of bed, still dressed in her underwear, looking for any sort of reaction from Rufus, who didn't look at her but examined his phone, seemingly oblivious to the lacy underwear she was wearing while standing a few feet from him.

"I need to go back to my room and get a couple of things done then I'll bring my kit through," he said, looking at her momentarily, still not seeming to register the way she was looking at him.

Oh my god, they both thought simultaneously but for completely different reasons, both misunderstanding the other completely.

She is so naïve and innocent, she doesn't know what she is doing to me, Jesus it's getting harder to remain focused. She must think I'm a real old fart to feel comfortable with her standing talking to me like that, Rufus thought as he went back to his room and knocked out a few press-ups to distract himself. He jumped in the shower to freshen up for the day and put his last clean shirt and underwear on.

He didn't even look at me, thought Victoria. *Even if he is gay, how could he not look out of curiosity? My gay friends still look at the opposite sex. They say they can admire the beauty, the form and definition, just not find it sexually attractive. I know I can look at other women and know they are beautiful. But he didn't even seem to know I was in my underwear. He must think I am a real munter.* She got in the shower bewildered.

She was disturbed by Rufus coming back into the room. She had been day-dreaming for longer than she thought. She hopped out of the shower, wrapped the towels around her body and hair and looked out from the bathroom. Fortunately the heat of the shower accounted for the flush in her face as he looked up at her.

"Come on Victoria, what have you been doing? Did you go back to sleep or something?"

"Yes, sorry Ru, I sat on the bed and just drifted off. I'll be ready as quickly as I can."

She dried and dressed herself in the bathroom wondering if he believed her. By the time she returned to the bedroom, she could see room service had delivered their breakfast, Rufus had laid it out and prepared the room in readiness for them.

Chapter Fifty-Two

Braddock was on the secure line to Sir Peregrine Dennis, as soon as he got into the office and read the update on Tanzania.

Dennis was sitting in his office at Vauxhall, overlooking the Thames, reading his morning briefing papers which had been left on his desk by his secretary.

"Good morning Sir Peregrine," Braddock said.

"Oh hello, Robert; to what do I owe this call?"

"I thought you'd be interested to know about a little update on our friends, the Conways."

"The Conways?"

"Yes, you know; the couple who were kidnapped in Tanzania?" Braddock said frustrated, wondering how Dennis could not remember the names of the couple they had been discussing for the last few days.

"Oh, yes of course," Dennis lied; he was distracted reading a report on suspected Chinese government sponsored hacking.

Braddock could immediately tell that Dennis wasn't listening; he had that vacant sound about him, not engaging in the conversation.

"We have intercepted some traffic indicating they are on the move."

"Oh, really?" Dennis's voice was monotone responding on auto-pilot. "Put it on a BJ will you, there's a good chap," and terminated the call.

Braddock couldn't believe his ears. He was furious. He had diverted resources at the behest of the COBRA committee meeting, he was paying overtime out of a budget that was being squeezed until it squeaked, he believed that this was a government priority, and he had been summarily dismissed by this public schoolboy, Cambridge graduate, sycophantic, upper-class snob, who had not even listened to what he had to say – and if he had then he wouldn't have given him his full attention.

He considered his options: he could raise it at the next COBRA meeting and do Dennis's legs in front of the minister, Dennis's boss, but he would have to be careful how he managed that one. He could phone Major Fraser and tell him about the intelligence, because after all, it had been agreed at COBRA that SF would be kept up-to-speed on all intel. He could approach the Under Secretary of State, and brief her off the record, but she was public school as well, and despite all of the changes in British society, the old school tie still had a great deal of influence and loyalty so it wouldn't take long for it to get back to Dennis.

He knew there was no love lost between SF and The Firm, and the major was definitely not a public schoolboy. He decided to contact Major Fraser. The only thing he needed to decide now was: would it be overt or covert. It didn't take him long to decide – it would be covert, behind Dennis's back.

He picked up the phone and dialled Major Fraser's mobile number, knowing the capabilities of his own systems and that of other countries, but knowing both his and the Major's phones were encrypted, Robert Braddock didn't want to take the chance of discussing anything on the phone and arranged to meet the infamous soldier for a coffee.

Mad Frankie Fraser grabbed the opportunity with both hands. He knew that Braddock was intimidated by the wily old spy, and he guessed that he knew far more about what was going on than he was being allowed to divulge. He was out of the his office and at Charing Cross Tube station in under ten minutes, on a Northern Line train, and was in Brent Cross in under thirty minutes.

+++++++

Nick Cooper, Head of Station at the British High Commission in Umoja House, Dar es Salaam took the call on his encrypted mobile phone from Esther.

"Mambo," said Cooper.

"Poa," said Esther in the traditional, informal Swahili greeting.

"Are you ok?" asked Cooper.

"I need to meet straight away," said Esther.

"Agh, that will be difficult," Cooper was torn; he knew that if Esther was calling him, it was really important and almost certainly involved the Conways. "I have an appointment with the High Commissioner in five minutes. Can we say two hours in the lagoon?"

Esther understood the code for the location and continued.

"This is very important, and is about our guests, I am sure you want to meet and discuss their position as soon as possible."

"Yes I understand that, but the High Commissioner is not a lady that appreciates being stood up on a scheduled appointment, two hours is the soonest I can do."

"Ok boss, but I think you will regret delaying our meet."

"Perhaps, Rafiki, but I can't do anything about it," said Cooper, thinking more about his personal career, buttering up the High Commissioner, relying on her support as well as Sir Peregrine's. "Surely nothing is so important it can't wait two hours, and then I assure you I will be with you and you will have my undivided attention."

I know I will, thought Esther.

"Hakuna shida, see you at 1030," said Esther.

Chapter Fifty-Three

Rufus and Victoria ate breakfast while he prepared her for the ten o'clock call. He took several calls and answered texts as they ate and role-played. As usual he tried to predict the way he thought the call would go for her.

"Unfortunately you are going to have to go over old ground. They are going to repeat a lot of what Wisdom, erm, James said to you."

"Is that his real name? Wisdom? Well he didn't show much wisdom when he kidnapped my mum and dad did he, eh? Has he not heard of the great Victoria Conway?"

"Ha ha, he didn't know what a fearsome, feisty, gutsy girl he'd be talking to did he? And neither do these guys, so we have to be just as focused, just as determined and work just as well together. Are you still comfortable with the way I set things up?"

"Definitely, I get so much help from you like this," Victoria replied, meaning every word.

They both looked at the clock as it approached 10a.m.

"Are you ready? We want to show how reliable we are and we will phone at exactly ten. Relax, some deep breaths and let's do this."

As usual it took several attempts to get through to the phone which was answered by Eddie.

"Hello," was the simple answer.

"Habari za hasubui," said Victoria trying to ingratiate herself a little with the man at the end of the phone.

"And what news do you have of our money?" came back the unemotional response.

"It's still early in the morning, but I have been to the bank and explained I will be transferring a large amount of funds from UK banks to the bank here..."

"Stop there, there is no need to transfer money from your British banks to Tanzanian banks, to withdraw, to bring to us, which will all take time and give your soldiers the chance to capture us. I will give you the details of a Luxemburg Bank account into which you can transfer the funds. Once I have it confirmed that the transfer is complete, I will release your parents."

Rufus had put his hand on Victoria's arm, ensuring she remained quiet, giving Eddie the chance to speak.

He showed her the prompt *Time.*

"That will still take time for me to get that amount of money together..."

...*Trust.*

"I am in constant contact with people back in Britain arranging the sale of my parents' house, and getting the money arranged for me. And how do I know that you will release my mum and dad when I have transferred the money?"

"You don't, you will have to trust me. Why would I want to keep them any longer than is absolutely necessary? But you are in no position to argue about how to deliver the money to me..."

Agree... Victoria looked at the prompt and at Rufus and he nodded silently, confirming that he wanted her to agree to the condition.

"When you tell me you have the money, I will give you the details of the account and not before. I will release your parents and phone you to tell you where they are. It's simple if you do as I say."

"Ok. I will do as you state, but as I said, it will still take me some time to get the money into the bank, and I don't want to mislead you at all. I am not a rich woman..."

"Stop," he interrupted her again. "Do not try and tell me you are not a wealthy family. We know who you are. We know what your parents do and we know the British government will pay to get one of their ambassadors back..."

"Pardon?"

"Now, think about what I've said and call me back when you have reconsidered your position."

The phone went dead. After he double-checked the call was cut, Rufus nearly diverted from his own post-call procedure after that revelation.

"Well done Victoria. That was nice and calm, and amicable. How do you feel?"

"Confused, I don't know what he meant. Who does he think is an ambassador?"

"We'll come to that in a minute, because I am wondering exactly the same thing. So if they call back, it will probably be about your confusion over the introduction of that title, we need to check that his meaning of the title ambassador is the same as ours, ok?"

"Yes, I think so. How do you want me to ask him?"

"Well, if I were you, I would ask him straight, there is no point trying to be vague or oblique. I'd say who do you think is an ambassador? And where do you think they are ambassador to? Now do you have any idea what he means? You've told us the truth about your parents haven't you?"

"Of course I have. If one of my parents was an ambassador, I would have gone straight to the Foreign and Commonwealth Office."

"But you don't know what your mum did as a job. You've told us that."

"Yeh, I know, but she sure as shit wasn't an ambassador. I would have known. We would have travelled all over the world. And Dad worked in a bank."

"Did Mum disappear for long periods of time?"

"No, not that long, no. Ru she was NOT an ambassador."

"But you don't know what she did?"

"No I know we've established that haven't we?"

"So why do they think that one of them is an ambassador, unless they are just trying to confuse you, and disorient you? I can't see them doing that. Perhaps it's a case of mistaken identity and an ambassador was travelling around on the same sort of itinerary as your mum and dad. I'll set Don on to that straight away. He'll have to do some research with the F&CO if they'll tell him. And I need to text Orla."

Rufus set to work on his phone and tablet, updating and tasking his two colleagues.

Victoria sat wondering what on earth was going on again. *Why did everybody have to speak in riddles? Do everything so secretively and furtively. Surely there must be a simpler way than this?*

She sat watching and listening to Rufus, wondering how this was all going to end.

Meanwhile, Orla was thinking the same thing for different reasons; she was cursing they had arrived, at what seemed to be their destination, in the light, and that limited her opportunities to get out of the pick-up.

They eventually stopped after nearly six hours' driving through the night. She heard all sixteen doors open and slam shut, concluding that all the occupants of the vehicles had got out. She could hear shouting and calling between the men, and the squeal of metal hinges, echoing and protesting about the lack of oil as metal moved against metal, and assumed something big was being opened or closed.

It was frustrating for her, but she knew she had to remain calm and patient while there was activity around her. She wanted to get out and stretch her aching body and examine the bruises she knew were going to be all over her, and two contradictory sensations overwhelmed her: more than anything she needed water and a pee. She examined the last few drops of her meagre water supply – if she drank it, her focus would change slightly as she would know she had no more, but if she kept a drop back, psychologically she would feel better. She knew she could drink her own urine if she had to; something she had done many times in the past and that would have killed two birds with one stone, but things weren't that desperate – yet. Even though it was going to get even hotter under there through the day, and she questioned her own ability to withstand the energy-sapping heat without any water to sustain her, she knew that breaking cover was out of the question until darkness fell, and hoped that she could last until then to have a drink.

She undid her webbing belt pushing down her trousers and knickers to her knees, wiggling her bottom and lifting it slightly to free the trousers and their attachments. She pulled the hessian sacking under herself, ensuring her pelvis was still slightly raised and she peed; a long relieving steady stream of urine. The hessian soaked up most of the warm, salty fluid, but inevitably some escaped and trickled downhill wetting her back. She couldn't roll out of the way, or raise herself; she just had to soak it up.

I thought I'd left all this behind when I left the army, she thought, imagining the attractive sight she must be presenting.

She retrieved an identical carbon fibre blanket to Rufus's out of her webbing and unfolded it to give her a little protection from heat of the flat bed and the wet of the urine, but it wasn't intended for that: when she went to the boffins in SRR and told them of her idea, she never dreamt she would be using the blanket in these circumstances.

She allowed herself a little day dream, wondering whether she would have made her fortune by manufacturing the blanket herself. She had designed it as a waterproof ground sheet for O.Ps and its secondary use was as a hedge scaler: several times on jobs, they had been thwarted by dense hedges and she had come up with the idea. When going rural they would usually work in a minimum of pairs. The first operative would boost the second up to the top of hedge and the blanket would be simultaneously unfurled, the carbon fibre weave creating an impenetrable protective screen from the thorniest of hedges.

She had designed a loop in each corner, so that the operative who was over the hedge could hold the loops, while the first one could use one of the loops as a stirrup to boost themselves up and over. The blanket would be pulled over for reuse.

It was an immediate success and used by Special Forces across the world, and she never made a penny.

After what seemed like an eternity, she slowly, gently, ever-so-carefully lifted the tarpaulin a fraction of an inch. She knew, like every wild animal knows innately, that the eye is drawn to movement, and so the more slowly she lifted the tarp, the better.

She identified the best cover to utilise later, and surveying the rest of the compound – for that was what she was in – she could see an eight foot wall all around, topped with razor wire. From her position she couldn't see the gate, but had to assume there was one and that it would be guarded and there would be guard patrols around the compound. She surmised that the rusty hinge sound she heard earlier probably came from the gates.

She settled back down as she felt her phone vibrate, and read Rufus's text.

Chapter Fifty-Four

Cooper and Esther met on the eleventh floor roof top bar at The Holiday Inn, on the corner of Upanga Road and Azikiwe Street in the city centre. The roof gave a panoramic view of the city down to the harbour and the opposite shore line of Kigamboni. They looked identical to the scores of businessmen that were meeting in the bar, doing deals, bidding for contracts and planning business initiatives. They found a high table in the corner of the roof top, a little away from the other meetings.

"Habari za hasubuhi," said Cooper.

"Nzuri," said Esther, in the more formal greeting. Nick always liked to use a little Swahili, but wasn't confident enough to conduct meetings, or intelligence updates in the language. He was wired with his covert microphone, so that he didn't miss anything, but he liked to be confident that he understood everything that was being said, and there was no misunderstanding.

They exchanged small talk while they waited for the waiter to approach their table and take their order. It was important in most African countries to spend time talking about family matters, health and welfare, before business matters, and it is often regarded as insulting when westerners ignore the important pleasantries of a meeting.

Esther ordered a coke and Cooper ordered a Gin and tonic, loosened his tie, and wished that he could take his jacket off, but couldn't as the bug was sewn into the lining and he would have to put it behind him, over the bar stool.

Esther looked at him, thinking it was still a little early to be drinking alcohol, and as Islam forbade it anyway, he would not be touching a drop personally.

Their drinks arrived and the waiter left and they got down to business.

"What's so important Ismail?" using his source's real name.

"They've been taken, bwana."

Excellent, thought Cooper, *so our friends have taken the bait?*

This part of the operation had been instigated by Esther, at Cooper's behest. He had planned it all and had just been waiting for Esther to contact him to let him know that al-Shabaab had been drawn into his net, so that he could alert Sir Peregrine.

"Who have? The Conways?"

"Yes bwana. The Pirates went and took them in the night, with Wisdom and three of the others. They left me out of that part of the operation, as I am useful in other areas. Your idea to make them think that he is a British ambassador, travelling anonymously worked perfectly."

"Tell me what happened." Cooper's voice was urgent and excited, as this had the beginnings of a great coup for him but sources had a terrible habit of telling you what they think you want to hear, which has got western intelligence agencies in trouble in the recent past, so he needed to double-check everything, so when Kumi made contact he could corroborate everything.

"The pirates, bwana, they went last night, took the two mzungus, the Conways, Wisdom and the others."

"Ok, so tell me in detail what happened, and who do you mean by 'pirates'?"

"You know who I mean, al-Shabaab bwana."

Cooper did know, but he had to make sure they understood each other completely.

Cooper was giving him his undivided attention, and congratulated himself that he had left his jacket on to record the conversation."

"Ok Ismail, let's start from the beginning. I need you to go through this in detail, from the start, don't leave anything out, no matter how small a detail or how inconsequential you think it might be," said Cooper in an urgent business voice.

"Ok bwana," Ismail said, thinking, *yes, you want to talk to me now don't you, you arrogant British shit. Have I ever told you something was important when it wasn't? Have I ever given you wrong information? I risk my life for you, and the few measly dollars that you pay me. And you treat me like shit. If I didn't need the money to keep my nyumba ndogo, my beautiful Sia, then I would tell you to fuck off, but she is such a sweet little sexy thing, I can't do without her, and I need your damn money to keep her in that little house, so we can spend time together, away from my harridan wife.*

Cooper settled down to listen to Esther, not bothering with his note book and pen. He was trained to remember information and a note book and pen tended to be a barrier to the conversation, anyway he would have it all recorded if he needed to review it.

Esther explained everything to Cooper, who frequently interrupted him to ask questions, which annoyed Esther intensely, thinking *I'm getting to that, just let me tell you what I'VE done, not you, what I've done risking my life with those pirates, for you and your Queen.*

+++++++

Back in London there was indeed another meeting taking place simultaneously on the same topic. Robert Braddock met Mad Frankie Fraser for coffee as arranged, in which Braddock updated him on the Sigint, and Dennis's reaction when he had told him. He could see a vein throbbing in the major's temple, as he fought off the rage that was threatening to inundate him. Major Fraser did, in fact, control his rage... just... as he knew he had to remain calm and focused. He knew he would have probably been a member of the General Staff if it wasn't for his temper, which he had learned too late in his career, to keep in check.

He double-checked everything with Braddock, to make sure he understood correctly, and to ensure he was not being set up to fire blank rounds. He thanked Braddock and marched back to the tube and his office, on a mission, determined to be on the front foot when COBRA met again in twenty-four hours.

Chapter Fifty-Five

Deidre and Martyn were manhandled from the pick-up trucks and dragged into the ramshackle building.

Martyn was blindfolded and led away; they shoved him into some sort of underground cellar, banging his head, elbow and shoulder as he fell in and temporarily lost consciousness.

They had gone from the frying pan into the fire. When they first heard the commotion, they thought they were being rescued. They had different emotions thinking that the British government had sent Special Forces to rescue them and they would be free and flying back home to Britain, to a hot shower, good food and a comfortable bed. When they realised what had happened they couldn't believe they had actually been taken by far worse, more ruthless men than the ones who had taken them in the first place. They still couldn't understand what was happening or why it was happening to them. And now they were in even worse conditions, if that were possible, than the ones they had been in. After an excruciating car journey, they now found themselves in tiny cellars beneath an industrial unit. It was like being buried alive: there was no air, no light, no room to move and very little sound. They were actually in the converted mechanics' inspection pits in the building. Since the site had been closed up and trucks no longer could or needed to be serviced, the pits had been changed to make-shift "prisoner" cells. The smell of diesel and diesel oil, fetid body odour, and of the faeces of previous residents of the pits still lingered, making them both gag. Deidre didn't know what was worse; the conditions in which she was now being held or the knowledge that the bandits were directly above them and could finish them off at any time.

Martyn was completely burnt out. The stress that he had been under had turned him into a zombie, the living dead. If he had the cognitive ability to choose between a bullet in the head or another day in captivity, he would choose the bullet. Tears trickled down his face, although for all intents and purposes he was not crying, but he could not stop the tears coming. He tasted the salty moisture on his tongue, and it was the only thing that persuaded him that he was actually still alive. Their clothes were soiled, stinking and putrid, their hair was matted and Martyn's beard looked like it had the left-overs from a kids' party squished into it.

Their new hosts were armed to the teeth and forced Deidre to sit on a chair. She was alert and surveyed the building in which she was now ensconced; knowing she didn't have the skills to escape, but still needed to remember detail. She was committing distinctive features to memory so that if necessary she could identify the building in the future. She took in the high small four-pane windows, the old colonial advertisements and logos on the wall; the two still discernible through the discolouring of years of blazing sunlight, cigarette smoke and vehicle fumes, were for the *Austin* car company and another was for the *Jowett* commercial vehicle company. She noted the position of the manager's office, all things that were as permanent as anything ever is in Africa.

"You will write out your full details on this paper for my colleague," said one of the men. He was a tall slim man, with a scarf wrapped around his head and a scarf across his mouth. He was wearing pseudo military clothes, and from what Deidre could see, he was heavily armed, with grenades clipped to his belt, a pistol on his side and what she assumed was an AK47.

"What do you mean? You know who I am, you have my passport and everything."

"DO NOT QUESTION ME. You will write out your details, or I will drag up that excuse of a husband of yours and execute him now."

"I'm sorry," said Deidre, "I wasn't trying to be awkward, I thought I was making it easier for you."

"Do not think, just do it."

Deidre picked up the pen and wrote out her details in her immaculate cursive writing for which she had been well known in her previous jobs, completing her full name, date of birth, home address and employment details. That sheet of paper was removed and handed to a young looking man, who walked to a corner of the room and started typing into his laptop. Deidre was then given another sheet of paper.

"The same for your husband," said the leader.

"Babu!" shouted the young man from across the room, as a term of respect for the older man. The young man approached the older man and explained that he could not read the writing and therefore could not carry out his job.

The older man looked like thunder and back-handed Deidre across the face, making her fall off the chair.

Deidre had never been struck in the whole of her adult life, and it came as a tremendous shock to her, and even though she could feel the tears welling up in her eyes, she refused to let them see that she was hurt either physically or mentally.

She picked herself up and sat back on the chair. She put what she wanted to say to the back of her mind and apologised.

"I'm sorry, it's just that I am so nervous my writing isn't what it usually is," she lied.

Her captors showed no compassion at all, and Babu put another sheet of paper in front of her.

"Write," he said.

"Whose details? Mine or my husbands?"

"Your details you stupid whore."

Deidre capitalised all the words this time, so that each letter was perfectly formed and legible and handed the paper back to Babu.

He snatched the paper out of her hand and handed it to the younger man again, who ran back to his laptop. The rest of the gang were sat around a small television, eating and drinking, showing very little interest in the proceedings. They had locked and bolted Martyn in his cell and appeared quite phlegmatic about the whole thing.

Babu then placed another sheet of paper in front of Deidre.

"Now mzungu, write his details, and make sure we can read it."

Deidre capitalised Martyn's details for them, she did not want to be struck again and could taste the blood on the inside of her mouth. She handed the paper to Babu, who grabbed her by the elbow and pulled her over to where the young man was working. He sat her down and watched the young man interrogate the internet.

She was amazed at the sites he was accessing, realising she merely scratched the surface of the 'net when she carried out an everyday search, but this man was mining deep into the depths of the digital world, unearthing all sorts of data she never thought possible.

She could see he was using a program called Maltego, absent-mindedly thinking about using it when she got home.

They cable-tied Deidre's hands, and put a black hood over her head, she heard the cellar door being opened and then the ground rush up to meet her as she lost her footing and fell into the pit.

She broke her fall with her hands, but broke her wrist in the process, hearing the bone snap as much as felt it. She could feel and hear the blood pumping through her head fearing she was going to faint with the searing sudden pain. The hood over her head making her claustrophobic, amplifying the pulse she could hear, making it echo through her whole head.

She heard Martyn being dragged from his pit, he was blubbing like a child, crying and sobbing and begging.

Thwack Martyn was either slapped or punched followed by a microsecond of silence as if somebody had sucked the entire atmosphere out of the building. Martyn gasped for air and there was a voice she recognised as Babu's.

"Now Ambassador..."

Ambassador? Thought Deidre, *What is he talking about?*

"...your wife has provided us with all your details, which we will cross check..."

"Ambassador? What do you mean ambassador?" Martyn was gasping for air and trying to think at the same time. His reactions were a good second slower than Deidre's and lightyears slower than his captors as Deidre heard another crunching *thwack*, which Martyn had clearly not seen coming and it sounded like he took the full force of the blow. She heard him collapse to the ground and start coughing a rasping, gurgling cough, as if he had been on twenty a day all his adult life.

"We know you are trained, Ambassador, but so are we, that is why we have got Lady Hanson to give us all the details we need first."

Who's Lady Hanson? Thought Deidre.

Martyn was on the floor gasping for breath and groaning with pain. He was not a physical man, and certainly not a violent man. He had never been punched in his life.

After, what seemed like an eternity, Deidre heard him croak.

"Who's Lady Hanson?"

"Come, come, Ambassador, please do not treat us like fools. We are professionals. We build our intelligence carefully and slowly in great detail. We know everything about you, as confirmed by your wife, Lady Hanson."

Martyn was just about to deny knowing anybody by that name, but came to his senses just in time and kept quiet.

"Now, you will complete this sheet of paper with all the requisite details, and just remember that we have already had our information confirmed by your wife."

Martyn didn't know what to do, he could only tell the truth, he didn't understand what was going on, or why they thought he was an ambassador. If he lied he would, presumably, contradict what Deidre had said, and get a beating; if he told the truth, they would think he was lying and he'd still get a beating. He decided he had to write down the truth and picked up the pen.

He completed the form in his best handwriting and told the whole truth about them and handed the form over to Babu.

Babu looked at the form, and could immediately see that his details corroborated Deidre's. He was furious and shouted at his men.

They ran to Deidre's pit, dragged her out and removed her blindfold.

"The British Foreign Office is clearly very clever and well used to lying. Lying about British colonialism, lying about Islam; and the pernicious dogs have taught you both to lie too. Now you will tell me the truth," he shouted at his men again and they took hold of Martyn's left hand, forced all of his fingers down, into a fist, except for his index finger and lay that flat on the table.

Babu calmly walked over to the wall of the building, picked up a machete and walked back with an exaggerated swagger to where Martyn was quivering with fear.

"PLEASE. PLEASE," Martyn squealed.

"We have told you the truth!" shouted Deidre. "I don't know who you think we are."

Another series of commands in Swahili, and Babu's men pinned Martyn down, while the other held Deidre facing him.

"You have a count of three to tell me who you are, or your husband loses his finger," said Babu in a baleful voice. "One..."

"We have told you the truth," said Deidre, looking Babu in the eyes. She looked at Martyn who was clearly incapable of stringing any coherent words together.

"Two..."

"I am Deidre Conway, Martyn is my husband of thirty-four years, we live..."

"Three." *Thhhhhwwwump.* The machete came down on Martyn's finger, slicing it clean off.

Martyn didn't even register what they had just done to him.

Deidre looked in disbelief, completely dumfounded as to what had just happened. Her jaw fell open, and her body started shaking, and then she let out her first sign of weakness and emotion as she emitted an ear-piercing scream.

Outside, Orla heard the scream, and could only imagine what was going on, but she knew she was powerless to do anything about it and cursed herself, but she knew that any pre-emptive action would not only mean her death, but would also sign the death warrant of Deidre and Martyn. All she could do was text a sitrep to Rufus.

Chapter Fifty-Six

Victoria felt like a spare part as Rufus made telephone calls and Skyped Don, in which they seemed to talk in riddles; had conversations in Swahili and was texting like a teenager. After what seemed like an eternity, Rufus sat down with her.

"Sorry about that Vicky, but without Orla here there seems to be more than twice the workload. I'll update you on everything, but first there is a change of plan and we are going to redeploy to a local airfield and start putting some calls in. Hopefully Don will get us a fix on your mum's phone and I'm going to fly up and pay them a visit."

"What? You're not going anywhere without me. Not again. You keep telling me we're a team, but as soon as you want to do something you drop me like a ton of bricks."

"It's not like that Vicky, the local air force is doing me a favour by giving me a lift, they shouldn't be doing that and I plan to parachute in to Mikumi."

"Well arrange for me to come with you." Victoria folded her arms over her chest and stuck her chin out. Rufus felt uncomfortable, he didn't want Victoria to come, but if they needed to make another phone call, it would be useful to have her with him. He was in a dichotomy. He could get her driven up, but that could waste valuable time. He decided it was safer for her to stay in Dar.

"I'm sorry Victoria, you can't come with me it's too dangerous."

"Rufus, I'm coming. I've done a tandem skydive and I know it's possible. I know you are an expert parachutist from your previous job, we could do the same and you could still land us on a sixpence."

"But..."

"No buts Rufus, you know you can do it, you know I'm safer with you than anywhere else in this forsaken country, and you need me with you."

"I've never done a tandem jump in combat conditions though Victoria."

"But you have done one? You know what you are doing; it's the same principle isn't it?"

"Well, yes."

"You need me to talk on the phone don't you?"

Victoria was using a technique Rufus had told her about known as the "Yes cycle", by getting him to agree to a lot of closed questions.

"I'm a doctor aren't I?"

"Yes."

"So I could be useful, couldn't I?"

"Yes."

"That's settled then, I'm coming," said Victoria.

"But Victoria..."

"I've told you, no buts, I'm coming."

Rufus considered what Victoria had said, and it did all make sense, except she wasn't combat trained, but he could hide her in a L.U.P and call her forward when it was safe.

He decided to go with it. He called Issa and explained his predicament. Victoria could see him pacing back and forth, gesticulating with his free hand while he spoke to Issa in Swahili. She couldn't understand a word, but knew that Issa was raising the same objections as Rufus had, she also knew that Rufus was using the same arguments that she had used on him to convince Issa that it was the right thing to do and probably a few more too.

Eventually after much pacing, Rufus turned towards her and gave her the thumbs up sign and big white-toothed grin. She jumped up out of bed and threw her arms around him and mouthed, "Thank you" and skipped off to the bathroom like a schoolgirl. Rufus watched her disappear into the bathroom and day dreamed for a second or two, shook himself to his senses and continued with his conversation with Issa.

They agreed a plan and Rufus cut the call. He walked to the bathroom door and called through the door to Victoria.

"Victoria, we need to be ready in fifteen minutes."

She opened the door slightly and looked at him with bright sparkling, happy eyes. I'll be ready you don't need to worry this time."

Rufus's gear was ready and he pored over mapping on his tablet. Don Skyped him and gave him his best estimate at where the phones were pinging. He sent an annotated map electronically to Rufus's phone to assist him. Due to lack of accurate, detailed mapping they had to use the A7 MSR, as their point of reference and agreed on a drop zone just to the north of it. They estimated that this would give them about a two-mile tab to the stronghold. Don took over Rufus's tablet remotely and set the route for Rufus to take. Rufus would not be able to take the tablet along with him, so he compared things against the mapping on his phone.

While they were talking there was a gentle knock on the door and Rufus got up and let Victoria in. She was grinning like a Cheshire cat because she was ready in under fifteen minutes, and was ready before Rufus. She had dressed sensibly and appropriately, in her lightweight boots, cargo pants and layers of upper clothing. Rufus was suitably impressed with her.

"Back with you mate and Victoria is here now."

"Hi Victoria," said Don. "Are you sure you want to do this? It's not for the faint-hearted."

"I couldn't be more sure of anything Don," said Victoria.

"Ok, but it's not the films you know, it's uncomfortable, cold and…"

"Dangerous, I know. Don. I'm doing it."

Rufus was shrugging his shoulders behind Victoria so that Don could see him, in the 'I've already tried and it's pointless. What can you do? She's a woman,' universal male gesture.

"Ok. Ok. I just wanted you to know what you are getting yourself into that's all."

"Thanks, now I'll leave you two to carry on with your planning."

She moved out of the way and sat on the edge of the bed, double-checking the small amount of personal effects and medical equipment she was taking with her, while Don and Rufus continued with their discussions. After a few more minutes they wrapped up and Don wished them both the best of luck.

Chapter Fifty-Seven

Cooper finished his meeting with Esther and returned to Umoja House, to the inner sanctum of the Chancellery, where his secure comms were in place.

He called Kumi, to corroborate what Esther had told him, but the phone was not switched on. He prepared his report for the attention of Sir Peregrine Dennis. It took him the best part of an hour, even though he was an experienced touch typist.

As soon as Esther had mentioned that al Shabab were involved, he knew that Dennis would want to be informed even if he couldn't verify it at the moment, he thought Sir Peregrine might be able to go through GCHQ. His and Dennis's plan had worked beautifully and al-Shabaab had taken the bait just like Sir Peregrine had predicted. He thought about his handling and tasking of Esther and how good he had been. That nobody but he could have controlled Esther the way he had, and was imagining himself giving lectures on agent handling around the world, this had been text-book.

He hoped that his signal would be for British eyes only but suspected that Sir Peregrine would class the intelligence as "two eyes" for the information of the Americans and the British only. Cooper didn't know the bigger picture, and there was always a bigger picture, but he guessed that Sir Peregrine would be trying to curry favour with the Americans, but they would not want to share this information with any of their other allies, but he also knew that the Americans would want to get in on the action if it meant they could possibly disrupt or kill any members of al-Shabab who had caused such havoc to shipping and communities around the Horn of Africa.

He believed that this was the first time that they had ventured this far south along the Eastern Coast. They were getting more and more desperate, or confident, depending on how you looked at it. He had put them in the cross hairs at his first attempt; it really was an ideal opportunity to cause some major disruption.

He sent his report as "Flash" knowing that Sir Peregrine would want to see the intel straight away and that the duty officer would inform him. He didn't appreciate quite how quickly things would move. It seemed that before he had even stood up to make himself another cup of tea, the secure phone was ringing and Sir Peregrine Dennis was on the line.

"Ah, Nick," said Dennis in his friendliest, matey voice. "I've just seen your report on the Conways. Most interesting, most interesting. Damn fine work old chap. You've graded the intel B.2.5 from your source Esther I see."

"Yes sir," replied Cooper.

"Even though it is uncorroborated?"

"I've graded him B.2 for the past three years sir. All of his work has been spot on for us. I've got him by the balls as his mistress, Sia, is on a retainer from us, and if ever I feel he is wavering I turn up the heat through her to put some financial and emotional pressure on him. You know the sort of thing. She really is a delightful woman. Very willing and game for anything, as far as I can make out."

"Yes, yes of course Nick, good work, good thinking," said Dennis, admiring his protégé's devious methodology, a carrot and stick, far more subtle than they used to be in the Cold War days, but that was when you knew the enemy, it was another country. These days it was an ideology, not any single country, not even any single religion, contrary to popular belief, but a plethora of extremist, anti-capitalist, anti-west, anti-democracy, anti-sodding everything as far as he could make out, and it was their job to keep the UK safe. "I'll get straight on to Braddock from GCHQ and see if they've got anything for us."

Forgetting that Robert Braddock had tried to brief him earlier, but he had been too engrossed in another little project of his.

Dennis ended the call and was straight on the phone to Braddock at GCHQ.

"Good afternoon, Robert, old chap. How are you?"

Robert Braddock's antennae was on alert straight away, *the pretentious, supercilious twat never phones me unless he's after something.*

"Good afternoon Peregrine," replied Braddock in his most sociable tone. "I'm fine thank you, how are you?"

"Excellent form old chap, excellent. Now old chap, about the Conways."

"Yes," said Braddock, wondering what had piqued Dennis's interest, when just a few hours ago, it was like he had never heard of them.

"I was tied up this morning I'm sorry, preparing an urgent paper for the PM," he lied, "and I'm afraid I was a little distracted when you called, and you sort of caught me on the hop, so to speak. I felt a little embarrassed this morning, and so I'm phoning to apologise."

Now Braddock knew he was lying, Dennis hadn't got an embarrassed cell in his body, he was incapable of the emotion, in fact he was incapable of any emotion.

"Oh please Peregrine, you don't need to apologise, I know how busy you must be." Braddock maintained his equanimity, but inwardly cursed himself for not having the guts to tell Dennis exactly what he thought of him, but he didn't want him as an enemy, not in their closed nepotistic world, it wouldn't do him any good at all. Anyway, he knew that Frankie Fraser was on the case, and while Braddock was not manipulative like Dennis, why have a dog and bark yourself?

"I need a briefing on the Conway situation immediately," said Dennis, not even acknowledging Braddock's good manners and reverting immediately to type.

Braddock couldn't believe the effrontery of the man, but agreed to be with him in fifteen minutes.

CHAPTER FIFTY-EIGHT

Rufus insisted they had a light afternoon snack in the restaurant before they got a taxi to the TPDF base a couple of miles away. Victoria was not in the slightest bit hungry, but he adamant she ate something.

"You don't know when you are going to eat again Victoria. You need energy, because when we get the LZ we will still have at least two miles to TAB to the stronghold. Now eat."

Rufus shovelled food into his mouth, and stuffed some high energy bars and snacks into his kit bag. Once he was satisfied Victoria had eaten enough, they caught a taxi to the TPDF base where they were met by Rufus's old friend Issa.

Victoria observed the warmth with which Issa greeted Rufus, hugging him and grinning from ear to ear, she knew he was putting his head on the chopping block for helping his friend like this, but he owed Rufus and Victoria thought that even if he didn't owe Rufus some favour, he would still have done his friend a favour, because she could see the affection, no love, that he had for Rufus.

After several minutes of talking in Swahili, and several bouts of raucous laughter Rufus introduced Victoria. She was examined from top to bottom and Issa immediately started talking in rapid Swahili, clearly teasing Rufus, the only phrase she thought she heard him say was 'nyumba ndogo', obviously asking Rufus if she was his mistress. Fortunately they were too busy talking to each other to see her colour up, and by the time they turned back to her, she had regained her composure.

Issa, the pilot and Rufus all sat down and agreed a flight plan. Issa could not let the plane stay up for too long for two reasons: the expense; and the possibility of being caught misappropriating military property, therefore as soon as Rufus and Victoria had exited the plane the pilot would fly back to Dar es Salaam. That was fine by Rufus, the fewer noises and planes over the site the better as far as he was concerned.

Rufus and the pilot sat together and started their calculations: they worked out altitude and wind direction, glide ratio and speed of descent. Rufus didn't want to go above 20 000 feet, because they would need oxygen above that height. Some people thought 20 000 feet was too high, but he had jumped from that height before and was quite confident that he would be ok. It didn't really matter too much if Victoria fainted because she didn't have to do anything anyway.

Even when they landed, his feet would touch the ground before hers and he planned to leave her at the drop site for her safety and his speed. But he had to be far enough away from the bandits to give them no cause for concern. The wing he had was nowhere near as good as the 6:1 ratio HiGlide wings the regiment used and with their combined weight he calculated a glide ratio of 2.5:1, or from 20 000 feet a glide distance of 50 000 feet, or nearly ten miles. They planned the LZ to be two miles from the stronghold, meaning the DZ would be twelve miles from the stronghold when they exited the C130, this was ample for his purposes, his main concern was engine noise from the plane, but at nearly twelve miles out, and with no radar or other military grade surveillance equipment, that would be fine. He would be able to use his phone to navigate them to the planned landing zone, where he would stow the unwanted kit and "yomp" to the stronghold.

After they had agreed the DZ, Rufus called Victoria over and explained the parachute system to her.

He started by explaining the way they would be harnessed together and that she would effectively be sitting in his lap. He went on to explain all the safety features which would make their jump a lot safer. The parachute itself is just a large wing, which is flown by the "pilot".

Rufus explained all the technical details to her, the number of cells, the leading edge, the sharks' teeth, the square footage the maximum load; he showed her the secondary chute and CYPRES (Cybernetic Parachute Release System) technology to deploy the reserve automatically if they were exceeding a vertical speed of about 115 feet per second at a predetermined altitude at around 2000 feet, effectively meaning they almost certainly couldn't and wouldn't crash land. He explained the only time this would happen was if he was unconscious for any reason and ran through the rudimentary techniques for steering the 'chute so that Victoria could land them in relative safety.

He described how they would be using a technique called HAHO, or High Altitude High Opening, not what she had done before with a free-fall element. This meant that they could fly, or glide further, leaving the airplane to return to the airfield without going anywhere near their

LZ. He'd lost Victoria after the first few sentences, but his enthusiasm for the subject was infectious and she absolutely knew that he loved parachuting, knew what he was doing and that she would be safe.

She stared at him, not listening to a word he said, just looking admiringly. She had to shake herself into paying attention because after Rufus had finished the safety briefing he prepped her for another phone call. Issa had arranged a small office for them, where they would not be disturbed and put a guard on the door to stop anybody inadvertently walking in on them. Rufus insisted that the guard stood on the outside of the door, so that he couldn't hear what they were saying.

Rufus and Victoria discussed what they expected to happen during the call. Rufus was upbeat about it all.

"Right Victoria, we have a few things we can use to our advantage here; he said call him back "when you have reconsidered your position", or something like that."

"But I haven't reconsidered my position. Neither of them were ambassadors."

"So that's what we tell him, we reiterate that he is wrong. Say that you have been onto the F&CO back in London and enquired whether either of them was employed there in any capacity. He might ask you who you spoke to, so you can say the HR department, who called you back to tell you that neither of your parents had ever worked for them. Ask him what he thinks their names are, and if he gives you different names reassure him that your mum and dad are who they say they are and, do you know their dates of birth?"

"Of course I do."

"Give him their dates of birth. Ok?"

"Yeh ok."

Rufus's phone vibrated and he could see a text had come in from Orla:

Scream inside s, hold.

Rufus put his phone away and continued with what he had planned to say.

"He's also accepted that you are on your own and cannot raise the sort of money he was talking about. So we can build on that one. Lower his expectations, but not too much. We don't want it so low that we run out of wriggle room."

Rufus knew he had to prepare Victoria just in case they had a threatening call. He assumed that the bandits must have made some sort of booster in their stronghold, otherwise they would not be able to phone out when Orla couldn't, anyway, that was of no matter to him at the moment.

"Remember Vicky, we have to be prepared for the threat of violence, or even apparent acts of violence over the phone -they know that you can't see what is happening and it is easy to play act apparently horrific acts, without you knowing what is going on. It's a sort of psychological warfare. Now even though most of these are threats, or acting, just as we are acting our end of the phone, you must behave like it's real; I want some good emotion coming over the phone from you. Ok?"

"Yes, ok." said Victoria.

They rehearsed the call, including Rufus making, and carrying out threats, and when they were ready Rufus keyed in the contact and pressed call.

"Uh."

"Hello," said Victoria.

"Uh?"

Victoria looked at Rufus, confused. Rufus realised that Eddie had given the phone to somebody else to babysit, as he was not expecting their call yet and was clearly preoccupied with something. He tapped a prompt *This is Victoria.*

"Hello, my name is Victoria and I was talking to somebody on this phone last night."

"Uh. Hold on," silence ensued and then they heard an angry voice say, "Hello?"

"This is Victoria."

"What the fuck are you doing phoning me now?"

"I'm phoning you like you told me to."

"What?

"You said, "Phone me on this number when I have reconsidered my position", well I have. I wrote it down so I wouldn't make any mistakes."

"Ah good, so you accept that your father is an ambassador?"

"No, I have considered all of the evidence available to me and I have contacted the British Foreign Office. I have to tell you that you have the wrong people, neither of my parents is or ever was an ambassador."

"What? Are you a crazy woman? You phoned me back just to tell me I was wrong?"

"I thought I was doing what you asked me to. I thought it was important that you know the truth – that you have got the wrong people. My mum and dad are just ordinary people."

"Fuck off. Do you think I am an idiot? It is opportune you called, as we have just been questioning your parents and perhaps you would like to join in the fun. We have already sliced off one of the ambassador's fingers..."

Rufus and Victoria looked at each other in confusion and Rufus put his finger to his lips.

"Your mother is next, unless you tell me the truth. Now remember, we have already questioned them and got them to admit who they are, although your father has lost a finger in the process. Now slowly tell me your father's full details."

Rufus mouthed the word "truth" to Victoria.

Victoria played her part wonderfully putting a lot of emotion and pleading in her voice. "Please, don't hurt them, I beg you, they are just ordinary people who have done nothing wrong."

"Their details," came back the malevolent voice.

"Um, Mum, Deidre Miriam Conway, born 22.12.1952, her maiden name was Dench. Dad is Martyn Gerald Conway born 14.8.50." Victoria was looking into Rufus's eyes who was looking straight back at her, nodding imperceptibly, encouraging her that she was doing the right thing.

"And what are their jobs?"

"They are both retired."

"What WERE their jobs, you stupid whore."

"Dad was a bank manager, Mum had several jobs and I never really paid attention to what she did."

"LIAR," roared the voice down the phone.

Rufus was encouraging Victoria to continue.

"My dad worked for the bank all his life, he rose to Bank Manager, before they closed the branch and then he took over a call centre," telling the bandits exactly what she had told Rufus, "he hasn't worked for some time now."

Rufus and Victoria could hear shouting and screaming in the background and the voice came back on the line.

"Choose a finger."

"What?"

Rufus showed Victoria a prompt *Change the subject. DO NOT CHOOSE.*

"I AM TELLING YOU THE TRUTH," shouted Victoria down the phone "Dad worked for the bank for nearly thirty years in Lincoln, in the east of England. He loved his job. Mum used to carry out research I think."

"HOLD OUT HER HAND," they could hear the voice shouting. They could hear a woman crying in the background.

Rufus had prepared another prompt *Injury = Problems= Treatment.*

Victoria picked it up immediately.

"SEPARATE HER FINGERS."

They could hear commotion in the background and stifled voices.

"What is the benefit to you of injuring them? It will only lead to more problems for you, they are old, their blood is thin and they will need medical treatment. I am a doctor and I know that they will need clean dressings and treatment or they will die and then you will not get your money."

Rufus was impressed she had got everything he would have wanted her to get in if he had had time to role-play and she had turned the situation round to make the issue about the bandits' money, not her parents.

Thwuuummp, followed by a horrendous scream.

"That was your decision," said the voice. "Your mother has just lost her thumb," and the line went dead, just as darkness was descending in Tanzania.

Chapter Fifty-Nine

It was mid-afternoon in the UK when Don took a telephone call from Frankie Fraser, who he knew well and often saw at D Squadron reunions. Don, like all of the major's men and ex-men respected him tremendously as a soldier and a leader of men. Don had seen him stand up for his men in circumstances where lesser officers would have backed down. He had seen him ball senior officers out for their incompetence, when they had endangered his beloved troopers.

"I need to see you at the office, as soon as" said Frankie Fraser in his unmistakable voice. No preamble or explanation was offered or needed. Don knew that if he needed him, he really did need him and knew he didn't want to discuss anything over the phone and resisted the urge to ask questions, which he knew would not illicit any meaningful responses.

"OK. boss, I can get the rattler down to Euston this afternoon and tube it over to the office and be there for five."

Don knew that Frankie Fraser would not call him out-of-the-blue and get him down to London unless it was important, and so he left Ed with some instructions and enough work to last him a week.

Ed's association chart was getting bigger and more interesting by the hour and Don knew they would have to go to Vauxhall at the end of this to give them their intelligence that they had developed. He went on line out of habit and booked his return tickets, and was gone out of the door, with everything he might need within fifteen minutes of receiving the call from Frankie Fraser.

Chapter Sixty

A few minutes after Don was leaving their offices, Orla lifted the corner of the tarpaulin, judging that it was dark enough to move around if she was careful.

She had had to use all her self-discipline to maintain cover. She was aching all over, and longing to stretch out her stiff, battered muscles, but she knew that personal admin would have to wait.

She knew Don would be searching for her with all of the skill and techniques he had at his disposal, but she had to conserve her battery and also make sure it didn't light the whole campsite up if it went off. *Damn smart phones*, she thought to herself, *they are brilliant, but the battery life is piss poor.*

She was confident in her husband's technical ability, after all that's why he had been DS at the Det and part of E Squadron, and knew he would brief Rufus, and she knew, knew beyond any shadow of a doubt that Rufus would be coming for her. She knew that nothing would stop him getting to her; the only question was whether he could get to her in time.

She listened intently, to the sounds of the night. The general chaos and shouting in the compound, the screeches and roars from without, at the first throws of darkness. As things settled into the evening routine she just heard the odd brief conversation, as the guards went about their business in a casual, lackadaisical, unprofessional manner.

She took the safety off her weapon and as stealthily as any stalking leopard she emerged from the tarpaulin and made her way to a large pile of disused, unwanted scrap: there were doors and timbers, old car seats and all sorts of machinery thrown in a pile by a tree. She had identified this spot as the best cover for her, giving her maximum protection from prying eyes. She burrowed into the mound of rubbish, disappearing from view again and created a little space for herself.

She had a much better view of the compound and could see a large 1950s style industrial single-storey building in a state of disrepair. There was a large roller shutter door in the centre of the end of the building, with a small pedestrian door to the side. She couldn't make out what type of locks and security was on either door from where she was, and that would have to wait until later. The paint was flaking off the walls, exposing the brickwork and the roof appeared to be corrugated iron.

She knew she needed water and wanted food, the food could wait, but she had to get some fluid inside her. She knew she was dehydrated after staying in the back of the pick-up all day, and she knew that lack of water could get her killed: her senses would be dulled and her reaction times slower. They had it emphasised over and over the importance of keeping the body hydrated, and one statistic she could remember was that sport scientists claimed a thirty per cent reduction in performance in elite athletes at just a two per cent water loss. She didn't know how much she had lost but she was sure it was more than two per cent. Her pounding head and increased heart rate told her that much.

She surveyed the area looking for any obvious water sources. She could see one guard, who she guessed was meant to be patrolling, already lying on the floor, apparently fast asleep. She considered drinking the water from his canteen on his webbing, but decided against it the threat of HIV from the bottle was too great a risk.

She could see a down-pipe coming off the roof into a large barrel and decided she had to get some water inside her. She moved around the side of the building, senses on high alert, watching and listening. She made her way to the barrel and filled two disused dirty drinks cans, resisting the temptation to drink the water immediately.

She got back to her hide, and went through the process of preparing the water: removing her sock she had been wearing for the last thirty-six hours, and carefully poured the water out of the cans into her sock, desperately trying to get as much of the liquid into her bottle as possible; she nearly filled her bottle from the two cans, ensuring the bigger foreign objects had been filtered out by her sock put the water purification drops in her bottle, put the screw cap on and shook it.

She turned the sock inside out and shook all the detritus off it, put it back on her foot and replaced her boot, ready for action.

Chapter Sixty-One

Rufus quickly double-checked the call was terminated before he allowed Victoria to speak. She was staring at the phone, her mouth agog, unable to comprehend what she had just heard.

"Oh my God, they've hurt Mum," said Victoria stifling the tears and sobs that were growing in her; everything now getting more real.

"We don't know that Victoria. I told you that they know you can't see and they are playing games with your mind. Your imagination is your biggest enemy now, because that is what you are doing, imagining what they have done. We have got to focus on the 'now' not be anchored in the 'then' because there is nothing we can do about it."

"THAT'S EASY FOR YOU TO SAY. THEY'VE JUST FUCKING WELL CHOPPED OFF MY MUM'S THUMB AND YOU SAY 'FORGET IT.'

"That's exactly what I am saying Vicky: we don't KNOW that they have done anything; we can't immediately do anything about it; and it will affect you if you wallow in it, and thereby endanger your mum and dad. WE HAVE TO STAY FOCUSED, in the now, not the then." Rufus thought of an analogy for her. "If you were doing your finals and you made a mistake in one paper or practical what would you do?"

"Put it out of my mind and concentrate on the next one."

"Exactly. And that is precisely what we have to do now. We are where we are Vicky, and we can't go back, so we have to focus on the here and now."

"I know you are right Ru, and I'm sorry I'm shouting at you."

"I understand Victoria and I don't take it personally. It is only right that you should get emotional, and now we have to stop any more threats or harm happening again, and we have to ensure we get your mum and dad safely released. I thought you did really well on that call, you picked up what I meant straight away, and I honestly don't believe he has harmed your mum. It all sounded very convincing, but I don't think they did. There was something missing for me, and I can't put my finger on what it was."

"Really? You really believe that was acting?"

"Yes I do. And now we have to prepare you for another call coming back in."

"How can you say that was acting? I heard the thud as Mum's thumb was chopped off, I heard her scream."

"Did you? Or are you entering into their world and buying their illusion? You didn't see any of that did you? I think they would have put your mum on the phone to crank up the pressure if they were really going to hurt her." Rufus had to choose his words carefully. He didn't want to belittle Victoria, and at the same time he didn't want to look like an over-optimistic idiot.

He had to raise her hopes and keep her positive, but at the same time keep her level-headed and realistic. He deliberately minimised what the bandits were potentially doing, rather than use expansive prose which could have made Victoria's imagination run wild.

"I can understand exactly what you are saying Ru, it's just that it's all so personal and horrific. I never knew there were such evil people in the world, and I've seen a few appalling injuries, it's just that now it's personal I guess."

"That's exactly right Vicky, it's personal to you, but to them it's not. This is business. Imagine yourself at work as a doctor. You have to remain detached and dispassionate in order to think clearly, make calm logical decisions to do the best you can for your patient, while the family, to whom it is personal, get wrapped up in the emotion. Does that make sense?"

"Yes it does. Oh, I'm so pleased and lucky that you are here with me." Victoria looked at Rufus as if she was ascribing him mystical qualities.

For once Rufus could see the way Victoria was looking at him and decided to get back to business as quickly as possible. The chemistry between them was increasing, and he had to keep it in check, or he would be guilty of what he was just telling her about: emotion and becoming involved.

"They could phone back anytime now Victoria so let's just think about what you will say if they do, ok?

"Ok."

"I think you would still be upset, do you?"

"Yes, of course I am, I don't need to think about that one, I will answer the phone snivelling, as if I am still crying."

"Perfect. And I think you would want to speak to your mum."

"Yes I would, I want to ask her if she is ok."

"And your dad? They said they had already sliced his finger off."

"Yes of course, I'd forgotten about Dad, oh no, poor Dad. Do you think they really cut his finger off?"

"I don't know. I think probably not, because I don't understand why they wouldn't use it against you, make you listen to it if they really did it. Or perhaps they are interrogating..." he cursed himself for using such an emotive word, "um, questioning your mum and dad and trying to put pressure on your mum to answer questions like they did with you, but they can't couldn't fake it like they can over the phone. I really don't know. I just hope he's alright."

"Me too, so I will ask about both of them and their injuries."

"Exactly. And then, if they are injured, I think we should emphasise that causing more injury will only lessen the likelihood of them surviving and thereby also lessen the chances of them getting their money that you are in the process of arranging. Emphasise that you are in the middle of all the arrangements, it is nearly done, dangle that carrot for them. And if they haven't harmed them, we should thank them and tell them there is no need to harm either Mum or Dad, to persuade you to get them their money. You know they are serious people and all you are trying to do is get their money as fast as you can."

"Ok. I understand, but you will have to have your prompts ready to remind me about some of these things, when I am talking to them my mind goes blank sometimes."

"That's ok. Vicky, and you know better than most the medical reasons why you go blank, but also use your medical knowledge to explain the dangers for your parents and link it like you did last time to the money, always make the issue about them getting their money. But you are doing brilliantly, I'm pretty well taking a back seat and letting you get on with it now."

"Oh, Ru, thank you, but you are such a liar."

"I'm not, you are doing really well; you learn, think and react quickly, just do me a favour and remember some of this stuff when you are a top-jolly consultant that you are still dealing with people."

"Ha ha, that seems a long way off, another world, but yes I will and thank you so much. I'll never be able to repay you for your kindness and all you have done for us."

"Well let's get your mum and dad back first, then we can all celebrate together, but we had better get going. Issa will be waiting for us."

As they exited the room, Victoria said, "He loves you you know."

"Pardon? Where did that come from?"

"I mean in a manly comradely way. He really admires you, and I would call it love."

"We respect each other and go back a long way, he's a good guy," Rufus said, a little disconcerted at Victoria's statement. "We don't see each other very often now, and when we do, we have a lot to catch up on."

They found Issa, and he led them out to the airfield changing room, where they donned their combat gear. Rufus helped Victoria into her harness, making sure it fit her properly, tightening up the buttock straps and couldn't help noticing how the straps accentuated the curves of her ass. He had to remind himself again, he was not on some sort of date, he was working and she was his client.

Next he put on the rig, getting Issa to double-check the fitting and strapping. They walked out to the waiting C130, the good old, reliable work horse, Issa accompanied them out into the evening darkness. The base was nearly pitch black, as it was on the generator back up, and all non-essential lighting was switched off. Victoria could hear recruits being bawled at by their training staff somewhere in the gloom, and it all gave the base an eerie, feeling which made her shiver. She didn't think of herself as a superstitious person, but a shiver ran down her spine, making her shudder, as a few whispy clouds scudded across the waning moon. She didn't want to show either man her concerns, and what she took to be as her weaknesses, so she tried to dispel the feeling of inadequacy and insignificance and walked with them to the plane.

They stood at the bottom of the ramp which led into the vast cavern-like belly of the Herc and Issa wished them both a safe trip, giving Rufus a hug, which told Victoria, more than any of the favours he had done for him, just how much he thought of his old friend, and wondered what it was that engendered such camaraderie and loyalty in the military.

They walked up the ramp and were greeted by the jump-master, one of a five-man crew needed to operate the monster of a plane. Victoria looked in amazement at the C-130J-30's hold: fifty-five feet in length, capable of carrying ninety-two passengers or sixty-four airborne troops or two M113 armored personnel carriers with a payload of 45,000 lbs. The two of them strapped themselves in, and looked utterly lost and insignificant in the gloom.

The huge turbo-prop engines increased to operating speed and deafened Victoria who could no longer hear the jump-master and just accepted she would do whatever Rufus told her.

The enormous deceptively agile giant taxied to the runway and although Victoria had flown numerous times, she wasn't used to sitting on a bench laterally to the plane, and the acceleration pushed her sideways into Rufus. Rufus's body didn't move a millimetre, it was like bumping into a mature tree, and Victoria felt comfort in his strength and solidity, believing that the man who she only met a few days ago would do whatever it took to get her parents back.

As they made their way to the DZ Rufus put his mouth next to her ear and regaled her with stories about Africa and the wildlife. An Afrikaans Professional Hunter friend or PH as they liked to call themselves, Tertious Ventor, had told him: the fact that hippos don't swim, but walk on the bottom, due to the bottom of their limbs being solid and are considered the most dangerous mammal in the world; that rhino have very poor eyesight and so tend to charge first and ask questions later; that leopards are mainly nocturnal and that lions are really cowards, and that if one charges at you, you should stand your ground and it will run away.

When he had finished they reversed positions so she was shouting into his ear.

"So we have got to be more wary of the hippos, rhinos and leopards than the lions? If you think I am just going to stand there if a lion charges me, you must think I'm mad."

"Well ask yourself this...who can run faster? You or me?"

Victoria pointed her index finger at him, nodding in his direction.

"So which one of us will the lion catch first?"

"I don't want to think about it," folded her arms and made it quite clear, this topic of conversation was over.

Chapter Sixty-Two

Sir Peregrine Dennis could not believe his luck; he was sitting on a gold mine of intelligence for which his cousins in the Company would forever be in his debt. He had corroborated intelligence giving him the whereabouts of an al Shabab cell that they had been trying to track for at least two years.

They had wreaked havoc in the Indian Ocean and the East Coast of Africa. They were suspected of the deaths of several Americans, and the Americans were like the Israelis, they had very long memories, and even more importantly, they had a very long reach. Even though they were in debt up to their eyeballs, the Americans still threw massive resources at the war on terror.

He picked up the phone and made a call to his counterpart at the CIA, Andreas Bornkamp, and arranged a meeting for that evening. Time was now of the essence and he wanted to give Andreas the best chance he could to rid the world of these unscrupulous, evil men, and earn himself a great deal of kudos in the process.

He called his secretary and told her to get his driver ready, to cancel his meetings for the rest of the day and prepared himself for the meeting.

A short time later he was sat in Andreas's office and admired the view across Grosvenor Square. He superciliously considered the situation with mild amusement, the situation that meant the embassy of the most powerful country in the world, together with other prestige buildings in London, was actually owned by the Qatari Diar Real Estate Investment Company. Dennis mused about what would happen if the Qatari's tried to evict the Americans, or wanted to enter their own property? He wondered how the Americans had got themselves into such financial difficulties, and whether they would ever regain their place as the economic and industrial powerhouse of the world. Or whether they would suffer the same slow, painful ignominious downfall that the British had suffered for the past sixty years? Privately he hoped they would, as he smiled his snake smile and exchanged small talk with Andreas.

"We must play squash again soon," said Andreas, remembering the thrashing he had taken from Dennis a couple of months previously. He had been practising since that game, because he was a lot younger and fitter than the Brit sat opposite him, and could not understand how he had been beaten so comprehensively. He was looking forward to exacting his revenge very soon.

"Mmmmm, whenever you have some free time Andreas old chap."

"Um," replied Bornkamp, looking at his diary, "how about next Tuesday lunchtime?"

"Oh," said Dennis, slightly taken aback by the urgency of the younger man and consulted his diary. "I will have to move some appointments round," he lied, "but that should be ok."

"Ok, I'll book the court at my club for, say, one o'clock?"

"Yes fine old chap, just let me know when you have booked it." Dennis didn't want a rematch, he knew he had fluked the first game and was in no rush for a second encounter. He would simply inform Bornkamp that he could not rearrange one of his very important, non-existent, meetings and would have to cry off.

The two men then settled down to business.

"I have some source led intelligence, supported by GCHQ, in which I think you will be very interested. It pertains to our friends from the Horn of Africa." Prolonging his moment of glory in the eyes of the CIA, who, he knew had been trying to pin down this group for the last two years. They had used the NSA, sources, satellites, Navy Seals, but had not been able to get a definite fix on them.

"Oh good. What about them?" asked Bornkamp.

"I have recent intelligence that Abu Faud has just relieved a criminal gang of a little package," said Dennis enjoying toying with his counterpart.

"You mean the guys who have just taken your two Brits to Mikumi?" asked Bornkamp in a deliberately naïve, innocent tone, enjoying stealing the Brit's thunder.

Bornkamp saw Dennis's shoulders fall a millimetre and the self-satisfied, smug look disappear from his face, for a split second, until Dennis regained his composure and readjusted his mask, which would have been imperceptible to a less observant man. He was overplaying his hand slightly, as all he had was intercept intelligence, and no real meat on the bones, but there was no way he was going to let Dennis revel in his coup. He would have to play this one tactfully, with a real poker face to illicit all the British Intelligence without disclosing his own paucity.

He surmised with good reason that Dennis would not have come to his office, unless he was confident of his intelligence and wanted to show off. That Dennis was too arrogant and needed to be brought down to earth was not in doubt, but for the moment Bornkamp needed him and access to the source, directly preferably, but if it had to be through the Brits then so be it.

"Yes, old chap," said Dennis, recovering his composure. "HMG thought they should assist you in any way they can in your hunt." Dennis naturally reverted from the first person singular to the third person plural, as he altered course from trying to grab some kudos for himself, to spreading the disappointment among other anonymous bureaucrats.

Bornkamp decided to press home his advantage and knew that Dennis, for all his experience, was jealous of the American's power.

"We have tasked the USS Carl Vinson, with eliminating them," said Bornkamp, stretching the truth to breaking point.

Dennis was immediately impressed. He knew the American navy was a formidable force. The Carl Vinson was a Nimitz Class Aircraft Carrier and an awesome weapon indeed, carrying up to ninety aircraft alone. At a cost of about $4.5 billion and with a total crew of around 6000, this was a statement of intent by the American.

Dennis knew that the Carl Vinson would be accompanied by six surface vessels and two submarines – an asset of that value never went anywhere alone. He felt green with envy that his younger, brasher less erudite colleague had the power to deploy such resources.

To rub salt into the gaping wound Bornkamp continued, "We have just trialled Carrier-borne drones, and this is going to be the first combat mission for one of our X-47 b stealth drones, called 'Odin's'. The navy boys are really excited about it." He was enjoying rubbing Dennis's nose in the dirt.

"Well anything HMG can do to assist..." Dennis had to rescue something from this debacle. "But you do realise there are two British nationals involved in this don't you?" he said trying to buy a little bit of thinking time.

"Yes, of course, and we will do everything we can to ensure their safety. But the American national security comes first and these fuckers have been roaming around killing folks and kidnapping people for fun, earning millions of dollars to swell the AQ coffers, spend on fast cars and better boats and it has got to stop."

"Is that your intel you have with you?" asked Bornkamp, indicating the file on the desk that he had noted Dennis had placed there with such assuredness a few minutes earlier in full view of him, like a prized trophy.

"Yes, yes it is old chap," stammered Dennis picking up the file, subconsciously protecting his once treasured possession.

Bornkamp knew that he had impressed Dennis with mention of nuclear powered carriers, and robotic drones and wanted to press home his advantage.

"Well let's see it then. You wouldn't want your l'il ol' country cousins making a mistake now would you?" affecting a hick accent, holding out his hand to relieve Dennis of the docket.

Dennis submissively handed over the file and sat back in his chair while Andreas went through the intelligence.

Chapter Sixty-Three

Mad Frankie Fraser was on a mission. While he was waiting for Don's arrival, he reread Robert Braddock's BJ with growing anger as he pieced together the catalogue of lies and deceptions told to them by Dennis.

He was furious, but determined to keep his anger in check as he had other people to think about: Deidre and Martyn, who he had never met and did not know, but seemed to be very nice people and were the reason behind the mission; he had twelve men, most of whom he did know, ready to go to battle to save them, and he was determined to give them the best possible chance to do just that and get out of there alive; and there was Rufus and Orla.

He considered his options and knew he would have to go back through COBRA to sanction what he wanted to do. That meant he would go head to head against Dennis, not that he was bothered about that, Dennis couldn't affect him: he was nearing retirement, would not get promoted again and didn't care what the wanker thought of him anyway, but he would expose Braddock, unless he was careful and he was bothered about that.

He knew Dennis was a vindictive, unscrupulous, manipulative operator and Braddock wouldn't stand a chance.

After liaising with Hereford, he contacted Captain 'Deano' Richards on the Chagos Archipelago and gave the order to move forward to the FOB at the TPDF base just to the north of Dar es Salaam. Captain Deano Richards, nick-named after the famous English rugby number eight, mustered his assault group of twelve men and gave the order. They were ready in minutes; their equipment was always ready, their Bergens packed, it was just a matter of gathering their few personal effects as they doubted they would be returning to the archipelago after the mission.

They packed all their equipment into two cigar shaped containers that would be dropped with them.

All bar two of them knew Rufus Stone personally. Some of them had served on the same squadron and respected him hugely.

He was a firm and fair SSM, a bloody good soldier, and good bloke which gave them a little added incentive to go into battle, if ever they needed it. They filed into the body of an identical Hercules to the one Rufus and Victoria would be jumping out of later.

The plan was to change aircraft from the C130 to a Sea King helicopter, which would deliver them to the DZ at 0100 local time, TAB to the RVP by 0200 and mount the DA at 0300, the time when the scientists say our body clocks are at their nadir, when our reactions are slowest, our senses dullest and gave the patrol the greatest advantage.

Their RAF crew knew their drills well, they worked with them permanently – they were airborne in the time it would take a commercial airliner to just load their passengers.

+++++++

A short time later a second C130 rose into the night sky and in no time at all, the jump master was indicating that they should get ready.

They stood up and Rufus pulled Victoria back into his body to clip her harness to his, Victoria started to tremble, this was real, she was going to be jumping out of an aeroplane into the night sky strapped to another body that now had complete control over her destiny.

"Sorry Victoria, this may feel a little uncomfortable, but once we are connected properly you should have a little more 'space'."

Whilst he was fastening the webbing hooks, Victoria felt full body contact; she closed her eyes and despite the environment and the predicament she found herself in, the trembling that was running through her felt even more charged.

All her senses were heightened; she could smell Rufus', slightly musky, manly aroma, and his heartbeat seemed to be pounding through her shoulder blades with a rhythmic sensuality.

His hands reached around her breasts and momentarily as he fastened the chest hooks, she laid her head back onto his shoulder in an involuntary movement as he moved down her torso towards the thigh hook points. Rufus just thought she had moved her head to offer him better access, but for Victoria she lost herself for a surreal moment and just felt a sense of willing surrender, losing herself, feeling a delicious excitement.

"Is that good?" Rufus's lips were close to her ear and sent shock waves through her.

"Mmmm," she murmured, then her eyes shot open as she realised where she was and what was about to happen. She shook herself out of her brief reverie and made sure that she was comfortably and securely attached to Rufus. "Yes, as good as it's going to get I guess," she shouted back over her shoulder.

Rufus gave her shoulder a comforting squeeze and they moved towards the doorway. The jump master opened the huge rear doors of the lumbering Hercules, allowing the wind and engine noise into the cavernous interior, reverberating around the old crate, giving a tangible sense of their height and speed.

The jump master concentrated on their exact position and when he was sure they were at the right position he gave Rufus two taps on the left shoulder. Rufus gave him the thumbs up and walked Victoria towards the end of the ramp. Victoria was expecting to stand on the edge and count to three, so was taken by surprise when Rufus just launched them out of the aircraft. He immediately deployed the 'chute and Victoria felt the jerk of the webbing as the chute stopped their free-fall into the infinite darkness.

She looked up and saw the Hercules banking away to the right to return to Dar, while Rufus concentrated on flying them to the LZ. After a few minutes, Victoria began to relax in the still darkness, the wind whistled past her.

There was no sensation of speed or descent as she had no reference points. She just had to "sit back and relax" in the words of the world's airlines. And she did just that, with her head against Rufus's chest, virtually sat on his lap, forgetting about the reason she had just jumped out of a perfectly good airplane, lost in the reverie of her time with Rufus.

Rufus was concentrating on wind speed, direction, descent and navigating them to the intended LZ. He had never jumped tandem in combat conditions before, and the controls were a lot more sluggish, he had to work harder to ensure they were on course, he didn't want to land short and give them more miles to cover and he didn't want to overshoot and potentially alert the bandits.

He had his iPhone strapped to his forearm where he could see it and constantly made tiny corrections to account for the changing thermals. As they descended, the air got thicker and warmer and they both became more comfortable after the initial shock of the freezing, thin air as they exited the plane.

Objects and shapes on the ground became a little more defined each passing minutes as they gently glided through the now warm African air, from about 3000 feet, Victoria could hear the sounds of Africa: lions roaring and elephants trumpeting and she came back to her senses, that she was falling to earth and was going to land very close to a game reserve, in which wild animals were free to roam, hunt and kill; animals that had adapted to their environment and landscape, who had evolved into very effective killing machines.

She was sure that a game reserve or a national park wasn't fenced like a safari park or a zoo and that the animals didn't know where they were supposed to hunt. She pressed her back into Rufus's abdomen a little harder to feel the reassuring firmness of his torso, and relaxed slightly in the knowledge that he was one of the most highly trained, proficient soldiers in the world.

Rufus was concentrating on flying them into a clearing, which they could see quite clearly in the bright moonlight.

Victoria was preparing herself for the impact of landing, as the ground seemed to be rushing up at them more quickly than she had anticipated, then at the last second, she felt Rufus pull on the toggles and they landed softly and silently on the ground. Victoria could hardly believe how gentle the landing was, no impact whatsoever.

+++++++

Orla decided it was time to break cover again and start her diversionary tactics. She didn't know how long it would be before Rufus arrived, so she decided to spread some alarm and fear amongst the ill-disciplined terrorists.

She decided to target the sleeping guard first, reasoning that he must be very tired to fall asleep at this time of the evening, and he must be ill-disciplined to allow himself to fall asleep, and therefore not a very good soldier if he did wake and discover her. After crawling over to him she could hear his rhythmic low breathing.

Very slowly, she cut the laces in his boots, removed the water canteen from his webbing and shoved dirt and gravel in the barrel of his weapon which was just lying next to him then crawled back to her hide, reluctantly poured away the water and looked for her next target. It was military folklore about the Ghurkhas doing the same sort of things to the Argentine soldiers on the Falkland Islands in 1982, and she hoped it would have the same effect.

Orla checked the time and gauged it was now safe to drink her water- using it sensibly, sipping it at first, feeling the fluid wet her parched tongue and throat and felt it descending though her chest, like icy tentacles. It was tempting to drink the lot in one swig, but again her discipline and training kicked in and she knew she had to drink slowly, a little and often.

She looked around for tools and equipment that could help her and began to stockpile some kit that might come in handy, using the cover of darkness to move around the compound, assessing the quality and quantity of the opposition: there were sleeping guards everywhere. They hadn't just nodded off through boredom – they had blankets and pillows, made themselves really comfortable. Something was taken from, or done to each of the guards; she could quite easily have slit their throats, but she reasoned the psychological warfare would be more impactive.

Although they were deeply religious, they were also highly superstitious and would see many of the things as witchcraft. At the first guard she got to, she could see he was sleeping on a white pillow, and used a piece of burnt wood to draw a devil on it, and carried on to the next guard; he was sat on a chair leaning backwards, with his bare feet resting on an old oil drum. She approached him from behind and used a long twig to hook one of his sandals that he had discarded on the ground. The stick bent under the strain of the weight of the sandal as she slowly lifted it, she worried that if she moved it too quickly it would spring upwards and crash into his leg. Once she had secured the sandal she slowly edged backwards, making sure she didn't knock into anything.

Once around the corner out of sight used the stick to place it high on a branch in a tree. She identified the next sleeping guard she would target and crawled through the brush, which seemed to be the dumping ground, scrambling through a pile of old animal bones, the smell of which nearly made her retch. A small prick of her thumb to draw some blood and drip on the guard's white shirt would do the trick. She had caught one of the chickens which roamed freely around the compound and secured it in the hide as her last secret weapon.

Eventually she returned to her hide and used some rope and a sheet she had found, tying it to a branch of a tree, keeping one end of the rope in the hide. Although it looked exactly as it should to her, she understood the possible effect it would have if she could start panicking the guards. Panic is organic which can spread from person to person like a virus if it remains unchecked, so she had to find the right catalyst.

After about an hour of creeping around the compound, she was finished with her preparations and returned to her cover where she could get some well-earned rest. At least she didn't have to worry about rain or cold tonight, like she had in the past.

Chapter Sixty-Four

Rufus of course was unaware of the events taking place thousands of miles away, to the east and west of him, he was concentrating on the job in hand: the rescue of Orla, Deidre and Martyn, and protecting Victoria. He secured their LZ and stashed the chute, ensuring that only the most curious person with the keenest of eyes would be able to see anything untoward.

He removed the Glock from his waist and handed it to Victoria.

"What are you doing?"

"I think you should have this. If anything happens, then at least you have a weapon to protect yourself."

"Ru. I've never even held a gun, let alone used one."

"There's a first time for everything Victoria. You might need it; we just don't know what will happen. I'll feel better if you have it."

After more discussion, Victoria eventually accepted the pistol, and put it on her waist, helped by Rufus. It felt alien to have the lethal weapon strapped to her body and thigh.

He texted Orla with their usual prearranged message, which he had saved in his phone:

Hi Orla, have you heard the news today?

Yes I was shocked by the announcement.

Are you ok?

No, I've got stomach cramps.

Rufus knew he was free to text her with his plans.

At LZ with Victoria, 2 ms frm u. ETA 2000. Advise re approach.

After some time Orla replied by text, *Approach from the east, await my signal. Force of approximately 30 men, poorly trained.*

R, was Rufus's reply.

He checked his Bergen and arsenal of weapons, two miles wasn't far, but he still ensured everything was stowed correctly, secure, where it should be and where he wanted it, in case of any surprises.

Victoria watched him, silently going through his procedures, *Oh my God. What am I doing? Am I in love with him? Is it just the halo effect because of the situation? I've certainly seen that before. But he* ***is*** *everything I want in a man.* Victoria shook her head as if to shake the thoughts out.

Rufus was concentrating on the job in hand, completely focused on what he had been trained to do and aware of his surroundings, the sounds, the smells and movements of the night-time jungle.

+++++++

Dennis left the embassy forlorn: he had gone there with high hopes of gaining credibility and kudos with the Americans, delivering them one of their most wanted targets; instead he had been ambushed by Bornkamp, stealing his victory from him.

He considered his next move, primarily how to cover his own back. He pace was much slower back to the pool vehicle, his shoulders, slightly hunched and the weather seemed a little more damp and overcast to when he had arrived. Still, no one need ever know that he had tried to sacrifice the lives of a handful of innocent British citizens to protect the overwhelming majority of the population.

As Dennis made his way from the embassy, Bornkamp was straight on the secure line with a video conference to Langley and the Pentagon. He had provisionally called the meeting prior to Dennis's arrival and enabled the audio feed from his office to let all the people he was now looking at hear his conversation with the British spy.

They had brought together some big hitters and decision makers quickly to assess and if necessary authorise action. At the Pentagon was Assistant Secretary of Defence, Chuck Martinovitch, the senior politician present. Martinovitch was a hawkish no-nonsense Republican, who was known for his bullish attitude. It was well known that he often didn't see eye to eye with some of the senior pentagon staff, who believed that winning the hearts and minds was as important as winning the battle. On screen with him were: Rear Admiral Karen Banner and General Ed Hutchinson, from the Joint Staff office. The Directorates of the Joint Staff at the Pentagon are complex, behemoths. The Joint Staff is divided into ten groups, or Directorates: two management and strategic Directorates and eight functional Directorates all given the prefix J, and runs from J1, Personnel and Manpower, to J8, Force Structure, Resources and Assessment. Rear Admiral Karen Banner was Director J2, Intelligence, and General Ed Hutchinson was Acting Director, J3, Operations. Both had an entourage of advisers and analysts to assist them.

On the line from Langley were: Director of Intelligence Stuart Wheeler, supported by Steven Hessayon, Director of the Office of Asian Pacific, Latin America and Africa Analysis (APLAA) who was supported by his own analysts and an analyst from the MENA region (Middle East and North Africa).

Associate Deputy Director Bill Massey, Head of Operations for Military Affairs from the National Clandestine Services which deals with clandestine CHIS intelligence and support of military ops with his analyst was there to assess the veracity of the British CHIS intelligence and be the liaison to the military, depending upon which course of action they decided on taking.

Stuart Wheeler, at ASD Martinovitch's behest opened the meeting, thanking everybody for finding time in their busy schedules and dropping what they may have been doing to attend the meeting. He handed over to Steven Hessayon who summarised the information to hand very succinctly.

"Ladies and Gentlemen, we have corroborated intelligence that this man..." he pressed a button on his remote control and the face of Abu Faud appeared on the large screens at the three sites, "Sheikh Moktar Ali Hashi Farah, more commonly known as Abu Faud, is holding two British nationals hostage in Tanzania." He pressed another button and a map of the world appeared, zoomed into the continent of Africa, zoomed further to the east of Africa and then focused on Tanzania. We can, with one hundred per cent certainty place him in a compound in the Mikumi National Park area with at least fifteen cohorts, three Tanzanian criminals and the two hostages.

We have redirected one of our Titan recon satellites to give us coverage of the area, and up-to-the minute intelligence.

We have several options on which we must decide:

1. We can take the whole group out with a drone strike. The USS Carl Vinson is cruising with her Strike Group to the East Coast of Africa and is capable of launching a drone NOW. With no danger to any of our personnel.
2. The British SAS have an assault team, moving forward to a FOB from some island in the Indian Ocean that they still own, and will be good to go in two hours.
3. As previously mentioned we have one of our satellite assets, Titan IV B in a geo stationary orbit over the area, which could surveil Abu Faud and potentially lead us to senior AQ leadership. We have intelligence that Faud is in frequent contact with, this man," another click, "Mahfouz Kamel Wasfi, the undisputed head of AQ, and is busting his balls to be accepted into the inner sanctum. Andreas, is that the gist of the story so far?" asked Hessayon.

"That's about it sir, we have our own intercept data, corroborated by the British Elint and also by Humint, a British source. The trouble is they are just thinking about the rescue of their two adventurers and not seeing the bigger picture of being able to disrupt and destabilise al-Shabaab, which is one of the major funders of AQ, through its piracy and kidnapping enterprises. By taking out Abu Faud we would strike a blow not just against al-Shabaab but against the whole of AQ."

Bill Massey spoke up.

"We have to think of the longer game here. We have a good source into this group and we should let them run, if we manage this correctly it could lead us to much bigger fish. We could get the British to re-infil their source into the group, together with the satellite feed and the intercept data, this has massive potential. Ladies and gentlemen, we are talking potentially about the biggest deal since OBL was taken out."

"There are too many 'ifs' and 'coulds' in there for me," said General Hutchinson. "A bird in the hand is worth two in the bush and we should take this son-of-a-bitch out while we have the chance. He is personally responsible for the lives of at least eight of our troops, countless millions of dollars in piracy activities and the deaths of other nationals."

Rear Admiral Banner was more circumspect and wanted more information.

"Has our bird been able to identify Faud at all?"

"No ma'am," replied Jack Parker, one of the analysts, "we have good pictures of several of the group leaving the building, but not Abu Faud."

"Thank you. The British source: what do we know about that? What is their motivation? How was the intelligence obtained? If they are running the source how long have they been running 'em? When did the intelligence come in? How did they grade it? Have we spoken to the Tanzanians about taking action in their sovereign territory? Have we considered the collateral damage to the hostages and our relations with the Brits? The devil is in the detail ladies and gentlemen and we need the detail before we can make an informed decision."

"Andreas?" said Stuart Wheeler and all eyes turned to the screen to look at the man in London.

"Thank you sir," said Bornkamp, attempting to hide the sarcasm in his voice. "I am told the Brits have been running their source for the past four years. For the past two years the intelligence has been graded B.2, the best you can get from a CHIS in their system. The intel is hot off the press, literally less than five hours since the Brits got it. That corroborated our and their Elint which was twelve hours old. We've now tasked our bird with the monitoring of Faud's cell and have an up-to-the minute visual, audio and technical feed. We are ninety per cent sure he is there. The Tanzanians won't be a problem; they rely on western aid to survive – although the Chinese are getting in there fast. Every Op has a chance of collateral damage, but we have to consider the greater good..."

"The greater good in whose eyes?" interjected the rear admiral. "We can no longer treat the world like our own play thing, there are phalanxes of nations and interests lined up against us, waiting for us to make this sort of gung-ho blunder. And these people are our closest allies, the Brits stand by us through thick and thin. If we are going to do anything we should speak to the prime minister and use their SAS, that way we have more chance of rescuing the hostages, capturing the bad guys AND most importantly from a political perspective, we are not implicated at all."

"We have no assets on the ground that could assist the British at such short notice. They are all tasked in other theatres and even if we wanted to re-task them it would take too long. If the Brits are good to go, then let 'em," said Ed Hutchinson.

Chuck Martinovitch had heard enough. "Ladies and gentlemen. As I see this we are in a win-win situation here. We now have bird overhead giving us an instantaneous feed, which we can now lock on to the phone of this Faud fucker; we have the means and ability to strike from the USS Carl Vinson. Faud must not be left to run, we have lost too many terrorists by letting them run to get to the bigger fish, who then come back to bite us on the ass. We take him out with a Hellfire from a drone. We have publicly stated that we will hunt these terrorists down, that are threatening the American way of life, we have the opportunity to strike at the head of al-Shabaab and demonstrate that they do not mess with the US of A. We procrastinate we lose. Make it happen."

What Martinovitch had failed to mention was that he was a non-executive director of TZR electronics who supplied the navigation systems to the X-47 B Avenger, and a successful mission would see shares rise, orders increase and a very welcome bonus to ASD Martinovitch.

+++++++

Don walked into Major Fraser's office just before 5pm and the building was still quite busy. Frankie Fraser was sat at his desk reading a document, but immediately stood and greeted his old friend. They had started in the SAS together and it was clear to Don that Frankie was a driven man and a natural leader of men. He always put his men before himself, ensuring they were well looked after. He argued that he would expect them to do extraordinary things for him, so it was his duty to look after them.

They sat down and briefed each other on what they knew, both of them becoming more frustrated, the more they found out.

At the same time Sir Peregrine decided to phone the major to give him the 'heads up' on the American situation, reasoning that he would look like the good guy in the soldier's eyes, doing his utmost to help him. He phoned the office to get the major's number, which he should have entered into his phone when introductions were made and business cards exchanged on the first COBRA meeting. Unfortunately for him, not lowering himself to such a demeaning act at the time cost him vital minutes.

Simultaneously Ed phoned Don and briefed him on what he had intercepted. Don immediately stopped Ed and put his phone on loudspeaker for Frankie to hear as well.

"Go ahead Ed, we're both listening in."

"I've just picked up some traffic back to Langley and Washington which suggests the yanks are going to use a drone to strike the stronghold."

"What? How?..." started the incredulous major.

"You don't need to know how Frankie," said Don. "Go on Ed."

"The spook over here has quoted somebody called Dennis as giving him the heads up as to where the stronghold is and they are prepared to launch a sea-borne drone from one of their carriers."

Major Fraser erupted. Ed wondered what on earth was happening on the other end of the phone. Don took the phone off loud speaker.

"Don't worry Ed, the major was just letting off a bit of steam that's all."

Once Frankie had calmed down Ed continued the briefing filling the two men in on what he knew. They disconnected the call and Major Fraser swung into action.

He got Don to call Robert Braddock on his behalf, while he called the offices of Dame Cunningham-Black and updated her, putting her on stand-by for further information. He called Deano, who was still in the air, and was patched through via the Herc's communications systems.

When he had his ducks in a row he called Sir Peregrine Dennis, knight of the realm, defender of the shores, who was still waiting for the call back to give him the soldier's number. Fraser resisted the urge to go apoplectic down the phone, concluding this would be counterproductive to his plans. Instead, he asked if he could visit Sir Peregrine at his office with Don to discuss developments and for Don to give him a brief on what Rufus and Orla were doing.

This fell into Dennis's plan perfectly and he readily agreed to the meeting, assuring Fraser that he would make the necessary arrangements for them to enter the building.

They arrived at Vauxhall just before 6pm. The building was still a hive of activity and as promised they were allowed through security, once they had had all their means of communication and photography removed from them for safe keeping. They entered Sir Peregrine's office and Frankie Fraser made the introductions,

"Don, meet Sir Peregrine Dennis... Sir Peregrine, Don is the best friend and colleague of Rufus Stone who you know all about and husband to Orla."

"Pleased to meet you old chap," said Dennis.

"And you," said Don expecting Dennis to insist on first names, but it was not forthcoming and he took an instant dislike to the man. His handshake was too limp, his smile was disingenuous and he never maintained eye contact. Don could immediately see why Frankie Fraser detested the man so much. Little did Don know that Frankie had set him up; Frankie knew that Don's temper was equally as bad as his, it just needed the right buttons to be pressed, and his guess was that Sir Peregrine fucking Dennis would press them all in one, unthinking arrogant go. It would also enable him to shield Braddock from any vengeance Dennis was able to exact.

"Now old chap," started Dennis, Don gave Frankie a bemused look, viewing Dennis as an anachronism of the old SIS. Don had been part of E Squadron, the ultra-secret SF unit attached to SIS and had never come across such a supercilious idiot as Dennis. Frankie Fraser just shrugged his shoulders.

"We have a bit of a delicate situation. It seems your colleagues have bitten off more than they can chew down in Tanzania. It would appear the Americans have been able to intercept communications between your guys and the bad guys and have obtained further Humint that the group holding the hostages are actually an al-Shabaab clan led by a man known as Abu Faud. Abu Faud is an extremely dangerous man believed to be responsible for numerous piratical acts and murders. My information is that they intend to strike the stronghold using hellfire missiles as soon as possible..."

Don, of course, knew Dennis was lying and was attempting to deflect the blame and cut across the spy, the way Frankie had suspected he would.

"Stop right there you fuckin' fuckwit," said Don, who was not a diplomatic man and believed in talking straight, whoever he was talking to. He had "beaten the clock" because of this frankness and if he didn't like something he said so, no matter what rank or position.

The SAS operated a classless society and Don still did. "If you call me 'old chap' again I'll fuckin' rip your smarmy fuckin' head off and shit in the hole. They are not my 'colleagues', Orla is my wife and Rufus is my best mate and if "we have a bit of a delicate situation" you'd better tell me right now what the fuck is going on because as of now I hold you directly responsible for their lives."

Sir Peregrine was not used to be being spoken to in such a forthright, insulting manner and looked at Don aghast.

Don smiled and added, "Just so we know where we stand, "old chap"."

"Now look here, ol...erm, my friend."

"And I'm not your fuckin friend, my name is Don, now tell me the fuckin' truth before I start to get a little annoyed."

"Um ...."

Frankie Fraser had only met Sir Peregrine a couple of times at COBRA and had not seen him on the back foot before. He was completely flustered and out of his comfort zone, he could usually use his upbringing and position to intimidate people but Sir Peregrine had never met an ex SAS NCO whose wife and best friend were in immediate danger.

"Um, right. My information is that the cousins are going to launch a drone strike as soon as possible. The USS Carl Vinson is steaming to the East of Africa and I believe is making the final preparations to launch the drone. They intend to take out the whole clan or cell in one go."

"Tell me something I don't know. We gave that intelligence to Major Fraser here nearly one hour ago, so why are you only just telling us? I'll tell you why you knobber, it's because you are the fuckin' source for the yanks and you have been trying to calculate how you can get yourself out of this fuckin mess."

"I've already phoned the minister and alerted her," said Frankie "GCHQ are tasked with a live feed to your ops room, as authorised by the minister herself, who I think is briefing the PM as we speak. The minister has also authorised access for Don to use "all and any of your available facilities to secure the safe rescue of Deidre and Martyn Conway". She also, retrospectively verbally agreed for me to move my troops forward. So, now we all understand each other I suggest you make the necessary arrangements asap. Old chap."

"Listen in," said Don reverting to his military days to grab Dennis's attention. "You are going to get me to your ops room, and get me on the secure sat to Langley so I can talk to Steve Hessayon. I am still DV'd and cleared to use this building from when I was with E Sqaudron, AND authorised by the minister so you can get me in there without any delays. We can offer them a much better solution than blowing everybody to kingdom fuckin' come."

Chapter Sixty-Five

While his best mate was verbally beating Sir Peregrine up, Rufus was getting the same treatment from Victoria: they argued for five minutes over whether she was safer going with him to the stronghold or staying at the LZ.

"After the stories you told me on the plane, you expect me to wait here? You must be joking. We get to the stronghold, as you keep calling it and I make the phone call then, and not before."

Rufus might have been great at negotiating with kidnappers, but he was utterly out of his depth with a determined, angry woman. She won the argument hands down; part of him was pleased that she was going with him, he was just worried about her when the action started, but reasoned he could leave her well out of the way at the compound, and when he and Orla had secured it, she could enter and treat any wounded.

He loaded up his equipment, leaving Victoria to carry her small medical supply bag. A load that he was quite comfortable with, he had gone into battle carrying much heavier loads: it was common for Special Forces to carry 150lbs to 200lbs of gear, worth tens of thousands of pounds. Although it was dark and the bush was dense they made good time. While they walked, Rufus used his wind up generator to put more power into his cell phone, there was no point leaving it until the battery was flat, he might not be able to do it then.

They heard all the sounds associated with the African bush and some that weren't: lions roaring, elephants or rhino smashing trees to bits. Victoria couldn't believe the destruction the elephants wreaked on the trees. There were hyenas laughing, birds that sounded like they were from Jurassic Park; a couple of times they disturbed birds, which panicked and took off, flapping their wings furiously, breaking the small branches around them. It was magnificent, frightening and evocative all at once. Victoria was determined not to hold Rufus's hand and show her fear; and to keep to his pace not just so he didn't have any justification for leaving her behind, but also for the security being close to him gave her. They moved through the high grass, listening intently, waiting for the strike from a 300lb lion, or the trampling of a herd of 500lb wildebeests. Instead, they heard the snuffling and foraging of warthogs and the scampering of impala, startled by their presence. She saw prehistoric looking birds, shoebills according to Rufus, which somehow looked even uglier and more threatening in the darkness. And the mosquitoes and midges drove her to distraction, swarming around her head and legs, finding a way through her clothing to bite her ankles and knees. She didn't know what she was more worried about, the walk to the stronghold, or arriving there.

After about forty minutes they were in sight of the compound. It looked like an old industrial site that had long fallen into disrepair.

Outside looked like a truck graveyard, with trucks of all shapes and sizes, abandoned. Some were wheel-less, some had been cut up for either the scrap value or to utilise the metal on another vehicle or on another project, such as providing shelter. The African flora was doing its best to camouflage the waste area, growing voraciously through the doors and windscreens, around the bodies and wheels. Rufus viewed the area with the trained eye of a professional soldier, assessing the cover it provided him, and at the same time the potential cover it provided his enemy.

He scanned the fore, middle and background, taking in detail that his experience told him was important, while instantly dismissing the inconsequential. He planned where his "killing ground" would be if his enemy broke out of the compound to attack him. He determined where his cover would be and where his fall-back position would be. Although he was a believer in Field Marshall von Moltke's assertion that no plan survives the first contact with the enemy, he also knew that preparing himself properly could save their lives; going through the drills, rehearsing scenarios in his mind, meaning he wouldn't have to stop and think. He who hesitates is lost. He would just let his sub-conscious take over.

After a few minutes surveying the area, Rufus had identified all these things and took Victoria forward to take cover behind the trucks. He spoke to her in quiet tones telling her what to do if shooting started, which basically consisted of getting behind the engine block of the truck and stay there until the shooting stopped.

Although it had been less than an hour since he had last texted Orla, he still went through the same routine to ensure she was free and able to text back.

Chapter Sixty-Six

Sir Peregrine organised access for Don and Frankie, Don insisted that he be allowed to bring his phone and laptop into the building and have them available to him in the ops room.

While arrangements were being made he called Rufus and not for the first time in his life cursed the vagaries of cell phone communication. The automated female Swahili voice cut in "Tafadahli..." which Don presumed meant 'Sorry' and would go on to say, 'the person you are calling is unavailable'. He cut the call and decided to text both Rufus and Orla, he used the same well-rehearsed routine to ensure they were able to communicate freely, by the time Dennis's secretary was back in the office he had established they both were and asked Rufus for a sitrep.

Frankie Fraser and Dennis looked at each other, the atmosphere in the room was palpable, the spy chief was very conscious about his status and standing in the eyes of his subordinates, and he maintained his air of superiority while they were around, but when they were on their own he looked sheepishly at the two men.

Sir Peregrine decided that it was beneath him to escort them to the ops room and broke the silence:

"Armstrong," he commanded, actually using his secretary's name for once, "take our guests to the fourth floor and ensure they are given access to all the facilities they need. You will be the liaison officer assisting them throughout their time here." At which he stood up and left the room, without a word, a shake of hands, or God forbid, an apology, as if he had done nothing wrong. Don just looked at him in amazement wondering how people like Dennis seem to populate the higher echelons of most organisations.

Armstrong escorted Frankie and Don to the fourth floor. The lift had smart technology which secured every floor. Don had to present his proximity card to the reader, while Frankie Fraser and Armstrong placed their hands on the screen. It seemed to take for ever to get through each of the security measures, and Don kept looking at his watch counting the minutes down. The lift's sensors counted the number of people entering it and the number of people who had entered their access details and if the two figures did not match, it would not move, ensuring that nobody could just 'hop' into the lift at the back of other users and get a 'free ride'. Once on the fourth floor they had to pass through another three security doors, by means of fingerprint and retinal scans to enter into one of the many communications suites. Don thought he had seen state of the art equipment before, but this was something else.

"I'll show you how everything works," said Armstrong.

"Not at the moment," said Don. "The first thing I need is to be patched through to Langley specifically to Steve Hessayon."

"Yes sir," said Armstrong.

"My name is Don, not fucking sir, remember that and we'll get on just fine."

"Ok. Don," said Armstrong as he arranged for the connection to be made.

Meanwhile Don sent a text to Rufus and Orla as he needed to boost their signal. There were limitations to the power of the SIS, CIA, NSA and GCHQ, and not even they could create a signal in the middle of Africa, just like that, not without taking some serious equipment out, or knowing some pretty low-tech nerdy stuff, like Don. He sent a text to both of them asking them if either of them had in their kit the electrician's tape and bag tie-twists that he had given them before they left?

After a few moments Rufus replied that he had and Orla replied that she hadn't got any of the gadgets that he had supplied.

Chapter Sixty-Seven

1810 Zulu

The satellite kicked in and the video link to Langley was up and running: Don spoke to Steven Hessayon, Director APLAA. Unknown to either Frankie Fraser or anyone else in the room, Don had worked with Steve when he was a field agent in the Special Activities Division serving in Afghanistan. They had been through some pretty hairy stuff together, which always has a habit of bonding men, in a way no other experience can.

"Hi Steve," said Don.

"Don, my man, how're the bollocks?" this was the usual greeting from Steve, which emanated from his fascination of British soldiers' use of the word 'bollocks'. A truly utilitarian word, used to describe good or bad, regret or happiness, a thing of beauty or one of hideousness.

"They're a little tight right now Steve. Orla and Ru are in Tanzania at the moment..." there was no need to explain who Orla and Ru were to Steve, as he had been at Don and Orla's wedding, at which Rufus had been the best man "and I understand things are about to heat up for them."

"Shit man, I had no idea they were there as well."

"No I guess you didn't. Steve, we have to delay this strike. We have a twelve man patrol RVing with them in approximately five hours. Give Orla and Rufus a chance to see through their mission, and who knows they might even be able to deliver Abu Faud to you on a plate."

"Yeh I know about the SAS team Don, the trouble is Assistant Secretary Martinovitch has instructed the strike to go in now, he's gotten himself all fired up about it."

"NOW? Hell man, you can run rings around him, some of the stunts you've pulled in the past. I only need a few hours – surely you can delay him by that much?"

"A few? That's the trouble with you Don you'll never give me an exact figure. But I can give you one. The asshole Martinovitch is due back here at 1800 hours, which is 2200 Zulu and he will want answers. That's just under four hours."

"Four fucking hours. Jesus Steve. I need six, just another two hours, surely you can delay for an extra two hours?"

"No Don, not four fucking hours, that bird has got to be airborne in two. We will need to examine the recon images first and the strike goes in in three hours twenty minutes, that's all I can buy you. Martinovitch is prowling around like a grizzly with a bee so far up its ass it's tickling his tonsils. He'll have my ass for breakfast if I don't deliver. Three hours twenty to the strike going in, and remember, the bird will be in the air well before that and if he comes back early the strike will go in early.

"Ok, Ok. I'll get straight onto Rufus and Orla to tell them and instruct them to let me know if there is the slightest hint on Faud doing a Donald."

"Doing what?"

"Oh sorry mate, a Donald Duck, its rhyming slang, leaving the place. I thought you'd have heard it."

"I'm putting my bollocks on the chopping block here for you Don, we want this guy; we want him bad."

"And I'll make sure you get him Steve. I give you my word. We won't let you down just buy me as much time as you can, and keep me updated will you?"

"I can't give you a minute more than the three hours twenty Don. I can't get you any more than that, so you'd better make sure Rufus and Orla are well away from the place." Steve knew he was pushing everything as far as he possibly dare, he also knew that Don would almost certainly come back to him, asking for more time, which he simply could not buy him.

"Thanks Steve, I owe you one."

The video link was cut and Armstrong approached Don.

"I think you should have a quick lesson on how this equipment works, it's normally a five-day course, but I can show you the basics in a few minutes and it WILL save you a lot of time and confusion."

Armstrong gave Don a headset and explained that this science fiction looking gadget was in fact a sleeker version of a fighter pilot's Integrated Helmet and Display Sight System (IHADSS). It tracked Don's eyes and he could operate everything with speech and eye movement and blinking. The computers were all voice operated. He could speak directly to the SAS team just landing in Tanzania, while simultaneously patch in to Langley. He could dictate texts and send them without touching a keyboard. He had sight of the images from Titan IV, giving him a bird's eye view of the scene. The beacons that the troopers carried on their webbing gave him an exact fix on them and their position relative to the compound. He surveyed the

Command and Control log in front of him, scanning the entries, showing that a bug had been remotely placed in Orla's phone, but although they had tried to do the same to Rufus's they had failed for some reason. It was clear that SIS had been working in the background of this kidnapping and a few pieces of the jigsaw started to fall into place in Don's mind.

When he was satisfied he knew the rudimentary operating commands he voice dictated a text to Rufus, instructing him to wrap the household ties around the phone aerial, or if it hadn't got an aerial, around the whole phone and fix it in position with the electrician's tape that he had supplied. This created something called the Tesla Coil effect: extraneous information that Don sensibly did not supply to Rufus, as he did not need to know it to make the phone work.

Next he dictated a text to Orla asking if she could get hold of an old radio antennae or some tin cans, as he already knew she did not have her technical bag with her.

Rufus got straight to work, while using the luxury of the trucks and darkness for cover. Orla just looked at the text from her husband and wondered what planet he was on? In fact she had to look at the text twice to make sure she understood it. There was lots of rubbish around the site, but she could hardly get up and walk around scavenging for old cans or aerials, so, cursing him, she had to simply reply *Standby.*

Don was cooking on gas now; he had everything he needed at the blink of an eye. He instructed one of the technicians in the room to set the electronic wall clock to three hours twelve minutes, the exact time he had left to save the Conways, Victoria, his wife and best mate.

He surveyed the space age facility, with its clean lines and quiet efficiency, and imagined what Orla and Rufus were dealing with in the back of beyond.

After a few more minutes Rufus's hushed tones were coming through Don's headset.

"Hi mate," said Rufus quietly, he didn't whisper as the sibilant nature of a whisper carries further than speaking quietly. "This is pretty fucking awesome. I went from one bar to full signal. How did you do that?"

"Great Ru, I'll explain how it's done later. I have a lot of information for you to get your head round."

"Ok. Don, go ahead."

"Right we have..." Don paused for a beat as he checked the electronic clock he had put on count-down, "two hours fifty five minutes to get you out of there before all hell is let loose: the American navy will carry out a drone strike on the compound at 2130 Zulu, blowing it, and everybody inside it to kingdom come. Deano Richards is leading a twelve-man patrol which is en route to the stronghold, and due to the limited time frame, they will have to HAHO directly to you, far too close for my liking, so any diversionary tactics you and Orla can employ will be useful. ETA of the team to your position, 2300 Zulu. That is ninety minutes after..."

"The drone strike," Rufus finished off for him. "Fan-fucking-tastic."

Chapter Sixty-Eight

1845 Zulu 2hrs 45

"I have full White Command facilities, I have eyes on you, eyes on the compound, eyes on Deano. I have fully integrated comms. I am in touch with Langley and will be given sitreps from them. I repeat at 2130 Zulu a hellfire missile strike will be made on the compound."

"Fuck me sideways Don. First of all, you and Deano have to rethink their plan and get them here a little quicker to give them a chance of joining the party, or it's going to be down to Orla and me. Vicky and I are ok. but Orla is inside the compound, she'll be blown to holy hell, along with the Conways and the bandits, unless we can get her and them out."

"I know, mate, I've just given Orla some instructions on how to boost her signal so I can talk to her. Standby, I've got a text from Orla I need to answer to get her up and running."

Inside the compound Orla had used the cover of darkness to move silently around. She climbed into several cabs looking for tin cans or aerials and in the fourth cab she found exactly what she was looking for, she hoped.

She got back to her OP, and texted Don that she had an old square looking radio antenna with about five feet of flex.

Perfect, replied Don. *Wrap about two feet of the flex around the phone and put the antenna as high as you can.*

Orla did what she thought Don meant and was amazed to see her signal jump almost immediately to a full signal, the only problem now was that she was running dangerously low on battery. She put her Bluetooth earpiece back on, to reduce the sound level and called Don. Like Rufus, she spoke quietly rather than whisper.

+++++++

1850 Zulu 2 hrs 40

Steve got on the video link to Don.

"The Avenger is launching as we speak buddy. You'll have access to the imagery shortly," as Steve spoke, the Titan satellite split its imagery and showed the launch from the Carl Vinson and the compound simultaneously.

"Yeh got it," said Don.

"Time to target is 1 hour 30 minutes, and hopefully I can delay the strike by another forty minutes for you."

"Cheers pal, you're the bollocks. I owe you one."

The Avenger took off sedately, climbing steadily to its operating altitude of 60000 feet and a cruising speed of 300 knots. Time to target: 1 hour 30 minutes. It was paradoxical that it looked so peaceful, graceful and benign and yet was going to reap such destruction.

Don's headset showed him Orla was calling, a blink of the eye and she was connected.

"Hello darling, this is another fine mess you've got me into," sharing their familiar Laurel and Hardy joke.

"Hi, love. There is a lot to tell you, but in a nutshell I'm in an ops rooms at Vauxhall. I have eyes on you via an American bird. Rufus and Victoria are outside and there is a twelve-man patrol led by Deano Richards en route to you. We have..." Don looked up at the clock "two hours fourteen minutes to get you and the Conways out of there before the yanks light the place up like Sydney Harbour Bridge on New Year's Eve."

"Roger that. My battery life is low, so I don't know how long I can talk for. Can I speak to Ru directly?"

"Yes you should be able to now. You will all be on talk through, like a conference call."

"Roger that Don, if I disappear my battery has run out."

Don let Orla and Rufus talk directly, to discuss their plans and preparations and turned to Frankie.

"Boss can you plan me an alternative approach for Deano."

Although Frankie was the senior figure in the room, he knew that Don was the right person to be leading the operation because of his technical expertise and was quite comfortable with supporting him.

"I've already started that Don."

"Good"

1900 Zulu 2 hrs 30

Don viewed his data and could see Captain Deano Richards and his team were still forty minutes from the TPDF base in Dar and gave the 'call' command.

"Deano, how are you doing? It's Don Ward here, speaking from Vauxhall."

"Bamm-Bamm", a nickname not used by anybody except Rufus and Orla for a long time, "how are you doing fella?"

"Good mate, good, except I have Orla and Pebble out in Mikumi, and you there. Frankie Fraser is just plotting an alternative solution for you, as your plan does not get you to the stronghold in time." He brought Deano up-to-speed.

With a blink of the eye he brought Rufus and Orla back into the conversation.

"I need to get some semblance of Command and Control into the situation. I can coordinate things from here, I am White Commander, Deano you are Delta Four-Zero. Over."

"Delta Four-Zero, Roger White Command, over."

"Ru you are Purple Commander and Orla you are Purple 1. Over."

"Purple Commander Roger. Over."

Purple 1, Roger, over."

"Everything comes through Vauxhall, White Command. Understood? The Shermans have authorised a drone attack, in, erm two hours twenty seven minutes, which I have pushed back as far as I can. Delta Four-Zero, sitrep please."

"We are thirty-five minutes from Dar. The Sea King Commando is being readied for take-off and we should be good to go at 1950 Zulu. We are a twelve-man patrol equipped and authorised for Hostage Rescue. Our flight plan is due West from here, and our ETA to the DZ is 2200 Zulu; ETA to the RVP is 2300 Zulu. Over."

Orla, Don and Rufus were doing the calculations in their heads: no matter how they did it, it did not get the troops to them in time. They were on their own.

"The alternative is HAHO from the C130 using our updated insertion methods. The Heelo can RV with us there for exfil and Casevac. Revised RV will be....2030. Over."

"Confirm 2030 Zulu please Delta Four Zero. Over," said Rufus, unable to understand how they could possibly shave one hundred and fifty minutes off their ETA.

"Standby all units. Over," said Don, turning to Frankie. "What are these updated insertion methods he's talking about?"

"We've developed the use of wing-packs since you left Don. It has revolutionised insertion methods, the blokes will fly in at 100mph in their suits. They'll exit the plane and fly to the LZ far faster than the old ram air wings you and Pebble were developing. If they had their jet-powered suits, they would have got there even faster, from even farther out, but they haven't, so the wing-packs will have to do."

"Ok boss, can you confirm Deano's calculations for me?"

"Confirmed," said Major Fraser.

"Equipment?"

"That's the best bit, we've taken and adapted the Sherman's drone technology to fit wings to the equipment containers and one of the troopers is able to control and direct the container, just like flying a model glider, all at over 100mph. It takes practise to be able to control your own flight and that of the container, but the boffins had come up with a way of attaching sensors on the finger pads of the suits to control the flight of the container. As long as the tube and its pilot are the lead jumpers, the rest of the team follow them. We've inserted from two hundred miles out using it."

"Fantastic," said Don.

Don brought up mapping on the screen and the computer did the calculations for them: a twelve-man stick from the C130 was the fastest most preferable option, getting them to LZ 500 metres from the stronghold by 2020 Zulu. Ten minutes to orient, prepare themselves, and the short TAB to the RVP. The programme was designed to show alternatives, using the parameters and variables input by the operator: the next fastest, but riskiest was the fast-rope option, with an ETA of 2140. There was no alternative.

"White Command all units: Delta Four-Zero to proceed by fixed wing, ETA to RVP." Don glanced at his display "2030 Zulu. The computer simulations show this to be the fastest of our options. Over."

"Delta Four-Zero-White Command. Roger. Over."

"Delta Four-Zero. I will get one of the techies to send you a satellite image of the compound, so you can start your IA plan." Don spoke in military shorthand for 'Immediate Action'. "I know it doesn't give you much time, but it's the best we can do. Over."

Don and Frankie could see the progress of the huge military plane on their screens. Orla updated Rufus on her preparations and what she could see of the layout of the compound. Don instructed one of the aids to listen in to their discussions to confirm from the imagery what Orla was saying and fill in any blanks she couldn't see, and to keep him updated on the situation in there. He could hear Rufus and Orla talking, planning their next moves, but he tuned them out and glanced at the clock.

1920 Zulu 2 hours 10

He and Frankie discussed tactics again. All they could do was provide information, intelligence and technical support. Both men wished they were there, but both knew the job they were doing was vital. They needed everything to work perfectly to stand any chance of affecting a successful hostage rescue. They had no time for surveillance, no time for dialogue to ensure that Deidre and Martyn were actually there and alive, they just had to do it and rely on Orla, Rufus and Victoria.

Chapter Sixty-Nine

1930 Zulu 2 hours

Don instructed Frankie Fraser to get hold of Dame Cunningham-Black, update her and bring her up-to-speed.

After a brief conversation Major Fraser told Don that she was on her way to Vauxhall asap, and had agreed their decisions. She was on the phone to her counterparts in Tanzania, keeping them in the loop.

"White Command all receivers: the time is... 1935 Zulu, one hour fifty-five minutes to the Deadline. White Command-Delta Four-Zero Commander, sitrep please. Over."

Although Don could see exactly where the plane was, he wanted Captain Richards, Rufus and Orla to all have the same information.

"Delta Four-Zero-all receivers. Five minutes to DZ, ETA remains 2020 to LZ, 2030 to RVP. Over."

"White Commander- Purple Commander, can you put a tactical call in on my instruction? Over."

"Affirmative White. Over."

"White Commander-Purple 2, have you prepared any sort of divisionary tactics? Over."

"Affirmative White. Over."

Dame Cunningham-Black came on the line to Frankie.

"I've spoken to the PM and the Defence Secretary and the Tanzanian president and apprised them of the situation. You have authority for an armed intervention."

"Thank you ma'am."

"My eta to you is 1945," said the minister, getting used to the military jargon she was hearing so frequently.

"White Commander all receivers: Stand by. All receivers, the time is now 1935 Zulu, one hour fifty-five minutes to H hour. We have a Go Go Go."

At that moment Orla and Rufus knew that twelve of their ex comrades were exiting the C130 high above them in the night sky, hurtling towards them to wreak havoc and destruction on the terrorists.

Don viewed the imagery, knowing he had a little down time to refocus, wishing he was out there with them.

Don's headset showed him that Al was calling from Langley.

"Hi Steve." said Don in quite a cheery positive voice.

"Bad news I'm afraid Don. ADS Martinovitch is en route here now, ETA, err, 2100 Zulu."

"Christ on a bike Steve, that only gives us..." Don looked at the clock and did the calculations, "one hour twenty-five minutes"

"I know Don, there is some serious political pressure coming down to get this guy. I can delay the strike until he gets here, claiming I wanted him to see the hit in glorious Technicolor, but I can't do any better than that. I'm sorry pal."

"It's not your fault Steve," said Don regaining his composure. "We just have to deal with it, thanks for the heads up."

Chapter Seventy

1940 Zulu 1hour 20

Frankie got back onto the minister and briefed her as she was arriving at the building.

Don re-entered the new timings into the computer: he knew it didn't affect the options it just reduced the time on the ground for the blokes. It meant Orla and Rufus would have to prepare things for them.

"White Command-All receivers. Be advised H hour now 2100 Zulu. Repeat 2100 Zulu. Received Delta four-Zero? Over."

"Delta Four-Zero received," said the remarkably calm and clear Captain Richards, Don couldn't hear any wind or background noise, and if he wasn't able to see the imagery of the twelve men flying through the air, from the beacons on their helmets, he would have doubted the fact that he was actually flying through the Tanzanian sky.

"Received Purple Commander? Over."

"Received White. Over," replied Rufus.

"Received Purple 1? Over."

"All received White. Over," said Orla.

Rufus briefed Victoria on what was happening, leaving the detail about the Americans planning a drone strike out of the explanation for the time being. He knew he had just under thirty minutes to prepare

Victoria for the call she was going to have to put in to the bandits so he started preparing her.

"We need to put a call in to the stronghold soon, to preoccupy them. Orla has prepared some sort of diversion in there and between the three of us we will create enough confusion to distract the bandits from our initial assault. If we can create enough chaos between us, it will give them the edge they need."

"Why the rush Ru?"

Rufus decided to tell her the truth. "The Americans are planning a drone strike on the building..."

Victoria gasped in shock, her hand over her mouth. She, like millions of others, had seen the video footage on the television of the American drone strikes.

"...We have to make sure that your mum and dad are out of the building by midnight."

Victoria looked at her watch and could just about make the time out at 10:40. "That only gives us one hour and twenty minutes."

"Yes and the team are about forty minutes away. Leaving us about thirty-five minutes, to get in, overpower the enemy, rescue your parents and get out of here which is cutting things fine."

Chapter Seventy-One

1945 Zulu 1 hour 15

Dame Cunningham-Black entered the room with her entourage. Major Fraser took the responsibility, together with Armstrong of acquainting the minister with the room and the update. She was a very intelligent woman who took all the information in first time, she knew she had to leave the mechanics of the operation to the military men, but there were ways she could try and help.

She spoke to Armstrong.

"Would you mind getting me a link to Assistant Secretary of Defence Martinovitch please, Keith?" Armstrong looked in amazement at the minister, somehow she had found out his name and her polite, yet determined manner, was a breath of fresh air. He got straight onto the job.

Don focused the imagery in his headset. He could see the guards at the compound, lazing around playing cards. He wondered just how powerful this optical satellite was, and allowed himself a few seconds of down time as he zoomed the satellite onto the cards of one of the guards, he could see the cards more clearly than if had been standing over him, he didn't know what game they were playing, but it didn't look a very good hand to him. After a couple of seconds of awe at the power of the thing, he was back on his game. He checked the time: 2000 Zulu.

The minister withdrew to one of the ante-rooms servicing the ops Room, and even though she had closed the door behind her, they could hear her raised voice as she spoke to ADS Martinovitch.

Chapter Seventy-Two

2000 Zulu, One hour

In the compound the atmosphere was quite relaxed among the al-Shabaab terrorists. They had become blasé, over the past few months: The westerners always said they would not pay publicly, but they always did. The internet was a wonderful thing for applying pressure, and when they uploaded images of the two unkempt depressed hostages the pictures would spread around the world on news broadcasts and people surfing through the social media sites. They had a Facebook account and they would put it on there, until somebody reported it as inappropriate, but by that time it would be too late it would be out there and could go viral. The same for YouTube: Abu Faud enjoyed the irony that he was using western corporate monoliths for his own purposes to attack the very institutions they supported.

They would alert Al Jazeera, who would down load it straight away, and it would be picked up by other broadcasters who would play it to the millions through their televisions. The pressure would build on the government which would say one thing publicly and do another privately. They had made millions over the last few years.

+++++++

At the same time Orla was double-checking all of her little surprises. She knew Rufus would be briefing Victoria and called him. "I'm running really low on battery here, so if I lose power completely, I'll begin my diversions at twenty…"

"Orla? Orla? Can you hear me? Oh shit, shit shit, Orla's battery has gone." Rufus got straight on to Don, who had overheard the conversation.

"Ok mate let's think about this. Can you get in the compound with Victoria and put in a call on my command? Over." It was a rhetorical question really. Clutching at straws.

"Negative. Over."

"No. I know you can't so we are going to have to figure it out. If it was us, what time would we start a diversion, knowing Deano is going to RV at 2030? … Standby, I can see some activity in the compound by Orla's hide. Over."

There was indeed activity, because Orla realised what had happened, and knew that her husband was watching what was happening in the compound, she was out of the hide, in the open, laying on the ground in full view the American satellite.

"What's she doing?" asked one of the ops room staff.

"I don't know," replied Don, looking at Frankie quizzically. "She knows we can see her so she is doing it deliberately, whatever it is. There's nobody else near her is there?" He switched to infra-red to detect any other heat sources that may have been close to her, but she was alone. Don zoomed in on her and it looked like she was fiddling with her watch.

They all peered at the screen unable to figure out what she was doing. She was pointing at her watch and then messing around with it.

"She's going to set her watch to show us the time she intends to start her diversionary tactics," said Frankie.

They all looked at the screen and could see the light of her small functional Casio flickering on and off as she appeared to be resetting the time. They watched and waited for her to hold the watch to show them the time, but it never happened. She kept doing the same thing, over and over.

"No, she's not doing that, if she changes the time on her watch, she doesn't know what time it is to coordinate with Rufus and us. No, she's doing something to tell us, but what?" said Don.

The minutes ticked by… they all watched the screen as Orla eventually slid back into her hide, reasoning that if Don had not picked up her signal by now, he never would.

"Fuck!" shouted Don. "Could anybody see the time on her watch?"

Everybody shook their heads in embarrassment and frustration, feeling they had let Don down in his attempt to save his wife's life, feeling the responsibility weigh heavy on them. Just then, Dame Cunningham-Black reappeared from the ante-room bringing the mood of the room down even further.

2010 Zulu 50 mins

"The imbecilic, cretinous, irresponsible, fatuous, asinine, blithering buffoon," seethed the minister. None of her staff had ever seen her so incensed. She never criticised anybody publicly, always choosing to keep her thoughts to herself, so they knew she was furious. She regained her equanimity and asked one of her aids to get hold of the PM.

She addressed the rest of the room:

"First of all, I'm sorry for that little outburst, but I've just got off the phone to the most ignorant man with whom I've ever had the displeasure of dealing. Unfortunately the Assistant Secretary of Deefence," another uncharacteristic show of displeasure as she accentuated the American pronunciation, "is not prepared to delay their intended strike by even one second. I'm going to speak to the PM and get him to speak directly to the president, but time is going to be tight to put it mildly. I'm sorry," she disappeared back into the ante room to speak to the prime minister.

Frankie could feel the energy draining from the room: that could be disastrous, if people felt defeated they were; he knew he had to do something to get them a little victory and bring the energy back up.

"Is everything recorded in here?" he asked the staff in general.

"Yes, we have to, all communications, all decisions and all vid...all videoed...shit, we have Orla recorded we can watch her again and see if we can decipher what she was doing," said Armstrong.

"Get to it then, asap," instructed Fraser

2015 Zulu 45 mins

They all watched the video replaying, willing an inspirational thought to pop into their heads. Don was just planning to put a call back into Rufus to plan their next course of action, on the basis of not knowing Orla's intentions, when Keith Armstrong shouted from behind him.

"Hold on. I've got it... It's Morse Code. Look, she's using the light of her watch to send us a Morse code message. See dot dot dot dot, dash; dot dot dot dot dot; dot dot dash dash dash; dash dash dash dash dash; dot dot dot dot, dash." He held up his notepaper to show them.

One of the other staff had brought up Morse on the internet and projected on to the screen while the video showed Orla repeating her signal.

"Four, five, two, zero repeated? What does that mean? asked Armstrong.

"Brilliant Keith, you're right, you've just started reading it halfway through the message that's all," said Don, "she's not leaving a gap between the sequences, it's 2045, she's going to make her move at 2045. Received Purple Commander? Over." Don felt a wave of pride and emotion sweep through his body, that his brilliant, talented beautiful wife had been so resourceful.

"Received, White Command. We will be ready to make our call by 2035 on your command. Over."

"Received Delta Four-Zero? Over."

"Received White. Over," said Captain Richards as the whole of his patrol hurtled through the sky at over 100mph. It didn't leave them much time at all, but it was what they had and they had to deal with it. The patrol was ready and focused.

+++++++

Dame-Cunningham Black was on the phone to the PM's principal private secretary, who was fielding the call.

"I am well aware that the PM is at the EU dinner, but I need to speak with him again now, this is not up for discussion or debate."

The minister looked at the electronic clock, in the ante-room which was identical to the clocks situated outside in the ops room: thirty-five minutes and forty seconds to go… and counting.

After what seemed an interminable delay, the PPS came back on the phone and said, "He's coming now, he will be here as soon as he can."

"Thank you," as she looked at the clock: thirty-three minutes and twenty-seven seconds.

+++++++

The SAS patrol silently landed in a small cluster five hundred metres from the compound. They opened their cylinders and prepared their kit while Captain Richards spoke to Don.

"Go ahead Delta Four-Zero.Over."

"We've secured the DZ, ETA to RVP confirmed as 2035. Over."

"Delta Four-Zero received. Over. Purple Command understood? Over."

"Purple commander received. Over."

Rufus returned to his preparations with Victoria, while Don and Deano, finalise details. Don still had exclusive use of the Titan Satellite, focused on the compound and could see that everything looked peaceful, the calm before the storm.

Steve appeared on the video link from Langley. Although he was patched in to the operation he still asked, "How's it going Don?"

"It's going to be tight Steve. Any time you can buy us will help. Do you know our minister has been on the line to Martinovitch?"

"No I didn't, he's not here yet. Did she persuade him to delay the strike?"

"From her reaction when she came out, I don't think so; her staff said it was the angriest they had ever seen her, he made a real impression on her. Anyway she's on to the PM now, I would think to get him to phone the president."

"They'll have to be quick, you've got thirty-one minutes. Tops."

"Tops? I thought H hour was 2100?"

"That's what I'm planning, but if he gets back earlier, what can I do? The drone is in position, locked and loaded, ready to go."

"Ok. Steve, thanks, keep me updated will you?"

"Sure will buddy, I'm keeping the link open now, you'll know what I know."

Chapter Seventy-Three

2030 Zulu 30 mins

"Are you ready?" Rufus asked Victoria "Remember we keep them on the phone, no matter what, we've got to keep them occupied so Orla's little surprises have maximum effect."

"I know Ru, I know." She was getting nervous now, she knew that the lives of her parents depended on her, if she didn't do her job properly, Orla couldn't do hers, and the SAS couldn't do theirs and her parents would either be shot by the terrorists or blown up by the Americans.

Rufus used his phone before he gave her the go-ahead.

"Call going in now, White Command. Over."

"Received Purple Commander, you are good to go. Over."

"A few deep breaths Vicky, get yourself grounded and prepared." He squeezed her hand, hoping to give her strength.

She nodded and he pressed 'call'.

As he touched the button, Victoria's worst nightmare appeared: a pride of lions; a huge male, six fully grown females and four cubs.

Rufus stopped the call, before it connected and put his hand over Victoria's mouth, pulling her towards him. He hoped he wasn't going to have to test old

Tertius Ventor's theory. They stayed motionless, hoping the pride was just transiting between one hunting ground and another AND they had just eaten.

Rufus wanted to look at his watch, he knew he had to get Victoria on the phone as soon as possible, but couldn't afford to move or make a sound. He knew if they attacked he would have to stand and make himself big at the very least, he couldn't afford to shoot one of them, not unless things got really hairy, a gunshot would put the compound on high alert, perhaps even bring the terrorists out to check what was happening.

At Vauxhall, the team watched powerless at the infra-red images of the eleven heat sources walking slowly towards Rufus and Victoria. They all held their breath and froze, as if they were the ones in danger from the beasts.

The massive male stopped and sniffed the air and turned towards the two of them. Rufus could feel Victoria stiffen. The lionesses followed suit and crouched. He could just about see them in the darkness as they organised themselves into attack formation: one man versus seven fully-grown lions, in their own back yard.

Rufus had to make a decision; time was ticking away and the lions were getting closer. He decided to charge: controlled aggression; the hallmark of good soldier.

"Stay here and get under the wreck if you can," he whispered in Victoria's ear. He pulled the Glock from her holster, thrusting it into her hand. "Use it if you have to." He knew that if he could spook just one of them, the others would probably follow suit. He removed a poncho from his Bergen, took his weapon in the other hand and charged directly at the big male, waving his poncho for all his was worth. The lion stood his ground, his massive head and mane getting bigger as Rufus got closer, beginning to question his rash decision... at the last moment, true to Tertius's word, the lion turned and ran, followed by the lionesses and cubs.

Rufus didn't know how much time he had bought them as he hurried back to Victoria.

"Ready?" he asked, far more in control of his senses than Victoria was of hers.

"Are you completely mad?" she asked, but relieved to be joined by the black-clad captain.

Rufus knew there was no time for discussions, recriminations or eulogies; they had to get to work.

"Vicky, we need to put the call in for your mum and dad and we need to do it now."

Victoria was on auto-pilot.

"Deep breaths and get ready," he said as he hit the call button at 2035 Zulu.

Inside, the telephone rang and Abu Faud answered.

"This is Victoria. How the fuck are my parents?" she said without any preamble.

They had decided to be direct and forthright after the last telephone call, but Rufus hadn't expected this.

"They are both with me, that is all you need to know."

"I want to fucking-well speak to them. NOW."

Rufus decided not to let her get too carried away...yet.

"Don't you believe me?"

"Of course I believe you, where else would they be you pr..." Rufus had put his finger on Victoria's lips to stop her ejaculating the insult, and mouthed the word "worried", and mimed a deep breathing action. Victoria took a deep breath and continued... "I just need to speak to them. After what you have done to them I am worried about them, I am a doctor and know what a trauma like that can do to elderly people."

Rufus was relieved to be joined by the SAS patrol. Deano gave hand signals to the patrol, that immediately set about their work: three troopers took up defensive positions to secure their holding area. The rest disappeared into the night towards the compound. Deano Richards joined Rufus and Victoria.

"Ha ha, they are fine, a little bleeding will not kill them, but my men are getting impatient, they need money to buy food to feed their villages, they need money to clothe them. When am I going to get my money?"

This had worked better than Rufus expected, he still wanted Victoria to speak to her parents, but Abu Faud had raised the subject of the money, so they could pursue that train of thought now, which is exactly where Rufus and Victoria wanted to take it.

"I hope to have some friends and associates contact me within the next hour, telling me if they have secured your money. As soon as they let me know, I will call you and we can arrange to get you your money. But I HAVE to talk to Mum and Dad first."

Victoria sat cross-legged on the bush floor looking straight at Ru who was as alert and attentive as ever, listening for all the nuances coming over the phone, picking up on words for Victoria to echo or mirror or turn on the kidnappers. She took strength as he smiled and nodded encouragement at her. She felt a little uneasy being so assertive, but Rufus had explained that in reality she would not simply hand over any money without knowing that they were alive AND that this Abu Faud had the ability to release them back to her. He likened it to buying a car without ever knowing if the car existed, nobody in their right mind would do it. With the troopers surrounding them, they could relax about any imminent threat from the lions, or anything else for that matter.

"You will only get your money after I have spoken to my parents. I am not going to hand over a single shilling, dollar or pound until I know they are ok."

"You will speak to your parents when I say so."

Rufus encouraged her again, with a mime of being tough and resolute.

"AND YOU will get your money when I speak to my parents. Do you really think I am going to give you millions of dollars without any proof that you have my mum and dad, that would just be foolish. I am getting your money, but only on condition that I can speak to my parents first. I may be many things BUT I AM NOT FOOLISH."

Rufus realised they were at an impasse, and it was a battle of wills, who would blink first. He decided to give Victoria her head and let all her emotions flood out.

"YOU BASTARDS. I'VE FUCKING-WELL TOLD YOU I WANT TO SPEAK TO THEM. YOU'VE TORTURED THEM. YOU'VE TORTURED ME. ALL I WANT TO KNOW IS THAT THEY ARE ALIVE AND SAFE. WHAT IS THE HARM IN THAT? WHERE IS THE WEAKNESS OR DISHONOUR? WHAT SORT OF INHUMAN BASTARD ARE YOU? CALL YOURSELF A MUSLIM? I HAVE MUSLIM FRIENDS WHO WOULD NOT WANT TO BE IN THE SAME FUCKING ROOM AS YOU.

Rufus thought she was going to burst in tears, and she wanted to, but she was determined to be strong for her mum and dad and show this bastard Abu Faud that she meant it.

Abu Faud bridled at being spoken to like that, and at the same time, admired the girl's spirit. He shouted out some orders and a few moments later he came back on the phone.

"I will allow you to speak to your parents, to demonstrate to you I am a man of honour. I hold no grudge against you or your parents, I am a professional and I will deal with you as a professional."

Deano and Rufus both knew that time was ticking, they both automatically checked their watches: 2039, but unless they had proof of life and proof of control in the compound, there was no point risking their lives. It was essential.

Rufus held up the word *apologise* on his iPhone.

Victoria looked at him as if he had gone mad. Why should she apologise? He was the one in the wrong. He was the one that had threatened and tortured her parents. He was the one that was holding them hostage.

Rufus could see the defiance in her face and body language and tapped his iPad again to reinforce the point.

"I'm sorry," said Victoria.

Rufus was gesticulating to develop the theme.

"I'm sorry I insulted you, it's just that I am getting very tired and very upset," and at Ru's insistence she started to weep down the phone, "I. I. I just want to know that they are ok. Is that too much for a daughter to ask for?"

Unseen by Victoria and Ru, Abu Faud handed the phone to Deidre. "Hello love. How are you?"

That is typical of her mother, always thinking of the welfare of the rest of the family before her own predicament.

"I'm worried sick Mum. How are you?"

"I'm ok. Your dad's a bit shook up though, but we will be alright. Where are you?"

Deano gave the thumbs up to the rest of the patrol as they readied themselves. One minute until Orla's diversionary tactics began.

Rufus and Victoria were on the same wavelength and before he could get his signal to her she answered without hesitation. "I'm still in Dar es Salaam. I suppose it is a silly question to ask where you are isn't it?"

"Yes love, I haven't got a clue where we are..."

Rufus and Victoria could hear a commotion in the background and then Abu Faud, take over the telephone. "Are you happy now?"

Rufus mouthed the word "Thanks".

"Yes, thank you for letting me speak to my mum. Is my dad alright? Can I speak to him please?"

Victoria heard the muffled incoherent words of her father on the telephone, she was a hundred per cent sure it was her dad, but could hardly make out what he was saying, "Bictoya. Ishtha chu?"

She guessed was "Victoria. Is that you?" and answered the question.

"Hello Dad, it's me Victoria. Hang in there, I've got the money to pay to get you home, it won't be long now."

"Cuufl," was the mumbled reply.

Rufus and Victoria looked at each other. Victoria shrugged her shoulders and raised her eyebrows and Rufus mouthed the word "careful" with rise of his eyebrows.

"Are you saying to be careful, Dad?

"Ess."

"I will be careful Dad, I'm in a safe place and nothing can happen to me. I'm in Dar es Salaam getting the money together. It's you that needs to be careful. You'll be alright I promise. I promise I'll get you out of there as quickly as I can." Victoria had said that as much for Abu Faud's ears as for her dad's. Rufus had told her that one of the bandits would almost certainly be listening to any conversation she had with her parents, and so to always treat it as such.

"Now, Miss Conway, when will I get my money?" cut in the unmistakable tones of Abu Faud.

Rufus and Victoria heard a scream both over the phone and coming over the wall from the compound. They guessed Orla had started her work.

"What's that?" they heard Abu Faud ask to an unseen colleague.

Rufus gesticulated that she had to keep going, had to keep his attention on the phone and on her, now she could get aggressive.

"I will have the two million within the hour and you will be the first to know when I do. And if I find you have harmed a hair on their heads I am going to get people to hunt you down like a dog and inflict the same horrors on you as you have on my family."

"You are in no..."

Another shout from inside the compound, followed by more commotion as guards started to panic. Abu Faud was distracted and Rufus needed him to concentrate on the phone for as long as he could. He stood up with Victoria and began to walk towards the compound.

"Oh yes I fucking-well am you bastard, you are the one that is not in any position to make threats..."

Inside the compound Orla had spread panic and terror. At 2045 exactly she sacrificed the chicken for a good cause. She held the bird under her left arm, taken its head between her right index finger and middle finger and ripped the poor bird's head clean off and threw it out of the hide. The chicken ran, squawked and flapped its way around the compound waking up the sleeping guards. The chicken, the 'ghost' blood on shirts and pillows, laces cut or sandals missing, put the poorly educated, superstitious Somalis into a blind panic.

2046 Zulu 14 mins

Rufus and Victoria could hear them shouting clearly now as the four remaining members of the patrol headed towards the compound. Unseen by Victoria the assault group scaled the walls, simultaneously setting off a deafening explosive charge at the gates.

"Keep going Victoria," Mouthed Rufus.

"What is going on, what is all that noise?" she shouted into the phone.

Abu Faud had to appear to be in control of the situation but was disoriented, he didn't know whether to stay on the phone and deal with the woman that was going to give him $5 million or deal with the rabble of his soldiers outside.

"What are you going to do with your $5 million? Are you going to share it equally among your people? Or are you going to keep it yourself? Whatever you do, I'll find you." Victoria knew she was waffling, she couldn't concentrate with everything that was happening, but Rufus was exhorting her to carry on. "That's the trouble with people like you, you set yourself up as some sort of Robin Hood and end up taking, taking from everybody."

"You don't know what you are talking about..." the line went dead as he eventually realised his attention was needed outside.

2052 Zulu 8 mins

In Vauxhall they could see the action taking place and hear it over Captain Richards's head set. Dame Cunningham-Black had reappeared and was watching the unfolding scene in awe. She had persuaded the PM to contact the president and could only hope he would intervene in time... Eight minutes to get everybody out of there.

Rufus could hear the shooting, the familiar controlled bursts of scything rounds leaving the troopers weapons. The noise seemed to be abating more quickly than he anticipated. He got on the line to Don.

"Purple Commander moving forward. Over."

Chapter Seventy-Four

2055 Zulu 5 mins

By the time Victoria and Rufus got through the gates the well-drilled, professional soldiers had completed their job of securing the compound. They could see a large group of terrorists laying prostate in the dirt, having their wrists cable-tied by the troopers. Orla rushed over to them, and as much as they all wanted to hug, they knew that the job was not yet done. They rushed over to the old maintenance building where they knew Deano would be.

The SAS troopers rounded up the three bandits that had given up without a fight in the ramshackle old building.

"There's no sign of Deidre or Martyn, here Pebble," said Deano.

"They're here somewhere Deano. We had proof of life and proof of control while we have been here."

Deano knew him and knew he would be a hundred per cent accurate on something as important as this. The two of them heard the communication from Don.

"Missile launched. Four minutes to impact. You need to be out of there in three minutes thirty seconds."

Rufus spoke to Don imploring him to assure the Americans the compound was secure and Abu Faud was captured, while Deano approached Abu Faud. “Where are Deidre and Martyn?”

Abu Faud focused on the floor six feet in front of him. He remained perfectly still and silent; his breathing did not change in the slightest.

Deano grabbed him by the throat. “We have three and a half minutes to live. Where are they you bastard?”

Abu Faud still focused on an imaginary point somewhere in the distance refusing to make eye contact with the SAS officer or even acknowledge his existence.

2057:45 Zulu 3 mins 15 seconds

One of the NCOs, SSM Alcock approached Abu Faud and pulled out his Glock, he put the pistol against the temple of Abu Faud.

“Three minutes ten seconds,” said Don.

“Listen you wanker. He’s an officer. He cares about the Geneva Convention and shit like that. Me? I don’t give a fuck and there won’t be any witnesses will there?” He pulled back the trigger. “Now where the fuck are they?”

Abu Faud let a grin disturb his lips, a self-satisfied smile. A knowing smile, because he knew the soldier would not pull the trigger. He knew they were running out of time and that any minute now he would become a martyr in the Holy Jihad and that he would take the ambassador, his bitch of a wife and all of the infidel soldiers to their deaths. Deaths he was sure they feared more than him. He kept repeating his mantra of “Allahu Akbar’ to himself, to block out the annoying voice of the doomed soldier.

“Three minutes. Guys, you’ve got to get out of there.” There was no panic in Don’s voice. That was the worst thing he could do. He had to relay the pertinent information calmy and clearly. He still had to abide by the communications doctrine of Accuracy, Brevity and Clarity. He returned his attention to Steve.

"For God's sake Steve, you can see what is going on as well as I can, abort the strike."

"I can't. Martinovitch is in direct contact with the Carl Vinson, he's instructed them to continue."

Don had a split screen again, showing the satellite imagery and the view from the on-board camera on the Avenger.

Rufus and Victoria watched with growing anxiety, they had got so close, had come so far, they couldn't be thwarted at the last minute. They looked on at Abu Faud, calm, stoic.

Victoria looked on with concern: she was a doctor and had taken the Hippocratic oath. She would tend to the wounded whichever side they were on, once she had found her parents and everybody was out of there.

"Two minutes fifty seconds," said Don.

"What's happening?" Victoria asked Captain Richards. "Where are my mum and dad?"

"We don't know Victoria. From what Rufus and Orla have said they are in here, but these scumbags won't talk and we haven't got time to carry out a systematic search.

"Two minutes forty," said Don.

Abu Faud simply laughed at the impotence of the westerners with their morals and ethics. *In war there are no ethics or morals*, he thought to himself, *it's kill or be killed. They have their rules of engagement that they have to obey. That's what makes them weak. That's why we will win.*

"Two minutes thirty seconds to impact. You need to get out of there now."

Victoria walked up to Abu Faud; the man who had tortured her parents physically and her mentally.

"Where are my parents?" she asked in a very calm, controlled voice.

Abu Faud knew people. *She is a doctor, not even a warrior. She has cried, she has screamed, there is no way she will do anything to harm me. She is a weak woman. She will meet our maker with the rest of us.*

Abu Faud smiled as he focused on the floor again. It was the last thing he ever did: as if in slow motion Victoria raised her right arm from her side and shot him in the head with the Glock. The first time she had ever fired a weapon. She didn't even watch him fall and approached the next prisoner.

Being a doctor is what she *does,* being a loving, caring daughter is what she *is*. She didn't even stop to consider the rights and wrongs, the moral dilemma of taking one life to save two. Or even two lives to save two. She was saving her parents' lives and would do *anything* to keep them safe, and if that meant a life sentence in prison, then so be it, they were her parents.

Rufus moved to intervene, but Captain Richards and SSM Alcock, stopped him.

"Two minutes twenty seconds."

"Where are my parents?"

"They are in the cells. THERE..." screamed the man on his knees in front of her. He had misjudged her once, thinking, like the now dead Abu Faud, that she wouldn't pull the trigger, he wouldn't misjudge her again as he pointed and gesticulated to the hidden ex mechanics' inspection pits.

At Vauxhall, Dame Cunningham-Black's phone rang and the prime minister gave her the bad news: he still hadn't been able to get through to the president. Everyone in the room looked at her expectantly, hoping the strike had been aborted on the command of the president, but the shake of her head told them all they needed to know.

"One minute fifty."

The troopers found the recessed handles and lifted the heavy sound-proofed doors hiding the couple. The troopers were joined by the others and they all took in what they saw. Both Deidre and Martyn were alive: they could see them moving. They had hoods over their heads and their hands were secured behind their backs. They were caked in dust and dirt and dried blood. Martyn started screaming, not knowing what had gone on above his head for the last few minutes and believed that he was about to be brutalised again.

"One minute fifteen seconds to impact."

"Purple Commander-White Command. Both hostages alive and in our care, over."

There was no celebration at either of the facilities watching the scene unfold. The voyeurs were watching their screens, being a party to the scenes in front of them. All of them knew how close this was going to be. They all had one eye on the electronic counters, inexorably counting down the time to zero, when the building and all those left inside would be blown to kingdom come; the other on the images being beamed back from the nose cone of the Avenger.

Deidre showed no reaction at all, she was resigned to whatever they would do to her.

The troopers jumped down, took off the hoods and hauled the couple out of their intended tombs. There was no room to manoeuvre the bodies in the confined space and it seemed to take an eternity to manoeuvre the dead weights.

"Fifty seconds to impact."

They struggled to upright them so that they could be lifted out of the pits. Helping hands grabbed clothes, or got under their armpits to haul them up.

"Forty seconds."

The two troopers followed them up, out of the pit with one easy bound.

"Twenty seconds."

The two biggest strongest troopers, Hobson and Willetts, hauled Deidre and Martyn over their shoulders. Another two troopers grabbed the kneeling prisoners and started running them towards the doorway. Everybody ran as fast as they could among the jumble and detritus that littered the floor, stealing vital seconds from their bid to escape.

"Ten seconds."

The two prisoners needed no encouragement and were actually pulling at the hands of the escorting troopers trying to run faster.

Don was counting down "Nine… Eight…"

He watched the satellite images and along with Dame Cunningham-Black, in COBRA and the team in Langley, he counted troopers out of the building. He could see Orla escape, and was slightly relieved, together with six of the SAS patrol and two prisoners, but no sign of Rufus, Victoria, Martyn and Deidre or Willetts and Hobson. They were all transfixed on the images being beamed to them from thousands of miles away, incapable of influencing what was about to happen. The drama was unfolding before their very eyes and they were mere spectators.

Troopers Hobson and Willetts with Deidre and Martyn over their shoulders were running the slowest, weighed down by the cumbersome bodies they were carrying, and their kit. They were accompanied by Rufus and Victoria, giving them as much assistance as they could. There was no way that Victoria was going to leave her parents behind, not after coming this far and getting so close. And there was no way that Rufus was going to let the three of them down. He had signed up to rescue them and he would either get them out of there, or die trying. He took hold of Victoria and started running her out of the building behind the two troopers.

The rest of the patrol and the prisoners were clear of the building, running as fast as they could to take cover from the impending explosion. All except Captain Richards, who re-entered the building to help his men.

Don and Frankie could see the officer, the leader of men, taking responsibility and tried to stop him, knowing he was returning to certain death.

"White-Delta Four-Zero, get out of there. Two... One... Impact." He was focused on the satellite images in his headset and saw the streak of the missile as it impacted into the building at 950 mph. He heard the explosion through his headset, took it off and threw it on the desk in frustration and anger.

The seven of them: Deidre and Martyn; Victoria and Rufus: Hobson and Willetts, and Deano were nearly at the door when the missile struck, blowing the building to smithereens.

Chapter Seventy-Five

Everybody in the two ops rooms watched the images on the big screen. The building had disintegrated, there was dust and rubble, billowing everywhere but there was no anticipated pyrotechnic display. Don and Frankie waited for the searing white flash to appear which they knew would accompany the explosion, but it never came.

Don put his headset back on. "White Commander-Delta Four-Zero-Two. Sitrep. Over."

"Delta Four-Zero-Two. The missile has failed to detonate. Standby we are going to search for survivors, over," replied SSM Allcock.

"Standing-by. Over."

The satellite imagery was shrouded in dust and smoke and none of the observers could see anything of any use.

They switched to infra-red to see the heat sources moving through the haze, as they went to where the building used to be.

Don blinked and made the connection to Langley. He could see Steve sitting calmly in the foreground, but his attention was drawn to the large, overweight figure in the background: the adjective probably does not exist in the English language to describe ADS Martinovitch's rage, but incandescent and apoplectic might just come close.

The new, state of the art, multi-million dollar missile had failed to detonate. Not only was it an embarrassment, it would cost him personally. In his own mind he had already spent some of the money that would have come to him from the bulging order books which would have resulted from a successful mission. He was like a raging bull, shouting and blaming the navy, the army, the CIA, the Brits; everybody he could think of, and then with a slam of the very heavy door, he was gone.

At last Don and Steve were able to speak and be heard.

"Did you see that?" asked Don.

"Delta Four-Zero-Two-White Commander, over," as the patrol cut across the conversation between Vauxhall Cross and Langley.

"Delta Four-Zero-Two go ahead, over."

"We have seven, repeat seven casualties. We need urgent Heli-vac for at least two of the injured. Will update you ASAP." SSM Allcock despatched one of his men to the ground outside the compound to prepare the LZ.

"White Commander, understood. Standby. Steve I'll get right back to you."

"White Commander- Zulu Quebec-One, over."

"Zulu Quebec-One receiving, over."

"White Commander-Zulu Quebec-One, proceed immediately to the LZ for casi vac, the ground is secured and under our control, over." Don could already here the rotor blades whirring in the background, as the pilot had pre-empted the request.

"Zulu Quebec-One, understood White. Zulu Quebec-One- Delta Four-Zero-Two, eta thirty seconds, over."

"Delta Four-Zero-Two -Zulu Quebec-one, understood, LZ is being prepared outside the compound."

All SAS patrols have a trained medic who is a fully 'badged' trooper, and has specialised in medicine; had some of the best and most exacting training possible, because where they are needed, there is no second opinion or back-up team or A&E. Trooper Green was the medic in this patrol and he had his work cut out. First of all he had to triage: to prioritise his casualties from P1 to P3 and he had to do it quickly. This was the way he would tend to the most severely wounded first checking airway; breathing; circulation and disability all seven of the occupants of the building had been blown off their feet and thrown several feet across the floor. Hobson and Willets were the least badly injured; minor disability: P3. They had helmets and full body armour to protect them. He got two of their comrades to help them out of the building and moved on.

Next he found Captain Richards: because he had been running back into the building, he had taken the force of the blast to the front. His vital organs were well protected, but he had a laceration to his face, and a broken humerus – he would live:P3. Perhaps not quite the handsome debonair man he once was, but the scar would give him a certain attraction which he would no doubt make the most of.

He reached the four civilians: Deidre clearly had a broken femur and clavicle, presumably as a result of being thrown from the shoulder of either Hobson or Willetts and landing awkwardly, her face was battered and bruised but otherwise she was ok. No danger to the airways, breathing or circulation, again P3. Trooper Green decided to leave her where she was, rather than risk moving her.

One look at Victoria, who was also just regaining consciousness, told him she was ok. Unknown to either of them Rufus has shielded her from the full impact of the blast, and other than having a full grown man thrown into her and knock the stuffing out of her, she would be alright. Which would be a help, she could assist him.

Martyn was in a worse shape: his head had taken the force of a flying object and there was a gaping hole in his skull, and he had stopped breathing: P1. Along with these more serious concerns he had a broken left humerus, which was compounded; and he appeared to have a double break in the tibia and fibula of the right leg. Orla was back in the ruins of the building by now and Trooper Green enlisted her help as he moved onto Rufus.

"Do you know anything about artificial respiration?" he asked.

"A little," she replied.

"That's good enough. Check Martyn's airways: he's stopped breathing and it may just be a blockage. Let's hope to fuck it is, or I'm going to have to put a P1 hold on him," essentially meaning, that although Martyn was critical, he would be left to die as the medic had to prioritise: if he had stopped breathing due to the blast then he was dead anyway, his only hope was a blocked airway.

He got to Rufus, who was unconscious: he had taken the force of the blast on his back, he appeared to have a broken right femur and ulna, again presumably where he had fallen, but more worryingly he had a large piece of shrapnel sticking out of his back, which may have punctured a lung. The medic quickly assessed the casualty: P1. He diagnosed a hemopneumothorax due to the shrapnel, which meant he had blood and air inside the chest wall outside the lung, Trooper Green's concern was that if he allowed the pressure to build, it would develop into a tension hemopneumothorax and kill him.

He looked up as Orla shouted over.

"He'd swallowed his tongue. I've cleared the blockage and got him breathing. What do you want me to do now?"

"Nothing at the moment. Just keep an eye on him. He's got a broken arm and leg and you will do more damage if you try and move him. He should be Ok. now, thanks." *Good. P2,* he thought *only one P1 to deal with.*

They all looked up slightly as they heard the unmistakable sound of a helicopter's rotor blades approaching.

Victoria was now fully conscious and came over to the medic. She could see him getting a chest drain out of his medical kit to insert into Rufus, the man she now admitted to herself that she loved, the man who had possibly given his life to save her parents, who might have made the ultimate sacrifice to help her. She fought back the tears as she medically assessed him. She chided herself for getting emotional, as that would not assist him or anybody else. He had reinforced that over the last few days and she knew how important it was to be objective, calm and focused. She looked at the SAS medic and knew he was carrying out a procedure that she would never dream of attempting, even after seven years at medical school. It was a very specialised procedure and she decided she would be better employed tending to her mother and father. She reached into the medic's bag, having lost her own in the confusion, and grabbed some gauze, bandages and sterilizer, left the two men and went to assist Orla with her parents.

She reached her dad first and checked what Orla had done: he was breathing, it was shallow, but he WAS breathing. She agreed with the trooper's assessment and would not move him until the stretcher arrived.

She moved on to her mother, now sitting among all the rubble and dirt. Victoria bound her mum's arm to her chest in order to take the weight off the clavicle and helped her outside to the fresher air, away from the carnage inside.

Trooper Green began inserting the chest drain. First of all he measured a hand's depth down from the armpit; cut down on to the rib, roughly in line with where the seam of a jumper would be, pulled the cut of flesh down over the intercostal space and then performed a blunt dissection through the muscle to avoid cutting any blood vessels. Once he was through the chest muscle, he pushed his finger in and swept in a 360 degree arc to ensure there were no smashed ribs and that the lungs were not sticking to the chest wall.

As he worked, he was joined by Captain Richards, and Orla, who had done everything she could for Martyn and Deidre and left them in the capable hands of their daughter. They watched in admiration and wonder as he grasped the end of the chest drain tube with a set of forceps and pushed it in to the hole aiming towards the shoulder blade. He was working with such calm, deft precision, it belied the circumstances.

Captain Richards left the medic and joined SSM Allcock and together they took charge of the situation ensuring all of the prisoners were secured, they despatched men to retrieve stretchers off the Sea King to carry the wounded to the chopper.

Once Victoria had supervised her father onto the stretcher and helped her mother to the helicopter she returned to Trooper Green to see if he needed help.

She had been in a few operating theatres, but she had never seen anything like this: they were in the middle of a destroyed building, with rubble and carnage all around them, and this medic was performing as if he had everything under control, on a pristine operating table, with bright lights and a team of anaesthetists, and surgical nurses surrounding him. She had been told by colleagues how professional the Special Forces medics were and now she could see for herself.

He got the tube where he wanted it and stitched it into place, securing it with tape to stop it coming out. The tube was attached to a bag with a one way valve to let blood and air out but nothing back in.

Victoria got on her hands and knees next to Trooper Green and checked Rufus's vital signs: he was breathing and although his pulse was weak, there was a pulse.

Captain Richards contacted Don.

"Delta Four-Zero-White Command, over."

"Delta Four-Zero, go ahead, over."

"Delta Four-Zero, we have five P3 casualties, one P2 and one P1 who will need immediate heli-vac. The compound is secure and we have numerous prisoners. Standby for exact numbers. Over."

"Received Delta Four-Zero. A second Sea King has been arranged and is en route to you for further transport of yourselves and your prisoners. ETA 2215 Zulu. Over." Don didn't need to add *in whom we, the Tanzanians and the Americans will be very interested.*

Trooper Green was still working on Rufus, but satisfied that he was now stabilised, he reviewed the others in his mind and couldn't believe how lucky they had all been. *How had it not detonated?*

Chapter Seventy-Six

Don kept one eye and ear on the proceedings in Tanzania and returned his attention to Steve, who was grinning like a Cheshire cat.

"Hi again Steve. That was close, too close. And we are not out of the woods yet, I don't know who is injured or how badly."

"Yes, sorry pal, it was the best I could do." Steve was now sat in the ops room on his own, while the others either relieved themselves, or stretched their legs.

"Pardon?" said Don. "What do you mean? What did you do you old fox?"

"Somehow the missile's detonation system was disarmed just before impact. I guess the president would have made that call if he had the facts, but I haven't got a clue how that could have happened."

"Oh you fucking glorious wanker," exclaimed Don.

Fortunately Steve knew this was one of the highest compliments that Don was ever going to pay him.

Then reality struck both men. Even without the warhead detonating, the shockwaves emitted from the impact of an object travelling at that speed could easily be enough to kill somebody.

Don refocused and from his momentary euphoria, he had a sudden bout of guilt that he was semi-celebrating and yet they still had casualties, possibly fatalities.

He watched the scenes courtesy of the satellite and could see the activity taking place, but couldn't distinguish who was who in the monochrome images.

"White Commander- Delta four Zero. Sitrep, please. Over."

Don heard the unmistakable tones of Captain Richards over the airwaves.

"Delta Four-Zero, repeat we have seven casualties: five walking wounded: myself and two troopers, from the blast; two troopers with grazes from the firefight; two seriously wounded: Mr and Mrs Conway and one critical patient: Rufus. We have sixteen, repeat sixteen captured suspects. All other suspects appear to have either been killed in the firefight or the blast."

Victoria looked at the officer, not sure if that was a deliberate lie or a mistake. As she looked towards the back of the premises, where they had all been standing and where the missile had impacted, she realised that there was nothing left. No bodies, no furniture, no walls, nothing. There would be no evidence of what she had done, but still she did not want anybody to lie for her, she had not and would not ask them to.

Don, knowing that there would be others listening and that as the techie had told Frankie only a few minutes earlier it was all recorded: "Confirm seven casualties, sixteen prisoners, all other suspects dead from the firefight or impact. Over."

"Confirmed White. Over."

"Status of Abu Faud? Over."

"Delta Four-Zero. Faud took the full impact of the missile. He is dead. We should be able to get a DNA match from some of the tissue spread. Over."

"White Commander-Delta Four-Zero, received. Be advised: the Tanzanian People's Defence Force are despatching two more heelos to assist in the transportation of yourselves and the prisoners. We are in the process of arranging holding facilities for the prisoners. HMS Sutherland is prepared to receive the casualties. Good luck and well done, out."

Don turned his attention to the minister, although he was no respecter of titles or position, he did respect honesty, guts and balls and she had displayed all these attributes over the past hour, he had really warmed to her.

"Thank you for your help and support ma'am, we have taken seven casualties as you probably heard, but no fatalities on our side yet, no thanks to ADS Martinovitch. We had a huge slice of luck there."

"Thank you Don, and thank you for everything, for keeping me in the loop and for coordinating everything so magnificently. My attentions will now be focused both internally, which I am sure you are aware of, and needs no elaboration from me; and Mr Martinovitch, I'm sorry I couldn't dissuade him from continuing with the strike, but both HMG and our Tanzanian friends will be making representations to the president in the strongest terms about the irresponsible, reckless actions of that man. We had authority to act in the way we did from the Tanzanians, a sovereign state, but the Americans did not. It could get pretty acrimonious especially with their recent track record. As you know I've already spoken to the PM who is beside himself with rage. Unfortunately none of that helps you or your comrades at this present moment does it? Is there anything I can do to assist? Do you want me to make any calls to smooth the way out there?"

"That would be a great help ma'am. I don't know what sort of facilities we've got on the Sutherland, but we may need to evac straight to Jo'Burg."

"I will ensure there are no problems or delays either end for you. Is that everything?" she asked.

"Yes thank you ma'am."

"In which case, I will take my leave of you. Just one more thing Don, when your colleagues return to the UK and are well enough to come to town, I would very much like to see you all for lunch to get an honest assessment of what we can do better in the future. Liaise with Simon and he will see to it that you are prioritised whenever you can make it. Cheerio and I hope your friend makes a full recovery."

+++++++

At the stronghold Rufus was stretchered to the helicopter accompanied by Orla, who wouldn't leave his side. It was at least two hours back to the Sutherland, anchored just off Dar, possibly slightly more and it was touch and go whether he would pull through.

Deidre and Martyn were carried out next, accompanied by Victoria and Captain Richards.

"Bastard! This is all your fault!," shouted one of the prisoners, sitting with his hands tied behind his back.

Victoria looked over at the group. "Who said that?" she asked the Captain.

Captain Richards approached his men and they identified the prisoner who had shouted, and brought him to the Captain.

"What did you say?" asked Deano of the man that was clearly not one of the terrorists, but one of the original kidnappers, who himself had been taken hostage by al-Shabaab.

"I said it's all their fault."

"What do you mean?" asked Victoria, but before she could get an answer, she was rushed to the helicopter to make the journey with her parents, Trooper Green, Orla and Rufus.

Chapter Seventy-Seven

The three casualties were taken straight to HMS Sutherland, accompanied by Victoria, Orla and Trooper Green, still tending to Rufus.

Surgeon Lieutenant McAllister accepted them into her medical department. She quickly realised that while she was well able to tend to Deidre and Martyn, all she could do for Rufus was stabilise him, to get him on to a better equipped medical facility.

The choice was simple, an eleven hour flight back to London or a four hour flight to Jo'burg, where the South Africans, as the most technically and medically advanced African nation, would take care of him.

Orla was the closest thing he had to family apart from Myree and Suvee, and she decided she wanted him on the shorter flight. Surgeon Lieutenant McAllister agreed with her, that the quicker they got him to a proper medical facility, the better chance he had of surviving. Victoria felt empty, she wanted to be involved in making the decision for him, she wanted to take some responsibility for him, but how could she? She had only known him six days, didn't have a recognised relationship with him, but felt a special bond with him, for him. She felt guilty that he was injured, possibly fatally, saving her parent's lives, and realised that he was protecting her from the blast as they ran out of the building, because there was no doubt in her mind that he could run faster than her and could have got out of the building if he'd wanted to.

Dame Cunningham-Black was as good as her word and everything was in place to get Rufus to Johannesburg without any bureaucracy or red tape. He was in the operating theatre at Sandton Medi-Clinic, Johannesburg nine hours after the missile struck.

Chapter Seventy-Eight

Two days later

Victoria sat in the private hospital room at Sandton Medi-Clinic, watching over the still unconscious Rufus. She felt like her whole world was collapsing about her. She was beside herself worrying about Rufus who was still critical. She wished Orla and the Surgeon Lieutenant had decided to send him to the UK but, as Rufus would have said to her, it would be pointless focusing on what could have happened; she had to deal with what had already happened.

Orla was outside talking on the phone to Don who had as full a picture as anybody was ever likely to get. He had been able to talk to everybody and pieced the events together and told Orla what he knew.

He had been with Frankie Fraser when Deano, contacted him.

"He told us the prisoner, who they now know is Wisdom Mwakimbwla had refused to say anything else at the compound until the British soldiers spoke to a member of staff at the High Commission, named Nick Cooper and gave them the number to phone. Deano said he'd phoned Cooper and his reaction was typical spook. He said "Nobody is to speak to the prisoner, and I mean nobody, until I see him back here." So like the good obedient troops we are, we completely ignored the order and began questioning Wisdom as we waited for our heelos to pick us up. Our charm and natural wit soon encouraged him to talk openly to us."

He continued, "Wisdom said nothing about his relationship with Cooper, he didn't need to. What he did tell us was that the original job was a set-up, arranged with him by the mzungu to collect the insurance money. It all had to be made to look realistic, but it was never meant to be a kidnap, it was supposed to be a straightforward murder and the body fed to the lions in one of the game parks. That was what was arranged, but the stupid mzungu prat never envisaged any of this happening, didn't think that by spending money like water it would make the bandits do a double cross. He said the mzungu had had enough of the marriage and wanted it all ended and hatched this plot to carry out murder and the pay-out would just be a bonus. But Wisdom reckoned they could take both of them and get ten times the money they were being offered for the murder, do a little work for the British on the side and play both sides off. What he never thought about was that the Victoria would employ a specialist and it all got out of control. While he was concentrating on trying to get money out of Victoria, al-Shabaab got in on the act and kidnapped the hostages, Wisdom and his gang."

"Ok Don, stop being a smart arse and tell me which one is responsible for all of this."

"All in good time my love. Meanwhile the Firm and the Company lose sight of the little people. The Firm was double crossing us and the kidnappers, trying to bring al-Shabaab in on the act, so they could take them out and contacted a local bunch of goons to take you and Ru out, but you know all about that, don't you?"

"Just get on with it," demanded Orla.

"The Company were in on the act as they had their sights on Abu Faud, and wanted to run an intelligence gathering operation against him and his network, but they were being, overruled by ASD Martinovitch who, get this, is a non-executive director of TZR electronics, and who supplied the navigation systems to the X-47 B Avenger, the missile that nearly killed you, and if it had, it would have been the first operational sea-borne drone launched successfully."

"You're beginning to piss me off now," said Orla "WHICH ONE WAS IT?"

"We made some assumptions when we couldn't find employment history for Deidre, thinking she probably worked for MI6 or a similar organisation, then her phone was being used for all the telephone traffic, it was only her that we heard from at the stronghold for some time as if she wasn't really being held captive, but Martyn was, so it all pointed to her. We couldn't find any employment history because there is none. She has seven degrees and after bringing Victoria up she had always carried out voluntary work, in charities and societies. The admin roles she had were just a hobby, something to fill her time around her studies. She was a full time student."

"Oh my God," said Orla "I'm really getting confused here Don, was it Deidre or Martyn?"

"Well, you know I asked Vicky for Martyn's phone when we first went to their house and she couldn't find it?"

"YES."

"She couldn't find it because he had taken it with him, so he could contact Wisdom."

"So it was Martyn?"

"Yes, that's what I've been telling you, we made the wrong assumptions. The bank he worked for has branches all over the world and organises exchanges and a branch manager from Tanzania came over to Britain some time ago and got friendly with Martyn and they kept in touch. When Martyn was hatching his plan he contacted this other manager and coerced him into putting him in touch with somebody who could do a job for him and that was Wisdom. I don't know what dirt he had on this other manager, but he apparently supplied the name quite readily."

"Jesus Don, how's Deidre?"

"She's in bits as you can imagine. She thought they had the perfect marriage and were on the perfect holiday. Apparently he had been planning it for ages. He was so cheesed off with her for never having worked a day in her life, always taking degrees in different things and working for charitable organisations. He resented her for him having to carry on working at the bank, even when he lost his job as branch manager, which was a real dent to his pride. They downsized and he held her responsible. She thought he loved his job, and thought she would emaciate him if she became the bread winner while he stayed at home. And there's another twist: Martyn says that Deidre knew all about it and they were just going to collect the insurance money together. She says she knew nothing about it, and that's why both of them are going to be questioned back in the UK. So it's a real cluster. Now can you just go and break the good news to Victoria?"

"Oh Jesus H Christ Don. Are you kidding me?"

"Well somebody has got to tell her."

Orla walked back in trying to decide how she was going to break the news to Victoria that she had just been given, but before she had time to broach the subject Victoria burst into tears and poured her heart out to her while they sat at Rufus's bedside.

Orla knew that Victoria was besotted with him; it was clear from everything she said and did. That came as no surprise to her; it was none of her business, but she didn't think things would work out the way Victoria envisaged, but hey, she had been young once, done foolhardy, reckless things – some she regretted, most she didn't. But she didn't want Victoria to raise her hopes that there might be any possibility of Rufus ever being anything more than her negotiator, the man who had helped her throughout the most traumatic period of her short life. It was natural that Victoria had given him some sort of mystical, hero status.

Orla was trying to think, and listen to Victoria at the same time, but she couldn't stop wondering about what she had just been told by Don.

She looked at Victoria, pitying the younger woman, whose world had been turned upside-down and was about to implode, but there was no way round it.

"Let's go for a coffee Vicky, we need to have a chat ..."

THE END

Available Soon...

The Accident

Who can you trust? Who do you believe?

In whose hands do you put the life of your daughter?

When Alan Ferguson, the National Crime Agency's number one Subject of Interest's prized Jaguar XKR-S is stolen, he embarks on a vendetta of violent retribution and cruelty to retrieve both his car and status.

A psychopathic monster, who will stop at nothing to retain his standing at the top table of the British underworld, he kidnaps Atikah, the young daughter of Hashim bin Saif: the innocent Emirati buyer of the vehicle.

Rufus Stone and his team at 22Red are called in to help, and meet their match in Ferguson's trusted Lieutenant and ex South African detective, Johannes, who is as technically adept, surveillance conscious and determined as they are.

Running parallel to the race to rescue Atikah, both sides know they have a mole and endeavour to identify the informant before it is too late.

This fast paced and gripping read takes place on the Sandbanks Peninsula (Dorset's millionaires' playground), the United Arab Emirates and East London.

For more information please see the author's website:
www.grahamrabone.com